CW01623931

Nine L… at!

By

Kym BB

Shield Crest

© Copyright 2025 – Kym Billington-Baddley

All rights reserved.

This book shall not, by way of trade or otherwise, be lent, re-sold, hired out, or otherwise circulated without the prior consent of the copyright holder or the publisher in any form of binding or cover other than that in which it is published and without a similar condition including this condition being imposed on the subsequent purchaser. The use of its contents in any other media is also subject to the same conditions.

ISBN: 978-1-917525-39-8

MMXXV

A CIP catalogue record for this book
is available from the British Library.

Published by
ShieldCrest Publishing,
Boston, Lincolnshire,
PE20 3BT England
Tel: +44 (0) 333 8000 890
www.shieldcrest.co.uk

Dedications

When writing this novel, my mind wandered to those people unfortunate enough to lose their jobs through no fault of their own. So, I dedicate my book to all those people who find themselves in this situation. As the saying goes "where there's a will there's a way", so keep strong and focussed and all will be well.

To my husband, David, I thank him for his patience that has surpassed all else, the reading and re-reading, the countless spelling and grammar checks let alone the constant reminders to get the book finished.

Also my many friends for their time, effort and dedication in supporting me through this journey.

I would particularly like to mention: Karren Roberts, Jan Billington, Helen McKay, Carol Cadman, Jani Neilson and Lesley Smyth.

And last but not least ShieldCrest Publishers for their belief in my book and helping me to get it into the public domain. I would particularly like to thank Leigh Stephenson for all his support throughout this very exciting, if not somewhat daunting, journey.

Contents

Preface

Nine Lives, No Cat takes the reader on a journey of survival, love and revenge. The tale is set in a toxic and brutal organisation where nine people find themselves on very different journeys in the space of a few weeks. Some try to survive on their willingness to 'do anything' to prove themselves while others take the long and winding road to the unknown. For added support, they promise to meet regularly at the newly formed Wine O'clock Club, a place where they can share their experiences and their life journeys as they try to make sense of what has happened to them. It is a story of survival. Their chosen pathways vary, their characters intertwine, and their success rates are not always that promising.

Health is hope and hope is everything. Enjoy this life. We are just passing through, so never be improper, and try never to be rude. Now then, sit back and immerse yourself in all this book has to offer—oh, and remember your raincoat when it's raining, and always return your library book!

Disclaimer

Any similarity between characters in this novel, living or deceased, is purely coincidental.

Chapter 1 - Introduction

"Blah, blah, blah, blah, nonsense, bullocks! Who cares about facts and figures? Who wants to read a textbook? What matters is the juicy bits, the real-life stories, the nitty-gritty of life and what it brings."

"So, readers, gather your thoughts as you come on the journey with me. Grit your teeth for the boring bits – they're tiny – *but* the scene must be set. Don't sweat the small stuff; instead, get on the rollercoaster and take the ride of a lifetime. No one's perfect, as you're about to find out."

Have you ever been had? A forty-minute management presentation and a few expletives later landing you squarely and unfairly without a job! Well, that's the fate that awaited all nine of those dedicated, hard-working, enthusiastic and honest individuals who had given, between them, more than forty-five years of service to an organisation that was now treating them as 'surplus to requirements' in the 'new, exciting' and newly unveiled structure laid before them.

In the blink of an eye, the man once considered a knight in shining armour was now the very devil in the room. They had thought he was about to recognise and appreciate the ambition, drive, and enthusiasm that each of them had to better their careers and send them on the path to success. Instead, they found themselves forced to listen to an endless list of mistakes and wrongdoings, mathematical equations that failed to add up and a round of inconsistent outcomes leading to the position each one now found themselves in. They couldn't help but hope that the nightmare would soon be over.

The notion of entering a room full of union representatives, several human resource professionals of various rank and file – as well as the Devil incarnate himself, wasn't an ideal situation to even contemplate. As such, the 18th February 2010 was not the best day in the life of each one of those nine people. Once they had been part of a strong and vibrant team. They had looked out for each other in their daily quest to achieve those dreaded organisational objectives.

So today was going to be different. They had all received emails a few days before instructing them to report to the said office for a consultation. When they had arrived, they were divided into two teams to receive the official news. Now, they were all leaving the room with the heavy burden of knowledge that 'everything is disposable'. This made that particular Thursday afternoon very different from those that preceded it.

With a median age of forty-nine years and an average service spanning twelve years, what would the future now hold for each of those individuals? Well, who knew and how many people cared anyway, when in real terms it wasn't happening to them? In a team totalling twenty-one people, nine people represented 43% of that workforce. Of those nine people, six were female and three were male.

This is the story of those nine people from the moment the news broke to the journey each one would now travel to reinvent themselves trying to find their pathway to success and their place in the world.

If you ever find yourself in a similar situation, don't give up; instead, be strong and take heart. You've heard the saying 'When one door closes, another one opens', so watch and listen. Observe everything around you and try to make sense of your situation as you slowly and methodically work your way through the plethora of information heading your way. Although you can't see it right now, your life is just beginning...

Chapter 2 - Character Building

Ever heard the phrase 'character building', i.e., the way you face and cope with the situation will make you stronger? Bollocks! Shit happens; deal with it!

Today there is a buzz in the office. Like little bees, each one of those nine people is trying to justify their worth in preparation for their relentless search for new employment. There is some talk of retirement, part-time working and self-employment.

Funny really, whilst turmoil envelops those affected, the rest of the office is carrying dutifully on, trying to concentrate on meeting their objectives whilst being mindful of the delicate situation that surrounds them. Nothing in this department will ever be the same again—even the name has been changed ready for the relaunch of a whole new department. This department will be populated by an entirely new set of staff headed by none other than the Devil incarnate himself. In the trial by fire, can he perform? Can he take the organisation to new heights? Is he overambitious or just a pure genius? The next few months will decide his fate. By this time next year, he will become the new god or be reviled for his poor decision-making and made a scapegoat, leaving him following in the wake of those nine very capable staff.

Why would a large and bold figure, formidable in his business approach and direct speech, require his personal assistant to be promoted to the dizzying ranks of business manager in the blink of an eye? Kudos? Status? Evidencing his importance? No recruitment process, no opportunity to apply for this 'new and exciting' position, just a new job title attached to her email correspondence soon after his arrival? Nia, the new Miss Moneypenny! And boy, did everyone know it! Her transition from a meek and mild individual, unsure of her future role within the organisation, to a rottweiler suddenly massively protective of the Devil's diary, meetings and time management made her a force to be reckoned with and somewhat impenetrable! This was to be the new task: Who could break the code? Who could access the Devil's gate? Who could douse his fire… who dares wins!

Such a lot to cope with. How would each of the nine staff members fare on their journeys? Well, let's introduce you to the characters and you can make up your own mind.

The Devil Incarnate

He was big, bold with a huge presence. Charming and charismatic, and with a huge portfolio of experience, he was not afraid to challenge the norm. With a friendly disposition, he was assertive, strong, with an opinionated stance, making him a formidable presence. This coupled with his smart pinstripe suits, brightly coloured ties and fancy socks slipped into polished brogues gave him style and panache worthy of a city gent. Dark curly hair with a hint of grey gave him a charming look and with his swarthy tanned skin one could be forgiven for mistaking his ethnicity. But he was truly English and unmistakably from the North; his warm and friendly accent gave way at times to his hearty, deep-throated chuckle drawing people to him with a feel-good factor of exchanged pleasantries. Could this man be like Marmite, Teflon, or something that you really don't want to hit the fan? Time will inevitably tell as the intrepid journey takes shape.

Clearly a devoted son, he chose to commute at least one hour each way to work to ensure that he was easily available to his ageing parents. Health issues prevented his father from living the life he would otherwise have chosen, and such was his condition that carers were required around the clock to see to his every need. No other family members were in the picture; the Devil lived alone, and work was very much his life. Unmarried and with no partner, he usually spent a large proportion of his time at work or at home working. Judging by the length of his emails and the times sent, he was known to burn the midnight oil.

Loneliness and isolation formed part of the Devil's life. Since he often worked late to further his career, he was known to be fidgety and awkward in social situations. His body language usually showed his disengagement, with his left or right flank carefully placed side on to his audience. He would then usually avert his gaze too. What did this mean? Could he be trusted? Was he bored by those that present before him or just disinterested desperately wanting to bring his own agenda to the fore? Time would tell. He was new, he was different, and he wanted to make an impact.

A three-hour commute each day allowed him the luxury of driving his new Mercedes Benz, steeped in leather, and polished to a shine not dissimilar to his brogues. Diamond black, this stylish two-seater sports model slipped neatly into a parking bay identified specifically for the Devil. A marked bay was the only way he could park given that he usually made excuses for his lack of mathematical genius when working out simple equations, waxing lyrical that maths is not his strong point. Maybe he needs a 'Tim Fix' (but more about him later) to function as his park assist!

Nia Shaw

Well, here she is in all her glory, the one and only Miss Moneypenny, glad to be of service and fiercely protective of the Devil. Small and petite, with blonde shoulder-length hair and outfits that became her neat figure, she usually walked on eggshells when dealing with the affected nine. Her now elevated position gave prominence and style to her once dowdy, dreary attitude of 'woe is me'. Her new job belied her age and appeared to have been the long-awaited injection of collagen that now became her. Wrapped in confidence and with a new swathe of ambition she gathered the clan and ensured that each would now take a seat in front of the Devil himself to hear the results of the so-called consultation. She truly was the Devil Woman. What power she must wield to be able to dictate the order in which those nine people would sit in front of the Devil. Nia, you could hold their hand, hug, and comfort them as they enter hell or simply show them in and wait for fate to play its part. Which approach would she choose?

Chapter 3 - All The People

1. Rupert Hope

Here he is, the man responsible for the mess those nine people now found themselves in. Because of his lack of panache, leadership, dynamism, and very poor communication style, many of those nine people truly lay the blame at his door. With the teams' wealth of experience, knowledge educational attainments, why did the organisation allow him to lead them like a lamb to the slaughter for nigh on ten years? Performance management, setting objectives and Key Performance Indicators didn't appear to be part of his management style. Return on Investment based on quarterly outputs was never achieved and delegation of targets to other departments never took place. So why, you might ask yourself, was his team to be punished for his inadequacies? Answers on a postcard please.

He was in his mid-forties, of a medium build with a ruddy complexion often referred to as a 'healthy glow' from all the running and cycling activities he did. Now keen to remove himself from the firing line, his days were spent secreting himself in his office, usually only appearing when needs be to make a cup of tea or fill up his water bottle. A true 'no hoper': means well but fails. Calm and well controlled until challenged, then out of nowhere you will witness a terrible show of temper with fists clenched and banging on the table to a face ruddier than ever, contorted and twisted with the display of temper. Clearly two sides to this man with the seniority of the job role protecting his uglier side.

Because he didn't follow the company's structural and reporting requirements, the staff were disempowered and needed information to perform well was missing from the loop. They were mushrooms in the dark, dormant, and dank awaiting the chance to spring into life. Apart from one of those nine staff, he failed to lead the rest. He failed to listen, and he failed to action culminating in yet another dark place each one of them had to feel their way out of. As his life was on a high. He was favoured and protected, nurtured and mentored. He had a chance; he had the opportunity to better himself. He had access to Continued Professional Development (CPD) and accompanied Rupert to meetings that most people had no chance of attending. Why would this be the case? What did Denzil have that others lacked? What was his penchant; how did he get the job in the first place (he was extremely late for the interview), and why was he now being protected?

2. Denzil Drum

Trumpet voluntary, here he is: 'Cometh the hour, cometh the man'. The one and only Mr Drum. Oh, how many of us wish he were distant!

Denzil is smart, sophisticated, stylish and walks with an air of confidence akin to a lion stalking its prey. Drumroll please (if only). Pray, silence for the dynamism that is Denzil Drum as he struts towards his protector, teeth whiter than white and a smile to melt your heart. Behind him flows a trail of Givenchy wafting through a stifled, silent, saddened office marking his territory as he goes. Today is his day, the day of reckoning, the day he's to be elevated to the dizzying heights of seniority. How can this be? What has he done? Why is he being promoted and why is he being protected?

Late for everything, but with charisma and charm, he's able to fool even the most intelligent of men. What's more, he is a man of many words but who, in essence, says nothing. With the prowess of an athlete, his honed body hides a bumbling idiot who's lost his way.

Lastly he is a sharp dresser and keen to please. On this day, his radar has him heading straight to Rupert's door ready to 'do business', whatever that means.

3. Tim Crocker

Is it a gerbil, is it a mouse or is it Tim? He was a man small in stature, slightly stooped, bottle-top glasses perched on the end of a slightly red nose, shuffling along as though his size 8 feet were too big for his small weedy frame. He usually wore ill-fitting trousers, crumpled and short, with dowdy grey socks that failed to meet their mark exposing a glimpse of white flesh on each leg. All this was topped by a tweed jacket that appeared to have shrunk, a shirt that had no idea what an iron looked like and displaying what Tim probably had for breakfast. His hair had only a nodding acquaintance with a comb, let alone a pair of scissors and he had very untrendy nose and ear hair too.

That said, if you could comprehend his mumblings, you'd have the makings of a highly intelligent individual not unlike Q from the Bond movies. Always the bridesmaid never the bride, Tim brought the intellect and knowledge to the table. Never one to shine, never one to bask in all the glory, he hid his light under a bushel.

He had recently relocated from the valleys of Wales, but travelled back there are often as he could. With an elderly mother and a brother in rehab, Tim had a duty to his family. He had a purpose and his mission in life was to care for his family.

Now in his mid-fifties, work was everything to Tim. Home was a one-bedroomed flat, devoid of character, family, pets, warmth, and charm. Instead, it was filled with gadgets, computers, and hard-wired machinery that littered each room like detritus.

4. Fee Shand

Fee Shand was a very stylish, delightful and delectable woman who habitually addressed people as 'darling'. Hashtag Posh is certainly no understatement. With years and years of service (as she keeps telling everyone), she knew her job. She also knew her mind and she surely knew what she wanted. Intelligent, experienced, and more than capable, Fee was no shrinking violet. Cross her and you'd know all about it! She was not one to suffer fools gladly; there were no outstretched arms to welcome people in but if you successfully breached her defences, you would have made a friend for life. Fee was fiercely protective of her job, its content and her sidekick. Be mindful to keep your distance until she's ready... Ms Shand will see you now.

Thrice married, thrice divorced, she spent her time waxing lyrical about her ex-cardiologist husband (who keeps her in the style to which she is accustomed) with whom she shares two children. Now in her early sixties, Fee knows that this job is her last chance saloon.

Petite, attractive with thick grey hair cut beautifully into a sheer bob framing her pixie nose and bright eyes, she slipped comfortably into her regular chair positioned as such to oversee the office. Delusions of grandeur spring to mind. That said, she's probably the longest-serving member of the team and a very valuable one at that.

Fee would often lock horns with Rupert and as such can easily forget the chain of command resulting in her beautifully red painted lips drawing back and dripping blood at the mere sight of Rupert—never mind being able to tolerate the utter drivel that emanated from his dry, cracked mouth. Knowing when to retreat is the key, but is not a skill that Fee Shand has and nor will she ever.

5. Anne Leigh

Behold the Fee Shand assistant, fiercely loyal to her master, keen to please, not one to rock the boat but instead known for steadying the oar for a safer crossing. The loyal, faithful servant docks her cap at the mere mention of Ms Shand. 'Fetch me, get me, bring me...' all too familiar for this overworked underpaid skivvy. Anne would normally stay late to show willing, and arrived early to be all present and correct. She is not a particularly attractive women, rather on the plump side with long, dark hair that sits perched on the crown of her head. This was usually adorned with a variety of brightly coloured bandanas enabling a cascade of colour to intersperse her glowing tresses.

Dowdy skirts circle her thick waist, fully pleated to add additional layers to her already fat hips! Anne was always the one to tuck in her blouse, shirt, vest... any top that struggled to get past her already tightened waistband. Not necessarily American tan but they might as well be, grey, off-white, orange, purple and even red stockings can be witnessed clinging to her legs throughout the winter months. Thank goodness she had a shapely leg otherwise all hope would be lost.

Thick-rimmed glasses sit neatly on her rounded pink cheeks, framing a set of gorgeous dark pools hidden from sight by every blink of those long, curled lashes that revitalise her eyes every few seconds.

Yes sir, no sir, three bags full, sir, is Anne's motto to her master. Yet in her own formidable way she had a dogged determination, a willingness to succeed and a passion to embrace life, whatever it may hold.

Anne was hopelessly in love with the one and only love of her life, and had been for several years. He treated her appallingly. It was on, then it was off, then it was back on again. In between, he would be off sowing his oats as and when he felt like it. How could this be, was he her Mr Right? Could she tame him and make him her own and if so when would this happen? In the meantime, she hung onto his shirtsleeve hoping that the worm will turn.

Anne lived in a very tidy flat, a stone's throw from work. She had a fastidious regime for cleaning and was extremely tidy. You could drop in any time and would see that nothing would be out of place. Her life outside of work was not full, she was a daydreamer and a 'what-if' person. The only consistent thing in Anne's life was her cat. A ginger tom rescued as a kitten and now displaying a blue collar with a small bell indicating a true sense of belonging. He had ginger stripes, a white-tipped tail and a white face, which gave give all the hallmarks of a Bengal tiger, so he was aptly named Tigger. This little bundle habitually sat joyously on her plentiful lap padding and purring to his heart's content. 'The wonderful thing about Tiggers, is Tiggers are wonderful things... and he's the only one!' (Courtesy of A. A. Milne.)

6. Millie Knott

One of the newest members of the team, loved by many, revered by few, Millie had an engaging smile, and an enigmatic personality coupled with a sense of style. She was not particularly pretty but made the most of her assets. She was big breasted, with a nipped-in waist and a muscular leg, giving the impression of an energetic, sporty female who enjoyed the outdoor life.

Upon joining the organisation, she was handpicked by Rupert as chair of the selection panel and seconded by Denzil, she gave an unforgettable interview. She was charismatic, engaging, thoughtful with a knowledgeable presentation that would be hard to beat. As the first candidate in, she prepared well, sat opposite the chairperson on a panel of three and ensured full eye contact and engagement throughout.

With the voice of an angel and the heart of a lion, she took control. This was one job that Millie wanted, and this was one job she knew how to get. Cool and calculated, she answered questions with great articulation, poise, knowledge, and confidence. She paused in the right places, laid claim to many successes in previous job roles evidenced by glowing references, all of which left no one in doubt who was best placed for this role.

The eyes of the whole team were now fixed firmly on Millie; she made a move using her pièce de résistance—her killer smile. This girl was going places, and she knew it.

Unbeknown to Millie, the office staff were busily betting on each candidate as they came through the door ultimately trying to choose the successful candidate. They based their guesses entirely on looks and engagement as each one took the only chair available, in sight of the full office, and nervously awaited the outcome of the selection process.

7. Mel Carter

A kinder more genuine person you couldn't hope to meet. With a warm engaging smile, accompanied by a bounce in her step and an outstretched hand you couldn't help but feel an immediate strong engagement with this woman upon first meeting her. She had shoulder-length straight hair with glints of silver grey, a neat little figure, glasses resting neatly on top of her head and wore heels high enough to make anyone giddy. She danced around the office as though her time on *Strictly Come Dancing* was reaching its finale.

She was the glue that held the affected nine and the rest of the office together. Never one to make a fuss, she was calm in a crisis, oozed affection and often became a solid shoulder to cry on when required. So, whose shoulder was Mel going to cry on?

Not long back from her honeymoon, she glided along as if on a cloud. Her love for her new husband and children took precedence over all else and not even the potential loss of her job was going to spoil her happiness. What a stalwart, what a true gift; what a wonderful woman she was! Even in the darkest hour, her bright light shone through to give hope to so many. Boy how everyone was going to miss this woman!

During our time on earth, we meet many people from all walks of life. Some we gel with and some we don't but each one of us deserves our place in this world. So, what place would the wonderful Mel take up in the future?

She met and married her new husband very quickly. It was her second time around and she wasn't taking any chances of losing him. A chance meeting in a supermarket, a brief exchange of numbers and a few discussions later, and the romance began its journey. Now she was surrounded by new family members since both she and her new husband had children and grandchildren. Life is but a dream and one that Mel didn't want to wake up from.

8. Cleo Melville

'Ride 'em Cowboy' a Country and Western girl at heart, this fiddle- and guitar-playing granny married to a musical genius was in it for the ride! Sporting grey fitted trousers, a cotton shirt, and flat shoes, she took no prisoners. Studious with an eye for detail, she was also the perfect proofreader. Graduating in English language and keen to exceed her current role, Cleo worked extremely hard to pass several Information Technology courses to position herself as one of the IT consultants within the organisation.

She was very articulate, and she spoke with an air of decorum. This aside, she was a woman not to be messed with, one who always had an answer, and the right answer, given her extensive knowledge base. She was a credit to the organisation, a forerunner. She was a woman of great integrity and one who could easily lead given half the chance. She had a quiet disposition which was interesting given how much she was missed when absent. She was very astute, had a good brain and wasn't afraid to use it. She loved her job, and her job loved her.

9. Rene Norton

Young, vivacious, motivated, enthusiastic, and keen to succeed, Rene was a breath of fresh air. Married, with a very young son, she wanted to achieve the best possible outcomes for her and her new family. Her youthful appearance and smooth slightly tanned skin implied she was not a UK native but someone from much further afield. She created a conundrum when her accent suggested otherwise. She was a pretty woman who spoke with a slight Irish accent, picked up whilst trying to learn English from *Father Ted*, one of the few English television programmes she could receive in her native Argentina. She drew people in with her alluring good looks and attractive accent.

And there you have it, the ill-fated nine, who had nowhere to run and nowhere to hide and now, they were, lined up, blindfolded, and awaiting their fate. The Devil incarnate, the new kid on the block: What might he have in store for his intended victims, handpicked to meet the so-called 'needs' of the organisation?

Are you ready?

Chapter 4 – So Long, Farewell

Rodney Marco (known as Marco to his friends and colleagues) was the man responsible for all the chaos when he chose to adopt his pal from another organisation. This was meant to be his defining moment, the action that would escalate him to penultimate success. He'd known the Devil incarnate for several years and honestly believed that his impressive track record would enhance the organisation bringing Marco the accolades and success he felt he truly deserved.

Marco was a kind and generous man, yet he was often passed over for further promotion due to his inability to engage with the right people at the right level. He suffered with a stutter, made worse when he was nervous or uncertain of a situation. This prevented him from having a confident telephone manner and speaking with some authority when engaging in conferences or any kind of public speaking. Those who knew him understood him and made allowances for his sometimes-slow delivery of information. But, this was not enough for Marco. He craved the adulation and recognition of the very top man of the organisation, and he felt by sourcing the Devil, he had the best chance of achieving his ultimate goal.

He knew that the Devil's entry would displace several people within the team but to him it was worth the risk. He justified his decision by carefully outlining who, in his opinion, was not up to the job and who, through the Devil's own work, could be disposed of. He wanted to rejig the team by holding onto its current leader, Rupert Hope, his pal for several years and getting the Devil Incarnate to reduce staffing levels without laying blame at his door. Was this the right decision or was this in fact to be Marco's downfall?

The Organisation

Like the Pacific Ocean, wide, vast, deep, cold, and blue, this once slick oiled machine had flowed sweetly and gently like a river entering the sea and resting calmly at its destination. Today it was anything but. It struggled to advance over rocks and waterfalls, aggressively rushing into crevices that took each wave captive, battering it relentlessly into submission. This once buoyant kingdom's crest was fast falling into the abyss.

Like a captain on a ship, the Devil incarnate was to lead his new crew to victory whichever way he knew how. He was to be ably assisted by his First Mate, Marco, who would gently steer the way using his knowledge, expertise, and experience to break the waves, creating a pathway to victory. Together were they to become a formidable force?

A butcher, a baker and a candlestick maker... who was the more creative, the more use or even essential? Well, it all depended on the circumstances. Each could use their hands; each had precision at their fingertips; and each had a learned skill making them all valuable assets.

Rub-a-dub-dub, three men in a tub? A Marco, the Devil and Hope. As the tub listed, the baker thought, *Don't put all your eggs in one basket*. The flank of the Devil attracted the butcher and Hope began to pray. One oar, three men and a tub.

Complex organisations need strong leadership, vision, and achievable targets. Each of those affected nine had the skills and knowledge to carry out their jobs to a very high standard, what they didn't have were the appropriate channels to allow this to happen.

Large organisations can be cumbersome, and many contain the great, the good and the also-rans. They are made up of several departments, some fighting for survival and recognition, some ambling along, all out to make a difference. For this department, change was imminent. The storm was brewing and the change in the wind direction meant that the team had to face the challenges head on.

"Ahoy Devil!" We're coming for you!

That fateful day saw nine people given their notice. Recompense was a handsome package made up of three months' salary and any outstanding leave paid in full. The deal was, take the paperwork to a designated solicitor and assure signature before said exit date allowing the Devil his highway to hell. Once signed there was no going back and only two months before exit. Alternatively, each staff member could hang onto their job until re-evaluated and re-graded and fight for it at a later stage with other staff known to the Devil and invited in by the Devil. Was this enough time to sort the wheat from the chaff? Who will do what, when will they do it and what will become of that once buoyant team? All but one chose the exit strategy. The beating heart of Denzil Drum decided to take a different path, one that would see him securely elevated to the hierarchy prior to his mentor's departure. How could this be, what influence could Rupert have at this stage of the game? Did Denzil pick up enough skill and knowledge to fool even the Devil? Surely not? Well, this is how things panned out and as contracts concluded, desks emptied, files handed over and laptops returned, Denzil had a new view of the office from his careful positioning in Fee Shand's chair. You couldn't write it, or could you? Broadly smiling and lording it over the other eight, Denzil began to settle into his new position, one step up the ladder, one step closer to the Devil and at least eight steps further away from his so-called colleagues.

Departure took on different guises, it was a staggered approach. Some of the eight had annual leave to take, some decided to be paid for their annual leave entitlement and some just gave up the ghost and went early unable to bear the thought of goodbyes, handshakes and 'oh we're really going to miss you' nonsense. So, let's take you through who did what, and why.

Chapter 5 - People are People

Rene Norton, young, sweet with a whole future ahead of her. She opted to leave early and had already set her sights on becoming a nurse specialising in midwifery. It required a fresh new set of skills, three years of training with multiple examinations to sit, and a sturdy fountain pen. There was no doubt in anyone's mind that this girl would succeed in all she set out to do. She was very charismatic, engaging and most people that met her found her extremely alluring and were transfixed by her beauty and her soft Irish lilt.

Cleo Melville, older heading very much towards retirement but not ready to give up the ghost just yet, decided to take the money and run (literally). She secured a part-time job in her local library very close to where she lived and saw this as the ideal opportunity to indulge herself in her favourite pastime... reading. She was to say the least an avid reader of all genres so this couldn't have been a better choice for her overzealous but very productive mind.

Mel Carter, well with mixed emotions and a heavy heart she decided to literally cling on until she could cling no more. This organisation had been her life, her love, and her comfort blanket. It had seen her through a divorce, a bereavement, the loss of a dear pet, the celebrations of becoming a grandmother and ultimately the meeting of a virtual stranger in a supermarket to now becoming the most precious man on earth.

How hard would it be for her to leave all these memories behind and begin a new chapter somewhere else? And what of all her work babies, how would they get on without her, how would she survive unable to allow each one of them the time and kindness to lend them her ear. Her personality and demeanour drew her to charity work, and it wasn't long before she secured a full-time role in a hospice as an administrative assistant / helping on the wards type role. Absolutely an almost perfect fit for the type of person Mel was.

Millie Knott was devastated, she loved her job, excelled at her job, and could see no reason why she should lose her job. Millie set out to prove how indispensable she was. She drew up a plan of action outlining all that she had set in place, all that was still to take place aligning it to her future vision whilst ensuring it fitted within the organisational plans. She arranged through the "Rottweiler" to present her plan on a five-page flip chart presentation to the Devil Incarnate himself, God loves a tryer! She was sheer brilliance on the day, had an answer to all his questions, was very articulate and had even calculated the financial element ensuring she felt a positive outcome. She was particularly thrilled when the Devil requested, he keep the presentation, but it soon became clear that the Devil wanted the ideas and future plans alright but not Millie, so she scooped up the flip charts with a defiant no you can't have them and shaking with temper, she rolled them up and place them under her arm as best she could, now duly accepting her fate. Not feeling particularly motivated, she had a speech to make at a conference the next day with several partners she had been engaging with. As that day approached, she watched the clock, her speech was on the agenda for eleven a.m. At 10.40 a.m., she was still at home, and it was a thirty-minute journey to the venue. She had a strong urge not to bother turning up, but her conscience wouldn't let her do that. She got ready and left.

Although she arrived a few minutes late, she was welcomed by tumultuous applause. Totally taken aback she collected her thoughts and gave one of the best speeches of her life that day. On conclusion she was presented with a huge bouquet of flowers as a thank you from all the partners for her wonderful work and great achievements. Millie was overwhelmed and once off stage took herself outside to sample the sunshine and breathe in God's fresh air. So much so that she didn't notice a rather rotund gentleman sidle up to her, until he blocked the warmth of the sunshine from her face. Who was this unfamiliar presence and what did he want with Millie? Lurking in the background were two well-dressed gentlemen watching the proceedings.

Anne Leigh, down and out, feeling the full power of rejection, hung her head in shame and closed the world out seeking comfort in her beloved Tigger. How long would it be before she was able to pluck up enough courage to even seek out alternative employment let alone actually successfully attain it? Tigger purred lightly upon the warmth of her lap, gently cleaning his whiskers from ear to ear, content to be loved by his ever-adoring mistress. Seeking solace in Tigger, Anne recalled the previous few days and reminisced about her long-lost job and colleagues. Would she be able to find a job so close to her flat? How was she going to cope and would her ever-hapless love come running to save her from all this? Doubtful but there you have it. Anne left early; she needed the money and had to give herself time to face a new world where all now seemed strange and uncomfortable. She longed for familiarity and so suggested that the team keep in touch via a WhatsApp group and update each other as they went their separate ways. Maybe a Wine O'clock Club could help to ease the pressures of facing so much so soon?

Fee Shand was mad and unable to accept all that had been done to her; she created so many waves it was a wonder the ship hadn't already sunk. She was not about to give up without a fight and as such tried to box clever with both the Devil incarnate and Rupert Hope. Spitting feathers and unable to contain her annoyance, she fought a hard battle for many days. She saw out her notice period battle-scarred and unhappy, but she vowed to return triumphant. Her work was everything, it was what Fee lived for. She loved it, and it loved her. She excelled at all she did and felt crestfallen and bereft when it eventually hit her that she was to be disposed of never to return. She knew that given her age, it would be exceedingly difficult to secure another job and as such she may end up as that lonely old woman, living comfortably but scratching around for things to do. Maybe joining the bridge club, the wine club and going for the occasional gin and tonic with friends. Is this what her life was to amount to going forward? Fee was keen to keep in touch and felt that Anne's groups were a good idea and could even become a lifeline, so she too, signed up to the WhatsApp group and the Wine O'clock Club.

Tim Crocker, well poor innocent and naive Tim, no one to love him and nowhere to go. Gadget man fails to keep his job. So, Tim took the package offered and went early from the organisation. But what now, a trip back to Wales to seek solace with his mother and making the weekly trip to visit his brother or stay steadfast in his little flat trying hard to be dynamic and secure another role in a similar organisation? As a huge lover of tech, Tim was keen to sign up to the WhatsApp group, and, as he liked a drink, he also decided to join the Wine O'clock Club to drink beer. At least now he could keep in touch, venture out occasionally and share experiences going forward.

As news of the newly created WhatsApp group and Wine O'clock Club spread, all affected members of the team joined forces except for Denzil Drum, who was to remain the outcast of the team, and Rupert Hope whom everyone felt was not to be invited.

Rupert Hope hung his head in shame, locked himself into his office like a clam in its shell, only prising himself out for hot water, toilet breaks and to meet the requirements of Rodney Marco his pal and the Devil incarnate. He never issued any kind of apology or statement to his once-loyal staff but chose to stay hidden, praying that this torture wouldn't last much longer. Now thinner-faced with a permanent frown, his once smart demeanour had given way to a wizened old man barely able to stand upright. He opted not to be paid for any outstanding annual leave and to instead work a further month in the job, with maybe the option, or so he thought, that the Devil would change his mind, or an alternative role may present itself. As his departure date loomed, he arranged to meet with the team in secret so that one by one he could offer a token of regret in the form of a bouquet of beautiful flowers for the girls and handpicked Belgian chocolates for the boys. Needless to say, on his departure he received absolutely nothing not even the handshake of the now supremo Devil incarnate, never mind Rodney Marco. Goodbye Rupert Hope, have a nice life.

And there you have it, the fateful nine, all dealt with, all done and dusted, and all put out to sea to sail their own ships or maybe somebody else's.

Chapter 6 - Mother of Mine

"Hurry along Tim, pay the man," she shouted as his elderly mother alighted from the taxicab. Tim fumbled in his pocket and produced a £20 note.

"How much is it, driver?"

"It's £17.50, mate," said the driver.

Tim passed the £20 note through the hatch and waited eagerly for his change before placing his size 8 shoe in a muddy puddle.

On a wet, dank, and dreary day, the only positive was entering the brightly painted building. Tim shuffled up to his mother, the same song line playing repeatedly in his head: 'They tried to make me go to rehab, but I said no, no, no'! Every time he entered the building, it was the relentless repetition of those very sad words that pulled at Tim's heartstrings. Charles was always the favourite son, always the one to shine, always a free spirit to do as he liked and follow his chosen path whatever it may be. For the past four years, Charles had a been a full-time resident at Llandavyff Rehabilitation Centre, paid for in full every six months by Cecelia Crocker, his beloved mother. He was a smart, intellectual man, three years younger than Tim. Mother and second son both with the same initials (CC)—Carbon Copy. Enough said.

Making their way up to the check-in desk Tim ran his fingers around his already dirty collar causing him to splutter. "Do keep up, Tim, and stop fiddling with your shirt."

Tim could already hear a voice in his ear giving him the repetitive answer of "Yes, Mother, I'm coming."

As they made their way along the corridor, carefully keeping alignment with the green central carpet, Tim started to wonder what was to become of his life never mind Charles. Up one flight of stairs to yet another green carpet slightly faded with the bright sunlight, Tim felt very much like he was walking the Green Mile.

"There you are Mother! Why are you late?" said Charles.

"Ask your brother," Cecelia replied. "Anyway, how are you today, Charles?"

With no reply Tim interjected, "Mother's talking to you, Charles, the least you can do is answer her."

"Stop worrying about it, Tim, let Charles take his time and speak when he's ready. Isn't that right, Charles?"

Still no reply.

"I don't know why we bother coming, Mother. It's like trying to get blood out of a stone, and it's never any different!"

"Stop it this minute, Tim! Charles is your brother, and you need to respect that. Go and get us all a nice cup of tea, will you?"

Glad of the reprieve, Tim dutifully shuffled off down the stairs and along the corridor looking for the vending machine. Eventually he happened upon a slightly wonky, slightly rusty old rectangular box which appeared to be somewhat of an excuse for a vending machine. *Nice cup of tea out of that,* he thought. *You must be joking.* It had three green padded chairs flanking its sides, two to the right and one to the left. At that moment he decided to sit for a while and reflect on his situation and possible next steps. *The tea can wait,* he thought as his mind meandered off to explore the unknown. He must have been sitting there for all of ten minutes thinking of his next steps when he was rudely interrupted by a mop and bucket approaching his size 8s.

"Pick your feet up would you, mate; I just need to clean under your chair," said a well-built, slightly older man dressed in a blue or maybe off-white overall with a Llandavyff logo emblazoned on his left breast pocket.

"Oh sorry, there you are," mumbled Tim, as he quickly raised his feet.

"Are you visiting today, mate?"

Tim thought for a moment and was somewhat confused. Could this man think that Tim was an actual resident?

"Erm, yes I am," replied Tim. "I don't come that often as I live several miles away, but I try when I can to accompany my mother who visits my brother regularly.

"Who's that then, mate? Is he on this floor?"

"Nope," replied Tim. *Nope? Where did I get that from, am I mimicking the voice of the inquisitor?* "He's on the third floor"

"Oh, room number 12! Is it Charles?"

"Yes, it is. How do you know that?"

"You look like him and sound like him," he said followed by 'mate'.

Mate again! I am no mate to this stranger, Tim thought as he ejected himself from his seat removing any further obstruction that may complicate the matter. As Tim searched his pockets, he failed to find enough money to operate the vending machine to achieve his ultimate goal.

"Need some change, do you?"

"Oh yes please, I'm 12 pence short, can you oblige?"

At that moment a huge, rough, hairy hand shoved a twenty pence coin towards Tim.

"Here you are, mate, don't worry about the 8p, just hope the tea's worth it."

"Thank you so much," Tim replied as he pressed the given coin into the appropriate slot in the vending machine. A thought suddenly crossed his mind: How would he carry three cups of tea back up to room 12? With great care he imagined.

"Where have you been Tim?" asked his mother rather brusquely.

"Well, I had to go down a floor and find some change to bring back the required items."

"It's too milky and barely warm; I can't drink this!" his mother snapped, thrusting the small brown cup back at Tim.

For twenty-two minutes Tim and his mother tried in vain to converse with Charles. Today he seemed a little different. Although he was never one for small talk, you could usually get him to smile and nod acknowledging the company of his mother and his brother. Not today though. He sat quietly shuffling and fidgeting in his seat, eyes vacantly staring but not looking, Charles seemed more aloof than ever. He had once been a charming, charismatic gentleman with the world at his feet, an accomplished lawyer who had been admitted to the bar, with an air of confidence and often dressed to impress.

Tim wondered whatever happened to his smart, intellectual brother. From a tall, elegant stance and a voice that commanded attention to a now shrivelled, crumpled, and bent-over figure that could barely mumble a coherent word.

Just then Tim's phone pinged.

"Honestly Tim!" his mother said in annoyance.

Tim ignored her for once in his life and proceeded to investigate the ping. It was the Wine O'clock Club (WOC) invitation he'd been waiting for.

Thank goodness, he thought. *There is a God.*

* * * *

As Anne played with Tigger, she knew she had to get her life back on track. No job, an elusive boyfriend and a tidy flat she intended to keep so she went in search of alternative employment. She had worked out her finances and knew that she had some leeway before her money ran out.

So, what would it be, where would it be and what would she like it to be? As her thoughts wandered to her past life, Tigger suddenly dug his claws into her ample thigh causing her to jump.

"Tigger don't do that! It hurts," she complained. But it jolted her back to reality. Anne's eyes scanned the room and a photograph of her and Billy caught her eye.

Is he real? Does he love me or is he playing me? How can I get him to commit—mind you, do I want him to commit? Can I share my life with him, and does he want to share his life with me? Who knows? she thought as she eased herself out of her comfy chair to seek solace in a bar of Cadbury's Diary Milk, snapping it off in sizeable chunks to ensure that it sat securely on her tongue to melt away the heartache. No wonder her waist was getting thicker by the minute.

Turning her thoughts to her previous work colleagues, Anne decided to engage the Wine O'clock Club and one month after departure from the said organisation she contacted the group inviting them via WhatsApp to a 'catch-up' evening. With meticulous attention to detail, she planned a meeting on a Friday evening at seven thirty p.m. This would give everyone a chance to dine before coming leaving enough time to get ready for the meeting. She was excited to see what everyone was now doing, and if anything had changed. She was particularly beside herself knowing that she would again meet up with Fee Shand, whom she had a profound respect for and whom she longed to emulate in every way.

Just then the kettle boiled. She poured the hot water into her favourite mug, bought for her by the wonderful Fee Shand, with 'You're simply the best' painted on the side in black ink, Anne proceeded to fill the mug up to the maximum level, just above the word 'best' to ensure that she had a full mug of hot chocolate. With that, she took the mug, reclined in her favourite chair (well, her only comfortable chair) and with a click of the remote settled down to watch her favourite soap.

Glasses perched on her nose, Tigger on lap, she couldn't help but feel comfortable with things as they stood right at that moment.

Who needs a man anyway, they only disrupt what you already have, she mused, as the *Coronation* theme tune echoed from the television.

* * * *

"Quiet please," said Cleo as three young students entered the library. "Can I help you?"

"Yes please," replied one. "We are looking for books on sailing."

"Follow me," replied Cleo as she led the trio past the history section. "Now then, here is the section on sailing and it goes from the basics of navigation right the way through to nautical examinations. This section covers a multitude of vessels from wind-driven to engine propelled. Is there anything in particular you are looking for?" she asked as she thought maybe they want the section on Stand-Up Paddle Boarding or canoeing.

"Not really. We're just interested in all sorts of sailing from sport sailing to ships. Cooper is set to join the navy in a few months," one of the lads stated as he placed his skinny arm around who was now identified as Cooper.

"Oh, I see, well maybe you need to be researching ships and submarines then, Cooper?"

"Maybe so," he said with a sheepish face which had now turned bright red.

"Not for me," said one of the other lads. "I want to learn to sail properly—you know, hoisting a sail and letting nature take its course, that's what I call sailing."

"Well, I'll leave it with you for now; just let me know if you need any further assistance."

With that, Cleo left the happy trio and returned to the check-in desk to assist what seemed like a very impatient gentleman.

"Three weeks late, I'm afraid. Forgot I'd even got the book. How much do I owe you, my dear?"

My dear? thought Cleo. *I don't think so; how patronising!*

She took the book from his grasp.

"Thought I was going to have to wait another three weeks before anyone came to the desk," he said, his face deadpan.

"Well, I'm here now and that will be £21 please."

"£21!" he retorted.

"Yes, it's £1 per day for the first month and then it rises sharply, so thank your lucky stars you've returned it just shy of one month."

Payment made, the so-called gentleman turned on his heels and left without another word. Cleo picked up the late arrival in preparation for a return to its long-awaited home, now where to place such a title, *To be Improper would be Proper, if it wasn't deemed as Rude*?

Erm... Cleo thought for a moment and filed the book under the Philosophy section, as she wondered if she might see him again.

Cleo was due to finish her shift at five thirty p.m. leaving enough time for a bite to eat before the seven-thirty Wine O'clock Club gathering. She was excited to see what everyone had been up to since their departure from the Devil Incarnates grasp.

*   *   *   *

"Oh, do shut up, Hugh! I am sick and tired of hearing about your new life, your new love and your bloody job. Some of us have got other things to think about, you know."

"Mum don't be like that. He's excited and keen to share what he's been doing, aren't you, Dad?"

"Well only if your mother wants to hear it, Matthew."

"Mother doesn't want to hear it; I've got enough going on with my own life, Hugh, without worrying about yours," Fee Shand said.

Hell, hath no fury like a woman scorned, Hugh thought. This was especially applicable to his ex-wife, Fee Shand.

"Just because you lost your job, Mum, don't take it out on us."

"I'm not, Matthew, but it seems all your father wants to talk about is his own life. I have no job; I'm trying to work out what to do next and some moral support wouldn't go amiss. Anyway, who wants a cup of tea?"

Fee Shand's ex-husband and son had called unexpectedly thinking they would surprise her. They did that alright, but she was none too pleased.

"I am due out tonight to the first Wine O'clock Club and I really don't want to be late. They'll all be there, and I need to catch up on all the gossip."

"Hey, don't tell me, Mum, but will your ever-faithful, diligent, dogsbody assistant, what's-her-name be there as well?"

"Matthew don't call her that! Her name is Anne and yes of course she'll be there, she's organised it all. More tea anyone?"

Fee was keen to see the back of her so-called 'boys' so she would have time to deliberate and pontificate on a suitable but glamorous outfit for the evening's event. She had carefully scanned her wardrobe a few days before picking out at least three outfits that would suit the occasion.

A little black number, very Audrey Hepburn but probably a little sombre for a joyful event, a gorgeous red two-piece with a knee-length skirt and front-buttoned jacket nicely teamed with a white blouse was inching ahead if it wasn't for the navy fitted bodycon dress that enveloped her petite figure and really enhanced her beautiful grey hair. That's it, she'd decided, navy dress, navy high heels, topped off with a pale grey coat that finished just level with her knees. Outfit chosen, Fee Shand was ready.

Let the fun begin, she thought as she hailed a black cab in the pouring rain.

* * * *

One month in and Rene was feeling the pressure. A light blue uniform had replaced her once flirty short skirts and tight blouses. Her beautiful hair was now pinched back in a rather untidy elastic band bunched up at the nape of her neck any old how. Even though her makeup was now more muted, her natural beauty shone through her chocolate-coloured skin, giving her a hue of gorgeousness worthy of a second look. Training was much harder than she'd anticipated. Exams were looming around every corner and shift work was proving difficult to adapt to. All this as well as a young baby and husband had made her life more than busy. Sensible as she was, there was a light at the end of the tunnel, and she knew anything worthwhile was always going to be demanding work.

Her thoughts skipped to the evening's event. Could she get off shift expediently? Did she have enough time to get home, bath Alfie say hello and goodbye to her husband and still be in time for the Wine O'clock Club meeting at seven thirty p.m.? It was going to be tight, but Rene was more than capable of living her life in the fast lane and once she'd made up her mind to go there was no way she was going to miss it.

Loud screams brought her thought process back to reality, "Rene can you get in here! The mother-to-be's cervix is dilating and baby is more than ready to make itself known to the world. One last gasp and out popped the most beautiful little boy you've ever seen, weighing in at 13 lbs and 3 oz. Rene handed the exhausted mother her newborn.

Hush little baby, don't you cry, she thought, and it was at that moment that Rene Norton knew that there was no other job like it in the world.

Having eventually given in to the Devil Incarnate, Mel Carter lifted her patient's head gently and allowed the young man to sip slowly from a plastic beaker carefully curved towards the mouth to allow a more accessible way to drink without excess spillage. She had been working at the hospice for nigh on a month, taking to her role like a duck to water. She loved it, absolutely loved it, and often wondered why she hadn't taken up such a role years ago. She was given a burgundy tunic and navy trousers to differentiate her from the medical team but allow her to evidence that she was staff. The job was made for her, kind and considerate as she was. She was also very much a people person with a caring attitude, and she soon won over the staff, patients, and visitors alike with her natural ability to connect and her immensely caring nature. Mel was one of those people that everyone wanted to be like; she never had a bad word to say about anybody and would always see the good in people.

Today she was on early morning shift, which meant she could finish at two p.m. and would have plenty of time to get ready for the Wine O'clock Club that evening. She was also off shift the next day which meant she could have a good night without having to worry about getting up the next day. It was rather fortuitous that her days off coincided with the Wine O'clock Club.

She often thought of all her colleagues, wondering where they were now, and what they were up to. She hoped everyone was okay, and she was excited to find out later that evening. She also reflected on the likes of Rupert Hope, Denzil Drum, the

Devil Incarnate and Rodney Marco and wondered **how** their lives had changed and what they were doing. Had they all made the right decisions, were they happy, and how was the organisation progressing now? Out of all the team, Mel felt most badly for Rupert. She felt that he had been dealt an awful blow when the realisation hit him that he was also in the firing line. Mel could see the good in him somewhere and as such found herself wanting to look him and up and check all was okay. She didn't though, as she knew that she was once one of those mushrooms hidden in the dark unable to break free and flourish due to the cycle of bad management.

Leaving behind her "best job ever" Millie complied with the rules, signed the paperwork, and left with a handsome package given her length of time in the job. She had settled well, befriended everyone after an initial struggle with Fee Shand (Fee thought she was conspiring with Rupert, and as such was the enemy). In a short space of time, Millie had the measure of the department. She was popular and worked with people from all walks of life. She was a smart cookie and could read a room in a second. So, what was to become of her now? Her departure had seen a rather rotund man approach her post conference and he now wanted to chat to her in private. "Can you collect everything from the conference please Carol?" she said to her assistant "and I'll see you in the coffee bar in fifteen."

With that, Carol left Millie and headed back into the hall. Millie stayed seated as the mysterious man closed in on her personal space.

"Hi there," he said. "Great speech, seems like you were very popular in there."

"Yes," Millie said hesitantly. She added, "Can I help you? Do I know you?"

"Yes and no," came the reply.

Oh, thought Millie, *what now?*

The stranger then proceeded to sit himself down beside Millie and take a cigarette packet from his pocket.

As he fumbled for his lighter, Millie said, "Do you mind? I'm not a smoker."

With that, the stranger did not light the Rothmans and politely returned it to his pocket. After what seemed like an age, the stranger introduced himself as Arthur Attley Junior or AA for short.

"Oh, the fourth emergency service," Millie replied with a slight chuckle.

"I've heard it all before, Millie, but touché for trying."

"Are you with those two guys over there, Mr Attley?"

"Oh, AA please, Millie," he replied.

"Okay AA, are you with those two guys over there, who keep looking this way?"

"I am Millie, I am."

Millie was now getting a little irritated as time was ticking by and she needed to collect her things soon, as the Wine

O'clock Club was beckoning. She decided to be a little more direct.

"What can I do for you, AA?"

"Nothing, Millie, it's what I can do for you!" came the reply. Perplexed and confused, Millie became impatient.

"I know I have intelligence, AA, but I have no idea what you are talking about and what you want. Therefore, can you speak plainly and quickly as I have places to go and people to meet?"

"Have you got any future plans; do you have any work lined up or are you still contemplating your next move, Millie?" came the reply.

Oh my God what is he talking about, she thought, *and what did her movements have to do with this stranger anyway?*

AA could now see she was agitated and as such pressed a rectangular business card into Millie's hand, stood up and quickly joined his two colleagues and was gone in a flash. Millie decided to ignore the card for the time being and shoved it into her jacket pocket without further thought. What time was it now, Millie needed to get a move on, she didn't want to be late for the Wine O'clock club, she really needed a large glass of Merlot right now.

* * * *

"Come in," said the Devil, beckoning as the Adonis of the office entered Hell. "Sit down, Denzil, and tell me what you've been up to over the last month. How are you settling into your new position and what have you changed?"

Denzil thought about telling the Devil he'd changed his car with his significant increase in salary but thought better of it. The air in Hell had now got the pleasantries of a Givenchy and Paco Rabanne mix, like one was trying hard to outdo the other. A loud knock sounded, and the Rottweiler herself entered the room.

"Would you like a coffee, tea or water, Denzil? I can throw in some chocolate digestives as well if you like?"

Gosh, Nia truly had become a Miss Moneypenny, swooning over the Devil and keen to impress, nothing seemed to much trouble.

"Coffee for me please, Nia," Denzil answered.

"I'll take a black tea," stated the Devil patting his rather large stomach whilst stating, "I'm trying to cut down, too much driving and sitting at meetings Denzil, and not enough exercise."

"I'll just leave the door ajar; I won't be a moment," Nia replied.

Denzil started to wax lyrical about his month in the job, lots of words but little was said. The Devil had made a conscious decision to let Denzil rabbit on until the coffee arrived at which point, he would stop him and get down to the real business at hand. In she came, tray in hand, china cups and saucers were the order of the day and true to her word, choccy biscuits adorned the rather large blue and white china plate.

"Will there be anything else?" she asked politely.

"Not for now," came the reply. "Please close the door on the way out."

"Very good," she replied, and with that she was gone, and the door was pulled gently to a close.

She truly was the Devil's woman, Denzil thought.

"Now then Mr Drum (Denzil thought this sounded ominous), you're not meeting your performance objectives!" the Devil yelled. "You had five targets to meet, and you haven't met any of them. Can you tell me why?"

Denzil thought for a moment and with a swift response and a flash of his pearly whites stated that all were midway and to reach their conclusion within the next two weeks.

"Denzil, I took you on and trusted what others said about you. I ignored my instincts and decided that given you were a smart young man you could step up to the task at hand. Now I am not so sure, you talk the talk, walk the walk but what are you achieving?"

Now fidgeting anxiously, Denzil was about to plead big style, his mind had wondered to his beautiful new car, bright red, a bit of an eye-catcher, low-slung, very sleek, and shiny with all the hallmarks of a Bond Movie. He thought it was a real babe magnet (yet to be proved) and he didn't want to lose it. Now back in the room with a jolt from the Devil, Denzil was about to face the fight of his life.

* * * *

"Dad, how long are you going to be? I thought we were going for an early morning run. It's nine thirty a.m. now and you're not ready!" shouted a female voice from the hallway.

"I'm just coming, love! I just had to respond to an urgent text."

With that, Rupert donned his running shorts and slipped into his vest. Nike trainers were the order of the day and off-roaders at that, given that Melissa wanted to run over the hills with the dogs. It was a dull day, warm but at least it wasn't raining as father and daughter set off with two dogs in tow.

"We'll run for forty to fifty minutes, Melissa, as I need to get back and the dogs will have had enough by then. It's hard work running these hills."

"Okay Dad, that suits me as I'm meeting Kathy at eleven in the coffee bar in town."

Rupert had spent the last month trying to find himself. He was bereft and lost. The man he once was had disappeared, he was much thinner now, had gone grey overnight and was forever trying to work out what had happened to him. His wife, although supportive, was pushing him to find work as they had a mortgage to pay, dogs to feed and university fees to find for at least the next year. She was a smart woman, bit of an intellect and fortunately had a job that could support Rupert and the family until such times as he found his feet.

The hills were hard going, and Melissa was well ahead. Rupert found running therapeutic. By letting his mind wander, he was more able to relax and try to come to terms with the ever-changing landscape. Where did it all go wrong for Rupert, was he such a bad man, did he treat his staff unfairly, was he a bit 'knowledge is power' or was he genuinely just totally misunderstood? He still had contact with Rodney Marco, they had become friends over the years and had often dined together at events. Rupert had also socialised with Rodney so was devastated when the Devil's presented plan saw his demise.

Still, he thought as he ran to catch up with his daughter, *at least I can catch up with Rodney and see what's going on albeit I can't get involved any more.*

Rupert had no idea that his once precious team had set up a Wine O'clock Club via WhatsApp which he hadn't been invited to. He knew he was disliked but he thought he'd left on reasonable terms ensuring that each team member had received a parting gift from him.

Once back, he showered and changed, grabbed a coffee, and made himself comfortable in his favourite seat by the window where he could watch the world go by. Melissa shouted goodbye and the door slammed. Rupert now had only the dogs for company as his wife and son had already left. As Beano, a gorgeous red-fox Labrador and Bandit, a black-and-white lurcher settled in front of the fire, Rupert looked down at them and thought, *Maybe this is not a bad place to be*. With that, he picked up his mobile phone and re-read the urgent text; it was from Rodney Marco.

Come over tonight dot, if you can dot; I want to talk, end. Rupert thought for a moment, closed his eyes to consider his options as he started to doze in front of the roaring fire.

Chapter 7 - Wine O'clock Club

It was here at last, the night they'd all been waiting for. It would be a night to remember, Anne thought as she pushed Tigger off her soon-to-be-worn dress. Anne had chosen a rather dowdy number, ankle length, floral, long-sleeved, and clingy paired with Doc Martens. Not the most flattering outfit for the already porky Anne but she liked it and that was the main thing. She decided to wear her hair loose for a change and popped in her contact lenses to accentuate her best feature, her gorgeous dark eyes. She sprayed a little Avon scent behind her ears, her neck and on both wrists.

She hadn't heard from Billy for a couple of weeks and wondered what he might be up to. Nevertheless, she was determined that this wasn't going to spoil her night as she slipped a flashy, sparkling cubic zirconia ring onto her middle finger. *Ready*, she thought, *one last look in the mirror,* as she grabbed her plain brown jacket, blew a kiss to Tigger and was off.

The wine bar was two blocks away from Anne, so she walked, forever thankful of her choice of footwear as she huffed and puffed her way to the entrance having encountered a heavy downpour of rain on the way.

Gosh, she thought, *I really need to do something about my weight.*

Thankfully for Anne, her chosen outfit had an elasticated waist giving plenty of room for manoeuvrability. She was nice and early, arriving a good thirty minutes before the start time. True to her usual self she was able to check the table booking, the position of the table and ensure that everyone attending would have a seat. She did all this before removing her now completely soaked brown jacket and placing it behind a chair to dry out by the state-of-the-art wood burner that was glowing gently in the dim light. She was excited and nervous at the same time. Was she a little plumper than when last she saw them? Would anybody notice, and if so, did she look okay rather than stunning? Okay was fine for Anne.

Single Ladies by Beyonce was playing in the background as Anne spotted her first member coming through the door. After a quick glance of the room, Cleo waved and smiled as she approached Anne.

"How have you been Cleo, you look lovely," Anne said as Cleo hugged her tightly.

"I've been fine Anne; I've been busy and not really had time to reflect too much on how I got here. Will be glad to see and hear how everyone else has been doing since we last met though."

"Thought we'd have a kitty, seems the only fair way to do it, what do you think?"

"Yes, great idea, how much are we contributing, Anne?"

"Shall we say £15 each and see how we go? That should give us around nine bottles of wine or eight if Tim is drinking beer."

"Sounds good to me, Anne. Shall we choose the first bottle? I'm ready for a drink."

With that, both Anne and Cleo sat down with a chilled bottle of Sauvignon Blanc and Cleo began to pour.

Next through the door was one bedraggled Tim, wet through, glasses steamed up to high heaven. He was just about able to see where the two women were sitting as he stumbled over to them.

"Hi there," he said. "What a terrible night! I've only just got out of the taxi around the corner, and I'm soaked already."

Both Anne and Cleo stayed seated and greeted Tim from a distance. His wringing wet musty tweed and squeaky shoes put them off.

"Sit down Tim, let me get you a drink," Cleo said. "It's a pint of mild, is it?"

"Yes, please Cleo; do you want some money?"

"Yes please." said Anne. "We've got a bit of a kitty going here if that's okay Tim, £15 per head.

Tim thought *That's a lot for my beer but hey-ho, it's all for a worthy cause.*

The music in the wine bar appeared to be on a loop and before very long, Beyonce was at it again.

Anne thought, *Oh my God I hope the music is going to change soon!*

This song immediately made her think of Billy and his lack of commitment.

The wine bar was extremely popular this Friday night; it began to fill up quickly with young attractive men, muscular, strong, and looking for love. Slowly but surely, young women started to enter the ark, usually two by two, linking arms, laughing, and having fun. Dressed in their finery, short skirts, tops that barely covered their breasts never mind their torsos, heels that reached the sky causing them to stumble as if already drunk. Made up to the nines, they would flutter their long eyelashes, pout their shining red lips, and scan the room looking for their next mate. What a game this was going to be and all to be played out in the presence of seven out of nine lives.

Next to make their entrance were Rene and Mel. They had arrived together and were sharing a rather wet brolly as they unveiled their outfits beneath two soaked coats. Waving vigorously, they rushed across to meet the gang and began to chatter incessantly before they'd even had chance to order a drink. That said, there was a cool bottle of Sauvignon Blanc adorning the centre of the table coupled with a lovely dark Merlot.

All up, stand to attention, the matriarch has arrived. Girls aloud, *The Sound of the Underground* was now playing at some volume and Fee's entrance was timed to meet the words *"the beat of the drum goes round and round"* as she set her gorgeous albeit wet shoes onto the beautifully polished wooden floor.

Anne was beside herself; she didn't know whether to salute, hug, kiss, or merely wait her turn as Fee peeled off her coat to reveal the most stunning outfit. Anne thought she had become more attractive over that intervening month than she had ever been. With a toss of her sleek grey bob, Fee Shand had arrived.

"Double G&T!" she shouted,

"Fee it's wine, red or white," Anne said.

"I'll take white then please," Fee answered and proceeded to muscle her way into the best chair with the best vantage point.

At that moment Tim thought, *Ah well I'll just move my coat, Fee wants to sit where Fee wants to sit*.

"Six down, one to go," said Anne at which point the door opened and in came Millie.

"Sorry I'm a tad late. Honestly, the traffic was a nightmare, and I was late getting home."

"Never mind, you're here now. What would you like to drink Millie?"

"I'll have a Merlot please and make it large," she replied as she shook the rain from her hair and took a seat between Cleo and Anne.

"Gosh are we all here now, Anne?"

"We are that," Anne replied as each of the seven began to settle into their positions ready for the first monthly update. It had been a while but as a remixed version of Barry White's *Let the Music Play* began to pump out of the speakers, all settled in for the next instalment.

Chapter 8 – You Got a Friend

Rupert woke with a start. *What time is it? How long have I been asleep? Pamela must have come home and nipped out with the dogs,* he thought.

He rechecked his phone. Marco wanted to meet at six thirty p.m. at the local Chinese. Rupert had just enough time to get there. He scribbled a note to Pamela, swilled his face in cold water and changed into a navy pair of Farra trousers and a pink polo shirt. Having popped on a navy jacket he was all but ready to leave. He couldn't image what Marco would want with him, but he was secretly hoping that there may be a way back for him as life hadn't offered him much since his departure.

Rupert chose to get the bus just in case he had a few more than intended with his Chinese. It was still raining hard as he alighted the red number 9 bus near to the restaurant.

"Should have worn a coat," he said quietly to himself as he ran towards the doorway.

As the rain pelted the windows, Rupert found it almost impossible to check whether Marco had made it indoors. As he approached the entrance, he wiped his black Hush Puppies on the doormat before entering the dimly but pleasantly lit restaurant. As he hadn't been given any further instructions, he seated himself in the waiting area along with a several people who were queueing for takeaways.

"One chicken chop suey, one pork and bamboo shoots, and one portion of egg fried rice please."

"Will that be all?" came the reply.

"Oh, and a portion of chips."

"Coming up, take a seat."

"Hi there." A young lad nodded to Rupert as he passed him to sit down. "It's mighty wet out there; I'll need a plastic carrier for my order, else I'll never get home," he chuckled.

"Indeed, you will," responded Rupert, now only half listening to this uninteresting banter.

"Next," shouted the rather stout assistant from behind the counter. It was a never-ending stream of people filing in, soaked, dripping but very much battling the weather to get their Friday night fix.

"Can I help you, sir?" came a somewhat familiar voice. Rupert thought *I know that voice anywhere,* and as he looked up from his now somewhat drier lap, he saw Marco, hand outstretched waiting to greet him.

"Come on Rupert. I've booked us a table over there in a private corner where we have can some time to reflect on all that has gone on."

Rupert, rubbing his bristled chin, thought for a moment, and then followed dutifully on.

Marco hadn't changed one bit; that said, it was only a month since they had last met. Small and stocky, his dark hair greying at the temples, he was sporting a well-tailored suit in a pale grey with accompanying shoes. He was always a well-dressed man. He had a slight Cornish accent having lived most of his young life in Penzance. His voice was more cultured now displaying how far he'd come in his education and attainments in life. He was a friendly fellow, easy to converse with albeit he had a stutter, but he was great with people and made friends for life. Upon meeting, Rupert realised how much he'd missed Marco in his life.

"What are you having to drink, Rupert? You're not driving are you?"

"Whiskey and ginger, thank you, Marco, and no, I'm not driving. I came on the number 9, dropped me just across the road."

"Okay," said Marco as he beckoned the waiter. "Vodka and lime for me, no ice, thanks. Same as usual, Rupert?" he said as he opened the menu.

"Yes please."

"Two chicken, one with bamboo shoots and one with cashew nuts; egg fried rice times two, a portion of chips and some prawn crackers please."

"Thank you," said Marco. "Now, where do we begin?"

* * * *

A cacophony of sound made it difficult to hear all the details, with the Eagles' *Lying Eyes* now playing at full blast, several people on the dance floor, a packed wine bar and several people raising their voices to be heard, maybe this wasn't going to be the catch-up night that everyone had intended. That said, Rene, Mel and Cleo were off the starting line with their rundown of current activities. All three had new jobs, new lives and felt in control for the first time in ages. Each reacted differently to their swift departures from the organisation but all three still felt hard done to and clearly laid the blame at Rupert and the Devil's door.

"What can we do? We are where we are," said Cleo. "All paid up and away from the toxic organisation."

"Speak up, Cleo, that bloody music is making it difficult to hear you," said Tim.

She repeated herself for a second time with her volume now turned up a few degrees. All seven still had an axe to grind and felt that the Rupert would eventually find his feet doing something and the Devil would now be well and truly ensconced in the organisation getting to grips with his new team. One person more than anyone else felt a great angst and wanted revenge in some capacity or another and as such Fee set about convincing the group that 'where there's a will, there's a way'.

At that point, Millie had remembered her visit from AA and as luck would have it, she had the same jacket on that she'd worn when she quickly placed that business card in her pocket and forgot about it. Having explained to the group in a rather loud voice what had gone on, she proceeded to fiddle in her pocket to find the said card. After a few seconds and three pocket searches later, Millie revealed the card. Before she had chance to read it out loud, Fee Shand snatched it from her grip and carefully and silently read what was written. She then took the card, stood up and read out loud in a truly clear and precise voice what was written on the card in black ink: -

Got a problem, call on us.

All you need without the fuss!

On the reverse of the card, written in red was **'the devil's in the detail'**.

Please Call: with a number ending: **666**

What on earth was this? Who was AA anyway and why did he target Millie? Did he know something the group didn't, or did the group have something he wanted? What a conundrum.

Tim was uncomfortable. He wanted nothing to do with it; although he was intrigued, he felt safer in the knowledge that to do nothing would be the right thing. Was **this** card targeted at Millie or the wider group? Further investigation was required otherwise the puzzle could not be solved. As the drinks flowed, the card was placed back into one of Millie's many pockets. There it stayed as the night progressed. No one had forgotten what was on offer, but all had decided to park it until another day when each could think rationally without alcohol affecting their judgement.

Thank the Lord for that, thought Tim as he downed yet another pint of mild.

Chapter 9 - Loving Angels Instead

The company had been running for ten years, very successfully, under the direction of Mr Arthur Attley Junior. Mr Attley enjoyed heading up Avenging Angels (AA) as it did what it said on the tin. He had a reputation for getting the job done, quickly, efficiently and to the clients' total satisfaction. Discreet and to the point, nothing was beyond the company's capabilities. He had taken over from his father also aptly named Arthur which for ease of reference required no changes whatsoever to the company name. Arthur was a married man, getting on in years. He had a portly figure and a belly hanging uncomfortably over his Gucci belt; it was clear that he liked the finer things in life. His suits were handmade, and he had a visiting tailor to ensure that they were always let out in the right places allowing him the pleasure of eating whatever he liked.

Arthur had been married to Carol for fifty years and loved her more now than the day he'd married her. Five children later and living in a large, detached mansion, Arthur knew he had made it. Now a grandfather of six and preparing to hand over his company to his eldest son, he felt that his life was very much on track.

As his eldest son was named Elliott Andrew, Arthur asked Elliott to consider using his middle name for the business allowing AA to keep its trading name thus ensuring continuity under the new director. Elliott was happy to agree to this request. Elliott had a lot to learn from his father and was settling well into the business after spending eighteen months shadowing his father.

Arthur Attley Senior was a man of military precision. He had been a captain in the army and had served Queen and country for all his adult life. Now retired and well into his nineties, his days were spent in a military care home where he was extremely well looked after and very comfortable. The home was close to Arthur Junior and, as such, Arthur, his children and grandchildren would visit Arthur Senior regularly. This brought him intense pleasure as his wife of many years had passed some three years earlier.

There was such a likeness in both Arthurs: they had the same smart stance, the same attitude to work, and both were highly intelligent men with an air of authority. What's more, they were very personable with the ability to give orders and direction in a very assertive yet non-aggressive way. Both were immensely popular with their staff and both extremely generous. No wonder Avenging Angels was so successful.

Arthur Senior had always wanted to join the army; he made it is lifelong ambition and studied hard at school. He joined the territorial army at a young age to gain as much experience as possible. He loved uniforms and dreamt that one day he would don a smart military style suit and become a leader of men. It was in his blood. Visionary, personable with excellent communication skills, Arthur Senior was soon noticed. He was upright, aware, and with an unmistakable gait so it wasn't long before he came to attention of senior officers. By commissioned invitation, he accessed the officer's route and worked hard to ensure that he made it through the ultimate goal... becoming an officer and eventually a captain of men. His moment had arrived, and he intended to make the most of it. He had served in the army for thirty years by which time his health was failing, and his physical and mental stature had passed its peak. But, by gum, what a life of service he had given. He was totally respected by his men and honoured by all as he stepped down off the podium to begin his life as a civilian.

Once retired from the army, Arthur Senior wanted to hone his skills, to make something of himself and use what he had to better the world. He had witnessed so much violence and hurt, so much pain and suffering, that he knew he could become the sticking plaster for all those that bleed.

Arthur Junior, also a military man, had picked up more than enough skills from his father to ensure the continuation of a great business. As a youngster, he used to play with his father when the latter was home from war, listen to his stories and long to be at least half the man his father was. He had a chance as an only child and a son at that; he knew he could make his father proud. With no siblings to entertain him, Arthur Junior would research war, guns, fighting and battles to help to lay the foundations and embed knowledge in preparation for his father's harrowing but interesting stories. When his son was younger, Arthur Senior would teach him to shoot. Target practice was often a tin can on a tree; his father would then offer a big tub of ice cream if his son could hit the can in five shots or fewer. Arthur Junior soon became a perfect shot and could more often than not hit the can in one or two shots. Practice makes perfect his father used to say. So quite often Arthur Junior would while away the time in the garden shooting tin cans, much to his mother's annoyance. He wanted to be more than perfect when his father returned home on leave so that they could spend quality time together.

From a young age, Arthur Junior learned to fight. He was enrolled at the local judo and boxing club and under the martial arts law, was taught discipline, respect, and control which, his father felt, were all essential skills required for later life. As a child Arthur senior often shared a finger of shortbread with Arthur junior as a reward for all his efforts and hard work whilst his father was away. They would sit in the garden and Mrs Attley would bring out a cup of Earl Grey tea and a glass of fresh orange juice. One packet of shortbread biscuits accompanied the drinks which contained two oblong sugary fingers, one for Arthur senior and one for Arthur junior. Arthur senior used to tell his son that these biscuits were special and were seen very much as a reward for his men after a long-fought battle.

Arthur Junior was an accomplished scholar and as such went on to realise his ambition to also join the army entering Sandhurst as a Commissioned officer. This made Arthur Senior extremely proud of his son and often referred to them as "two peas in a pod". Arthur junior served for five years reaching the rank of Lieutenant. He was well respected in a secure and well-paid job allowing him the salary that would enable him to enjoy the finer things in life, just like his father before him.

As an only child he was well provided for and, as his father had pointed out, 'the world is your oyster'—whatever that meant, he used to think. In time Arthur Senior thought that his son could eventually join the business and run a tight ship. Arthur senior saw Arthur junior as the next guiding light of Avenging Angels with a ready-made job once he exited the army.

So, as the sibling business started to build, based very much on advice and guidance for those that needed help, Arthur Junior realised his fathers' ambition and went into the business post army.

Arthur Junior's other children, two more boys and two girls (he had always wanted a big family, being an on only child), stepped away from the business choosing instead their preferred pathways in life. His girls married young and had children quickly, so he became the proudest grandfather ever.

His boys chose vastly different careers. One became a public servant and the other opted for life on a farm, producing good quality beef and pork with lucrative contracts supplying local butchers.

His daughters, one a qualified nurse and one a teacher, had both cut their careers short to have children but cleverly chose careers that they could easily return to. Arthur Junior was blessed, and he knew it. He had a beautiful wife, gorgeous clever children, a father he absolutely adored, a lifestyle many would envy and a business that was going from strength to strength. What more could he ask for?

Chapter 10 - Dancing with the Devil

Now at the biggest crossroads of his life, was Denzil about to sell his soul to the Devil? With little choice and mounting debts (including his babe magnet), Denzil decided to ask for a lifeline.

"Give me another month to show you what I can do. If I fail within that given time, I will have no alternative but to hand in my resignation."

"One month from today, Denzil. If you fail me, you will literally burn in hell. I also have targets to meet and need to ensure that I meet them for the sake of my job. You need to achieve at least four out of the five of yours but five would clearly be better," the Devil snorted. "Now go away and get it done."

The door closed gently behind Denzil as he lived to breathe another day. He knew that he couldn't go on like this; he was clearly failing and had on many occasions been given a boost up by Rupert Hope, but now he was alone literally fighting for survival.

"Have a good day Denzil; I hope your meeting went well," shouted Miss Moneypenny.

If only she knew, thought Denzil as he legged it down the stairs and back to the comfort of his look-out chair in the office. His ship was fast sinking and with no one to bail him out he knew that he was in for a rocky ride. How could he steer the ship to calmer waters buying some time to douse the Devil's flames. As he thought deeply, his eyes closed. Sweat began to creep into his furrowed brow and the pain was clearly etched on his once bright, smiling face.

As the Devil sat back releasing his larger-than-life frame into the comfort of his leather-backed office chair, he also pondered on his future. He had made many of the changes required of him and made them very successfully too. What next, what did he want now?

His mind wandered to his father. How was he getting on? What life had he now got, and what more could the Devil do to improve it? Did he make the right decision engaging in such long commutes, he wondered, given his circumstances? Would he be better living a little closer to work and going to see his parents at the weekends? Did he want to live closer; might it give him the chance of building some kind of relationship with someone or was it too late for that?

A loud knock on his door interrupted his pensive mood and once again he was back in room.

"Come in."

It was his boss, Rodney Marco.

"Hello Marco, what can I do you for?"

"Well, I'm planning on seeing Rupert this evening; he still isn't working and to be honest he's on a downwards trajectory."

"Nothing I can do, Marco; it is what it is. I have completed what was required of me and as such have nothing more to say on the matter."

"But—"

"No buts about it. Now, was there anything else?"

Marco had agreed the Devil's position and was now being treated as though he were the minion.

"Can't you have a word? He's been a lifelong pal, and I feel somewhat responsible for where he now finds himself."

"No, no and no," came the reply. "He needs to sort himself out; he's had carte blanche in this organisation for far too long anyway, it is what it is, and you brought me in to clear up the mess in this office!"

With that, Marco backed carefully up to the door and made his exit.

"Gosh he's a busy man today, Marco," remarked the Rottweiler.

"In-in-deed," Marco stuttered as he left in a hurry.

Was the Devil incarnate about to move up a gear by replacing Marco? *How come was he so authoritative?* thought Marco. *Am I for the chop? Surely not,* he thought as he began to close his briefcase for the day. As he popped on his overcoat, he saw the rain lashing on the windowpane. He made one almighty dash to his car and started the engine. Another day done but what was he going to tell Rupert?

Chapter 11 - Abide With Me

"Going to the chapel and I'm going to get married…" *If only*, thought Tim as he stood outside breathing in God's fresh air. Three weeks had passed since the Wine O'clock Club.

"Oh, Hi Tim, nice to see you again. Shame it's under such sad circumstances," said Rupert as he shook Tim's hand.

"Hello Rupert, how've you been?" Tim replied.

"Well, I can't complain, Pamela is working hard at the moment helping to keep things afloat. I'm afraid I am struggling to find work but not giving up. It's not easy when you're a bit older, Tim."

"I know," said Tim with a sigh. "I'm still looking too. Most of the time I don't even get an interview. I spend ages filling in the application form and once sent off, never hear anything," he said with a sigh.

Just then who should roll up but Fee Shand looking resplendent in black, hair beautifully placed beneath a pill-box hat making the milliner proud. Her outfit was finished off with some gorgeous black lace gloves to add style to an already elegant look. She immediately bypassed Rupert and went straight to Tim, who wondered why he was so popular.

"Well, hello, Tim. How are you since we last met? Did you get home alright? Absolutely shocking weather wasn't it? All ready for the next one?"

Tim thought for a moment, four questions in quick succession with no time to answer.

Did Fee Shand require an answer, Tim wondered, *or it was it a distraction tactic played out in front of Rupert to save her speaking to or even acknowledging him? By gum, she is a conniving so-and-so,* thought Tim.

As the chapel began to fill, a piped version of *Amazing Grace* began to echo in the morning sunlight. With fifteen minutes to go, Cleo, Mel, Rene, and Millie entered the chapel stopping briefly to catch Tim's eye before walking solemnly into the pretty chapel to take their places near to the front. Millie had noted a somewhat familiar man sitting near the back of the chapel with another as she rushed to take her seat. Where had she seen him before or had she, she wondered as she politely nodded to acknowledge Rupert. He was already seated in the opposite aisle when in rushed Marco who hurriedly sat down beside him.

With no sign of Anne and the introduction of *Abide with Me* now engulfing the small chapel, the congregation was asked to stand as the pall bearers entered the main doors carrying a beautiful oak coffin balanced on each of their four shoulders. As they arrived at the altar, the coffin was placed gently on a wheeled bier in preparation for its final journey.

*   *   *   *

Anne was full of good intentions. She had prepared her outfit, fed Tigger and was about to exit her tidy flat leaving enough time to make the funeral. As she closed her front door and headed down the steps who should be coming the other way but the elusive Billy. His curly blond hair cascaded over his forehead, and his slightly tanned skin giving emphasis to those beautiful blue eyes and his strong muscular physique made him impossible to resist.

"Where are you going, Anne? You look lovely."

"Billy, what a surprise! You never said you were coming?" "Well, I'm here now," he said as he pulled Anne towards him kissing her gently on the cheek.

"Billy, I need to go."

"Really?" he said. "Come back inside and share this bottle of Champagne with me; I think we have something to celebrate."

"And what may that be, Billy? I never know where you are, how long you're going to be away and if you're even coming back. I spend most of my time on my own, well with Tigger, just staring at a photograph of you not knowing what's going on. There is no contact from you, let alone any commitment. I really can't go on like this."

"Have you been talking to that Fee Shand again?" Billy grunted.

"What if I have?" Anne said. "At least I can offload how I feel. She gives me good advice and supports me emotionally."

"Anne, I love you, I want to be with you. I've missed you!"

With those few words, Anne's heart melted as Billy pulled her close and began to caress in a way he had never done before. As the cork popped, the liquid began to flow, and Anne wriggled and writhed as if in heaven.

Tigger felt the view was most definitely not for him, so he scurried away through the cat flap to be greeted by the warmth and sunshine of the morning.

Well, I've missed it now, Anne thought as she pressed her ample breasts against Billy's warm and glistening chest. As he entered her once again, she groaned with delight. *'At last, my love has come along, my lonely days are over, and life is like a song' (Lyrics by Mac Gordon)* or so she thought.

*   *   *   *

With the final eulogy now complete and Eva Cassidy's *Fields of Gold* echoing through the small chapel, the oak coffin with its precious cargo placed carefully inside was gently making its way through to meet its maker, whoever that may be. The flaming furnace now up to temperature was ready to receive its next visitor. One final glance at the altar saw the lid of the coffin disappearing and for the very last time, the congregation pondered on the beautiful yet sad words 'You'll remember me when the west wind moves upon the fields of barley...' Then they filed out into the glorious sunshine.

The wake was to be held in the pub around the corner from the chapel. All the congregation had been invited. It was the most gorgeous day, the birds were singing, the pavements were littered with people going about their daily busy, sunshades, coffees in hand, jackets slung casually over shoulders, the sound of chatter and the hustle and bustle of the traffic made it hard to believe that a funeral had just taken place.

It was very evident from her stunning outfit that Fee Shand was going to make the most of the event, parading up and down like a peacock seeking the attention of a mate. She was mortified that Anne hadn't shown and decided that she would seek out her excuses post the wake.

Inside the pub, the bartender ushered them into a beautiful room set out with several small white poses adorning each table. It was five to a table with no set seating plan. There was a bar placed in the corner of the room, it was announced that the first round of drinks was on the house.

There was a stream of light coming from what appeared to be patio doors, and as Millie went to investigate, she found herself outside with the warm glow of sunlight on her face. What a lovely place she thought as she sipped her Prosecco reflecting on the service and life in general as she plonked herself down on a wrought iron garden chair thoughtfully padded with some bright green cushions.

In the silence of that moment, Millie came to terms with where she now was in life. Her thoughts were then rudely interrupted by a man she'd seen before but couldn't place.

"Hello again Millie," he said, his familiar voice ringing in her ear.

"Sorry, do I know you?"

"Yes, we met at your last conference, and it was sunny then."

"Oh yes, you're the man that asked if I had any future plans, isn't that right?" she said, while feeling unwilling to engage him any further.

"Well, have you?" he said.

"Do you know," she said, "I was just thinking of my options before you appeared." Millie then looked the stranger in the eye and added, "Oh you gave me a card; you were quite insistent. I was rushing, and you pushed it into my hand. To be honest I haven't even looked at it. Actually, I think I have it with me." She checked her pockets and pulled it out on the first attempt. "Arthur Attley that's you. I remember now, and you had two other guys lurking in the background. What can I do for you, Mr Attley—oops, AA?"

"Read the card, Millie. I need an extra pair of wings," he said.

As the afternoon moved to early evening, the wake concluded, and people started to drift away. What a sad day it had been, However, the weather was beautiful, the service, simple but quite remarkable, the attendance excellent and now at the closure of proceedings, life would continue on its merry way as God would have intended.

It would only be a couple of weeks until the next Wine O'clock Club, so farewells were brief finishing with 'see you soon'.

The congregation then departed into the early evening sunshine.

Chapter 12 - Three's A Crowd

Rodney Marco, brave, bold, or just plain stupid? Much of his life had been spent working for the same organisation trying to ascend to the very top but never making it. Now being spoken to and treated like an underdog by the very man he sought out to "shake things up." He was very fond of Rupert Hope and was as devasted as he had been when he lost his job. The instruction was to remove all staff whose current workload was concluding before they began to work on new projects, along with any identified staff supporting them. In Marco's eyes, Rupert Hope was not in this tranche. Perplexed as he was, he had to accept the inevitable and watch helplessly as Rupert prepared the leave the organisation.

During the Devil incarnate's first few weeks at the organisation, Marco and Rupert supported and respected him. They understood what had to be done and allowed the Devil to proceed. During those first few months, Marco, Rupert, and the Devil would spend time drinking at the local pub and Marco would brag about what a sailor he was. Rupert had been out with him on several occasions making a weekend of it at the local loch.

Marco owned a small Laser dinghy that he accessed most weekends. He was divorced with no children. His wife had left him for another, taller, better-looking more charismatic and charming gentleman called George. George and Mrs Marco soon became an item and there was talk of Mrs Marco marrying George in the not-too-distant future. This didn't please Marco, but he was between a rock and a hard place. If he wanted to continue to live in the marital home, he needed to accept the situation.

George was not only a looker he was also very wealthy and had met Mrs Marco at an art exhibition. Apparently, it was love at first sight (whatever that means Marco often thought). So, when not working, Marco spent his days on the water reflecting on his past life and thinking about his new one. He was lonely, angry, upset, unloved and worried what the future may hold. Now with the Devil not only taking control within the organisation but of him as well, he felt that he was experiencing what hell was like on earth.

As Marco pondered about his future, he wondered whether he should invite Rupert and the Devil to a weekend of dinghy sailing, a few pints and meal in the local. He thought that this may be a way to get Rupert back into the fold and for the Devil to soften up a bit and see what Rupert really had to offer. It would also remind the Devil who really was the boss. He knew that Rupert would be up for it, all he had to do was convince the Devil to take a weekend away from his parents and come and have a bit of fun.

The loch could be difficult to navigate when the wind blew in an easterly direction; it created a tide that made for heavy going. Marco would need to pick a weekend when the weather was at its best to allow both Rupert and the Devil to enjoy the experience.

Could he do it, could he bond them? Could he curry favour and gain control once again? If so, what was his plan?

Chapter 13 - Take Me Home

The road was long with many a winding turns and the traffic chaotic. Darkness engulfed the Mercedes as the engine purred gently through the night. A few more miles to go and the Devil would be back in the fold of his loving parents. How he longed for a relationship like theirs, warm, cosy, oozing love, and affection even in their later years. He felt betrayed, unloved, and very much alone, he thought, as his car glided to a stop on his parents' drive.

Another weekend of caring, another weekend of repetitive conversation with his father, where he would have to tell him time and time again a) who he was; b) what was going on at work; and c) explain why his father only saw him every couple of weeks or so.

With a similar stature to his father, his mother would often say to him, "While you're alive, your father will never be gone."

The Devil's father was now well into his eighties, diagnosed with dementia for the last four years, progressing quite rapidly, the Devil knew it was only a matter of time before his beloved father would need to go into a care home for the final days of his life. His mother, although spritely, had little or no time to herself due to his demands and his constant wandering. It was difficult at times, to keep a watchful eye on his antics.

Once settled inside the well-appointed three-bedroom bungalow, the Devil sat back with a large mug of tea, his polished brogues resting neatly by his feet, his suit jacket placed carefully over the back of the chair. He was now relaxed and ready to listen to his mother's tales of what had been happening over the past week.

"I can't keep living my life like this," she said. "I need to seriously consider what to do with your father. He's becoming really difficult, and I am struggling to dress and undress him at the moment, as he's fighting my every move. Can you help, son? Is it worth bringing in some extra help? I think I would prefer this to putting him in a care home. You are so far away now, I feel alone and uneasy and to be honest, I think I'm getting a bit depressed. Might it be worth getting a live-in carer, son?"

"If you think that's the answer, Mum, whatever you want, I'm happy to foot the bill. Anything to make life happier for you and Dad."

"Well, you're not here, are you, just when I need you the most. I know you have your work, and I understand that, so something has to be done."

"Do you want me to see what's available, Mum, and organise a time to see some potential carers that may meet our requirements?"

"Oh yes please son, can you make sure you're here when we see them? I'm not great at picking the right type of person, do you know what I mean?"

"Yes of course, Mum. I'll arrange it as soon as possible and travel up when we get a few to interview."

"Thank you so much son, I know it's a big ask given all your responsibilities at your new place of work but honestly I wouldn't ask if I didn't need the help."

"It's fine Mum. Now, let's enjoy our cuppa and you tell me what's been happening since my last visit."

The Devil and his mum settled in for the evening; his father was now fast asleep and peaceful, at least for a few hours. The Devil knew that he needed to work quickly otherwise his weekends would be clearly mapped out for him. He wanted more of a life outside of work and as such thought he'd get onto the care agency first thing on Monday morning.

Chapter 14 - Think Carefully

There came a knock at the door, which got louder with every thud of the door knocker.

Who could this be? thought Anne, while calling out, "Hold on, I'm coming." *Oh my God, it's Fee*, thought Anne unhappily as she partially opened the door.

"Come on, hurry up girl, I haven't got all day."

"And good day to you to, Fee," Anne replied.

"Well, where have you been?" she said as she made her way through the hallway, spying a wonderfully comfortable seat in the lounge, which was warm and clearly was where Anne had been sitting with Tigger before she was rudely interrupted.

"What do you mean?" asked Anne.

"Well, you didn't make the funeral. I waited and waited for you, and you didn't show, yet you said you'd be there." Before Anne had chance to answer, Fee went on. "It was lovely and there were lots of colleagues there, all wondering where you were too."

"Well," began Anne but and before she could get any further, she was rudely interrupted again.

"Don't tell me that fly-by-night is back please."

"I beg your pardon?" said Anne. "What do you mean?"

"You know exactly what I mean, Anne. Has the wanderer returned? That's the only possible reason you didn't show, because the ever-elusive Billy is back."

How can Fee be allowed to talk about Billy like that; what right does she have? thought Anne. *She's clearly not my boss anymore, so why am I listening to what she has to say!*

"Anne, you need to dump him, dump him, *dump him*, that's what I say!"

"Do sit down, Fee," Anne said mustering a modicum of decorum. "Would you like a cup of tea, coffee or a glass of something stronger?"

"A nice glass of white for me please, Anne," came the reply.

As Anne popped into the kitchen, Fee scanned the room, spotting the photograph of Billy over the fireplace. This prompted her to shout, "So where's he been then?"

Anne ignored her and thought she'd finish pouring the wine and pick up the conversation once back in the lounge.

Anne pulled up a stool and handed Fee her wine, Tigger meanwhile was playing with a ball of red wool on the floor. A moment of silence followed before Anne said, "Fee, I know you mean well, but my life is my life and what I choose to do with it is up to me, don't you think?"

"Well yes and no," Fee replied. "I don't want you to make any mistakes, Anne; it's bad enough we've both lost our jobs never mind anything else."

"Fee I'm fine. Actually, I've applied for a couple of jobs now relatively close to home, so fingers crossed."

"Oh," replied Fee, quite belligerently, seemingly unhappy to hear that Anne was getting on with her life. "That's good, then, when do you hope to hear?"

"Next week," Anne said.

"Brilliant," replied Fee.

With that, Fee relaxed into her wine and began to ease up on the intense questioning.

"If you must know, Billy *did* surprise me. I was all ready to attend the funeral and he suddenly appeared out of the blue. Hence my absence from the funeral. His job takes him away quite a bit, Fee, but he always comes back."

"Indeed, he does, Anne, like a bad penny always turning up."

"What have you got against him, Fee? He's a really nice fella, and I am very fond of him."

"That's the main thing then Anne, grab your happiness while you can."

Anne thought *That's a turn up for the books* and with that the subject of Billy was no more.

"Anyway, how are *you*, Fee? What's been going on in your life apart from the funeral?"

"Well, I'm still looking for some kind of part-time work, more or less impossible at my age, but I'm biting the bullet and giving it a go. The ex-husband is a still a pain and keeps dropping by, won't leave me on my own for too long, that said, I'm quite glad of the company sometimes. I do keep thinking 'what if'.

"What do you mean 'what if'?" Anne said.

"You know, what if we were still there, what if something happened to the Devil and we could all get back to where we were."

"Honestly, Fee, that isn't going to happen and anyway you have signed away your rights of ever returning to the organisation now. You've taken the money and literally run."

"I know, Anne, but have you ever heard of revenge?" said Fee.

"Gosh what do you mean, Fee?"

"Time to get our own back."

"No, no, no," said Anne. "Impossible, and anyway I have no idea what could be done and more to the point, who'd do it?"

With that, both sipped their wine while Anne tickled Tigger's tum. She refilled their glasses and both settled down with a few nibbles and snacks Anne had cobbled together at the last minute. It looked like Fee was here for the duration.

Chapter 15 - Pussy Cat, Pussy Cat

A beautiful small yet perfectly formed ball of ginger fluff, that is the only way Tigger could be described. He was the most handsome kitten of all time, stripped like a Bengal tiger with a white tip balanced carefully on his tail as though he had dipped his tail in a tin of white paint. He was one of a litter of five kittens born at the local rescue centre to a mother predominantly black with a hint of white through her tail and on the top of her head. All kittens and their mother had secured new homes, with the newly named Tigger sporting a blue collar and bell about to begin his new life with his human mum, Anne.

Tigger was a sophisticated cat, clever, streetwise and more than capable of looking after himself. He was very resilient, enjoyed a challenge, adored playing with most things and loved to explore and investigate his surroundings. He was a curious cat, to say the least.

Anne had always loved cats and had grown up with them in the family home. Her parents had two, a black-and-white cat called Zebra, and a pure white cat called Snowflake. She adored them both and as a schoolchild would often ask for their help when she got stuck with her homework. Anne had two brothers who also enjoyed the cats' company and all five on them could be seen playing on the local haystacks in the field adjacent to their house. Zebra lived until he was fifteen and died of a heart failure shortly after a visit to the vets diagnosed his condition. Snowflake went on to live another three years before she crossed a busy main road and just wasn't quick enough.

Anne's parents were heartbroken and decided that as they were getting on in years it wouldn't be fair to have another cat as they often live relatively long lives. That's when Anne vowed to get another cat when she was old enough and living an independent life.

My how time had passed and here she was with Tigger, thirty something, unmarried, a spinster through and through she thought, unless Billy were truly ready to commit. Tigger was Anne's life, she absolutely doted on him, no Kitty Kat for him, though. Instead, he would get slowly grilled fresh chicken with a hint of olive oil, sardines, fresh fish, canned tuna, and full fat milk! A highly sprung mattress, deep and soft, complemented by a rather snug, duck down duvet for Tigger to cosy up in close to his mistress every night. He was more than spoilt.

Although an outdoor cat, Tigger loved to be in at night, no prowling the streets for him looking for unsuspecting prey. He preferred the warm sunlight on his fur, rolling around on the small patch of grass Anne had at the rear of her flat, where a rather elaborate deckchair adorned most of the area. It was quite a sun trap to the rear and Tigger knew it. So, if he wasn't in the flat, you could almost guarantee that he'd be in the square patch (couldn't really call it a garden) sunning himself on the deckchair or the sliver of lawn to the right of it. Mrs

Campbell next door loved Tigger and would often call him to the fence where she'd stroke his beautiful ginger fur making him purr loudly with delight. She told Anne that she'd care for Tigger any time and adopt him if necessary. Mrs Campbell was a lovely woman, married to Norman for an age and both getting on in years now. Retired and living a very comfortable life, Mrs Campbell spent her days doing exactly what she wanted. *What a wonderful life,* thought Anne. "That'll be me one day," she told Tigger, "albeit a while off."

Tigger was now four years old and had grown into a lovely cat, he was extremely popular locally both with people and other cats. Dragon and Matilda, just a stone's throw from Tigger, loved to call on him and as a threesome they would wander off down the street to seek out 'what's new pussycats'. Very handsome that looked indeed, Tigger displaying his whiter than white bits against his gingernut body; Dragon, shiny black with a left white sock, and Matilda, slender, sleek with her grey fur resembling a fine velvet coat.

Chapter 16 - Tim Fix

Like a pendulum swinging back and forth, Tim felt that he was on the road to hell. Nothing but nothing was going his way and, to add insult to injury, his mother was on the warpath. She demanded she see more of him now he wasn't working.

Cecelia, you're shaking my confidence daily, he thought as she texted him again for the umpteenth time.

"When are you coming home?" she demanded. "You don't need to live there anymore by yourself, Tim. You haven't got a job and can't seem to find one."

Confidence booster, Tim thought. *How many times do I need to spell it out to her that I am not coming home and that I want to stay put?*

The mere thought of living again with his mother and being introduced as the one who didn't make it, didn't really seem that inviting to Tim. He understood that she was lonely; he understood that accompanied visits to his ever-wonderful brother Charles would make it feel more like home for both Cecelia and Charles.

Albeit Tim had a mathematical brain, it didn't take a genius to know that this situation would never work. He ignored her texts and made up his mind to contact her in the morning when he was feeling less irritated and tired. A more rational approach with whatever excuse he could think of would appeal to her gentler side. He would tell her that his phone was on charge, hence the missed texts.

With that problem now resolved in Tim's head, he resorted to a small whiskey and began the search for his ever-elusive headphones. His calculations had given him another two months or so to find work before he would have to start selling a few precious items to ensure that he remained in his flat. He could also sell some of his crypto currency if he had the mind to. That said, his overbearing mother would, if necessary, help with his finances, or so he thought. Best thing would be to secure a job as soon as possible, he reminded himself as he downed the last bit of Jura which had been watered down by the ice cube now virtually melted in the glass.

As he reflected on his life, his eyes grew weary and began to close allowing his mind to wander, evidencing what had gone on prior to his departure from the organisation. Tim had always been a 'safe pair of hands', called on for anything technical. With his trusty sidekick Cleo, both had a reputation for solving IT errors pertaining to complicated computer programming. He was never short of work; the organisation relied on his ability to comprehend and communicate difficult algorithms and not only trace but fix the problem at source. This was not something many people could do, so Tim's departure didn't seem to make any sense. Who would do this job now, who was capable of such a job and how was it all going to work? Tim had no idea as he drifted into a deep sleep, glass still in hand.

Charles wasn't coping with his confinement so well of late. He had become restless and moody with barely a word spoken to any of the care staff. He had one friend, one colleague, one man that he could confide in, one man that would listen to him and one man who had very much become his confidant.

Colin Clappin had worked at Llandavyff for nigh on fifteen years and had seen people come and go. He was a tall, well-built burly character, with forearms to match Popeye's. He had worked in the building trade since a nipper, at first helping his father and then later working for his uncle until he fell from the scaffolding and injured his back. Two steel rods later and a month in hospital at the tender age of fifty-five years, he had to consider alternative employment.

Welcome to Llandavyff, he thought as he took on the challenge of keeping the home at the top of its game. Maintenance person, cleaner, gardener and quite often driver, Colin enjoyed the variety of his job. He had seen people come and go over the years, he had made several friends, both clients and visitors. He was a very friendly guy although his appearance would lead you to believe otherwise. Dressed in what can only be described as a blue or off-white overall with a bright red logo on the breast pocket displaying the words 'Llandavyff Care', Colin made sure he greeted people politely and with a smile given he was generally considered to be the face of the company.

Colin had befriended Charles on his arrival at Llandavyff and helped him to settle into room Number 12. It was a pleasant room, overlooking the garden and south-facing so Charles had plenty of sunlight and warmth most of the day. He would often take Charles out into the garden using a manual wheelchair to ensure that Charles's upper arms continued to remain strong.

At first Charles grunted at the mere thought of conversing with Colin. However, over time, Charles learnt to trust Colin and he would open up about his previous life, his mother, his brother, and question how on earth things had to come to this. Colin was a superb listener; he often sat in the sunlight with Charles and let Charles wax lyrical about his previous life.

"I used to be a highly regarded person, a professional lawyer, Colin," he would say. "I had the world at my feet. I had a reputation that belies any of these fancy lawyers today." A moment's silence and he would continue. "But four years ago, my life changed forever, I made a fatal error that was to end my career and see me spend the umpteen years stuck in here trying to make sense of what I did and where I go next. I can't converse with my mother or brother anymore, Colin, as I have nothing to say to them. Both are very kind to come and see me as they do, but you know, I can well do without it. I don't want their pity, I don't really want their love, I just want to be left alone to get on with it, whatever 'it' is," he said.

"Honestly if there's anything at all you want or need Charles, you only have to ask," said Colin.

"Do I?" said Charles.

"Yes of course," said Colin.

"Well," said Charles, "there is something you can do for me Colin…"

With a long pause, he stared out of the window.

"Whenever you're ready," said Colin. And with that he closed the door to Number 12.

Chapter 17 - As Time Goes By

You must remember this; a kiss is just a kiss Anne thought as the months passed and Billy was nowhere to be seen. It had been six months since Billy had told her that he loved her and that on his return he wanted to marry her. Still without work, Anne started to apply for anything to give her a bit of money at least. She eventually got a cleaning job with a small company based locally, so she knew she could walk there, which she thought would also help her to get control of her ever-bulging waistline. She didn't want to become that fat lass that nobody wanted. Tigger was always there to console her, and he gave her hope. Such was her state of mind that the Wine O'clock Club was now on hold; she hadn't organised a get-together for months.

Tim was still looking for that ever-elusive job, but he was down-trodden and feeling low; things weren't going his way. He was just about managing all the outgoings of the flat but for how much longer he had no idea. He had even thought that returning to the family fold may not be such a bad idea after all.

Fee was still spitting fire and the dragon in her was still very prevalent. She still had no work and was much more reliant on Hugh's generosity, which really didn't please her. She was in fact a year older, making it even more difficult to find work. And of course, she wouldn't just take any old thing as she put it.

Cleo was still enjoying her job. The 'To be improper would be proper, if it wasn't deemed as rude' man (now named 'Raincoat Man' after he'd appeared several more times in the library in the same raincoat) still failing to converse and just milling around a variety of genres without what seemed any particular interest.

Mel was now working full time on the wards; she had more than proven her worth and as such was moved away from the administrative part of her role to enable her to concentrate on what the hospice thought she did best. She was in a happy place (in her mind) and thought that the organisation had done her a favour. She was enjoying her job much more than she ever had before. Her life was full; she loved her husband more than ever; her family were her everything. However, being a people person, she did wonder how her ex-colleagues were doing and as such thought about contacting Anne to resurrect the Wine O'clock Club.

Rene was firing on all cylinders; she was really into her stride, and nothing was going to stop her now. Confidence on a high, six months of training under her belt as a trainee midwife and, although feeling the pressure, really enjoying the challenges of such a fast-moving job. Always tired at the end of a shift, she still found time to cuddle Alfie and spend some much-needed time with her husband. Rene felt she had the balance spot on.

Millie had at last accepted the challenge and joined Mr Attley at Avenging Angels. Not sure what she had let herself in for, she decided to give it a go anyway. Her first few months were spent learning the ropes, she started by answering the 'red hot' telephone.

It seemed that everyone in the world had some kind of problem or issue. At first all she had to do was note the basic details, i.e., name, contact details and an overview of the problem. This would then pass to AA or another to investigate further. Millie felt that this was a good company, a company that could help people, a bit like a private detective agency, so she was keen to learn and get involved. The job paid her handsomely whilst in training, so it really wasn't to be sniffed at. *Whoo hoo!* she thought as she looked at her bank balance.

Rupert Hope, well he still had little hope of ever finding a decent job that could again bring him back into the fold. His wife, Pamela, had given up on his attempts to find something suitable and as such was working longer hours to try to keep on top of all the bills and outgoings. As such, Rupert found himself very much on his own. The kids had returned to university; there was only so much housework he could do; and the dogs were exhausted from all the running he was doing to alleviate the boredom and loneliness.

He had met up with Marco a few times and was waiting for him to organise this big sailing event he had planned in the hope he could at least talk to the Devil. A few months felt like years to Rupert and as such he began to get depressed. His once tidy self was now somewhat unkempt, his hair was greying quickly, his bristled chin and top lip now both painted silver and his long eyebrows were drooping into his eyes. His daily attire was a black Nike tracksuit, which made his already thinning body even thinner and a pair of off-road Reebok trainers, which at some point had originally been white. Rupert Hope was on a downward spiral.

Where was Denzil now? Had he made the grade, and did he meet those targets? Well, now was the time to find out. Denzil Drum, the sole survivor of the shake up, the only one to stay employed. Still very much the 'man about town', Denzil had managed to attain his objectives. He had met his targets through whatever means and had remained in the bosom of the Devil. Spurred on by his 'babe magnet' he went hell for leather, adopting whatever strategy he could find to stay employed and to stay in favour. Not always the right way to do things, but Denzil didn't much care. He needed his work, he needed his status and, as such, often got by through bribery and corruption to get what he wanted. For now, it was working. Not one to stand on ceremony; where there's a will there's a way, he always said, and Denzil truly had a will.

Billy don't be a hero, Anne thought as she lay in bed thinking about Billy. Where was he? How long would it be before she saw him again? *Would* she see him again, and where did he keep going?

"Unanswered questions," she told Tigger as she rolled over to try to get some sleep. The nights could be long and lonely, but Anne knew that one day her love would come again and this time she wasn't going to let him go.

As she started to drift, her mind turned to the Wine O'clock Club, and she made a mental note to organise another meeting sooner rather than later.

Well let's face it, she thought, *my cleaning job doesn't take up a lot of time and therefore I haven't got much else to do.*

"Answer the phone Millie, it's been ringing for a while!" shouted Elliott.

"I am just about to pick it up," retorted Millie. "Avenging Angels Millie speaking, how can I help you?"

"To be improper would be proper, if it wasn't deemed as rude," came the reply.

"I beg your pardon, sir?" she said.

"To be improper would be proper if it wasn't deemed as rude," was repeated this time with a little more urgency.

"Just one moment please. Elliott I am not sure who this is, and I certainly don't understand what they are saying. Can you help me please?"

Elliott marched across the office and took the receiver.

"Can I help you, sir?"

"To whom am I speaking?"

"This is Elliott, sir, a partner in Avenging Angels."

"Where's Arthur?"

"Well, he's still with the company but winding down to retirement; can I help at all?"

"No, I don't think you can," replied the caller brusquely and the phone went dead.

"Can we trace that call, Elliott?"

"No, the caller wasn't on long enough. Let's see if he rings again; I'll mention it to Dad when I see him tomorrow."

The south-facing garden didn't look so attractive anymore and Charles was fed up with his life. He was ashamed of what he had become and longed for his previous life, albeit stressful and fast moving. He had so much time on is hands that his mind often wandered to the what-if scenarios.

What if he hadn't made that fateful decision?

What if he hadn't taken any of those bloody drugs?

What if he swapped places with Tim?

What if his mother stopped paying for his care?

What if his mother died?

What if Tim died?

What if he died?

Well, it would be a way out for me, he thought.

"Come on Charles, open the door. Your mother's in reception and wants to take you out for a breath of fresh air and a coffee at the local café."

"Oh, sod it, I'm coming," he mumbled as he walked somewhat unsteadily towards the door to let Colin in. He plonked his tall but somewhat bent frame into the wheelchair lifting his feet up onto the pedals as best he could.

"You can't go out in your slippers, Charles. Where are your shoes?"

"Over there," he said pointing to the only upright cupboard in the room.

"Black or tan?"

"Fuck knows," he said.

"Okay tan it is then," Colin said.

*   *   *   *

God how I hate my life, Fee thought as she began to prepare for an online interview (have you ever! In all her time at work when did she ever do an online interview?). *C'est la vie*, get on with it then. She decided on a pale pink blouse and matching scarf, she felt it made her hair look decidedly smart and gave her complexion an overall glow. She accompanied this rather pretty look with some pale pink lipstick with the hint of a gloss shimmer. Bottle of water to hand, she was ready or so she thought. Computer on and whirring in the background, camera poised at a rather fetching angle, Fee felt she looked younger than her years. But she was nervous. It was like waiting for the death sentence. She breathed in deeply, glued to the screen, and awaited her next move. Glasses on or off? Could she see clearly enough without them? Oh! No time to pontificate, lights, camera, action you're on.

Introductions completed, the three stooges had her in their sights, "Now tell us a bit about yourself, Ms Shand."

For fuck's sake, she thought as she revved into gear. Onerous, tedious, boring, self-deprecating, she waffled on about how great she was and what she had to offer.

Twenty-two boring minutes later, the interview was over and the piggy in the middle informed her that they would let her know by close of play that day.

Fee didn't want the job; it was beneath her capabilities. She couldn't see herself as a first-line manager working in a tax office.

Is this what it has come to, she thought. *I'm not doing that, #boringasfuck*. She hoped she didn't get it. The online experience was something different and she thought would stand her in good stead for the future. She rather liked talking to idiots that weren't physically present; was this something Fee Shand could explore a bit more?

As Mel experienced her first hospice death, it hit her hard. The young man was one of her first patients and she had grown extremely fond of him. Although they tell you not to, it is very hard when you are a caring individual and put your all into the job. No one can prepare you for the devastation and grief that overwhelms your whole being particularly in someone so young. She took solace in the fact that she was with him in his last moments on this earth, she held his hand and stroked his beautiful blond hair, she felt she had comforted him in his final moments as his eyes closed and she watched the rise and fall of his chest for the very last time.

"Go gently on your way, young man. May God keep you safe in his presence until once again you are reunited with your loved ones," Mel said as the room fell silent and warm, wet tears engulfed her eyes dripping gently down her cheeks as she carefully caressed his now still hand.

Why is life so cruel, why do beautiful young people die? Why, oh why? she asked herself as she caught sight of her colleague across the room equally bereft at this young man's passing.

'Mother of mine, you gave to me...' Tim thought long and hard about that sentence. *What did she give me, apart from a load of grief? What did she want from me? Why am I that bothered anyway?* Well, Tim was at a crossroads and needed to decide which way to go. He was fast running out of luck with the job scene and money was truly at an all-time low. What could turn his fortunes around? What could a middle-aged man do to alter the path he was following? His mathematical brain had said no to gambling—not even the occasional flutter on the lottery, so he was feeling pretty desperate when he was interrupted by the mobile.

"Hello," he said not recognising the number or the soft tones of a gentle whisper transmitting down the phone. His head was spinning trying to make the connection. "Is that you,

Charles?" he asked as a process of elimination had led him to this conclusion.

"Yes, it is Tim; we need to talk."

"Here Tigger, Tigger, where are you?" Anne shouted as she rattled his food dish with a spoon. She hadn't seen him for most of the afternoon which was a worry as Tigger was as regular as clockwork when it came to feeding time. Anne knocked on Mr and Mrs Campbell's door to see if Tigger had paid them a visit. However, they weren't in, so she scribbled a note and popped it through the letterbox. Trying not to worry too much, she scoured the streets looking between the parked cars, down the alleyways and across the beautifully laid lawns and gardens of the nearby houses. No sign of the now very elusive Tigger. As she headed home, it began to rain, and Anne knew then that it would only be a matter of time before Tigger appeared as he hated the rain.

Stop worrying and relax, she told herself and she entered her front door, wiping her feet on her brand-new cat doormat she somehow knew that Tigger wouldn't be long.

Chapter 18 - Prince Charming

Don't you ever, thought Denzil as he was about to face his demons again. *Be confident, be smart, play the game and you'll be fine*, he said to himself as he was about to enter hell yet again.

Knock, knock knocking on heaven's door—not.

Denzil heard the dulcet tones of the Devil reply, "Come in, I've been waiting for you."

Checking his watch Denzil could see that he was three minutes late... not a crime he thought as he entered hell with some trepidation. Without the offer of a cup of coffee or a good morning, Denzil was greeted with "You can't do it Drum, you just can't do it," (Drum he thought, that sounds bad). I have given you more than enough warning so here you are!"

Hand shaking, Denzil took the piece of paper with 'WRITTEN WARNING' typed across the top.

"Much improvement needed, Drum, otherwise you'll be gone, and believe me, at the rate you're going, it won't take long!" the Devil bellowed. "Out of my sight, go... I'll see you in one month if not before," he shouted.

With that, Denzil was ousted by Miss Moneypenny and gone in a whirlwind.

Bollocks, bollocks and bollocks, he thought as he made his way out into the fresh air. *How much longer can I hold on; who can help me to survive? Where is Rupert when I need him? Bugger, I need some help.*

The mobile was ringing off the wall. Rupert was trying to buy some plants at the local garden centre when he was rudely interrupted by his mobile.

"Can you just hang on a minute while I get this blasted phone," he said to the assistant. "It must be important, or they wouldn't keep ringing. Hello?" he said somewhat irritated.

"Hello Rupert, it's Denzil. How are you?"

"Well, I'm okay," Rupert said, quite shocked to hear from Denzil.

"Sorry to bother you but..."

Oh no, thought Rupert, yet found himself saying, "But what?"

"I need your help, Rupert; I really need your help."

"I'll call you back this evening, Denzil; we'll talk it through, whatever it is."

"Okay that's super, Rupert. Thank you. I look forward to hearing from you. Bye for now."

"I'll just take the four David Austin Roses and the red and green acers please," Rupert said eventually completing his purchase.

"Thank you, sir; have a good rest of the day." The assistant smiled pleasantly and with that, Rupert was gone.

How many roads must a man walk down, before you get some smidgeon of success, Rupert? Planting was back-breaking, and it was a dull but rather warm day, so Rupert was constantly wiping his brow.

"What on earth was Denzil up to? What had he done now, mind you, why should I even get involved? It's not like I still work there now is it? Sod this I'm off for a cool beer and a sit down." Spades discarded, wellies off and hey presto, beer in hand Rupert eased himself into a rather wonky deckchair. Gently patting his beloved dogs, for the first time since his redundancy Rupert felt an element of calmness and serenity as he took in the sights and smells of his beautiful garden.

Kiss several frogs and you may get a prince, Denzil, but you'll be lucky this time. Luck has a fine timeline and soon runs out especially if you keep repeating the same mistakes.

Chapter 19 - Go Daddy, Go

He was late arriving; the new carer had already started and had been briefed by his mother. She appeared to be very efficient and effective and had already built up a rapport with his father. She was a slim woman with long blonde hair tied back in a neat bun and she exuded elegance and panache. She had a very calming voice that still carried authority, and she had a 'can do' approach.

"Hello," he said. "I'm the son."

"Well, hello there, nice to meet you. You look genuinely like your father I must say."

"It's been said many times before; I'm just a bit larger than he but yes there is truly a resemblance. My mother says that you are going to live in for a while and see how Dad goes."

"Yes, that's right. Your mum is finding it increasingly difficult to cope and really needs some help."

"Great stuff, which care agency are you from then?" "Nightingale's just down the road. I am the registered nurse there and often work with new clients."

"Where are my manners!" the Devil said. "Sorry, what's your name?"

"Oh, everyone just calls me Clem."

"Well, very nice to meet you, Clem. I hope my father behaves himself for you." He said, as he left the room to join his mother.

"She seems a lovely carer Mum, I'm sure Dad will get along with her and to top it off she's good-looking. We know what an eye for the ladies Dad has," he said with a wry smile.

"Erm, yes indeed, let's see how it goes son."

"Well, it's some company for you, Mum, during the week, which will be nice, and some new conversations to be had."

Clem had her own room and had soon made herself at home. She was positioned next to the Devils parents' bedroom; easily accessible should his father need anything. For now, his mother had vacated the marital bedroom and was sleeping in the small bedroom to the rear of the bungalow. With Clem ensconced in the second room and Dad in the main bedroom, the Devil found himself on the couch for his two-night stay. It was comfortable albeit a little short and narrow for a rather burgeoning frame. However, he was going to make the most of it and enjoy some quality time with his parents—well, his mum at least, and find out a bit more about the rather pretty, intelligent Clem during his stay.

The care company was to cost the Devil a pretty penny, but it was worth it to see the difference Clem's arrival had made, more or less straight away, to his mother.

This weekend is going to be a more pleasant experience, the Devil thought as he closed his eyes and started to breathe heavily falling into a deep slumber.

Mother, father, and son now sleeping deeply, Clem decided to acclimatise herself to her new surroundings. Used to manoeuvring in the dark, she crept slowly from room to room familiarising herself with ornaments, objects, furniture, rooms, pathways to exits, window and door locks. It took her all of five minutes to undertake a recce of the bungalow before she too, took herself off to bed in preparation for the start of a new journey.

Good night, Devil, sleep tight, sleep very tight.

Chapter 20 - Avenging Angels

"It was strange, Dad. Millie answered the phone and a man, elderly man, said 'To be improper would be proper if it wasn't deemed as rude'. What the hell does that mean?"

"I've no idea," said Arthur to his son. "Does Millie know?"

"No of course not, that's why I'm asking you."

"Well, I think we'll have to wait and see if he calls again."

"He knew you, Dad; he was asking for you."

"Don't suppose you traced the call?"

"Not on long enough."

"Okay, what's the order of the day, Elliott?"

The office was buzzing; work had increased tenfold, and Millie had surely been thrown in at the deep end. She was really enjoying getting to grips with the role and had taken several phone calls that had given her the gist of the company. Although she knew what the company stood for, she wasn't sure if she wanted to continue 'putting wrongs right' if you know what I mean. It wasn't the fact that wrongs needed to be righted, it was how this was carried through that Millie was struggling with. Not fully understanding the 'how' of the job role, she continued to learn and take note of everything that was going on in the hope all would become clear in the not-too-distant future. Her role for now was to answer the telephone, direct the calls, and shadow Elliott around the office. She also needed to pick up on his paperwork, his demeanour, knowledge and intellect when dealing with other staff and clients. Millie found this taxing and some days she would leave the office with what she termed 'brain ache'. That said, she wasn't going to let this fantastic opportunity pass her by.

Since she was now making good money, Millie wondered about her first step on the property ladder. She was considering moving away from a rental to purchasing a house all for herself. This was something she really aspired to and felt that in time once settled into this role she could start to explore the property market post probation.

She hadn't seen the gang for several months now and wondered how things were going. Although busy she would make time for another Wine O'clock Club meeting when one became available.

I wonder what Anne's up to these days, Millie pondered, as the phone interrupted her thought process.

"Good afternoon, Avenging Angels, Millie speaking, how can I help you?"

"To be improper would be proper if it wasn't deemed as rude. Is Arthur in, please?"

Quick thinking Millie replied, "No sir, but Elliott is here."

"I want Arthur," came the reply.

Millie asked for a trace on the call by gesticulating to the office staff. However, the caller quickly said, "Don't bother to delay this call to enable a trace, I just want to speak to Arthur."

"I'm so sorry, sir, he's not here. Can I tell you when he'll next be in and you can ring back then, or Arthur could even ring you back?"

With that suggestion, the receiver was replaced, and the phone went dead.

Not again, thought Millie. *What on earth does this man want with Arthur or Avenging Angels come to that.*

He had a soft voice with a calming and controlled demeanour. He wasn't rushed but quietly assertive. There was little trace of an accent except to say there was a softness present, somewhat like that of an Irish lilt. Millie imagined what he looked like, tall, slim, smart, with greying hair, clean-shaven with a slightly olive skin. He was probably nothing like, but his voice had conjured up this picture in Millie's mind.

Chapter 21 - We Need to Talk

The van pulled up and the back doors were flung open. An automatic lift transported a lonely, bent figure to the ground. Two burly arms later and Charles was face to face with Tim. Colin had come along for the ride and once his client was in a suitable place, he left him to chat with his brother. This was a monumental moment for Charles, fresh air, free and for the first time face to face with his brother without the constant interruption from their mother.

"You're looking well, Tim," Charles said.

"I'm not feeling it, Charles. Things are not going well since I lost my job," Tim said as he perched his rather small frame on the van lift. "Anyway, what's up Charles, and why have you suddenly decided to become more active? You seem different and certainly more compos mentis that you have ever been! Does the centre know that you've come out?"

"Yes of course they do; it's not a prison, you know, and Colin looks after me very well."

"Are you pretending to be someone else, Charles? You've been four years in that centre with barely a word to me or Mum and yet here you are now, parading around and giving orders to Colin like you own the place."

"Well, I've had time to think."

"Erm you certainly have," replied Tim.

"I want to leave the centre but need somewhere to live."

"Ask Mum," Tim suggested.

"No, Tim, you don't understand. I want to come and live with *you*."

"Fat chance Charles! You've got to be joking."

"I'm not, Tim. You are on your own with no job and I can help you to pay for the flat and keep things ticking over until you find suitable work."

"Absolutely no way Charles; the flat's too small for two people."

"It could be reconfigured to give us both the space we need and it's company for you with a bolster of cash to keep you living there."

"You won't get that wheelchair in there, never mind manoeuvring through the doors."

"I don't really need it, Tim. I use it because I'm lazy and I feel sorry for myself."

"Blimey Charles, has this all been a facade?! Are you well? Do you know what you are doing? What's more, have you any idea how much money Mum has spent keeping you safe, secure, fed and watered whilst you've been in that centre? My God! What's going on here?"

"Ask Colin, Tim."

"What do you mean, ask Colin? What's Colin got to do with it?"

"Ask Colin, Tim," came the same reply.

Not one to swear, Tim said, "Oh for fuck's sake, Charles, what the hell are you talking about?"

"To be improper would be proper if it wasn't deemed as rude," answered Charles.

"Eh, Charles? I am more than a little confused here. You expect me to take you in, rescue you from the centre, you have spoken more words in the last ten minutes than you ever did over the four years you have been in the centre. You are obviously much more physically able than you appear, and you have presented me with a man that goes by the name of Colin to discuss what's going on! Pinch me; am I dreaming? Is this a nightmare?"

"Just ask Colin; you won't regret it, Tim."

With that, Tim walked across to Colin.

"Well?" said Tim.

"Well, what?" replied Colin.

"Have you got something to tell me, Colin?"

"How long have you got, Tim?"

Chapter 22- Ring, Ring, why don't you give me a call

A deep sexy voice was in the throes of revealing their attire when the doorbell rang.

"I must go now; picture me as described and you won't be long. Have fun, my darling."

And with that the receiver went down.

"Hold on a minute, I'm just coming."

As she opened the door, Fee saw Hugh standing there with a bunch of roses in hand.

"Oh, it's you," she said.

Charming thought Hugh.

"Do you want to come in? Sorry, I was just on the phone. Cuppa or something stronger?"

"Have you got any whiskey, Fee?"

"Oh! What's up, Hugh? You only drink whiskey when you're on a downer and you need to talk."

"No all's fine, I just wanted to pop round and see how you're doing, that's all."

"Well, that's very nice of you, Hugh albeit not your usual style."

"Have you seen anything of the children?" Fee asked.

"Not for a few days. They're busy getting on with their own lives now; all feels like we're a bit redundant now."

"It's called growing up, Hugh. They'll be back in touch when they want something no doubt."

The phone started to ring. Fee ignored it and let the answerphone kick in. *I can't come to the phone right now so feel free to leave me a message.* The whirring of the phone suggested a message had clearly been left. It had no sooner stopped ringing than it began to ring again.

"Gosh Fee you're popular," remarked Hugh somewhat sourly.

"I'll just pop it onto silent, it's probably the girls from the book club calling about the latest novel."

"You look nice. Are you going somewhere?"

"No not really, I wanted to make myself feel better and you know me! A nice little black number does it for me."

"Indeed, it does Fee. You look lovely."

"Why thank you kind sir!" Fee replied feeling somewhat humbled by Hugh's compliment.

"Do you want to sit down, Hugh, or aren't you staying long?"

"Oh, go on then Fee, I need some company. I'm feeling a bit low today."

"Oh, Hugh... what's she done now or is it the kids?"

"Fucking hell, Fee, I just don't know what's going on!"

"What's going on with what Hugh? Don't tell me it's over when it's barely just begun?"

"No, it's work, Fee. I'm under pressure and I'm feeling it. I'm more than a bit stressed of late. Had a check-up with the doc and he says everything is simply fine and I need to relax a bit more, so I'm seriously thinking of going part-time."

"Oh my God, Hugh, are you sure?"

"Yes, I reckon so, don't worry about things, you'll still get your spousal maintenance," he said smiling and knowing Fee as he did. "I'm thinking of dropping down to three days a week. I want to play golf, go on holiday, and relax a bit more."

"What about the children's university fees though?"

"Well, they've only got a year or so to go, so think I can manage that."

"What does Ellen think?"

"I haven't told her yet; she'll probably go off the deep end and worry about how we'll make ends meet given all my other commitments."

"Well, it's all part of trading me in for a younger model, Hugh."

"Don't be like that, Fee, I still love you and always will."

"Well, that may be the case, Hugh, but you love her more... anyway whatever, the decision is yours to make and yours alone I feel," said Fee.

With that, Hugh settled himself on the sofa with a topped-up whiskey glass and waxed lyrical about his love for Fee and the life that they had shared. As he started to doze, Fee gently removed his arm from her shoulder and rushed to the answerphone. She had missed six potential customers. For pity's sake how was she going to get Hugh out of the way now! She could see that he had arrived in the car so decided to phone Ellen to come and collect him before he became completely comatose.

"Hi there, is that Ellen?"

"It is, indeed, who's this?"

"Oh, it's Fee Shand, Ellen, Hugh's ex, you know."

"Oh yes of course, Fee, what's up?"

"Hugh called around this evening and he's had a couple of whiskeys so can't really drive. He's falling asleep on the sofa; any chance you can pick him up at all?"

"Yes sure, I'll get the car and be there in about forty-five minutes," Ellen said.

"Okay thanks Ellen, I'll see you then."

With that, Fee completed her call and put the mobile phone to one side. Hugh was breathing heavily and had slumped across the sofa. He was clutching an empty glass which Fee left with him so as not to disturb his now soft slumber.

She straightened her dress, slipped on her high heels, and went to the phone. She always felt more of the part dressed to kill and ready for action. She picked the phone calls off one at a time, honing her skills to meet the needs of each client. She was getting rather good at this now and at times she felt a tingle of excitement as her voice took on a sexy, gruff, and breathless tone. She had decided to treat each caller as an individual and not have a prewritten script as this appeared too well prepared and staid. She wanted it to be spontaneous and free, with an element of surprise for each caller. This new role far exceeded working in the tax office; it was exhilarating, fresh and had given Fee as reason to live again and she was loving it. Her clients paid handsomely to hear her dulcet tones. Her bank balance was on the rise and her confidence was through the roof. Did she really need Hugh anymore? Probably not, but she wasn't going to tell *him* that.

Chapter 23 – Sending Out an SOS

"I can't do it anymore Rupert, I can't keep up with the Devil's demands."

"What do you mean, Denzil? What's the matter with you?"

"Since you left the organisation, the pressure on me has been immense. I'm in his office more times than I care to remember. He just won't leave it."

"Leave what Denzil?"

"Leave me alone! He's constantly monitoring my work; he's forever criticising me and he's now threatening to sack me unless I can meet his nigh-on impossible targets."

"You were doing very well when I left, Denzil, so what has changed?"

"You," came the curt reply.

"Me? What do you mean?"

"Rupert you were there for me, helping me to achieve, letting me shadow you and basically keeping me on the straight and narrow. I've not managed very well since your departure and unfortunately the Devil has noticed. I need to make some key decisions, Rupert, and have come to you for advice. I am under intense pressure and feel incredibly stressed all the time.

What's more, I am not enjoying what I do anymore and want an avenue out."

"Denzil you were quick enough to accept the offer when all around you were floundering; you even stepped into the lookout post while doing more than rubbing Fee's nose in it. You can't expect to have all your own way."

With that, Rupert added, "How can I help you now? I'm no longer a part of the organisation and never will be."

"Marco," came the reply.

"What about him?"

"You're still in touch with him. Can you get him to help to keep me afloat?"

"By doing what exactly, Denzil?"

"Getting rid of the Devil," came the reply.

"Denzil this is your fight now. I am trying to get Marco to give me an avenue back in, but it seems that the Devil has other ideas. Even Marco feels under pressure from the Devil; he told me that his superiority has been compromised and, as such, his seniority threatened. I am not sure that I have any influence whatsoever over what is now going on."

After twenty minutes or so, Denzil decided to call it a day. He had planted the seed, so he thought all he would now need to do was to sit back and watch it grow. Could this be the right decision for Denzil or was it to lead to his downfall a little quicker than he had imagined?

Rupert chose to ignore Denzil's pleas as he had enough troubles of his own. He had given Denzil the leg up that he required and now Rupert was out. Denzil was alone and needed to understand that any future decisions involving his career pathway now sat heavily on his shoulders and his shoulders alone. Did Rupert think that he could sort it out? Yes, he did and so Denzil was left to face the long road which he would walk one step at a time.

Chapter 24 - I am Sailing

It was a glorious day: The sun was shining, the birds were singing, and warm wind allowed the dinghy to launch first time.

Rub-a-dub dub, three men in a tub, Marco thought as the Laser dinghy sailed effortlessly along the blue water of the loch. A couple of beers apiece to appease any tension, two medium life jackets and an extra-large and they were gone, riding the crest of the wave. How this had happened not even Marco could work out, but here they were, not the best of friends but willing to compromise and bond as best they could.

Marco had chosen his light blue chino's, some slip-on navy sketchers and a blue v neck sweater supporting his well-co-ordinated light pink shirt which was poking out over his tightly knitted sweater. He looked like a well-heeled sailor and topped his outfit off with a rather fetching cotton navy cap sitting slightly askew framing his ruddy complexion.

Rupert was looking thinner than ever, his medium life jacket hanging limply on each side causing his off-white jumper to curl at the bottom as it caught the life jacket toggles. He was dressed in black jeans, black trainers and was supporting a rather crumpled cagoule in case of emergencies. He had chosen not to shave and had preferred the rugged, rather unkempt appearance as he knew he was to come face to face with the Devil and had opted for the sympathy vote.

The Devil exuded authority, his life jacket barely fitted where it touched but beneath it lay a man of sturdy foundation, a burly giant, dressed in a vibrant mix of colours for his very first expedition. Supporting dark green cords, a light green Barbour jacket, matching Barbour boots and a green tartan tweed cap, the Devil had come to impress and impress he did.

This was to be their first meeting as a trio since that fateful day when Marco had persuaded the Devil to take a break from his parent-visiting weekends and come and have a bit of fun on the water. To Marco's surprise the Devil had agreed to the invitation. But what the Devil was unaware of, was that Rupert had also been invited. Marco chose not to divulge that fact as he knew that the Devil would have turned down the invitation, so Marco decided to deal with the situation once it had arisen. It was then, that as adults, they could decide whether to sail as a team of two or a team of three.

The water was cold and clear, it was a calm day, the loch was reflecting the bright blue sky giving it a sense of peace and tranquillity. Although a reasonable size, the dinghy felt small carrying the bulk of the Devil, there would certainly be a lot more room if had declined the invitation. Getting him to 'heave-ho' proved difficult as he was slow, cumbersome, and awkward, not a natural sailor at all. Nevertheless, her didn't give up and showed great tenacity when put under pressure.

Marco had planned a few drinks on the opposite shoreline and then a return sail when the sun when setting to allow the beauty of the loch to encapsulate the moment and possibly build an allegiance and meeting of minds to top off what had been so far, a splendid morning sail and some evidence of togetherness.

The Devil began to relax, his big hands now showing signs of confidence, gone were the tightly gripped knuckles clinging to the side of the Laser dinghy, replaced by an ever-increasing growth of confidence in his fellow sailors and his belief in his own abilities to conquer the water. So much so, that he removed his life jacket to disrobe. He removed his Barbour jacket before clumsily replacing the said life jacket. Now with his shirt sleeves flapping in the breeze, the Devil's demeanour was much more relaxed. Marco felt a warmth towards him that he had never felt before. Was the Devil to become a great sailing buddy for Marco? Two grown men, both alone, looking for something to fill the void in their lives. Similar people working together in the same organisation, longing to explore and expand their current lives... could this be the start of a beautiful friendship?

There was a fly in the ointment, though: Rupert. He had his own agenda, which was to get back in the fold. He had gone several months now without a job, a purpose, and an income. It was beginning to show. Rupert had become somewhat impatient, aloof and at times curt. He wanted his old life back, he longed to be important once more, to wear nicely pressed shirts and fitted suits, a man out to impress whoever, whenever. You wouldn't think so to see him now, dishevelled, unshaven, thin and somewhat Wissen looking, the man had changed beyond belief.

"Jibe-ho Rupert," the Devil shouted. "Oh my God, Rupert *duck*!"

But the warning came too late. The boom swung around and hit Rupert fairly and squarely on the forehead knocking him sideways into the water. It was obvious from the way Rupert floated in the water that he was unconscious and was drifting away from the dinghy. There was a tinge of blood on the wooden boom mid-point just where it had collided with Rupert's forehead.

"Quick, he's in trouble!" shouted Marco. "Can you jump in?" The Devil no sooner heard the order than he stood up and leapt in, rocking the dinghy as he went. The impact of him hitting the waters of the loch caused the dinghy to ride on more than one crest of the wave and it took Marco all his skill to steady her.

The Devil awkwardly swam towards Rupert.

"I've got him!" he shouted as he turned Rupert over and grabbed him under the chin. Marco was impressed; the Devil had clearly done this before or at least had some training in it. It was now all too obvious to see that Rupert had indeed been knocked unconscious by the boom. He had a rather large gash, bleeding badly on his forehead and was in no fit state to help himself. After a bit of a struggle, the Devil managed to haul Rupert up out of the water and half into the mirror dinghy. It was now up to Marco to heave him into the boat.

"First aid kit," the Devil panted, "where is it? That gash is pretty ugly and needs tending to."

"Erm, I don't have one, it's usually just me or me and the kids and we don't go that far."

The Devil retorted, "No matter what, where or how far you're going Marco, you should always have a first aid kit! "Have you got a blanket at least?"

"Not really, you can use this old sheet that I clean the oars with if you like."

"For fuck's sake Marco, what kind of sailor are you!? We need to get him dry and dress that wound with something."

The Devil then pulled Rupert towards him and checked that Rupert was breathing by placing his face near to Rupert's mouth. He was also in a clear position to see the rise and fall of Rupert's somewhat skinny torso. Once he was satisfied that Rupert was breathing, he began to gently pat his cheek to try to bring him round.

After a few grumbles and groans, Rupert began to respond. The Devil then offered Rupert some water as he began to emerge from his semi-conscious state. He wrapped Rupert in the 'old sheet' to keep him warm. The gash on his forehead was nasty but contained so the Devil removed a clean handkerchief from his Barbour jacket, dabbed it in the loch and placed it neatly on the wound, mopping up the blood and skin fragments from Rupert's forehead. Once he was satisfied it was clean, he placed the cold compress on the wound then asked Rupert to lie still. He instructed Marco to head for shore.

Chapter 25 - Midnight

It was so dark; the streetlamps were flickering, and the rain was lashing on the tarmac road. There were some faint mutterings amongst the tip tapping of the rain but none that appeared to be coherent. It was now 6 weeks since Tigger had vanished, and Anne was more than bereft. She had visited Mr and Mrs Campbell many times over that period all to no avail. Tigger would be so wet, cold, and hungry by now she thought unless some kind soul had taken him in, fed him and kept him cosy and warm. Her mind was filled with angst, she had little sleep over the past weeks and longed for the return of her beloved cat. When you don't know what's happened it's even worse than when you do, she thought... at least if you know then there's an end in sight. How can Tigger have just vanished?

Billy hadn't been seen for at least ten weeks so all in all, Anne's life was now totally incomplete. She needed a shoulder to cry on and desperately yearned for the company of Billy as well as Tigger. The night was going to be extremely long she thought as the clock reached half past midnight. At least she wasn't working the next day so she could rest up best she could.

Her mobile pinged at 12.34 a.m. and as she reached to look at it, she saw a lovely photograph of Tigger set as the wallpaper on her phone.

"Oh, my gorgeous boy, where are you sweetie?" she murmured sadly. "I need you to come home right this minute so that I can once again caress you and keep you safe."

A tear rolled from her now very tired eyes and as it hit the pillow it began to make a damp patch underneath her cheek. She moved her head to avoid the said patch.

As she began to doze, her mind wandered back to her childhood cats and her parents. She felt sad as she thought about their passing and how short life can be. Eventually her eyelids closed, and she started to breathe heavily as sleep enveloped her body. Time stood still.

"Goodnight Tigger," she said in her dreamlike state. "See you soon."

Chapter 26 - Angel Face

Millie was learning fast, her job was moving like no tomorrow, she had mastered the basics and was moving onto more complicated stuff. Arthur was massively impressed with her talent to connect facts, so much so, that he had given her a small team of two to lead to test her abilities as a manager and visionary. Her job was very much about multi-tasking, engaging the client and ensuring all the necessary facts were assimilated prior to the case being accepted by Avenging Angels.

"To be improper would be proper if it wasn't deemed as rude." *What the hell does that mean? Who is making the calls, what do they want with Arthur or Avenging Angels or*, Millie thought, *what do they want with me?*

This hadn't crossed her mind until right this minute. Could this mysterious caller be after Millie rather than the Attleys? *Surely not,* she thought as the ringing phone once again interrupted her thought process. Millie decided to test her managerial skills, "can you get that please Stewart?" With a swift movement of his hand, her assistant lifted the receiver and spoke only to introduce "Avenging Angels." His silence attracted the office, his face was ashen, and he was nodding his head as if on trial for a profoundly serious crime. The phone call lasted all of 42 seconds as the caller spoke all of twelve words followed by "Tell Arthur." Stewart appeared more than complexed and found it exceedingly difficult to articulate the information received from the mystery caller. "Well, what's the gist of it Stewart," Millie asked. "That he'll ring again in two days' time and Arthur must be here to answer the telephone or else" "or else what" Millie enquired, "or else, that's all he said Millie." "Oh, for fuck's sake Stewart I'm so fed up with these calls, we are unable to track them or even identify the caller's voice, so what are we supposed to do with that information?

I need to get a life outside of work Millie thought, I need a distraction from all this, as much as I love it, subconsciously it's always there. Come on Millie lighten up, there is life beyond the realms of Avenging Angels. This immediately focused her mind on the Wine O'clock Club, time to catch up with Anne and the gang she thought as the phone interrupted her thought process. Did she still have Anne, Cleo, Rene, Tim, or anyone else's number to call? Millie made it her mission to deal with this "to do" task on completion of her working day. That surely had given her something to think about outside of work.

Chapter 27 - Savage Garden

Tim had noticed that the garden wasn't quite as well tended as it had been and asked Charles why this might be. He retorted "the gardeners left."

"Do you mean Colin, Charles, has Colin left, surely not?"

"Yep, he's gone without a word, he slipped through in the dead of night, and no one has heard from him since."

"How come Charles?"

"How the fuck do I know Tim, he's just gone, okay."

"Okay Charles, no need to get so uptight."

"Well, I have no one to confide in now, no one to help me along, no one to listen to me and no one tending to what was once a beautiful garden. I am more than pissed off with this place but at least Colin made it more bearable."

"Strange don't you think Charles, that Colin should disappear just like that, isn't it a bit out of character for him?"

"I don't fucking know Tim, why should I?"

"Well, I thought you were close, forgive me if I'm wrong."

"We were, but then yesterday he was acting kind of strange, and our conversation was much more limited than usual."

"How so?" said Tim.

"Bloody hell Tim are you trying to get down with the kids, where do you get that phrase from?"

"Oh, I don't know Charles anyway, what do you think?"

"I don't Tim, he's his own man and can please himself."

"Yes, Charles but he's been here for years."

"And your point being Tim?"

"Well, it just seems odd that someone of his calibre and length of service should just decide to leave and leave forthwith, that's all."

The walls to number 12 seemed empty now, the picture-framed window far less attractive than it was and one huge lump of a brother now far from happy.

Silence prevailed for some time before Tim spoke.

"What are you going to do now, Charles? Will Colin's departure make you rethink where you actually are in life? I know Mum would like that."

"Wouldn't she just, Tim, save her a fair penny if I was to leave this place, imprisoned here for four years, by God, she'd be raking it in."

"Blimey Charles, don't be so harsh. Mum has been brilliant and saved your bacon let me tell you."

"Do you think I don't know that Tim, what do you want me to do, bow down and kiss her feet, my Saviour my God."

"Charles don't be so callous; Mum has worked hard to bring you to this point and now here you are slagging her off, she would be more than heartbroken if she could hear you now."

"I know Tim, you're right of course, as you always are. I am an ungrateful son of a bitch."

"She'll be here at the weekend, so I think I need to tell her of my decision."

"Which is what, Charles?"

"Well, I want to move out of here and in with you."

"You can't Charles; I don't have anywhere near enough room, and more to the point, I don't even have a job to support me let alone you!"

"Tim, I want to do it and maybe we can compromise and ask Mum to help out until we're settled."

"Charles, she will *not* want both of us back at home living with her, two sons, no jobs and both with few or no prospects... doesn't sound very exciting, does it?"

"Tim, you leave Mother to me. All you have to do is agree on the strategy going forward and I can see to the rest."

With a huge sigh, Tim felt it time to leave.

"Look Charles, I'll see you at the weekend with Mum and we'll discuss how best to move things forward, but please don't take it for granted that you can move in with me. Maybe living with Mum maybe a better option for you and let's face it, you've always been the favourite son."

With that, the door closed gently too, and Charles was now left in what he saw as the abyss. Could he survive until Saturday? That was four days away. Colin had only just left, and he was already feeling somewhat bereft and confused. He sat back in his wheelchair close to the window to spy on the 'goings-on'.

Chapter 28 - Blue is the Colour

Darkness started to surround the dinghy; Rupert had turned a paler shade of white with lips nearly as blue as the loch. He was now in a semi-conscious state.

"Marco, how long to shore?" the Devil enquired.

"About twenty to thirty minutes, I think."

"You *think*," the Devil replied a bit derisively.

"Yes, we're heading in the right direction."

"Bloody well get a move on, man! Rupert just isn't looking well."

"If we call an ambulance now, we can get it to meet us as soon as we dock," the Devil suggested. "Give them the estimated time of arrival and the details of Rupert's condition."

"Which emergency service?"

"Ambulance please."

"Hello this is the ambulance service, how can I help you?" Marco began to stutter far more than usual, his words were somewhat incoherent, this coupled with a slight breeze and the swell of the water made it virtually impossible for the operator to understand what was required.

"Give me the phone Marco, swop places. You hold Rupert's head steady while I give some details to the ambulance crew."

After a brief explanation, an ambulance had been dispatched with the operator staying on the line to give some instructions on how to deal with Rupert and his head wound as they slowly pulled ashore. This necessitated the Devil relaying information to Marco who was trying his best to keep Rupert steady as well as navigate the boat. Twenty-two minutes and three seconds later, the boat landed to the sound of a siren and flashing blue light making their way along the shoreline.

"Is the patient still conscious, sir?"

"Yes, only just though," Marco replied.

"I'll leave you now then," the operator said. "I can hear that the ambulance has arrived, take care," and with that the receiver was replaced and Marco popped his mobile into his pocket.

Pamela had been home for quite some time and had read the scrawled note left by Rupert, stating that he had gone sailing with Marco and would be back around five p.m. As she let their beloved dogs out for their last pee, she couldn't help but feel a slight unease as darkness fell and there was no sign of Rupert. She had called his mobile several times, but it had gone straight to voicemail. After five messages, the first three displaying some irritation in her voice, she changed tack, and spoke with a more sympathetic and concerned tone.

Melissa heard her mother's voice.

"Your father hasn't come home from his sailing trip. Have you any idea where he might be? Did he say anything to you before he left?"

"Mum, I can't hear you very well; can it wait until I get home?"

Pamela replied, "Well yes, I'll see you soon."

Pamela then rang Theo; he too was somewhat perplexed.

"I'm nearly home Mum, I'll see you in a minute."

As the doorbell rang Pamela immediately wondered why Rupert didn't use his key.

"Hello there, Madam. Is it Mrs Hope? We are sorry to bother you at this late hour." Said the police officer.

A few moments later, the story had been relayed to Pamela. As she grabbed her coat, shuffled the dogs into the kitchen, Theo appeared.

"Your dad's had an accident and is in hospital," she told him hurriedly. "I'm going with the police to see him. Can you tell Melissa when she comes in, and then can you come to the hospital to see Dad and to bring me back home? Is that okay?"

"Yes, sure Mum; is he okay?" Theo said worriedly.

"I have no idea; all I know is that he hit his head and has a severe wound on his forehead."

Marco and the Devil stood up as Pam entered the hospital wing eager to discover exactly how Rupert was. There were two police officers, one in plain clothes and one in uniform asking both several questions. Pamela acknowledged them and was shown into an individual unit housing Rupert. He was unconscious, heavily sedated with several drips fed into both arms. His head was tightly bandaged with some bloodstains that had oozed though the dressing. Pamela pulled up a chair and held Rupert's cold and somewhat clammy hand. As she spoke, her voice was soft and comforting, her eyes very tearful and her words were disjointed and inquisitive.

"Rupert, what have you done? What happened to you? The kids will be here in a minute and the dogs are eager to see you."

No response. After ten minutes or so, Pamela was asked to follow the consultant into a private room.

"There has been some damage to the front of your husband's brain due to the enormity of impact from the boat's boom. Some fragments of wood have entered the wound and damaged the frontal lobe of the brain. Now we have no idea as to the extent of the injury given that your husband is unconscious. Because there are many functions carried out by the frontal lobes there are many symptoms arising from such an injury. We will have a better idea of the damage once your husband is conscious."

The Devil and Marco sat quietly in the hospital corridor as Theo and Melissa ran up to their mother.

"Is he going to be okay, Mum?"

"I don't know; he's unconscious at the moment and the doctor said we'll know more when he comes round. Marco, can you shed any further light on what happened?"

"He failed to 'come about' (swap sides of the dinghy) when we were tacking (taking a different course) and the boom hit his forehead with some force knocking him semi-conscious into the loch."

The Devil then interjected.

"I dived in and managed to haul him into the boat as we then made our way back to shore. His head received a nasty gash which we cleaned and held a cold compress to. He was drifting in and out of consciousness as we met the ambulance crew on the shore."

"Don't worry Pamela," Marco said. "Rupert is made of strong stuff; he'll be fine. We'll go now and catch up with you tomorrow, try and get some rest."

With that, both Marco and the Devil disappeared through the rotating doors and down the corridor. It was going to be a long night for Pamela.

Chapter 29 - Pray Silence

Cleo yawned as she placed the last few books on the shelf, it had been a late-night gigging at her local. She longed to put her feet up with a nice cup of tea but still had two hours left to complete her shift. As she placed the newspapers in a chronological order, she noted a headline in the local rag: *Man hospitalised after boating accident*. Although only a short paragraph and without naming the injured, it described a small dinghy sailing on a familiar loch with three sailors on board. Cleo's mind immediately shifted to the three young men that had entered the library some few months before, all interested in sailing of some capacity or another. Could this be one of those lovely young men? As she read a little further it soon became clear that it was a middle-aged man with little or no experience of sailing. How sad she thought as she then got the gist of the man's injuries. *Hopefully, all would be okay, and he'd make a full recovery. You just never know what happens right on your doorstep, expect the unexpected that way you can't go wrong*, she thought.

"Country roads take me home, to a place I belong," she hummed as she wheeled the library trolley through the bookshelves, stopping occasionally to tap her feet on the lovely wooden slats adorning much of the library floor.

With her mobile on silent during working hours, she had missed the WhatsApp alert sent accompanied by the date, time, and venue for the next Wine O'clock Club meeting. She was deep in thought as she entered the Philosophy section heading for Einstein as she bumped into a remarkably familiar face... she couldn't quite place him and then, hey presto, she knew it was Raincoat Man.

As he stared at her, totally pan-faced she decided to acknowledge him, given he was a visitor to the library.

"Well good afternoon, sir," she said looking straight at him.

"Huh" he replied, "is it?"

How rude, thought Cleo. She hadn't experienced anything good about this very bizarre visitor since her first meeting with him.

"Can I help you with anything?"

"No, you can't," came the reply.

"Very well, I'm just over—"

"I know where you are, just over there at that desk where you kept me waiting last time," he said indignantly.

With that unpleasant exchange, he sidled off towards the exit sign. Cleo thought for a moment and then decided to head towards the very book he had returned to the library a few weeks ago. Philosophy, a theory, or attitude that acts as a guiding principle for behaviour, erm...

The book *To be Improper would be Proper if it wasn't Deemed as rude* was nowhere to be seen. A slight gap where the book had once been placed, no card, no trace, no sign.

Had Raincoat Man whipped it away on his visit? If so, how could this be proven? Why would he do this? What the hell is that book about anyway? How was Cleo going to explain a missing book that had only recently been returned to the library after a month's absence!

As she gathered her thoughts and digested what had happened, she had noted that Raincoat Man had left the library. She hurriedly ran to the exit checking both left and right along the street, absolutely no sign that he had ever been there. And more to the point it wasn't even raining! How very odd she thought as she entered the rotating doors of the library pondering the situation.

By now she had made a mental note of this gentleman, hair colour grey, build stocky, skin colour lightly tanned, grey stubble protruding from his chin, eye colour unsure, accent well-spoken even posh but hard to say due to the irritation in his voice. Dress sense, erm... grey crumpled canvas cloth overcoat making him look a little bit unkempt. Some kind of brogues on his feet, black, brown she couldn't be sure. Cleo took out her mobile and made some rough notes there and then whilst she could remember the basic facts. She added the time, day, and date so she could see if there was a pattern to his visits if he came to the library again. Somehow, she doubted it as it appeared he had now got what he came for. She thought for a moment and decided to leave a note for her colleague that this book was now reported officially "missing "from the library.

Cleo had now noted the message from Anne about the next Wine O'clock Club and messaged back immediately with her intention of attending. A good old catch up, much needed Cleo thought as she proceeded with her daily tasks before closing time.

Chapter 30 - The Bells

"Oranges and Lemons said the bells of St Clements," Clem was humming to herself when the Devil's mother entered the lounge.

"Is everything okay, Clem?"

"Yes fine," she said. "I was just giving the room a flick around with the duster whilst I had five."

"That's exceedingly kind of you, Clem."

"Well, we aim to please."

"Would you like to sit down and have a chat?" the Devil's mother asked, showing her to the three-seater sofa.

"Oh lovely, but only if you've got time."

Clem I've got all the time in the world," she responded.

Clem had really warmed to the Devil's mother. She found her kind, sensitive, keen to please, communicative, passionate, and, most of all, interesting.

She had been caring for the Devil's father for nearly eight months now at which point his condition has become much worse and he was now receiving end of life care. The Devil was making frequent trips to see his father who was by now heavily sedated and very much bedridden. The Devil spent time sitting on the edge of the bed talking to his father about when he was a lad and how together they would play jokes on his mother to make her scream. All three would end up laughing so much that tears began to trickle down their already red cheeks.

"Those were the days, eh Dad?" he would reminisce, hoping for a glimmer of recognition that he was there. The Devil would take his father's hand and just hold it tightly as he watched the rise and fall of his chest.

The Devil was making the trip to his parents much more frequently now and staying longer. His mother had found some solace in Clem, which helped her to get through the days. Clem had become more than a nurse, she had become a friend, a confidante, and a necessity.

Watching his father sleeping, the Devil thought, *Where there is life there is hope. He and we all need hope. Hope... Rupert, how is he? Has he come round? How are Pamela and the children?*

The Devil looked at is watch. It was a bit too late to ring Pamela now, so he made a mental note to catch up with her the next morning.

Chapter 31 - Cry me a River

It had now been two days since Rupert's accident, and he was still in a coma. His hands were a pale-yellow colour with some crazy paving-like veins running through the middle. *They appeared a little odd but nothing to worry about*, thought Pamela. Although Rupert was now a funny colour, he had always displayed a ruddy complexion. When she enquired with the consultant, he explained that his body temperature had dropped due to being hypothermic and once it had risen sufficiently his normal colour would return, which may take a few days.

It was hard to see Rupert like this; he was usually such a healthy, athletic, and attractive man. Since his removal from the organisation, his life had spiralled somewhat out of control and all he had been trying to do was to get it back again. Who'd have thought it... a job loss, a last-minute decision to go sailing to try to get back into the Devil's good books and not be forgotten about and then...disaster.

"Come on Rupert, let's make you comfortable," she said, "and I'll see you tomorrow. Beano and Bandit send their love and are missing you something shocking. I'll bring the kids tomorrow; they want to come and see how you're doing."

With that, Pamela grabbed her coat, kissed Rupert gently on the cheek, gave his hand a squeeze and closed the door behind her, glancing back just to make sure he was okay.

The days just morphed into one endless loop for Pamela. She diligently went about her daily business yet felt in a bit of a fuzz, not quite knowing what she was supposed to be doing. She felt numb and vacant but tried to carry on with her life hoping and praying that things would turn out alright.

One large mug of coffee later and now joined by Melissa, Pamela sought solace in her in her daughter before proceeding off to bed ready to try to face another night without her beloved Rupert by her side. As she snuggled up as best she could, she reached out to turn Rupert's mobile off and that's when she saw it: large bold text. RUPERT, I NEED YOU! HELP ME PLEASE. No trace as to who the writer was, no phone number, no clues just this one big bold message written at 10.23 p.m. that evening. Would Rupert know who this was? What did this person want with Rupert and what was the urgency, Pamela wondered? *Very strange*, she thought as the light switch clicked off and darkness enveloped the room.

"It's not good news, Mrs Hope," he said having taken Pamela into a side room. As he stood there in his theatre attire with a junior by his side, Pamela could see his lips moving but had no idea what he was saying. As his sidekick nodded in agreement, Mr Hargreaves began to explain what was meant by sepsis. Blood poisoning, he said, was usually associated with an injury, fall, or shock and required antibiotics immediately to stop the infection from spreading.

She had been told that Rupert was showing obvious signs of sepsis in his extremities, specifically his hands and feet.

Although still unconscious there were changes in skin tone, a crackled appearance in both hands and feet that appeared to be slowly spreading up his arms and legs. Tests had proved positive, and antibiotics administered.

"We have managed to control the spread Mrs Hope, but we need to operate to ensure no further spread for your husband to have any chance of survival."

"*WHAT, WHAT, WHAT* do you mean? What the hell is going on!? Rupert, Rupert, Rupert!" she screamed.

"Mrs Hope your husband will die if we do not get control of the spread. Sepsis works quickly and can close down vital organs within minutes. We have it under control at the moment, but immediate surgery is now required to save his life. Will you sign the papers Mrs Hope? We need to act quickly."

"What does all that mean? what will you do to him?"

"It's hard to say until we have him on the operating table, but it will require some amputations to control the spread."

"Amputations, Mr Hargreaves? You want me to agree to have one limb, two limbs or whatever removed from my husband just like that? Do you know what you are asking me to do?"

"I absolutely do, Mrs Hope, and I do believe it or not really understand your dilemma, but may I just reiterate, Mrs Hope, Rupert will die if we don't operate immediately. Can you please give us your permission to at least try to save his life?"

As Pamela lifted a blue biro in her now vigorously shaking hand, she steadied the paper, skimmed the detail and through blurred vision she signed the consent at 03:35 hours. As her cheeks felt the warmth of her tears as they began to trickle down her now flushed face, Mr Hargreaves's sidekick led her back into Rupert's room.

"May God forgive me, Rupert, if my decision breaks your heart, but life is precious, and I will love you no matter what. I'll see you on the other side, my darling."

Pamela kissed his cheek, caressed his now purple hands and watched as he was led away to theatre. Unsure of what exactly they would find she curled up on a hard chair in Rupert's room to try to get some sleep. It was too early to call Melissa or Theo and what could they do right here and now anyway? So, Pamela, alone and frightened wrapped a blanket around her body as a source of comfort and tried to get some sleep. Fitful as it was, she awoke to the sound of Rupert breathing heavily. It was now quarter to eight, and Rupert had just returned from theatre.

He was covered with blankets with only his face visible. He looked peaceful, rested, and comfortable. Afraid to remove his bedding and be faced with whatever they had done to him, Pamela instead sat by him, gently whispering in his ear. There was a modicum of recognition so much so that Pamela was convinced Rupert was starting to emerge from his now three-day coma.

A lovely nurse entered the room and asked Pamela if she would like a coffee and something to eat. Pamela agreed to the coffee. She made her way to the sink and caught sight of herself in the mirror: hair unkempt, bags forming under her eyes and genuinely exhausted. She focused on the reflection of Rupert.

Oh my God, oh my God, what have I done, she wondered?

"Your coffee, Mrs Hope. Mr Hargreaves will be along shortly."

Pamela phoned Melissa and Theo and without informing them of the seriousness of their father's illness, she explained that he had required an emergency operation during the night. "We'll be there shortly, Mum," Melissa said.

"Both legs just below the knee and Rupert's right hand just above the wrist. We've managed to save his left hand," Mr Hargreaves said. "As we now have the sepsis under control; we expect Rupert to emerge from his coma within the next day or so."

"What do I say to him; how do I deal with this, Mr Hargreaves?"

"We will be with you to support you and explain to Rupert what clinical decision was made, why it was made and what this now means for his future."

Beneath the hospital sheets Rupert still looked like Rupert. His wound was healing and underneath that dressing was the handsome, kind, and loving man that Pamela had married all those years ago. She asked Mr Hargreaves if she could see what

Rupert's body looked like now. She had to be prepared for Melissa, Theo, and most of all Rupert.

As the sheets were removed, Pamela could see three heavily bandaged limbs or what was left of them... Left and right legs now short and stumpy making Rupert look childlike. She could see two arms but only one hand that was supporting just three fingers. Pamela found herself shaking and gasping for breath. The lovely young nurse quickly assisted her to a chair. After glass of water and a gentle squeeze of her hand, Pamela had gained some composure.

"Mum," came a voice.

Melissa and Theo had arrived.

Chapter 32 - Cheers

Happy Hour seven p.m.-nine p.m. All Welcome!

Just what Anne needed to see, great, super time to hold the next Wine O'clock Club meeting. As usual, Anne arrived early. She was dressed more casually this time as she had felt the need to be comfortable and sought solace in her grey leggings and baggy black top which had some light ginger fur clinging to the hemline. She wore white trainers trimmed with gold edging to add a bit of sparkle to her otherwise plain outfit. She chose to wear her hair down with no bands or clips to scrape it back and this time she decided to wear her rather trendy, tinted glasses so if Tigger came up in conversation, she could hide her tears behind the big frames.

Although she wanted the catch up, she was a bit nervous of the subject matters particularly if Fee started on like she was inclined to do. Anyway, she was here now, all was organised, so Anne decided to try to relax into the evening. The table chosen was by the window and had five chairs around it when Anne arrived, so she scoured the room for an additional two hoping that all seven invitees were able to attend.

As she had plenty of time on her hands Anne rehearsed what she was going to say about her job, Tigger, and Billy. From then on in she would play it by ear.

After what appeared an exceptionally long ten minutes in walked Mel looking very relaxed and very happy.

"Hi, Anne, how are you?" she said as she hugged her tightly. "My, it's been a long time, great to get together again. "What are you drinking Anne?"

"Well, I was waiting to see what people wanted, so Mel, shall we get a couple of bottles of red and white and run a kitty like we did last time? That seemed to work well and even Tim was happy with his beer."

"Yes let's," said Mel. She tossed a tenner into the middle of the table which Anne immediately matched.

Very soon there were six wine glasses and two bottles of wine on the table, a chilled Sauvignon Blanc, and a lovely dark Rioja. Both Anne and Mel chose the Rioja and as Anne poured, the wine swilled around the glass before settling neatly at the bottom.

"Cheers," Mel said.

"Cheers," Anne repeated as they downed the first sips of the dark, fruity, and rich wine. After two sips in came Rene and Cleo waving frantically in their excitement to meet up again, followed closely by Tim.

"You need to get a pint Tim; we've got a kitty like last time," shouted Anne.

Tim duly nodded and made his way to the bar.

How many of these can I afford, thought Tim. *Money is tight, but I don't want anyone to know.* He quickly calculated that he had enough change to down at least four pints and that would be it even with the bonus of happy hour.

As Tim found his way to the table, he took a sip of his beer before placing it safely down on a beer mat and in his best Welsh accent he said, "What's occurring?"

Oh my God, was he changing! What on earth had made him say that he thought? Mind you it brought a chuckle to the table.

"Tim you're chilling a bit, got a bit more with it since leaving the fold," Rene said.

Millie appeared next, hair tied neatly in a ponytail and looking very swish in a one-piece khaki jumpsuit she sat herself down closest to the Sauvignon Blanc and began to pour a large glass.

"Hi there, how are we all?" she asked. "Fabulous to see everyone again... oh, where's Fee, is she coming?"

"I would think so," replied Anne. "She hasn't said she isn't, let's put it like that."

"Erm... in her own time," Tim retorted. It was now 7.45 p.m. and still no sign of Fee.

"Shall I ring her?" Anne asked.

"No, she'll turn up at some point. If not, something urgent has happened as Fee isn't one to miss a do, especially a gossipy do!" said Rene.

The music in the wine bar was much more sedate this time and acted as a backing track rather than something that required a shouting match. Think it's a Michale Bublé track, the old romantic Mel thought. She had recently been to see him in concert and was keen to share the whole experience with everyone in minute detail. As the drink flowed and the conversations got under way, the bar tender sidled across with some nibbles, seven shots and some salt and lemon.

"Who's having Fee's?" Rene shouted just as the door opened and in she came.

"Sorry I'm late darlings, but work took me to a place further than I've ever been for ages."

"What the fuck does that mean?" Tim said. Not one to swear but he'd now had two and half pints of his allocated four pints and it was taking its toll on him. Funny how drink makes you lose your inhibitions and gives you the ability to speak as freely as you like.

As usual she looked drop-dead gorgeous with an added spring in her already sprightly step.

It was at that moment that Anne thought, *Oh bloody hell, I should have made more of an effort*.

"Anne how are you darling! It's been a while; how's that handsome hunk of a Billy? Has he popped the question yet given he seems to have popped everything else?"

With that more than embarrassing question, she slurped a huge mouthful of Rioja and proceeded to sit down beside Cleo.

Unfortunately, this placed her right opposite Anne, and in the best place to ask the questions. Anne Leigh, watch out: 'You are the weakest link, goodbye.'

As the night progressed, each attendee gave a brief resume of their lives to press to update the group, apart from Fee who couldn't stop talking about Hugh and the fact that he was thinking of reducing his working hours for a better work-life balance. Fee thought that this was absolute disgrace.

It was clear as the night progressed that some of the group had found their vocation in life and the removal of them from the organisation was the best thing ever. Rene was very near to qualifying as a fully trained midwife after one year then she had two years' probation (someone looking out for her) before she would be a free agent with the ability and skills to deal with lots of wide and varied situations.

She shared with the group that she was ready to have another baby, a sibling for Alfie once her first year's training had been completed. She clearly loved her job, bringing new people into the world was quite extraordinary and as such she felt very privileged and honoured to not only undertake the rigorous training but to also find out that she had a natural aptitude for it.

She completed her synopsis by standing and lifting her Sauvignon Blanc to her lips before saying, "Cheers! Here's to all new lives that enter this world; may they be long and happy." With that, she sat down to a "hear, hear" and loud clapping. At that moment, Rene was more than proud.

Tim was reticent to even began to describe his somewhat delicate situation. Even three pints wouldn't be enough Dutch courage. So, he chooses to sit it out in the hope that no one would notice and that other stories would take so long, he'd be forgotten.

"Fee, do you want to go next?" Anne asked.

"I don't," Fee replied somewhat indignantly. "It will take me the rest of the evening and no one else will get a word in edgeways."

As such both Tim and Anne were praying that she *would* go next leaving no time for anyone else.

Mel felt compelled to go next; she had a story to tell, and she wanted to tell it. Her job had taken her to new places, new experiences, and the total appreciation of life from a different perspective than Rene had seen. Mel rose quickly to her feet on Fee's refusal and before more wine had arrived at the table Mel was on her journey.

"Never underestimate life," she said. "As Rene marvels at the sight of new life entering this world so I quietly contemplate the end of life. Two vastly different spectrums, life and death with the middle dash, the descriptor as to how you live your life. I believe that life is impossible to live without hope; we all need hope." Mel then recited the quote from Martin Luther King: "'We must accept finite disappointment but never lose infinite hope'." She went on to talk about her first experience of loss in her job role and recalled the young blond man who quietly slipped away in the presence of Mel and her colleague. It was noticeably clear from her compassion and the tone of her voice that this job was meant to be, it was her destiny and vocation, and she wasn't going to let it go any time soon. Her reference to hope was to become her defining moment but she didn't know it.

As the third lot of wine was delivered to the table, the group had begun to slouch, yawn and stretch. The sound of the Rat Pack playing *The Girl from Ipanema* in the background enhanced their sleepiness but not before – you've guessed it – Fee Shand took to the stage. Twenty-five minutes later, she was still waxing lyrical about her phone sex role, her heightened sense of how good sex was in any capacity and the use of sex toys in the privacy of one's home.

People couldn't help but feel that this was all a bit near the knuckle, but it was clear she was making a particularly good living from it and that she was much better suited to it than working in a boring tax office. The money was good, the working hours were very much down to Fee, and she was her own boss. She had an amazing speaking voice that Tim felt would be incredibly sexy once in character; the thought of her speaking to him sent a tingle down his balls and he felt the shaft of his penis harden.

Cleo had little to say that could beat that, she was still at the library, still working part-time, and still very much enjoying it. The variety of people visiting made it entertaining and interesting. She was never short of something to do and enjoyed the mix of job roles entrusted to her. The job kept her on her toes as she explained how books were rank and filed and how difficult it was when something was misfiled or missing. Memory jogged, she went on to tell the group about Raincoat Man. As she recalled the book title *To be Improper Would be Proper if it wasn't Deemed as Rude*, Millie screamed and jumped to her feet.

"I don't believe it, Cleo. What did you say? Can you repeat it slowly and precisely for me once more?"

Cleo, a little perplexed, reiterated, "To be improper would be proper if it wasn't deemed as rude."

"Oh, my giddy aunt, Cleo! You've just helped to solve an ongoing mystery at Avenging Angels!

Millie, already on her feet, then outlined all the changes that had taken place in her life. She was quick and efficient telling everyone how much she was enjoying the job and how much she had learnt since starting. She was also enormously proud of the fact that she was now line managing two people, how exciting was that, she added. Everyone was listening intently dying for her to get to the bit about the phone call. She could see that they could wait no longer as Fee's fingers started to drum on the table.

"Okay here's the thing:" said Millie, "a gentleman caller has now phoned the office twice over the last three weeks. He is very sharp, short and to the point. The only thing he wants is to talk to Arthur— that's the director of the company. He doesn't want his son or anyone else, he just wants Arthur. He says the same thing every time he calls: 'To be improper would be proper if it wasn't deemed as rude'. What the fuck does that mean?" Millie asked. "Do you know, Cleo?"

"I have no idea, none whatsoever. All I can say is that the book was filed away in the Philosophy section. The bloke that brought it in was more than late returning it and had to pay a hefty fine. He was rude and I could barely be courteous with him, given his demeanour and aggressive stance."

"So," said Millie, "you've seen him, you know what he looks like. you've noted his clothing, his voice, his hair, face and body shape? You'd recognise him in a line-up?"

"What line-up; what are you talking about, Millie?"

"I reckon he's up to no good, Cleo. He desperately wants Arthur and will stop at nothing until he gets him."

"Erm... Tim interjected. "Millie, you're getting ahead of yourself, there might be a simple and reasonable explanation for his behaviour."

"Like what?" said Millie. "What is reasonable about repeating what we now know as a book title to an investigating unit like Avenging Angels?"

"Eh?"

"Really Tim, there must be more to it."

"Do we have an author, Cleo?"

"No, I don't think so. I checked the book on the library system, it's logged with no author. And get this, it's not very popular, this is only the third time it has been booked out or nicked this time."

"Who borrowed it before?" Rene asked.

"I don't know," said Cleo.

"Why would you return a book, pay the fine and then come back a few days later and pinch or maybe borrow it again? You wouldn't!"

Gosh these strange goings-on had really taken the pressure off Tim and Anne, and nobody seemed the slightest bit interested in what they had been up to. As the evening drew to a close, Tim had spied some loose silver sitting in the middle of the table which was definitely going into his pocket.

"Anne thank you so much for arranging yet another spiffing evening, it's been most enjoyable. How soon shall we do it again?" Rene asked.

"How about six months or so? Give us time to gather our thoughts thus far?"

"What about Raincoat Man and the book?" Millie asked.

"Maybe you and Cleo can further investigate, Millie, and let us know the outcome," Mel said.

"I think we'll do just that then. Cleo, are you up for it?"

"I am, I'm very intrigued to know what is going on, Millie."

"Okay we'll arrange something outside of this rabble."

And with that the evening was ended with Tim hopping back to grab the change off the table.

Chapter 33 - Don't Look Back in Anger

The next day Mel was reflecting on last night's shenanigans, she could see that most of the organisational staff had made giant leaps forwards and seemed more than happy with their lot. She thought about Anne and Tim who had little chance to update the group, given the goings-on with Cleo and Millie. Her thoughts then took her to the Devil, Denzil, Rupert, and Marco. How were they? What was going on in their lives? As far as she knew, the Devil, Denzil and Marco were still sailing the ship and Rupert was still searching for his ever-elusive job, or maybe he'd got one by now? Mel being Mel thought she may enquire through Miss Moneypenny; she still had some contacts with the organisation and just wanted to know that all was okay.

"Nia Shaw speaking, how may I help you?"

"Nia, this is Mel here, Mel Carter. How are you?"

"Oh, this is a surprise, Mel. Yes, I am fine, thank you. What can I do for you?"

"Erm, I was just wondering if you were still in touch with Rupert Hope; I was thinking about him the other day and was wondering how he was getting on."

"I've really no idea, Mel. Since he left the organisation, we haven't heard anything from him. That said, I think Marco was considering asking him to go sailing for the weekend but I'm not sure that happened. The boss isn't here at the moment, his father's very ill so he's taking some time away to be with his mother."

Mel said, "Oh I'm sorry to hear that, Nia."

"Well, I suppose it's life eh, Mel? Things are certainly not the same since you all departed; If it wasn't for Denzil there would be no trace of the team at all."

"Oh, is he still with you, Nia?"

"Barely," came the reply.

"Well, if you hear from Rupert, can you remember me to him? I know what happened wasn't right, but he did lose his job as well didn't he, Nia?"

"Yes, he did, and do you know, Mel, sometimes it's better the Devil you know."

With that, the phone went dead and Mel was satisfied that she had done her bit... for the moment anyway.

Chapter 34 - Drumroll Please

The weeks had turned to months and Denzil felt that he had a reprieve. The Devil was away from his desk for quite some time which give Denzil the breathing space he required to sort himself out. Work was more than tough; he was struggling and just couldn't find a way to rectify what had been going wrong. He was missing Rupert desperately, his guidance, his mentorship, his friendship, and his true belief in Denzil. What had gone so wrong? Was Denzil boxing above his weight? Many staff genuinely believed he was and if it hadn't been for Rupert, he would have been out on his ear long ago. Did Denzil make a mistake? Should he have taken the package on offer like everyone else? Should he have left with his head held high and gone on to start afresh elsewhere? Why had he been so blinkered or had he? Did he like lording it over the other eight, feeling the power and pure elation of keeping his job whilst everyone else was losing theirs? Did this make him feel important, worthy, favoured and in control?

It was Rupert who had put Denzil's name forward as a young and enterprising staff member, keen to learn with a confident manner and the ability to lead from the front. Not the impression others had of him. He was branded as lazy, riding on the back of others' ideas and work; he talked a lot but said nothing. His flashy suits, strong aftershave, and honed physique were merely smokescreens for his incompetence. He was always one to agree with the boss (whoever the boss was) and would be seen nodding vigorously in the background like Churchill in the car insurance ad. Nothing really added up with Denzil; it was hard to know who the real Denzil was. With few or no friends, Rupert was not only his boss but also his ally, his confidant and is friend. Treading water can only last for so long Denzil.

Why isn't he answering the phone Denzil wondered? *Last I saw him he told me that I was very much on my own, well I am but I need him, so where the fuck is he?*

After several unanswered calls, Denzil texted Rupert late one evening: "RUPERT, I NEED YOU... HELP ME PLEASE." This text remained unanswered.

His babe magnet might have been doing it for Denzil, but it was doing bugger-all to attract the local talent. It was an expensive car to run but Denzil felt that not only did he look the debonaire entrepreneur/man about town, but his car matched his persona, so why was he still single? Simples, ask his ex-teammates and they will tell you that he is a nob.

As the days went by, Denzil could not get himself out of the mess he was in and as a last resort decided to visit Rupert at home. That way, he could come face to face with him and get what he needed.

Dressed casually in a cotton jacket and jeans, he eased himself into his low-slung car. With his aftershave heavily perforating the small cockpit he switched the CD player on and chose Queen's *Don't Stop me Now* which came blaring out of the quadrophonic speakers. Tapping the wheel in time to the music, Denzil popped the gear stick into the drive position and off he went in search of Rupert. Not sure whether he was having an enjoyable time or a ball he thought.

Chapter 35 – He Ain't Heavy

I want to break free and break free I have!

Charles was out of the rehab centre for good, four years of being confined to Room Number 12 had ended at last. He had persuaded his mother to let him rent a flat near to Tim as a starting point on the proviso that Tim ensured that Carbon Copy Charles would be okay. Ceceila had paid one year's rent upfront for Charles to enable him to get back on his feet and rebuild his life. No money had come Tim's way, but he was okay with that as it did not make him beholden to his mother. Tim thought that a flat nearby was the lesser of the two evils, Charles moving in with Tim or Tim and Charles going to live with their mother, God forbid.

Tim made a point of visiting Charles rather than Charles visiting him, purely because Charles never knew when to go home and he definitely couldn't take a hint. This way both parties could get into a routine. Charles was surprisingly capable. After a few days, he ditched the wheelchair, stood upright showing his full six-foot-one-inch height (inherited from his father). Tim erred on the small side, like his mother. Aside of the height difference, they did look alike, same colour hair greying in similar places, same skin tone, eye colour and basic shape except Charles was just a bigger version. Both spoke with an educated Welsh accent albeit Charles's voice was much bolder, louder and way more confident.

Perhaps being a lawyer gave Charles the art of articulation of speech as well as an inquisitive tone making people unsure of his friendliness towards them.

Before his downfall he had been a brilliant lawyer: the go-to man, larger than life, strong, efficient, and massively successful, so much so he could command his own salary. Destined to go to Chambers and become a High Court judge, Charles saw himself there for ten years or so until retirement or attaining the age of seventy. Unmarried and keen to focus on his career, he steered clear of long-term relationships; he didn't want any distractions on his way to the top. Charles had trained in Corporate Law, the highest paying legal specialisation which saw him work on behalf of organisations. As a corporate lawyer, Charles engaged in drafting documents, structuring transactions, attending meetings, and negotiating deals.

Until one day he wasn't...

How can you go from top man to nobody in the blink of an eye?

Chapter 36 - Help me if you Can

In search of Raincoat Man, Millie was determined to find the underlying cause of this conundrum. She had arranged to meet with Cleo independently of the rest of the group; she wanted Cleo's full attention.

Questions flew around in her head. How could this be? Where did Raincoat Man come from? Who is he? 'To be improper would be proper if it wasn't deemed as rude'... what the hell did this mean? How can there possibly be a book with that title? So many questions, so few answers.

It was a beautiful sunny morning; the birds were singing as Millie skipped along the street eager to meet Cleo in the coffee shop situated at the end of the road. Millie always dreamed of owning her own tea shop, serving scones and Earl Grey was more than appealing to Millie. Set on the High Street to catch the passing trade, Millie felt that she could become quite successful with her gift of the gab and public interaction. Was this now a time to consider that option? Oh, how she wished she were a bit braver, living the ultimate dream she thought as she entered the coffee shop at three minutes to ten and identified a table close to the window, no sooner done and Cleo stepped over the threshold. Two coffees, a latte and a cappuccino, Millie and Cleo settled in for an investigative morning trying to join the dots.

"Have you read the book, Cleo?"

"No of course not, Millie; I've never even heard of it before all this."

"Well, he has phoned Avenging Angels twice now, both times asking for Arthur Attley, who is my boss. I have no idea what he wants with Arthur, and I don't think Arthur does either."

"Can we get the book, Cleo?"

"I don't think so, although it's logged on the system with no author. However, what I can't understand is why he would bring it back, pay the fine and then pinch it. It makes no sense at all."

"Do you think that he may return to the library?"

"No, not now he has what he came for, why would he?"

"So," said Millie, "we will have to wait for another phone call from him then. I can't see another way to trace this man."
"The problem is we don't know when he's going to call."

Exasperated and scratching their heads, they made some notes of what had gone on so far. Millie was desperate to have something tangible for Arthur. They began to summarise their findings thus far: one man, one raincoat, grey stubble, stocky, rude, impatient but with a sense of authority and very demanding. Not much to go on. Millie had a sudden thought: "To be improper" well he is, he has no decorum whatsoever, "would be proper" ugh, how can that be proper, "if it wasn't deemed as rude," well he is utterly rude. So, in essence he's rude so cannot possibly be proper. Is that right Cleo?"

"Oh, hell I don't know Millie! I can't work it out."

"What does he want with Arthur? Does he know Avenging Angels and what they stand for? Has he used them in the past? it's all very puzzling. Another coffee, Cleo?"

"Oh, go on then Millie, I need the caffeine fix."

To be improper would be proper if it wasn't deemed as rude.

"Let's take the words and try to reconfigure them, Cleo."

"Into what, Millie?"

"I don't know, let's just brainstorm and see what comes up."

"Proper / Improper – Opposites," said Millie.

"To be... erm, or not to be... a bit of Shakespeare," said Cleo.

"AA one of the letters are in there Cleo."

"And so are lots more Millie. Do you think there's some sort of code in there?"

"Well, it must mean something to someone, Cleo. Has Arthur absolutely no idea what this may be about?"

"No and neither do I, Millie. Can we stop now, it's making my brain ache."

"Do you fancy a scone or a bit of lunch? On me, Cleo, of course."

"Oh, go on, go on then, at least I've got something tangible from our meeting, Millie."

With that, the pair ordered more coffee, a cheeseburger and fries and a bacon and brie toastie accompanied by a side salad and chips.

Chapter 37 - Billy Don't be a Hero

The ever-elusive Billy, as he was branded by Fee Shand, suddenly reappeared working for White Wings Crematorium. Dressed smartly in a two-piece suit, white shirt, and black tie, he looked every bit the part. Fronting proceedings, meeting and greeting mourners, convening crematoria slots, one couldn't help but wonder what he was up to? It was very evident that it was Billy; he wasn't trying to hide. There he was with his blond hair cascading over his forehead; his upright stance and broad shoulders gave him a very distinctive gait. Why wasn't Anne aware of his job? Why did he keep disappearing, was it to undertake this role that he appeared to be carrying out so very well?

White Wings Crematorium was located sixteen miles away from Anne so why didn't Anne know what he was up to? What exactly was Billy doing at: -

White Wings Crematorium

Where we take great Care of your Loved Ones

Let Doves fly high up in the Sky!

A lovely way to say Goodbye.

Described as a final resting place for those we love. What they mean is:

Bodies are prepared for cremation by crematorium staff.

Bodies are tagged and all jewellery removed.

Pacemakers, artificial parts, and any non-fixed metal is removed.

A huge magnet removes any further metal detected post cremation.

Only one body at a time is permitted to occupy a furnace.

Furnaces sit at a temperature of between 1000° C and 1300° C at which point bodies enter the brick archway and burn for a period of two to three hours. Any bigger bones after cremation may be put through a cremulator to ensure that family recipients receive a smooth white dust-like powder that occupy urns or are dispensed into the sea, the land or sit all neat and tidy on the shelf of a loved one's home. Whatever the outcome of that dust, the process is repeated time and time again in the crematorium.

A very warm welcome awaits all those who visit.

Chapter 38 – Bye-Bye, Baby

"I'm on a rocket ship on my way to Mars on a collision course..." BANG! The mobile was still in his hand when he hit the chevrons warning of a sharp right-hand bend. His car crumpled on impact smashing his babe magnet solidly into his chest. No one could have survived such force; the police estimated speed on impact to have been at least seventy mph. The letters R... U... P... could be seen written in capital letters on his phone.

Denzil had been attempting a text when he took his eye off the road to write his message. His cotton jacket was neatly entwined in his chest and had turned red on impact. His jeans were twisted around the handbrake and had settled either side of the cockpit. Queen was still rocking as the car came to a halt in the middle of the road. The driver's door had been flung open, and Denzil was on show with half a metal chevron sticking upright from his chest. Denzil was no longer floating around in ecstasy. He never made his destination; he never got further promotion. The audience with the Devil was no longer required; his life was now cancelled.

Some weeks later the sun shone and the music played, the white posies on the table emitted a fragrance so beautiful that momentarily the vision of Denzil at his best had entered each of the congregation's thoughts. Rupert, although sad, was glad that Denzil hadn't witnessed what he'd now become. He took solace in the fact that Denzil had been his protégé, his would-be successor and Rupert truly believed that Denzil had solved the puzzle, that's why he was coming to see him.

As *Amazing Grace* echoed through the chapel, Denzil's coffin was wheeled in. Rupert shuffled to his feet using his good arm to now steady himself on his unfamiliar prosthetic legs. He managed to reach his full height, much to his relief, and once there he was able to view most people at eye level. It had been a long journey for Rupert, Pamela, and his children. His face had healed well and with his good arm he had the ability to manoeuvre his prosthetic legs over his two stumps. He was learning to adjust; he had no choice, but he realised that it was going to be an exceptionally long road. Most people acknowledged his situation and were sympathetic and understanding, giving him more time than they had ever done in the organisation. But no matter what, Fee Shand could not forgive or forget and felt very much that Rupert had got what he deserved.

What goes around, comes around, she thought. *He has been truly butchered.*

Denzil's mother managed to read the eulogy cover to cover with her head down. She managed to splutter out how wonderful her son was. She was a beautiful woman, full of warmth and love. Together with his two sisters and younger brother, Denzil's family had done him proud.

As the service concluded with "Go in peace to love and serve the Lord," Eva Cassidy's *Fields of Gold* echoed through the small chapel. Denzil's family were standing on either side of the doorway as the congregation exited. His mother, a small, delicate woman, wearing a black hat and grey dress, took comfort from mourners' words and comforting actions. As Rupert approached guided by Marco, Mrs Drum took his only hand and kissed it.

"Thank you, Rupert, for everything you did for Denzil. He spoke of you often with great pride and joy. He told me that he was your protégé and that you were his guiding light, teaching him the management style required to head up a successful team. I applaud you for that, Rupert," she said, with tears beginning to roll down her cheeks. She wished Rupert well on his journey of recovery and turned to greet the next mourner.

Chapter 39 - Love Hurts

He never made the funeral; he sent a wreath instead with the message, 'May you rest in Peace, Denzil'. It had blue and white carnations in the shape of a square cushion with a big red D emblazoned in the middle. It was laid amongst the other floral tributes but truly made its mark and could be seen from some distance. One couldn't help but wonder if it depicted D for Denzil or D for Devil? Only one person would ever really know.

Now, as the car came to a halt in the driveway, the Devil prepared to greet his mother who was now standing arms outstretched to receive her only son.

"I'm so glad you made it son; your father hasn't got long now."

The Devil entered the dimly lit room and could see his dad prostrate on the bed with a slight rise and fall of his chest. Clem was close by checking for vital signs.

"Hello," she said in a calm but sympathetic way. "I don't think it will be long now; his blood pressure has dropped and is breathing has become much shallower. Would you like some time alone with him while I make you and your mum a cup of tea?"

"That would be lovely, Clem, thank you so much."

With that, Clem stood up and left the room quietly closing the door behind her.

"Hi Dad, it's me, I'm here," the Devil said in a softly spoken voice.

The Devil took his father's hand and held it tightly hoping his father could feel his presence. He was immensely sad; his heart was heavy, and he could feel it in his chest, like the beat of a distant drum. In that moment the Devil felt calm; with his eyes transfixed on his father's face, he began to mumble some incoherent words followed by a quiet humming of *You'll never walk Alone*. He had no idea why that tune had entered his head. Barely ten minutes has gone by when his father's breathing became silent, and the hand that the Devil was holding had gone limp and heavy. The Devil felt all was lost. *My patriarch, my father, my soulmate, gone without a last goodbye*, he thought. The Devil raised himself up to his full height and called out to his mother.

As he and his mother left the bedroom, Clem was calling the GP for certification of death as well as organising the undertakers his mother had chosen several weeks ago.

"Say it loud, say it clear, you can listen as well as you hear. It's too late when we die, to admit we don't see eye to eye..." (courtesy of Mike and The Mechanics) was now running fiercely through the Devil's mind. He had good days and bad days with his father but no matter what, he loved him very dearly and would miss him deeply.

The path of life is filled with good intentions, the Devil thought, *but time runs out and we don't always get to say what we want to.*

He held his weeping mother close. They took comfort from each other and as they waited for the doctor, they openly wept like they had never wept before.

The bungalow was quiet when the Devil's father had departed. Suddenly it was just his mother, Clem, and him. No running around, no checking on Dad, no keeping quiet, no reminiscing with Dad, no one to tell the Devil that everything will be all right. Just the solitary figure of his mother standing by the window endlessly staring out at the grass. Although you know it's coming nothing can quite prepare you for when it does.

Clem agreed to stay on at the Devil's request until such time as his mother felt stronger and more able to cope. He was now hoping that she may move to be closer to him and his place of work.

Chapter 40 - Till Death Us Do Part

He sat resplendent in the sunshine, licking his white paws, contented and happy. His blue collar was catching the light and twinkling around his neck. The bell would tinkle as soon as he made a move. People were coming and going, cars were moving slowly up and down the drive, gates would open and close and still he looked on in splendour and adulation. He was petted several times a day, visitors loved him, he made them feel strong more able to cope.

"Here Tiggy," shouted a young blond-haired man as he made his way towards him. Was this Billy and was he shouting Tigger. Surely Not? A closer examination saw the young man pick the cat up and gently stroke his neck, making the cat purr with sheer delight.

"Daddy can Tigger come in now?" a little voice echoed from behind the car.

"He can indeed. Come on Tigger, time for tea."

The crematorium was closing for the day. Billy had been down to the roadside to put up the closed sign as Tigger followed him back up the pathway. Billy scooped Ethan up in one go and proceeded to enter the kitchen with Ethan in one arm and Tigger in the other. As he gently kissed Taylor on the cheek, he passed Tigger to her.

"Don't you think someone might be missing this lovely cat, Billy? He has been so well looked after; I'm sure someone, somewhere, loves him."

"Well, he's here now and seems to like us, so no going back for Tigger, eh Ethan?"

"No Daddy, I love him; he's a very handsome kitty cat and he sleeps on my bed."

"I think we'll give him a new collar, Ethan, what do you think? Maybe a black one with a little round name tag?"

"Yes, please Daddy, then we can truly call him our cat. Do you here that Tigger, you're going to get a new collar."

Billy and Taylor had moved to the crematorium several months ago when Billy got the chance to manage the business. He and Taylor had been childhood sweethearts and although they'd parted on several occasions before, it was like it was meant to be. Ethan was nearly four and had been brought up by Taylor when Billy 'drifted'. As time marched on, Billy wanted to become a proper father to Ethan and as such asked Taylor to marry him. They were in the throes of organising the wedding when Tigger came into their lives. Their wedding was to be a lavish affair given Billy was paid handsomely to run the crematorium. He was keen to tie the knot as soon as possible but Taylor wanted to wait until after the birth of their second child.

Chapter 41 - Annie Get your Gun

Many months had passed since Anne had seen her wonderful Tigger. Life was a drudge; she had become several pounds heavier, and her clothes were beginning to evidence the fact. A red rim now encircled her waist where her once nicely fitted clothing sat. She was clearly depressed, fat, frigid and forty... fuck! Who wanted her now? No cat to love, no Billy to love, a make-do job that paid the bills and no social life aside of the Wine O'clock Club she insisted on organising, mainly to keep her sane. Mr and Mrs Campbell next door would often interrogate her about Tigger. They meant well but fuck it, it was really getting her down.

As she reflected on her life reclining her favourite chair, she wondered what she may have done differently. Why wasn't she more like Fee, a go-getter, an attractive bubbly person that oozed confidence and panache? Is it possible to change your life? Did she *want* to change her life? What else could she do? She had now removed the gorgeous photograph of Billy and replaced it with an even bigger one of Tigger.

That ship has sailed, she thought as she placed it in the bottom drawer hidden amongst her old tat. *Take that you bastard, I hate you, wherever the fuck you are.* Love and hate... totally different meanings but very closely aligned.

Anne had to get on with her life; she needed new interests, renewed vigour and a reason to go on. Flicking through the local magazine, she'd spotted a gentle impact Zumba class. *That's what I need*, she thought, *something to get me moving and meeting new people. Half price taster, this coming Thursday in the village hall. Whoopee I'm off to that she thought, fuck knows what I'll wear but I need to do something.* A glimmer of hope came over her. She'd decided to do something positive, was this to be the start of something great?

Chapter 42 - When you are a King

One hundred and fifty thousand pounds a year is a lot to lose. *I was once a kingpin,* Charles thought. *I had a fantastic home and lots of like-minded friends. Where did it all go wrong for Charles? Well, how long have you got; how can you make such a hash of such a brilliant life? Easy, just follow Charles.*

Called to the bar at just forty-one, young, keen, and massively talented. Charles was ahead of the game, a slick, knowledgeable lawyer with the Midas touch. What could possibly go so wrong… well let me tell you.

Sex, drugs and rock'n'roll was his downfall, his party trick, his je ne Sais quoi. For one big burly bloke it was a long way to fall.

Charles could never really understand his sexual orientation, was he straight, was he gay, was he bisexual or non-binary, who knows he thought. Maybe I'll try a bit of everything. It wasn't long before Charles became entangled in a love triangle, a married couple keen to explore new things. Charles became the "playmate" the inbetweener, the one to be experimented with. He got immense pleasure from his visits, twice weekly trying absolutely everything under the sun. Bloody hell, half of it he didn't know existed!

As things progressed with this middle-aged couple, Charles got increasingly involved. It went from bondage, blindfold, ball gag, rope, cuffs, and flogger to a snort of cocaine to heighten the senses, a slug of whiskey to deaden any pain and a cock harder than a fist of steel. His love for this couple grew beyond belief, he longed to be with them all the time. His mind wandered when working thinking of his next encounter. He was driven by his needs and the sexual urges became his life. He spent more and more time away from the courts ensconced in the bed of this martial couple. The more he experienced the more he wanted to experience, the more he experimented, the more he wanted to experiment. His first taste of drugs had led him further into the drugs market, getting high, losing inhibitions, and experiencing heightened sex like never before. Fuck this was beyond ecstatic. He paid a handsome price for his experiences but to him it was more than worth it.

On that fateful day, Charles was leading the roleplay, he was the dictator, the leader, the powerful one. Having snorted several nostrils of crack cocaine and downed at least four large whiskeys, he was more than high. Both he and Brian changed into full-length, black PVC suits, having covered their rather large bodies in some talc to ease with the fitting. Charles insisted Brian placed a ball gag into his mouth. Then in she came, a small blonde, petite woman, pert breasts, nipped-in waist and a clean-shaven pussy. Ready for penetration, Charles thought. She danced around in thigh-length black leather boots, had a black leather strap tied tightly around her waist, she was truly ready for fuckin.'

"Lick my dick," Charles instructed as he slipped his rock-hard cock out of his now damp PVC attire. As she did so, Charles eased his hand deep into her arse ramming as many fingers as possible into that hole. He instructed Brian to lick her side on. It was pure elation for Charles, and he ejaculated after no more than three minutes.

"Again, again!" shouted Brian incoherently.

"Hang fire I need a rest."

The drink was flowing, all three were off their heads on crack cocaine when Brian fell silent.

"Okay Brian, we're ready now."

"Brian, Brian, come on, move yourself!"

"Brian for fuck's sake, come on!"

Chapter 43 - Red, Red Wine

The drive was long and slow. The Devil was contemplating his life and that of his fathers as he took the journey home from his parents' house. He was due at work the next day and as such was mentally preparing himself for the onslaught of activity awaiting him. He was sad and somewhat bereft. What did his life have in store for him now. Would his mother move to be closer to him or stay put where she knew most people and was very familiar with her surroundings. He had asked Clem to remain with his mother until such times as she was able to cope living alone. He was quite happy to pay for her companionship. As his car purred to a halt, he alighted with a heavy heart, opened the latched door, kicked off his trademark brogues and poured himself a glass of malt. Tomorrow is a new day, new beginnings, a fresh start. A slither of cheese with three crackers and two glasses of red wine sent the Devil into a sleepy state. As he changed for bed, he thought of Rupert and wondered how life was now treating him, shit he thought, as he pulled the duvet over his rather rotund frame and fell quickly into a deep sleep.

As daylight peeped through the curtains, the Devil was woken by the gentle humming of his alarm clock signalling six thirty a.m. Time to rise and shine. He was feeling a bit groggy and worse for wear as he tumbled out of bed and into the shower. Today was going to be the day he thought when an announcement would hail the arrival of a "new" Denzil. The

Devil hadn't been involved in the interviews given he was otherwise occupied with his father, but he knew a replacement was urgently required given the sudden departure of Denzil. As such he'd left Marco and two senior colleagues to appoint.

He arrived in plenty of time to meet up with Marco, having parked his beautiful Mercedes in his designated parking spot, this time without the need for "Tim Assist."

Knock, knock, knock, "come in, we've been expecting you." The Devil entered Marco's office and could see three men sitting in a row, Marco proudly positioned in the middle. "Nice to see you again, sorry to hear about your father."

"Yes, it was to be expected but all a bit surreal when it happens."

"Would you like a tea or coffee?"

"No, I'm fine thank you, a glass of water would be good." The Devil was now feeling a bit uncomfortable as Miss Moneypenny entered the room with a jug of water and four glasses.

"Close the door on the way out will you," said Marco.

"Yes, will do Mr Marco" came the reply.

"Now then, we have reached a decision on the replacement for Denzil, and we think that she will be a perfect fit for the job. She has a Doctorate of Letters, and we see her as a real asset going forwards. We also feel that a "shared knowledge of her and your experience" will help her to better understand your position and what you may expect of her. So, can you arrange to meet her sometime next week and decide on a strategy going forwards that will engage the team and renew the partnership arrangements that we have?"

"Erm, yes that's fine Marco, no problem."

"Oh, and Human Resources are doing an audit of educational attainment given Alicia is now joining us, they feel it's time to ensure that individual files are up to date and computerised. Can I leave that with you as well?"

"Yes, no problem, I'll get onto it straight away. Can I meet this young lady before next week and does she have a name?"

"Of course," replied Professor Lindsey, the strait-laced man sitting to the right of Marco. "Her name is Alicia Jenkins; she is actually Dr Jenkins daughter, so it's no surprise she has performed so well."

"Super," the Devil retorted as he raised himself to his full height to leave the room.

"I look forward to it."

With that, he was gone and for the first time in a long time he felt that he wasn't in control of the situation that he had just found himself in. Alicia Jenkins, do I know her, no, but some people in the organisation clearly do, so what's going on here the Devil thought as he manoeuvred himself awkwardly down the stairs.

"Be professional, be professional, be professional" a voice in his head was telling him. She is probably somewhat naive and inexperienced this Alicia Jenkins so how come she's done so well for someone so young. Has someone pulled a few strings for her? Oh, and who the fuck is Dr Jenkins? Time will tell thought the Devil, now then where did I put my certificates?

Chapter 44 - Life of Brian

"Brian, Brian, Brian, wake up will you... come on, breathe, honey it's me, wake up! For fuck's sake, Brian, stop messing about!" Mavis said nervously as she removed the ball gag from Brian's mouth. He was ashen grey and looked dead as fuck.

Fuck it, I've had it now, he thought. His thought processes were interrupted with "Can I have your name, sir?"

"Erm Yes it's Char..." he incoherently stated.

"Are you alright, sir?"

"Yes, I'm fine," came the reply.

"Sarg, the ambulance is here."

With blues and twos flashing, the police car came to a halt on the drive; Charles felt that his life was well and truly over. Although now standing tall in a gimp suit towering over the two police officers, Charles suddenly felt ridiculously small.

Charles thought, *Fuck it, I'm sold down the river now.*

The defibrillator sprung into life, more than we can say about Brian, who was pronounced dead at 4.03 p.m. that afternoon. No cause of death available until after the postmortem, where no doubt they would find plenty of drink and drugs in his system. As Mavis sat rigid with a soft pink dressing gown now covering her modesty, it was clear that she was in a state of distress. As the paramedic tried to comfort her, she stood up flailing her arms in the air, shouting some obscenities and then proceeded to hit Charles hard in his stomach causing him to fall backwards and vomit all over her newly cleaned suite.

Chapter 45 - Let's Get Physical

"One, two, turn, one two twist and breathe!"

Goodness this is harder than I thought, Anne said to herself whilst trying to catch her breath. She was more than glad she'd tied her hair up and decided on contact lenses, else her glasses would easily have slipped off her nose by now, given how much she was perspiring. As Lady Gaga belted out *Bad Romance*, Anne's pulse rate was heightened so much so that her cheeks were flushed with exertion and her panting increased.

I need to stop, she thought. *I need a break and a swig of water.* Just then the music ceased, and the instructor shouted, "Take five."

Thank the Lord, Anne thought.

As she slowly wiped her brow and missed her mouth with her water bottle, she spotted a small, attractive woman heading her way.

"Hi there, you're new here, aren't you? Is this your first visit?"

"It is indeed," said Anne as she tried in vain to wipe her sweaty palm on her towel before surrendering it to the stranger. With several droplets of water now cascading down her chin, she didn't feel at her most attractive but then when did she?

"Well, welcome to Zoe's Zumba. I've just started back and need to take it slowly given my condition."

"Very nice to meet you," Anne said. "I'm hoping to become a regular in time, I need to get a bit fitter first."

"You'll get there sooner than you think."

"Oh, by the way my name's Anne."

"And mine's Taylor," she shouted back as the music engulfed the room once more.

What a great class and so super to have met someone that I can befriend, thought Anne as she made her way gingerly down the steps and back to the car. *Well, if nothing else I've gained a friend and one that can help me to get fit along the way. How marvellous.*

Chapter 46 - Hideaway

It had now been three months since Colin departed Llandavyff Rehabilitation Centre. He was forced out after nigh on eighteen years, the management, the quality standards, the lack of professional and well-trained staff had just about gotten to him. Tough as he was, he had started to find the centre depressing, unfriendly and, more than anything else, unpleasant. He was torn about his decision based on Charles and how much he grown to like him and see him as a friend. That said, he could see that Charles was changing, becoming more self-reliant, stronger, and more able to cope with the outside world. He could see his strength of character, his charm offensive and his vast knowledge of life now beginning to emerge. If Colin was going to go, then now was the time to do it.

The centre's management team had not long been announced, it was time to bring the centre up to date with state of art devices tracking staff's every move and hidden cameras tracing any movement in the centre after lights out. It had become too much 'Big Brother' for Colin, so on a whim and a fancy he took himself off, without a word to anyone, especially management, he vanished taking with him only what he stood up in. He felt guilty leaving Charles without even an acknowledgment of his pending departure, but needs must as the Devil drives thought Colin as he quietly closed Llandavyff's door behind him for the last time.

The outside world seemed different now, less welcoming, cold, and intrusive Colin thought as he settled into a hostel some forty miles away from Llandavyff. How long could he stay here, unrecognised and under the radar? How long did he want to stay here; where was he going? What move was he about to make, if any?

Warm soup coupled with a warm welcome had eased his troubled mind, a shared bread roll with a rather scruffy, unkempt soul had given him some solace and peace of mind that people in general were kind, that he was doing the right thing, that yes, the home would miss him, but so what after his years of service. Charles troubled him but he knew time with Charles was limited so he surmised that a quick, dead of the night getaway was the answer to both their prayers. Someone else could carry the perplexities of Charles's mind, the unsolved puzzles that became more than just a game.

As Colin settled in for the night, his mind wandered: *'To be improper would be proper if it wasn't deemed as rude'... what the fuck*, he thought as his eyes became weary and his eyelids heavy. That conundrum would have to wait for another day, as sleep engulfed his tired body, and exhaustion got the better of him.

Goodnight Colin, sleep tight.

Charles was in what they called a 'holding cell' whatever the fuck that meant. He was dressed in an ill-fitting casual tracksuit borrowed from the police store, navy with splashes of white paint on both sleeves, purposely added to give it that trendy look. Believe you me, it didn't look trendy on Charles!

"So, Mr Crocker, you're here because a man has died, that man is—sorry, *was* Brian Ball. It is believed he choked to death having failed to get enough air into his lungs and as such choked on his own vomit whilst in a state of panic. Neither you nor Mrs Ball had noticed that Mr Ball was in distress. Is this correct?"

"Erm, yes, I didn't have any idea that he was even in trouble. I just thought he was messing about when he didn't respond to his name."

"And what about Mrs Ball?"

"" Well, I think she felt the same, honestly, it's such a shock, I don't really know what happened."

"How long have you been having a relationship with Mr and Mrs Ball?"

"Several months, might even be a year now."

"How long have you been taking drugs, Mr Crocker?"

"A couple of years, it started with spliffs and got a bit out of hand; to be honest I'm finding it hard to control the urge, but I am trying."

"You need help, Mr Crocker, to curb your addiction." The police inspector shoved a lukewarm cup of tea under Charles's nose and told him to drink it. "It'll help you think straight when you're interviewed under caution tomorrow."

"You mean I have to stay here overnight?"

"Oh yes indeed. A man is dead, you were there, you were high on cocaine; you have no idea what happened so until you do, this is your home," he said cold-heartedly. "Now drink up, get some shut eye and we'll see you in the morning."

"Rigor mortis has set in; I'd guess he's been dead for at least eight hours. Let's get him out of this gimp suit and assess what really happened."

Michael Jenkins had been the resident mortician at Steinway Hospital for ten years, so there was very little that he hadn't experienced. As an expert witness, he was very well versed in police procedure and a highly respected and competent medic.

"It's clear that his body is showing high levels of cocaine inhaled via the nostrils and he has several puncture marks on both arms indicating that some drugs – cocaine or another – have been regularly injected into this man through self-administration or via another. This might take us sometime to decipher the cause of death."

After the initial wait period for rigor mortis to wear off, usually around thirty-six hours, Dr Jenkins ordered the next phase. With Ian, his ever-dutiful assistant by his side, both men dressed in white suits with matching face masks began to lay Brian out on the table. They took several photos of his naked body positioned in differing ways to evidence the extent of drug entry. Brian would probably have gained much joy from this was he able to feel and see the extent of the touching and mauling to get him into the correct posture.

Blimey, thought Ian as Brian was at last laid flat in preparation for his postmortem.

"I don't fancy having all this done to me when I die, Dr Jenkins," Ian said.

"Well, you won't if you behave yourself and die a relatively normal death like most people.

"Scalpel, Ian, please."

Chapter 47 - Oh Baby, Baby

"Ellen, I'm going part-time, I can't cope with the pressure any longer. Three days is plenty, and I can still earn a good salary."

"What, to keep me in the life I've become accustomed to and look after the ex-wife's needs. I doubt that Hugh"!

"I'm doing this Ellen, it's a hard enough job as it is, so give me a break, the kids are entering the next phase of their lives, Fee seems pretty settled now, so why can't you accept the fact that this actually could be the right time for me, erm and you, to start enjoying some newfound freedom."

"I'm pregnant, Hugh."

"What?! *What*? What are you saying, Ellen; how could you be? You're forty fucking five, no way, *please*."

"Oh charming, just as I thought, two kids are enough for precious Hugh."

"Stop it this minute, Ellen! Have you ever thought of the age gap between us, I'm nearly sixty-nine for Christ's sake. I can't cope with a young baby at my age."

"Well, you know what Hugh, fuck you. I'm having this child whether you like it or not and yes, we'll require maintenance payments."

Ellen calmly picked herself up from the sofa and made her way into the hallway.

"Where are you going, Ellen?"

"Out of your way Hugh and to someone who might appreciate a new baby and even congratulate me."

"Ellen, listen—"

Too late the front door had slammed shut and Ellen's car engine was revving.

Bloody hell, thought Hugh, *what a fuckin' mess. I don't want or need this, three years with Ellen and now a new baby, please God no. I want to ease into retirement, play golf, go on holiday, enjoy meals out with friends and family. No chance with a new baby, no sleep, midnight feeds, nappies, sick, slobber, never mind the immense cost of a newborn. Oh my God what am I going to do?* thought Hugh as he slurped a full glass of Glenmorangie to ease his troubled mind.

"Hello, who is this?" Fee said as she heard a faint mutter and a bit of heavy breathing. Could it be one of her clients fooling around?

"Hello, hello... hi, is there anyone there?"

The phone went dead. *Oh bollocks*, Fee thought. *Tossers.*

Hugh woke up one hour and sixteen minutes later, shirt crumpled, tie stained with whiskey and a head that felt like it had been steamrollered.

Still no Ellen, so he got up made his way gingerly upstairs and changed into more casual attire.

Was he too hard on Ellen; did she deserve a better more positive response? How must she be feeling, he thought as he attempted to set the table for her return.

It was now eight minutes past seven and still no Ellen. Hugh was beginning to worry; where could she possibly be until this time? Was she at her parents, with her brother, down at the wine bar with Andrea or somewhere else Hugh couldn't immediately think of?

He had tried calling her mobile several times and had by now left five messages with no response.

Boy, he thought, *she must be really angry with me. I'll leave it until seven thirty and then I'll start ringing round to see where she might be.*

With that he decided to grill some salmon, accompany it with some freshly made salad and a few new potatoes. He knew that Ellen loved fish, so it would be a welcome surprise on her return. He had chosen a lovely bottle of Pinot Grigio to set the meal off.

"Cheers," Hugh said as he downed his third glass of Pinot. The fish was now done to a crisp, salad wilting in the heat and still no Ellen. After several attempted phone calls, Hugh gave up. No one was answering any of the calls and it was getting late. At approximately ten thirty he received a text:

Go to bed, I'm not coming home tonight, can't be bothered arguing with you. I'm staying at a friend's, might see you tomorrow. Signed E. With no kiss or any hug emoji to accompany the single letter E, Hugh clearly knew that he was more than in trouble. He left the dishes, downed the rest of the Pinot, and took himself upstairs where he fell comatose in a heap on top of the duvet.

An almighty crashing sound brought Hugh round. Dazed and bleary eyed, he glanced at the time: seven thirty-three and still no sign of Ellen. There was another loud bang whereupon he carefully removed himself from the bed and looked out of the window. Of course, it was bin day and there they were in all their glory, high-vis jackets, waving and shouting to residents who were now clearly up and ready for work.

OMG, Hugh thought, *what day is it; am I due in today?*

So much had failed to ease his already troubled mind that he decided to ease his conscience with a nice latte from the coffee machine in the kitchen. He perched on a breakfast barstool and considered all the feasible options. Nine a.m. seemed a reasonable time to ring Fee and get her take on it all... erm maybe not, though. He'd likely hear something like 'Told you Hugh, you never listen to me. Ellen was always going to want a child. Trading me in for a younger model! How dare you; serves you right.'

Hugh wasn't quite ready for this so decided to give it a miss.

Having checked his schedule, he saw that he was due in theatre at eleven a.m., which gave him plenty of time to brush up, gather his thoughts and get off to the hospital in plenty of time to meet his deadline.

Just then, the phone interrupted his thoughts.

"Hello," he said.

There was a slight pause at which point High could hear the breath of the caller.

"Hello," she said.

"Is that you, Fee?"

"It is, Hugh."

"What's wrong?"

"Well, I've got Ellen here and she's told me the situation. She came last night and asked me to promise not to call you when she arrived. She's now had a change of heart and is in a terrible state. Hugh, why are you being so unreasonable?"

"How strange, Fee. I called you last night and then changed my mind when I ran through all the things you might say to me, none of which you have repeated now."

"So, Hugh, what are you going to do?"

"What do you mean?"

"Well Ellen tells me she's three months gone, has been for her scan while being frightened of your reaction once you knew. And let's face it, Hugh, you haven't let her down."

"Fee this is nothing to do with you, this is between Ellen and me."

"So why has she come to my house then, Hugh?"

"Oh, I don't know, maybe because she thinks you know me better than anyone else."

"Well, I do, Hugh, every little detail."

"Can you tell her to come home or better still let me speak to her?"

"She doesn't want to converse at the moment, Hugh. I am letting her stay here until she clears her head and decides what's best for her and the baby."

"Is this really happening to me, Fee? I can't believe what's going on. Listen I need to go, I must be in theatre at eleven. Can you please tell Ellen that I will ring her when I'm home. Oh, and tell her I love her, and we'll sort things out."

"I'll pass your message on, Hugh. Have a good day."

With that the phone went dead and Hugh stood in a complete daze trying to comprehend all that was happening to him. Work was going to be extremely arduous today he thought as he attempted a Windsor knot in his burgundy silk tie.

Chapter 48 – Money, Money, Money

Toe-tapping Tim was ecstatic: he had just landed an excellent job in IT working for an international company located a ten-minute walk from his flat. More money than before, access to a pool car if required and an office of his own.

Pinch me, pinch me, he thought as he skipped his ungainly size eights across his new corridor of power. His thoughts immediately went to the Wine O'clock club. *When is it? I hope it's soon, I have something to celebrate, something to say. I am back in gainful employment!*

Charles, on the other hand, was less than enthused. He would now see much less of his brother; his mother would be constantly in touch, given that he would be much more accessible than Tim now. What's more, Charles needed Tim to try to keep him on the straight and narrow. Obviously, Tim hadn't thought of any if this when he accepted the job. *How selfish could he be*? thought Charles.

Tim had a new assistant, not quite on a par with Cleo but he would do, knowledgeable, keen, enthusiastic and one to please. Tim felt rather chuffed with himself when Stanley knocked on the door with a steaming hot mug of coffee especially for him.

Stanley, Tim thought, *does that name really suit such a smart, young up-and-coming IT professional... maybe.*

Tim settled into his role with great ease. His analytical mind had not forgotten him, and he soon immersed himself in the algorithms, megabytes, gigabytes and whatever was required to get the job done. He was in his element.

Cecelia would be proud he thought, as he had a moment to take in his journey and how far he had now come. Out of five candidates, he had excelled. His time had come: plush leather chair, a state-of-the-art computer desk with built in coaster for hot drinks, and to top it all off, a computer screen that would rise like a phoenix from the ashes allowing him to type, dictate or transcribe handwritten notes directly onto the screen. It was more than anyone could ask for; Tim was beside himself.

They had allowed Charles to go home after questioning but told him to remain local until the completion of the inquest in case any further issues arose.

Chapter 49 - Monday, Monday

Today was the day. *Alicia Jenkins, what a start to a dreary Monday morning,* the Devil thought as he clasped several pieces of paper close to his chest.

He had to be at the meeting hall for nine thirty and was already running late. As he turned the car engine over, it began to purr like a cat that had got the cream. Oh, how he loved his cars, bit like Denzil really, except the Devil was a much more diligent driver. An automatic suited his big hands. There was a Costa coffee now sitting neatly in the centre console, steaming away, emanating the aroma of a casual coffee bar somewhere in London twinned with a pan au chocolate or a raspberry muffin. His mind wandered to happier days and then back again to this drizzly, dank, dull, and very wet Monday morning. Could the wonderful Alicia Jenkins lift his rather sombre mood, or would she make it even worse? Well, he was about to find out.

His car found its own parking spot; automatic parking was something that the Devil loved once he realised that the car had a button to ensure that this would happen calmly and safely. It was a button he was truly going to use as often as possible now discovered.

As he removed his rather bulky frame from the vehicle, it moaned under the release of the pressure and soon settled itself back into position.

"Oh, don't forget your papers, Devil, you're sure going to need them," he said out loud. He straightened his belted Burberry mac and headed quickly into the hall out of the rain.

There was tea and coffee on hand and several little booths scattered around the hall to ensure privacy for individuals. The Devil sat himself near the door, displayed his name badge on his left lapel as he waited patiently for the ever-dynamic Alicia Jenkins. He had no idea what to expect, no idea what she looked like and really very little idea of why she was the preferred candidate for Denzil Drum's job. As he mulled all this over in this brain, in she came, and by gum, was she a stunner! He immediately knew that this would be her, by her elegant entry, her panache, her pure beauty, and her gorgeous long and stupendous glossy red hair. *Good grief,* he thought, *she's a looker. If she's as clever as she looks this truly is an appointment of a lifetime.* She was handed a badge at the entry, clearly displaying her name and as she stepped down onto the level, the Devil rose to his full height to make himself known and introduce himself.

Enchanted by her bright green eyes and soft Scottish accent, the Devil was more than smitten. As he invited her to sit, he watched her hair swish gently over her shoulder until it cascaded neatly across her breasts landing securely by her nipped-in waist. She was absolutely adorable, more stunning than you could ever imagine.

"Coffee or tea, Alicia?"

"Coffee please."

"There you are," he said handing her a large mug of steaming, freshly brewed coffee from the glass cafetiere.

"Lovely to meet you. Sorry I couldn't make the interview. My father died, and the funeral was on that very day. Anyway, I understand that you have been duly appointed into this role and come with a vast number of qualifications and experience. So, I hope everything will meet your expectations."

"I am sure they will. My father informed me of the job; he and Professor Lindsey are old friends. When the job was advertised, the professor mentioned it to my father, and I applied straight away. I see it as a terrific opportunity for me and one that will surely enhance my career."

"What is your ultimate ambition then, Alicia?"

"Just to be successful really. My father wanted me to go into medicine but it's not for me. He says as long as I'm happy that's the main thing. I think I'm really going to enjoy the job, and I am so looking forward to it."

"Well, that's great," said the Devil. Completely bowled over by her presence and stature, he had little to nothing else to say. "Lovely to meet you, Alicia. I will see you in a couple of weeks' time when you start in earnest. Oh, and don't forget your certificates, HR are updating their systems and want everything in one place. As a new starter that shouldn't be too onerous on you."

"No problem," she said as she stood up. She offered her delicate hand to meet the Devil's burly one and he tried hard not to squeeze it too tightly. The warmth of her palm melted his heart and sent a shiver down his already tingling spine.

God she is so gorgeous, he thought.

As he left shortly after Alicia, the thought re-crossed his mind: What the fuck am I going to do about my certificates?

Chapter 50 - Burn Baby Burn

God another week has gone by already, Anne thought as she donned her Zumba outfit once more. The only good thing to come out of these sessions was the fact that she now had a friend to call her own: Taylor. She was so pleased to meet her and was extremely excited to catch up with her again this evening. Her legs had stopped aching, her body was back to normal which gave her the impetus to go again and repeat last week's session. It must be doing her good she thought... right?

Anne arrived bang on time. As she entered the hall she scanned the room for Taylor, no sign of her as yet. She placed her water bottle and towel neatly in the back corner of the room, a place she felt safe, where no one was watching her fat self-parade on the dance floor and where she could go at her own pace without really being noticed. Doing something new took her mind off work, off Tigger, off Billy and onto something physical that was, she thought, going to work miracles.

"Hi there" shouted the very unfamiliar figure, "how are you?"

Anne looked around. "Sorry, are you talking to me?"

"I am," said the slightly rotund female figure now standing directly in front of her.

"Sorry, do I know you?"

"Erm no, but you soon will."

"Pardon?"

"One two and one two, now turn your partner around and repeat," came a voice over the microphone. The class had already started, and this unfamiliar figure had chosen Anne as her dancing partner, probably because there was no one else left in the room.

"I'm Becky," she said as she slipped under Anne's armpit. "I came last week but didn't get chance to say hello as you were talking to a rather pretty, petite young lady that seemed to know what she was doing."

"Oh yes, Becky, that was Taylor. Not sure she's here this week."

"Does she work at White Wings?"

"Where?" said Anne.

"White Wings."

"White Wings what?" said Anne.

"You know, White Wings Crematorium."

"Erm no, I don't know, where's that then?"

"Just down the road from here about fifteen or sixteen miles away"

"Well, how would you know that, Becky, if you don't know her?"

"Hold on Anne, let's get to a break and I'll tell you then. I can't talk and dance at the same time, it's making me short of breath."

After several more twirls and one final push-up, the class came to a halt.

"Take five!" the instructed shouted.

"Bloody hell, I'll need way more than five," Becky said.

"Me too," Anne giggled as they both retreated to their water bottles.

"Now then, you were saying, Becky?"

"Yes Taylor, I think, works at the crematorium down the road. I was there last week at my neighbour's funeral, and I am sure I saw her there. If not, it was someone genuinely like her. Think she had a little boy in tow, she was walking up from the crematorium gates."

"Oh, I don't know. I've only just met her; she seems very nice. It's a shame she's not here tonight."

"No doubt she'll be back, seems keen."

With that the music began and they were off again.

Another thirty minutes of torture, Anne thought. All good for the soul and if she kept it up there might be a remarkable difference in her appearance by the time she organised the next Wine O'clock Club meeting.

Chapter 51 - All You Need is Love

"Do you remember when you used to dream of what your life would be like as an adult? What you would do for a job, who you would marry, if you'd have any kids, where you would live, and generally hoping that you make all the right decisions to get where you want to be?

"So where does making the wrong decision, not being in a relationship, yet alone married, and renting when you should be buying sit within that equation, Cleo?"

"Erm, I don't know really Millie; are you talking about yourself?" Cleo asked gingerly.

"Well of course I am, Cleo, who else would I be talking about?"

"Millie, there are plenty of positives in your life."

Trying to be the ever-faithful friend, Cleo was determined to show Millie how far she had actually travelled.

"You have a great job, a vibrant social life, lots of friends and you're now at the point of considering the purchase of a house. What more could a girl want?" she said with a wry smile on her face.

"Yes indeed, you're right, Cleo, but do you know, I now long for the touch of a man's hand, caressing me closely so that I can sense the urgency of deep and true passion."

"Oh, a bit too near the knuckle for me, Millie, but I can understand all that you say."

"Anyway, listen hun, I'm going to have to go. Here's my half of the bill, and I'll see you in a couple of weeks at the Wine O'clock Club unless you have something earth-shattering to share with me before then."

"Bye for now."

With that Cleo was up and gone leaving Millie in the dreamy state of imagined love.

As Millie approached the counter, her thoughts drifted again to a lovely tea/coffee shop set just off the square, easily accessible to all, and dog friendly to boot.

"That'll be £23.47 please," the friendly assistant said with the ring of the till.

Millie presented her debt card and keyed in her pin; as she did so, she fumbled in her pocket for a bit of change, having noted the tip jar on the counter. Service was always good; the café was always reliable and, more to the point, very seldom closed. With that thought Millie took her hand out of her coat pocket and produced a £5 note from her purse instead which she felt was far more worthy than a few pence. In time, if she did open a coffee shop, she would try to offer a service attracting similar tips.

As she had the day off from AA, she contemplated what to do next as she left the coffee shop.

'To be improper would be proper if it wasn't deemed as rude...'

Hmm, could it be an anagram, a poem, an old saying, a famous saying, a by-product of a famous saying or was it just utter nonsense and gibberish? Who knows, she thought as she made her way down the sunny side of the street wrapped up her own thought processes. *My, how things have changed in a short space of time*, Millie thought. *Nothing stays the same; my dad used to tell me that. You think it does, but it surely doesn't.*

Chapter 52 - Brothers In Arms

"These mist-covered mountains are home now for me..."

Brotherly love hath no end, or so Charles thought, until Tim got the job of his dreams, that was. Charles was bereft. He had nowhere to go and no one to do anything with. What was to become of him now, and now he had his bloody mother, Cecelia, ringing him every five minutes now that she couldn't get hold of Tim.

His thoughts wandered to Colin. Where was he, what had happened to his so-called 'best buddy'? Why did he leave the Rehabilitation Centre in such a hurry? Did he think that Charles could battle on without him now? Who knew. That said, Charles was really missing his buddy, the one man that he had truly confided in. "To be improper would be proper if it wasn't deemed as rude." Colin knew it, Charles knew it but who else knew it?

Charles had settled somewhat into his new abode; he was beginning to feel it as they say. He had a few bits and bobs around him now, that made it feel more like home. His mobility had returned to a certain extent, his big six-foot-odd frame was now more upright and his speech much more articulate and beginning to evidence his previous life as a high-flying lawyer. Drugs had very much taken a back seat, given all the trouble they had caused Charles. He was now trying to concentrate on his future life, given that Tim had suddenly turned his life around with this super-duper job he had just landed. Honestly, the difference in that man was totally unbelievable! He was worried that Cecelia would now focus her attention on Tim's successes and Charles would get left behind. Although somewhat insignificant, small, unkempt and unnoticeable, Tim had a brain. He was a bright individual, and, given half a chance, he could most certainly run rings around the more intellectual of us. 'Tim Assist' as he was dutifully named by the Devil, was now more like 'Tim in Charge' Charles thought.

As he awaited his fate from the complexities of his sexual encounters with Mavis and poor old Brian, Charles made a promise to himself to never ever get himself into that scenario again. All he wanted was his old self back and maybe a good woman to keep him on the straight and narrow. But he was where he was, and no amount of wishful thinking was going to change that now.

As the dulcet tones of his phone rang out playing Vivaldi's *Four Seasons*, Charles lifted the mobile to his lips.

"Hello," he said.

"Well, hello. Is that you, Charles?"

"Yes, who is this?"

"To be improper would be proper if it wasn't deemed as rude," came the reply.

"Bloody hell, is that you?" Charles said.

"None other," came the reply. "Can you meet me later today at the coffee shop in town, Charles?"

"Erm yes, what time?"

"Shall we say three p.m.?"

"Okay, I'll see you then."

"Looking forward to it, Charles," and with that the call abruptly ended.

As Charles composed himself, he took himself off into the lounge, which was barely as cock's stride from where he was, poured himself a stiff whiskey and eased himself into his only comfy chair. He started to reflect on his past carefully bearing in mind what his future now might begin to hold for him.

His heart was racing; he was slightly sweaty, and he wasn't sure if it was from excitement or fear. What time was it now? Eleven o'clock... he had a while to go. As Vivaldi again interrupted his thoughts, he could see that it was the lovely Cecelia calling.

"Hello, Mother."

"Charles how are you; I've been trying to get hold of your forever. I can't get that wretched brother of yours at all."

"Well, he's working Mother, that's why. He's absolutely engrossed in his new job and loving it. He has a new lease of life, freedom like he's never had before and of course he's loaded, his job is paying him mega bucks."

"The tables have turned then, Charles. Remember when you were like that, an excellent job, a ladder that you could climb forever, the world was your oyster. Well, maybe now it's Tim's turn. I must admit I'm shocked that he has done so well, let's hope he keeps it up."

"Anyway Mother, what do you want?"

"Can we go out for lunch Charles? I need some company and want to chat."

"Well, erm... I have an engagement at three p.m. so can meet at say noon until about quarter past two."

"Charles, you know how I can talk, not sure if that'll be long enough."

"Take it or leave it, Mother," Charles heard himself say.

"Okay I'll take it. Shall I come to you?"

"Yes, otherwise I won't be able to make my next meeting."

"I'll book that Italian then, what's it called again Charles?"

"Minto Minto, Mother."

"See you later then."

"Yes, okay Mother, bye."

Fuck that's all I need, thought Charles. *Mother always phones, calls, visits at an inappropriate time. I must make sure she's very much disappeared before my three-p.m. meeting.*

Chapter 53 - Giant Steps Are What We Take

Arthur was tired, his business had been going from strength to strength and Millie had certainly added some variety into the mix. She was clever, had a nose for the job, instinctively knew how to manage situations and take appropriate investigative steps. She had really begun to show her true worth and by giving her a couple of staff to manage, her people skills were shown to be abundantly clear. This girl was going places and Arthur knew it.

It was clear that Arthur had a plan. For him, it was just working out when he was going to execute it. His bugbear was the Improper Man; he had no clue and so before his retirement he vowed to explore and resolve this case so that he could bring closure to the whole bloody lot. The whole of the AA team now had some involvement in this case. Millie and Stewart had answered the phone to him, but other staff members had listened in, so the stranger was beginning to take over office small talk, with many staff best guessing who he was and why he was calling. It ranged from the sublime to the ridiculous and as such Arthur was having great trouble focussing on the facts as they presented themselves.

One insistent man, one repeated saying, one targeted recipient of the message.

"To be improper would be proper if it wasn't deemed as rude."

What the fuck?! thought Arthur.

There was no pattern to his calls, they were intermittent and often came in when Arthur wasn't available causing someone else to receive the said call. It was very apparent that no one else could help him and that it was imperative that Arthur was the recipient.

Arthur was indeed winding down and, as such, spending much more time at home leaving Elliot to lead the team. He was enormously proud of his son and knew at some point that he was the most capable of all his children to make a tremendous success of AA and take it even further up the ladder.

Arthur began to drift, his thought processes wandering to a place far away, seeking out memories long hidden in distant places. He recalled his first kiss, his first real business deal, his first fight, his first attempt at sex with Hilary from three doors down—*not the best of experiences he thought as he chuckled his way to other thoughts. How did an army officer get to this very point in his life? Was Mr Improper someone from his dim and distant past? Was he out to right a wrong, give Arthur what for, seek some kind of revenge or merely trying to look up an old friend from days gone by? The latter seemed unlikely given the sense of urgency, persistence, and tone to his voice.*

No one seemed able to pin down an accent with Mr Improper. He wasn't on the phone long enough and repeated the same words using the same intonations and inflections in his voice and choosing not to engage much more with the recipients. Arthur was more than frustrated. He had been a Lieutenant in the army, how come he couldn't resolve this conundrum? *God help us*, he thought, *maybe I've utterly lost my touch.*

Chapter 54 - Nice to meet you

"Bye Mother, thanks for dinner. I'll call you, but I need to dash now. Will you be okay?"

"I'll have to be, Charles. Looks like you're going no matter what."

"Can you pay Minto Minto, and I'll settle with you another time?"

With that, he kissed his mother's cheek, and he was gone. She'd never seen him move so fast, spritely, lithe and certainly moving.

Where on earth can he be going and more to the point who is he going to meet? wondered Cecelia as she settled the £38.41 bill at the restaurant.

Now in a hot sweat and breathing like there was little or no air, Charles turned the corner to spy the coffee shop halfway down the street on his left. He glanced at his watch: three minutes to three.

Will he be in there? Will he be late? Will he even turn up? Charles thought as the bell rang once he stepped over the threshold. A quick scan round identified an elderly couple in the corner, hugging two mugs of what looked like hot chocolate, a young woman on a laptop near the window, two young lads fooling around on their phones and a young woman and older man behind the counter ready to take orders. There was no one else in the coffee shop.

"Can I help you there sir?" came a monotone voice from behind the counter.

"Oh yes please," said Charles. "One Americano with hot milk please."

"Anything to eat, sir?"

"No thanks, I'm just waiting for a friend."

"Sit down and we'll bring it over shortly."

"Thank you," said Charles as he spied a table facing the doorway with his back to the wall enabling him to see all the comings and goings in the coffee shop. Bang on three p.m. and no sign. Charles was just thinking how long he should give it when his thoughts were interrupted.

"One Americano with hot milk, sir. Enjoy, sugar's on the table."

"Oh, thank you."

Six minutes past, still no sign. Charles stared into his Americano watching the swirling milk fall from the jug turning his black coffee brown in an instant.

Chapter 55 - Climb Every Mountain

Each step was getting a little easier, each movement a little less painful, acceptance was now etched in the mind of Rupert.

I need to fulfil my life best I can, I need to be positive for my family. I cannot work on the notion of 'what if'. My family have been wonderful, and I need them more than ever now.

Rupert took one more sip of luke-warm coffee before he opened the back door and with his beloved dogs prepared to walk across the uneven terrain to the hills where he thought he might tackle a hill or two. He wanted to be useful, take his fair share of duties, not expect all and sundry to wait on him hand and foot.

Marco had kept in touch as had the Devil. Several visits from both had made Rupert feel a little easier. That said, any sort of role was now very much out of the equation. So, as each visit concluded Rupert found himself increasingly detached from their lives and felt that maybe sympathy and responsibility were now the main drivers of their visits. Nevertheless, he welcomed them and tried in earnest to hold an interesting conversation albeit he wasn't doing much.

The hills were just too hard to climb so Rupert made his walk shorter and less painful for himself much to Beano & Bandit's disgust.

"Hey," he said, looking down at them, "at least it's a start and I will improve."

Pamela was ready for work on his return.

"Can you manage to get yourself some lunch today, Rupert? And there are lamb chops in the fridge that will need to be popped into the oven around four thirty p.m. if that's okay?" She kissed his cheek as he then watched her stiletto heel slip smoothly into the well of the black BMW.

"See you later!" she shouted, and the car turned down the drive and onto the main road.

Another day seeking solace in my never-ending situation, Rupert thought as he poured himself another cup of coffee and carried in gingerly into the lounge. *She is marvellous,* he thought. *She could have left me, but she didn't. She's more than I could have hoped for... or is she,* he wondered?

Thoughts rudely interrupted by the phone, Rupert eased himself gently out of his chair. *Who could this be at this ungodly hour* Rupert thought. *It's only 8.43 a.m.*

"Hello," he said. "Hello who's there?" No reply, Rupert tried again "Hello, helloooo."

The phone went dead.

Bloody hell! Rupert thought. *It's taken me ages to get to the phone and some bastard has decided to cut me off!*

As he eased himself back into a comfortable position, the phone rang again.

Bugger it, he thought, *I'll let the answerphone kick in.*

After three double rings, click the answerphone spoke to the caller.

Three beeps and hey presto, "Good morning, Rupert," was the message captured. Rupert didn't recognise the caller's voice and to be honest not enough was said to even get a hint of who it might be. *Maybe they'll ring again*, Rupert thought.

As Rupert sipped his now lukewarm coffee his thoughts transferred to Denzil—a young man's life cut so very short.

I wonder what he wanted on that fateful day, why was he coming round to see me, what was so urgent that he needed to see me there and then given I was only just out of hospital and recovering at home?

It had now been over a year since his death, and nothing seemed much clearer to Rupert than the day Denzil actually died.

Bless him, he thought as he shut his eyes to catnap in the chair.

Chapter 56 - Isn't she Lovely!

Ellen delivered a beautiful baby girl much to the delight of Hugh. Fee was there to lend a helping hand and all's well that ends well, as they say. Hugh was forced to continue working full time for the sake of Ellen and now the much adored and loved Natasha. Albeit Hugh would be nearly eighty when Natasha hit eighteen, none of that seemed to matter right here and now. Hugh adored her, she had his eyes, his mop of dark curly hair and the olive skin tones of her gorgeous mother. Her blue, blue eyes were enchanting, and the proud father couldn't wait to show her off to all and sundry. Who'd have thought it, a few months ago things could have been so different. Fee was asked to be godmother at Natasha's christening, which she felt was more than an honour. She had already picked her outfit in preparation for her big moment at the event.

Things were quite different now. Fee had found her way in life, she was happy and contented with their lot, she was delighted to be godmother to Natalie and more than satisfied that Hugh had sorted out his differences and chosen what he felt was the right path.

As for the kids, well they are what they are, Matthew settled into a trainee Health Inspector role with an agricultural company hoping to become Head of Service before very long, he always did have his eyes set on career progression. As for

Miranda, she was off travelling the world for what she stated would be one year and then back with much more experience of life to settle herself by following in her father's footsteps into medicine.

Funny how life turns out, one minute you're coming and going not knowing what to do and the next, you're settled, happy, and really looking forward to the future.

Fee felt she had a lot to divulge to the Wine O'clock members at the next meeting.

I wonder if anyone else has such tales to tell, she thought as she gently pushed the wardrobe door closed, relishing the moment Ellen and Hugh had asked her to be godmother to the gorgeous Natasha. Could life get any better than this?

The nightmare of those nine lives were nearing their conclusion she thought. The sad and tragic death of Denzil, the abhorrent contracting of sepsis for Rupert brought on by a boating accident, and the introduction of who was likely the most powerful man behind those decisions: the Devil. You couldn't write it, really. The disappearance of Tigger was perplexing, and Fee was certain that Billy had something to do with it. As such, she would track Anne down at the Wine O'clock Club and try to get to the bottom of it all. In the meantime, she was going to kick off her shoes, down a couple of G & Ts and reflect on her next steps.

Chapter 57 - Raindrops keep falling on my head

As Charles transfixed his gaze on his rather steamy coffee, he failed to see the door open, and a rather portly gentleman enter. He only paid attention to this stranger when he pulled up a chair directly in front of Charles and slid himself and his rather shabby raincoat into place. It wasn't whom he'd expected.

"Hello, Charles," he said.

"Erm, hello" Charles replied. "Can I get you a coffee or something?"

"One espresso and two shortbreads please."

With that, Charles rose to his full height and walked briskly to the counter. Having ordered his companion's choice, he stood tapping the counter with his fingers impatiently waiting.

The assistant shouted over, "I'll bring it over to your table sir, won't be long."

With that Charles nodded and headed back to the table where this rather strange, grey bearded man sat huddled in his raincoat awaiting Charles's return.

"Well, what can I help you with?" Charles said.

The reply was curt, sharp, monotone, and delivered with pure precision.

"To be improper would be proper if it wasn't deemed as rude.

Remember your mother and your brother.

But also, do exclude.

The good, the bad, the ugly

And those that make you sad.

Repent at your leisure, relax, rejoice be glad.

To be improper would be proper if it wasn't deemed as rude.

Make way for the Devil and let his work conclude."

Perplexed and unsure of his next steps, Charles listened intently, actively nodding as the unkempt man delivered his speech. Totally confused by this message, Charles looked him in the eye and waited for a response.

"Don't ask any questions, Charles. Dissect the rhythm and follow the rules."

"What rules? Who are you; what are you to do with me? How have I got here? Honestly, I have no idea what's going on." "Where the fuck is Colin?"

As quickly as he came, the stranger slurped two mouthfuls of coffee, popped the two shortbreads in his pocket and was gone. No goodbye, no offer to pay for the goods, he upped and went without a backward glance.

What the hell? thought Charles.

Leaning back in his chair, Charles proceeded to try to digest the whole scenario. Luckily, he was able to jot down the rhythm albeit in bits, so as he sat swigging the remainder of his coffee he quickly and swiftly elongated the scribble until he had produced each word that had been articulated by the stranger in the grey raincoat. To be improper... where, if at all, had Charles heard this saying before? *Had* he heard it and if so, who was saying it? His ruminations were rudely interrupted by the appearance of the waiter.

"More coffee sir?"

"No, I'm fine, thank you anyway. Listen by the way, you don't happen to know the gentleman that just left do you?"

The assistant thought for a moment and said, "No but he comes in here maybe once a fortnight."

"Thank you," said Charles.

Erm... *think, Charles, think*.

At that moment, his phone began to ring, as he picked it up, he could see that his mother was on the other end.

Answer it now, Charles or wait until you get home and lose twenty minutes of your life, he thought.

"Hello, Mother."

"Charles, I paid the bill at Minto Minto. I loved it so much I've booked us in again for next week, same day, same time. I was going to see if Tim will join us."

"Why? Are we having a celebration?"

"No, I just thought that I'd like to treat my two sons at the same time, is that okay with you?"

Charles thought in a flash: *That's it, that's where I've heard the saying before, it was when I was with Tim and Colin from the Rehabilitation Centre. Colin had used the saying*. Charles was more than positive about that now.

"Okay, okay, okay, I'll check the diary and get back to you. It should be alright, not sure about Tim though," Charles said.

"You leave Tim to me, Charles, I'll get him there."

"Yes, super Mum, see you then, bye," and with that, Charles rang off.

Colin, where is he now, what happened, what has he gone on to do with his life and what has the 'Improper' saying got to do with him? Charles's mind was racing. *How do I work this out?*

The Devil... Charles remembered that he had been Tim's new boss, his brother's demise, and he also noted that this Devil bloke was far from popular. Tim had said he was supposed to be their saviour but turned out to be very much the Devil.

The more his mind recalled the many chats with Tim when Tim was at his lowest, the more he thought that he needed to contact Tim to see if he could shed any light on what was going on.

Colin, Colin, Colin, he thought as he made his way from the café out into the rain.

Remember your mother and your brother, what a conundrum. That coupled with Colin was more than Charles could take right now. He curled his collar around his already wet neck and made his way along the shimmering footpath hoping and praying that the pieces would all fall into place. He was smart but was he *that* smart?

Chapter 58 - Burn Baby Burn

"One, two, three and turn. Three burpees and stop."

Fitter with a more defined torso now, Anne was more than pleased with her progress.

At last, she thought, *I'm really getting there.*

The class was mega busy, and Becky was her usual upbeat self.

"How long have we been coming now Anne?"

"It must be at least six weeks Becky hey and still no sign of a that lovely girl I met on my first outing here. Maybe she's not well or has changed her mind about the class."

"I doubt that, Anne, she was dead keen. We could always pay the crematorium a visit and see if we can spot her?"

"We can't do that, Becky."

"Why not? It's a place and you can just go and take a look around at the beautiful gardens and headstones if you so wish, nobody can stop you, unless they're closed."

"Oh, shall we Becky, it's a good opportunity to see if we can find, what did you call her..."

"Taylor."

"Yes, Taylor and I'm sure she wouldn't mind a friend looking her up."

"Okay Anne, listen after class I'll WhatsApp you with some times and dates that may suit, and we'll go from there."

"Super, Becky. Thanks ever so."

Ten press-ups, five-star jumps, two laps around the hall and the class came to its conclusion.

Thank the Lord Anne thought as she wiped her rather sweaty brow, swigged her water and zipped up her hoodie.

"Good class again Anne."

"It was, indeed, Becky. Anyway, listen I've got to dash, so I'll await your messages. Bye Becky."

"Bye Anne," and with that they were gone.

Anne arrived back home to a hot shower and some homemade leek and potato soup. She ripped her French stick in half, spread lashing of butter on the bit she intended to eat and popped the rest back in the fridge. This is a time she'd feed Tigger and talk to him about his day.

Time had passed so slowly without him, but new adventures had given Anne a purpose again and she was still forever hopeful that Tigger would reappear. As for Billy, she was beginning to think that Fee was more than right now and that he had disappeared for good. She had placed his photo in the back of the drawer now and decided that her life needed to continue. It did mean starting all over again, but Anne was more than capable and very, very willing to give it a go. She couldn't envisage herself being single for the rest of her life, could she?

She was very fond of Becky and hoped that she would be true to her word and together they could seek out Taylor to try to understand what had happened to her. With that thought and a fully belly Anne ironed her apron, collected her cleaning trolley, carefully checked the content, and placed everything by the exit door in preparation for tomorrow's early start.

"My life is good, it could be better but for now, I have no choice but to sit it out and see where it takes me. With a little help from my friends maybe this time next year things will look vastly different."

Chapter 59 - The Bells are Ringing

Mrs George married Mr George on a glorious sunny day. Marco was now well and truly out in the cold. There was no chance of a reconciliation with his wife now and he never really envisaged that there would be. Well and truly alone, unloved, lost and with nowhere to go, Marco's ship had truly sailed, and he was left hanging onto the mast. What did life now have in store for him. He could never attain the wealth of Mr George, and he felt that was very much part of the attraction for the now Mrs George. She looked resplendent in white with her gorgeous dark hair cascading over her beautifully fitted bridal dress very becoming of her neat and trim figure. What to do now Marco thought. Fuck it, not much going for me, a Devil that thinks he's in charge, an ex-wife, a job that has lost its shine, an ex-colleague devoid of several limbs due to an outing arranged by him and now sitting here nursing an exquisite Glenmorangie courtesy of Mr George watching he ex-wife being twirled around on the dance floor by a very tall, dark and handsome man, oh and not forgetting rich! Aw well at least he got an invite to the wedding of the year albeit a little bit awkward.

"Marco, come dance with me."

"Really?"

"Yes, be happy for me and let's share a moment together for the last time."

With that, Mrs George whisked Marco onto the dance floor, and they began to sway to *One Moment in Time* by Whitney Huston, rather apt Marco thought as he twizzled his ex-wife around. As she drew close into him Marco couldn't help but say to her, "I still love you, you know, and I always will."

With that she kissed his cheek gently as the song rang out its final note.

"God bless, Marco. We have a history together and no one can ever take that away."

With that, she rushed over to her new husband and posed for several post-wedding shots. She looked gorgeous, she looked happy, and she was now ready to start a new chapter in her life which was more than Marco could say about his.

I'll look up Rupert over the weekend, Marco thought. *I need to see how the poor soul is getting on.* With that thought, he grabbed his jacket, waved goodbye to the newlyweds, and was gone. Have a nice life Mr and Mrs George. The wedding buffet didn't much appeal, so Marco made his apologies and left.

The next day, Marco made a point of contacting Rupert early in the morning before he forgot. The landline was ringing off the wall, so Marco diverted to the mobile. Three rings later and the mobile went to voicemail.

Bloody hell, you can never get anyone when you want them, he thought as he slammed the mobile down on the kitchen worktop. He didn't leave a message as he couldn't be bothered and when Rupert decided to pick up his mobile, he'd see that he tried to call. *Okay Marco what next? Boat trip, walk, briefcase, pub, or generally slob around. Eeny-meeny-miny-moe, boat trip it was.*

The loch was calm, the water was blue, the waves were gently lapping against the bough, it had been sometime since Marco had ventured out. He'd been twice since the sailing accident and both times he had sailed alone. So, third time lucky. He had always loved sailing but the tragic circumstances surrounding Rupert were hard to block out when you're on the same boat, same loch and similar sort of day weather wise. That said, he whiled away the time catching the sun's rays giving him that healthy glow many people envied. Two hours has passed in the blink of an eye as Marco pulled into the shoreline to moor up. Sailing is a terrific way of forgetting the present and just going with the moment he thought as he removed his life jacket and replaced it with a zip-up hoodie.

Once on shore he called Rupert once more, maybe he'd like to meet for a drink and a catch up. As the line connected, Marco could hear the dulcet tones of the mobile ringing out.

"Hello," came a voice from the other end.

"Hello, Rupert, is that you?"

"Well, who else is it going to be if it's my mobile?"

"Just checking"

"Is that you Marco?"

"It is Rupert"

"Where have you been?"

"What do you mean?"

"Well, I rang you earlier."

"Can't a man have a life, Marco? It's not all about you, you know."

"Only kidding, are you up for a drink later, Rupert, I can come your way to make it a bit easier for you."

"Well Pamela's working late, the kids are away so the only thing I need to do is walk the dogs. Can we say four p.m., Marco?"

"Yes sure. Where would you like to meet, or I can come and pick you up?"

"Yes, pick me up, Marco; it's a bloody nightmare for me to walk very far. I'm okay with the dogs but by the time I get back I'll need a bit of a rest."

"Okay shall I pick you up at four p.m. or just before?"

"Four p.m. would be good Marco; I'll see you then."

"Okay, bye for now."

Marco looked at his watch. It was just gone two, so he had time to get in, shower and change, grab a quick bit to eat and be on his way. He was feeling pleased with himself; at least he had some sort of plan for the rest of the day now, thank God.

Chapter 60 - Bad Education

Alicia duly presented her certificates of education all in order and top class to the HR Department. True to her word to the Devil, the expediency with which she delivered was quite remarkable. Beautiful, intelligent and no doubt out to make her mark, she was truly awe-inspiring and seemed to be very much loved by all who met her.

The same could not be said of the Devil, having searched high and low he was able to produce most of his educational attainments albeit the one most required and which the job rests were far from on show.

Why didn't they request this before I took up the bloody job? the Devil thought, *and then maybe I could have retracted the offer or gone before I was pushed. Instead, they've left it until a re-jig of the HR department, demanding all documents are scanned and go online for future reference. This is all very understandable and will make life easier all round but not for me and not at this time. God help us! What am I to do?*

A PhD in Chemistry is not something that can be easily hidden, it was the route to success and gave the Devil a job of a lifetime. Unable to produce it at interview he was asked to surrender it on his start date. With all the confusion and furore over job losses, reconfigured job roles, union and HR interventions, the PhD had been somewhat overlooked by his peers and wouldn't have raised its ugly head again if it hadn't been for the new online systems. If you haven't got a PhD then you can't magic one up from anywhere, so who was the Devil kidding? He hadn't got one, he had never had one; he didn't study for one so what was he looking for?

All very timely, Tim thought. *It couldn't have been easier if he'd tried. A hint here, a hint there, and hey presto, an online system to record all staff's education was up and running just like that. What a stroke of genius,* he mused, having not really considered the consequences. It was more about Denzil than anybody else but as luck would have it his actions had severely implicated the Devil. *How did I get away with that one*? he thought, as he tried to contain his rather smug smile. That saying Millie had, what was it? He thought for a moment and then remembered it was 'what goes around comes around' and he wondered could that really be true. Was there a God? Did he work in mysterious ways? *Well, it sure looks like it from here. So, two down but one not yet out, nearly but not quite. Come on, work your magic, this will play out exactly as you want if you carefully consider your next move and not let anyone get in your way.*

Chapter 61 - The Woman Next Door

Anne had no time to WhatsApp Becky, on arrival at her flat, an ambulance was in attendance at Mr and Mrs Campbell's. It was noticeably clear all was not well when Mr Campbell came rushing out to meet Anne. He was hysterical, "Anne, Anne it's Betty, she's unconscious and not responding to treatment. I think she may have died, she's in the kitchen, please come I need you to help me." With that, Anne rushed to his aid and entered the neat and tidy kitchen. Sure enough, there was Mrs Campbell lying prostrate face up on the cold tiled floor, eyes staring up to heaven. The room was silent, the paramedics nodded to Anne, and she knew for sure that Mrs Campbell was no more. Anne's mind wandered briefly to Tigger—oh, how he would miss Mrs Campbell and what was Mr Campbell going to do now?

Anne gently led Mr Campbell, Norman into the sitting room. It was warm and cosy with a dim lamplight emanating from one corner of the room.

"Sit here Mr Campbell, I'll make you a nice cup of tea once I've dealt with the ambulance crew. I won't be a moment."

So, in the dim-lit room, Mr Campbell sat duly obeying orders. He was numb, his world had suddenly fallen apart, two became one and one needed at some point to move on with their life. A small tear trickled from his left eye finding its way onto his now pale cheek meandering like a small river in a valley until it fell like a raindrop onto his lap making the tiniest damp circle you may ever have seen. This was followed by many more until Mr Campbell reached out for a tissue presented in a box by Anne. As Mrs Campbell's body was removed from the cold floor and the paramedics left the scene, Anne clung to Mr Campbell for all she was worth. Feeling his immense pain, she comforted him by holding him close to her ample bosom until his shaking and sobbing had somewhat subsided.

"What am I to do now, Anne? Half of me has gone! I will never be whole again; I have no idea how I'm going to cope." Anne soothed him, murmuring, "One small step at a time, Mr Campbell, one small step at a time."

Due to ongoing health issues, Mrs Campbell's age and the fact that she died at home, there was no need for a postmortem. This made the funeral date most expedient and Mrs Campbell's cremation had been set for the following week.

Armed with that knowledge, Anne sent a WhatsApp to Becky informing her of the situation and that she would now be attending White Wings Crematorium with Mr Campbell the following week. This seemed a much more plausible reason to be visiting the crematorium than simply just a visit. Becky said that she would come along and sit at the back of the church at Mrs Campbell's funeral. There was to be only one service which would be taking place in the church at the crematorium. The saying 'kill two birds with one stone' came to mind, but Anne decided to dismiss that thought.

Chapter 62 - Dear John—Oops, Colin

I *would have walked five hundred miles,* Colin thought as he pontificated about Charles and his steady life at Llandavyff Rehabilitation Centre. Did he do the right thing? Where was he going now? Who was he going with, and, more to the point, how was he going to get there?

With no simple answers to these questions, Colin collected the few belongings he had and left the hostel as quietly as he entered it. Time would tell as he stepped out into the chilly morning air. He took the 59 bus into the main town, where he entered Marks and Spencer's and bought himself some new trousers, trainers and a nice woollen navy jumper with a crew neck to match his dark-blue chinos. To add to his look he purchased a warm, pea coat in a fine navy and white check. A hidden zip with the addition of buttons to keep out the cold and gave him a sophisticated socialite look.

Revitalised by his fresh look, Colin headed to the nearest café for a spot of lunch. He ordered chilli con carne and rice, two huge hunks of garlic bread and a large pot of tea for one. He took a seat in the corner with his back to the wall to enable him to see the café patrons' antics. His mind wandered to Charles and Tim and that saying, 'To be improper would be proper if it wasn't deemed as rude'. Erm, ask Charles, ask Tim, and ask Charles again, hey then ask Colin. Ask Colin, what the fuck!

What did Colin know about being proper or improper? Colin thought long and hard and the only thing he could come up with was a bloke he used to know who was just never proper. Instead, he was always rude, always arrogant, always felt that the world owed him a living. He was also scruffy, and somewhat of an irritant to have around; could this be the bloke everyone seemed to be talking about? *No, surely not*, he thought as his chilli was delivered before him with a separate portion of rice on the side. *Gosh this looks delicious,* he thought as his mind wandered away from his initial thoughts.

Do I need to go back to source? Colin thought as he scraped the remains of his chilli onto his fork. *Do I need to meet with Charles and Tim, well Charles anyway? Is this action going to help to conclude what the hell is going on here?*

As he slurped the last dregs of tea, he had already agreed with himself that a return to base was necessary.

The phone was ringing off the wall with no prospect of it being answered.

Fuck it, Colin thought as the answering service kicked in. "Please leave your message after the tone." Beep... beep... beep...

"Charles it's me, pick up the bloody phone, ring me back as soon as..."

Then the dial tone kicked in.

Patience is a virtue, thought Colin.

Chapter 63 - The Heat is On

It was three p.m. sharp. Psalm 23 was accompanying the mourners to their pews. The mainstay was there for Mr Campbell: their daughter, along with Mr and Mrs Campbell's few friends and some distant relatives. All told you were looking at around twenty-one people in total. Mrs Campbell was very well respected, she was loved, she was a cheery soul and never one to give up. She loved life and life loved her. It was all incredibly sad that this day had come, and poor Mr Campbell would spend the rest of his life mourning his beloved wife, how sad, life can be so cruel in so many ways as Anne was about to find out.

As the funeral cortege entered the church, Mrs Campbell had four pall bearers, three from the undertakers and a fourth that looked vaguely familiar to Anne, she just couldn't quite see his face but there was no mistaking his beautiful blonde curly hair or so she thought. As the coffin was carefully placed towards the alter, all four pall bearers bowed and moved sidewards to take their place at the furthest point in the church making it nigh on impossible to see any of them.

A beautiful eulogy was calmly delivered by Mr Campbell's daughter, two further hymns, a sermon, a mention of Tigger (which pleased Anne greatly) and a closing *Abide with Me* concluded Mrs Campbell's funeral. This took all of thirty-five minutes from start to finish. As the congregation stood to allow the descent of the coffin, Anne could not help but shed a tear as Mrs Campbell's coffin waved its last goodbye to those she knew.

"God Bless you Betty," Anne muttered as she wiped her watery eyes with the back of her hand. She was trying so hard to remain strong from Mr Campbell. The wake was to be a small affair in the Rising Sun next door but three to the crematorium. At that point three of the four pall bearers left the church, leaving one behind.

Could it be, no, surely not, was it, is it, no, really, am I seeing things? thought Anne. *Billy... could that be him. Turn around will you*" thought Anne, as she spotted Becky out of the corner of her eye. *What was Becky doing, some sort of gesticulation towards what appeared to be a remarkably familiar figure. Fuck me*, thought Anne. *Oops don't swear in church... is that Taylor? Is that Taylor? Yes, it is, and who's that with her? A young boy, he looks about four years old. Is that Taylor's son?* Anne thought.

"Thank you for coming," Mr Campbell said as mourners departed the church heading for the wake. "Betty so loved living next door to you Anne," he told her as she held out her hand to him. "She was particularly fond of Tigger. Do you know, Anne, I thought I saw him earlier wandering around the crematorium. That said, he had a different collar, and I do get mixed up these days, probably wishful thinking," he said sobbing into his handkerchief.

Becky was calling to Anne.

"Over here," she said as Anne stepped towards her.

"Taylor, I thought it was you, how are you, how's the pregnancy, not long to go now. We do so miss you at class."

"I'll be back before you know it Anne," she said as she was rudely interrupted by a pulling on her skirt. "Oh Anne, Becky this is Ethan, he's four going on twenty-four."

"He's gorgeous Taylor, must have a handsome dad."

Taylor replied, "Oh he does, I refer to them as two peas in a pod. Here's his dad coming now." Just then a glimpse of fur caught Anne's eye and there was no mistaking who it was. "Tigger is that you, Tigger, Tigger!" she called out, at which point the most beautiful ginger tomcat came leaping across to Anne. She was absolutely in no doubt that this was Tigger. Different collar, fur slightly unkempt but no doubting this gorgeous ball of fur.

"Do you know this cat, Anne?" Taylor asked.

"Erm yes, if I'm not very much mistaken this is my cat, Tigger. He went missing over eight months ago. Funny, Mr Campbell had just said to me that he thought he saw Tigger. I thought he must be wrong, but do you know that this *is* Tigger, and he recognises me. He just has a different collar on."

"I'm confused, Anne. This is Tigger and he's Ethan's cat. We got him around seven to eight months ago. My husband-to-be said Ethan could have a cat. Tigger visited often so we just decided to adopt him."

"Billy!" Taylor shouted. "Anne thinks that this is Tigger, her lost cat."

Billy, Anne thought, *you have got to be joking.* She turned to see that very handsome man, with the blond curly hair cascading over his burly shoulders, that whiter-than-white smile and those beautiful blue eyes. There was no mistaking that this was her love, her long-lost love, this was her Billy, and this was Tigger, her long-lost and beloved cat.

"Pinch me Becky before I scream! Am I only dreaming; is this my eternal flame?"

"Close your eyes Anne and it will all go away. Breathe deeply and precisely and make it all go away."

As Anne did exactly that, her long lashes parted to reveal exactly the same situation.

"Oh my God, you've double-crossed me! You're living two lives, or you were living two lives. Billy, how could you, how could you do this to me? Taylor she's pregnant with your child no doubt and what about Ethan? Is he yours as well?"

Time stood still; Anne's head was in a spin. Becky tried to calm her down and Taylor was utterly confused. Billy hung his head in shame and asked if Anne and he could spend some time alone to try to work through this whole mess.

Becky, Taylor, and Ethan proceeded to Mrs Campbells wake, leaving Anne, Billy, and Tigger alone in the graveyard.

This was how it used to be, thought Anne as Billy guided her sobbing, broken self into the church. They sat for many a while with Tigger purring at their feet. Billy held Anne close, she could feel the strength of his arms holding her tight, the smell of his aftershave filled her nostrils with a sense of purpose, and she began to relax her taut body against his chest.

"I never knew what to do Anne, I've always cared for you and Tigger." "I didn't want to end it, but I knew I couldn't continue. Ethan is mine; Taylor was pregnant again and I want to get married and make it all right, do you see."

"No, I bloody well don't, Billy, what about me, what about Tigger, how could you, how could you do such a thing and leave me out in the cold with nowhere to go, no explanation, no nothing and then steal my cat from me, the one thing you know brings me peace, tranquillity unconditional love. "YOU BASTARD, YOU BASTARD, YOU FUCKING BASTARD"!

"You've even taken his collar off and adorned him with one of your choosing, trying to hide the guilt no doubt. YOU ABSOLUTE TWAT BILLY and to make matters worse, Fee was more than right about you! "How long have you been working here since you vanished from me no doubt. And what about Ethan, that relationship must have started before we even met. What is wrong with you, Billy? What gives you the right to be such an arsehole?"

Chapter 64 - Mr Attley, I Presume

Time and Tide and all that, Arthur thought, *wait for nobody, I'm not getting any younger, my life is great what more do I need? Not much*, he mused. *Maybe just to work out the conundrum that's been bugging the company. Who would want to contact me, what do they want with me, why am I so very interesting, do they know something that I don't?*

The more Arthur thought about this the more he puzzled, how many people had been in contact with this "To be Improper would be Proper if it wasn't deemed as Rude" man? Let's see: Elliott, Millie, and Stewart who all worked at AA. Arthur had not had the pleasure of having anything to do with him.

Thinking long and hard about his army service and that of his father's, was there anything hidden in his or his father's dim and distant past that could remotely link to what was currently going on? At that precise moment, Arthur could think of no one that would want to contact either him or his father.

To Be Improper... what is that? What does that mean? If you are improper, are you rude? Maybe or do you just do something that isn't quite correct? That said improper attached to an arrogant, self-effacing person may then seem clearly rude. So, in essence what have we got here: - a saying and an arrogant and rather abrupt gentleman. A gentleman who doesn't want to engage with anybody but Arthur. A gentleman who has connections, can move around somewhat freely, without detection and hound people to seek out Arthur.

As he puzzled over the logistics of trying to coincide with Mr Improper, Arthur's telephone began to buzz in his pocket.

"Dad it's me. That bloody bloke has been ringing the office again. Maybe you should come in over the next few days and see if he calls."

"And if he doesn't, Elliott, what then?"

"Well at least give it a try, Dad. I did say that you'd be here tomorrow at which point he stated that he'd ring back."

"Didn't he leave a number?"

"No of course not, Dad, he never does."

With that, Arthur agreed with his son that the following day he would complete a full day at Avenging Angels to try to solve the conundrum.

Mrs Attley was wating at the front door when Arthur pulled up on the drive. She waved sweetly to him as she peeled off her gardening gloves and held her hand up towards her mouth in a fist motion gesturing a mug of something hot was on offer. Oh, how Arthur loved her, really loved her! His life was so complete with her in it.

"I'm going into AA tomorrow. Elliott's asked me to pop in and see if we can track down Mr Improper man. He phoned today, and Elliott made the promise that I'd be there tomorrow so that whoever it is can catch me. So, I'll be doing a full day as

I'm not sure when hell ring if he does. Actually, do you know, I think it'll do me good to see Elliott in action and catch up with things in the office."

With that thought, Mrs Attley plonked a steaming hot mug of coffee in his lap accompanied by two pieces of shortbread, Mr Attley's favourite.

Chapter 65 - Lost in Thought

True to form, Marco pulled up outside Rupert's house just in time to see him closing the front door having waved goodbye to Beano & Bandit telling them that he wouldn't be long. It was two minutes past four and ten minutes past, by the time Rupert had made his way to the car.

"Okay, where are we off to, Marco?"

"Anywhere Rupert; where do you fancy?"

"I need to be back for six; Pamela's father is coming round for tea and to see how I am. I'll need a stiff drink before facing all his inquisitive questioning. He means well but it's bloody hard work."

"I just want some company for an hour or so and couldn't think of anyone better to chinwag with." said Marco

"Oh, thank you very much, Marco, I'll take that as a compliment," he said, meanwhile thinking *He's just going to go on and on about Mr George. Still*, Rupert thought, *it will give me a break from all my woes.*

The quaint old pub, the Plumb Duff, was pretty empty; the log burner in the corner was blazing away, so like a pin to a magnet, both Marco and Rupert headed for the seats directly facing the fire. Once seated, Marco put his coat behind the chair ensuring this was now his property as he stood up and edged towards the bar.

"Pint, Rupert?"

"Yes, please Marco, Guinness for me this time; I fancy a change from Mild."

"Okay, any nuts, crisps, pork scratching?"

"Erm no thanks, it'll spoil my tea," Rupert said with a sigh.

As both men cradled their respective pints, the fire crackled causing a burning ember to ignite a huge log engulfing the pair in its warmth. Each of them groaned and made themselves comfier and more settled for the foreseeable future. What a journey it had been for them since the introduction of the Devil. No one could have foreseen what would happen and how quickly it would happen.

For a few minutes neither of them spoke, both entwined in their own thoughts, memories, and circumstances. It was hard to believe that the engagement of one man could cause such disruption and displace so many people both from a professional and personal stance. Marco was upset; his actions had caused what was now seen as catastrophic circumstances. He hungered to be noticed, his possible ascension to power interrupted by his stammer and his inability to realise that the Devil was to be way more powerful than he had ever thought.

What a mess, what a bloody mess, he thought. *What has it all been for? Why did he do it, why did he rock the boat? Why did he let it sail into the abyss, rudderless and without a captain? What on earth was he thinking? Look what he's done to Rupert, his pal, his friend, his confidant.*

As Marco cast his eyes over Rupert who was now dozing in front of the fire, Marco couldn't help but notice how thin Rupert now was, how grey he was and how that once ruddy complexion had turned more yellow with dark circles shadowing both eyes.

Bless him, he's a fighter and the one thing about him is that he has never given up. When all seemed hopeless and lost, Rupert battled through. The rest of Rupert's life is going to be one constant battle, Marco thought as he was jogged back to reality by the burly rough hand on his shoulder.

"Marco, fancy seeing you in here at 4.35 p.m. on a weekday. I wouldn't have thought this was a pub you would frequent."

"Well, you neither. What brings you to this neck of the woods?"

"Business. You know what's is like... I have a few phone calls and visits to make tomorrow, so I thought I'd pop it for a bite to eat and a swift half. I'm staying across the way."

"Well sit down, take your mac off—oh by the way, this is Rupert. We used to work together."

"How do you do, Rupert?" he said as he shook the three fingers on Rupert's good hand.

Rupert looked inquisitively at him waiting for some sort of explanation as to how he knew Marco, but it didn't come. Although a stranger to Rupert, Rupert felt that he knew him, his mannerisms, his gruff deep voice. Although his appearance was unkempt, there was an air of authority about him that made him quite intriguing. Rupert knew one thing: his pint was definitely swift as it was gone in three swigs.

"Anyone for another?" he asked as he got up and headed to the bar.

"Not for me, thanks," said Rupert. "I haven't got much time."

"You've got time for another half, Rupert, surely?" said Marco.

"Ah go on then, but I must be way by five thirty at the latest else I'll be in trouble."

"Deep shit," you mean said the stranger as he headed to the bar.

"Who the fuck is that, Marco?"

"Somone from my deep and distant past. He's a bit rough now but means well."

"What is he doing around here do you reckon?"

"No idea. Last I heard he was heading off to New Zealand for a long holiday. He served in the armed forces but was pensioned off having suffered PTSD when some of his regiment were blown up in a tank while serving under his command. He looks way older than he is; I reckon it had a big effect on him. He didn't give the order to proceed but very much blames himself for the loss of at least three lives. Incredibly sad really, because he was such a proud man who had made a decent rank in the army and, until that fateful day, was going places. I know him from school; he always wanted to join the army. That was his life, his passion and his goal. Now I reckon he's a bit lost, like all of us really. Maybe we should start a club and call it The Lost Boys, what do you think?"

Marco gave a wry smile as what was now known as the ex-soldier returned to the fold.

"Got to go, Pamela will kill me if I'm not back in time. Marco, I can get a taxi if you like, and you can catch up with your childhood friend."

"No, no, no. I got you here and I'm taking you back, Rupert."

"Nice to meet you, maybe see you again," Rupert said as he struggled to get up and precariously balanced on his prosthetic legs.

"That can't be easy mate," Marco interjected. "He's doing very well, aren't you, Rupert?"

The ex-soldier said, "I'm around tomorrow if you fancy another catch-up, Marco. It would be nice to see you."

Chapter 66 - I Who Have Nothing

Anne cried all the way home; it was a very long sixteen miles. *How could he,* she thought. *What am I, useless!* came the reply in her head. She pulled up sobbing into a tissue when she spotted Mr Campbell's daughter who looked bereft and lonely. Even though Anne was feeling like shit, she stumbled out of her car and glanced across waving to Mr Campbell's daughter.

She shouted, "Are you alright? Would you like to pop over for a coffee?"

With that she made a beckoning gesture indicating that she would be pleased to have some company. Equally Anne was clearly glad of some normality.

Once inside Anne's flat, Mr Campbell's daughter settled into Anne's comfy chair and began to relax. The two women sought comfort in each other, and, as the day progressed, the pain had eased for both.

Anne had agreed with Sylvia (Mr Campbell's daughter) to keep a close eye on him over the coming weeks and ensure that he was looking after himself. This of course gave Anne a purpose and some positivity in her life. Sylvia agreed to check on her father in person every two months or so and made Anne promise to contact her should anything go awry.

And so, this was the way of Anne's world, she began to add Mr Campbell to her list of things to do. She visited him daily to ensure that he was the best he could be. In essence she became his carer, and although not paid to do such a job, Sylvia did ensure that Anne had everything she needed both for her dad and for herself. It was a win-win for Anne, which was unheard of. Sylvia held down a good, well-paid job so would offer Anne the chance of a holiday, some new furniture, a chance to regroup through spa days and massages by way of a thank you. Anne found all of this immensely therapeutic.

Slowly but surely, Anne began to recover. Her life was empty without Billy and Tigger, and some might have called her soft for relenting and letting Billy keep Tigger, never mind Taylor bagging Billy. But Ethan loved Tigger and Tigger Ethan and Anne could see that it would be wrong to remove her precious cat from that family fold. As for Billy, she felt that he never really loved her, and she had been just a distraction and a bit on the side when he had fallen out with Taylor and needed to seek solace. How on earth he had kept two relationships going Anne would never know but he did.

Fee Shand kept repeating herself like a broken record.

"Told you so, selfish bastard! You should have given him up years ago, Anne; you never learn."

If she said this once, she said it a million times until Anne grew some balls and said, "Do you know what Fee, fuck off! I've had enough of listening to you whinge on and on about Billy. It's my life and I'm now free to make all my own decisions now and they don't involve you sticking your nose in."

Blimey had Anne actually said this to Fee Shand, her boss, her ruler, her life? Yes, she jolly well had and now it was time for Anne to take the reins and lead the way as the next chapter in her life was about to begin. No Billy and more to the point, no cat, no Tigger but hope. Anne always had hope. Maybe one more visit to the Wine o'clock Club before putting paid to her previous life. Good luck Anne.

Chapter 67 - Bad Education

The PhD in Chemistry never transpired, the search was over, HR were no longer "human" when it came to any kind of explanation. There wasn't even a chance to bid farewell, Au Revoir or Bobs your uncle before the Devil hit the highway to hell with nothing but his briefcase and brogues. C'est le vie he thought as he headed down the road for the last time in his perfectly formed Mercedes Benz. The one thought had crossed his mind was, would he be able to keep his bright shining bit of metal. Marched off the premises is surely one way to go, out with a bang. Bit like Denzil really the Devil thought as he was escorted through his paces until his larger-than-life size frame was dutifully ejected.

The ship had sunk, no more listing in the waves, the abyss had finally captured the hearts of the dutiful Captain, his first mate and all who sailed on her. The ship had indeed become rudderless, and the crew had been left to their own devices.

The knock-on effect of the Devils antics burned deep into Nia, the rottweiler, her role now reduced to ashes had forced her back to a life of drudgery and insecurity. The transition was utterly amazing, back to where she had originally started. Be careful what you wish for, don't tread on anyone on your way up for you sure as hell will meet them on the way down. Hard lesson for Nia to learn but learn it she did.

Marco had some questions to answer on his return to work, how did the Devil manage to keep everyone at bay whilst desperately seeking out the evidence he required to secure his future. Life has a habit of biting you on the bum when you're least expecting it. At least now Marco had a chance or so he thought, and maybe this move could help Rupert? Although that ship had sailed Marco always had Hope.

Chapter 68 - Mr Improper

Colin met up with Charles and Tim, eventually. They discussed Mr Improper (or Raincoat Man as he was known to others). Tim laid claim to knowing this gentleman from the Plumb Duff, where Tim had started to attend the weekly quiz. He described him as an intelligent man, very articulate when he wanted to be, but a slovenly and unkempt look had warned people off him. He wasn't often in the pub and Tim believed that he lived outside of the local community but was in the area at times undertaking some contractual work. He was a prolific reader and when he was around, he would often visit the library. He was a grumpy and angry man and certainly didn't suffer fools gladly.

Mr Improper was keen to source a book called "To Be improper Would Be Proper if it wasn't deemed as rude." The said book was nestling in the library where Cleo worked. It had disappeared from the library shelves months earlier and after some considerable time Mr Improper returned it to the library. Apparently, he was asked to pay a hefty fine, which he did under protest before Cleo safely replaced the book in the Philosophy section of the library.

Not long after its replacement Cleo had seen Mr Improper visit the library once again. He wasn't friendly and sat staring out of the window a lot of the time as if he were contemplating his next move. That move came sooner rather than later. In the blink of an eye, Mr Improper had once again left the library, titled book under his arm and gone. Cleo could not understand what was going on.

The book had always been logged on the library system by its title but with no author, which was strange.

Charles admitted to meeting Mr Improper in a café, a chance meeting set up via a telephone call. Just through the description that Tim had given, Charles knew that it must be the same man. Charles recalled the café owner telling him that Mr Improper visited the café every two to three weeks when he was in the area.

Charles was really pleased to see Colin and he started to reminisce about their time at Llandavyff. It was clear to that Colin and Charles truly did have a bond, which appeared to be much more about love than just friendship.

Chapter 69 – So We Meet Again

"Good morning, AA, how may I help you?" said Millie

"To be improper would be proper if it wasn't deemed as rude," came the reply.

"Arthur!" shouted Millie. "It's him."

Arthur, now rather portly, shot from his chair like a spring chicken to get to the phone. He managed it well, hurling himself across the office like a tennis ball catapulted from Djokovic's racket.

"Arthur Attley here, how can I help you?" Albeit slightly out of breath, he was composed and ready for the response. None came. "Hello, Arthur Attley here, is there anybody there?"

Sweet as you like came the reply: "Two pieces of shortbread, Captain, if you please."

Arthur froze, his eyes now wide open, his stance as if he were on parade, he proceeded to straighten his jacket and then out came his reply. "Is that you? Is that really you?"

"To be improper would be proper if it wasn't deemed as rude," the caller said.

Arthur was now the colour of the photocopying paper; he was shaking and really needed to sit down. Millie rushed to get him a chair. She pushed Arthur into it as best she could; he was still rather rigid but as his knees buckled, she managed to catch him in the base of the chair.

"Two pieces of shortbread indeed!" Arthur said out loud.

Was this some sort of code? did Arthur now know the identity of Raincoat Man? Had this conundrum now been solved with two pieces of shortbread?

"Meet me at four p.m. sharp at the two shortbreads café and you can tell me what you want," Arthur said.

With that the phone was gently placed on the receiver and Arthur breathed what appeared to be a sigh of relief.

When did he last see Mr Improper/Raincoat Man? What was the man doing in the area and why was he seeking Arthur out? What did this random book title have to do with anything, and what was so urgent that needed to seek Arthur out in the first place?

It was going to be a long day for Arthur, who now sat sipping his Earl Grey tea. Staring at the swirling slice of lemon, he thought about how to approach said situation. One man from his platoon stood out from all others and this, although Arthur didn't know it was to be a bond for life. Together they had been through the good, the bad and the ugly coming out the other side somewhat unscathed but scared by their experiences. For each man, the two pieces of shortbread gave them each the sweet taste of paradise encapsulated in two oblong fingers, a buttery biscuit, and a sensation of melting on the tongue eased the pain and pressure of war. The buttery biscuit became the symbol of peace for both men. A tradition that would die with them.

Chapter 70 - Gotcha!

Tim never meant to hurt the Devil, he just wanted to teach him a lesson. The Devil was cruel; he didn't suffer fools gladly and picked on those whom he thought of as being weaker staff to enable him to exert authority. Tim took the brunt of his 'little man syndrome' jokes, his off-the-cuff remarks about clarity of speech aimed mainly at Marco but Tim also took it personally. Tim was never one to really excel, to push forwards as his mother kept reminding him and he knew in his mothers' eyes that he could never be as good as Charles. You see Cecelia and Charles were carbon copies of each other and could do no wrong, whereas Tim and Cecelia well never the twain shall meet. So, when Tim had an opportunity, he took it.

Before his departure from the organisation, Tim had been working on an up-to-date HR system that could relate each individual post to their qualifications, job roles and titles and the department in which they worked. It was all but finished when Tim was rudely disposed of not allowing him time to complete what he had started. Cleo had also been working on this project which required a few algorithms completing and a program written to automatically attach each qualification to each staff member listed in the database.

Tim had reached a point whereby the system needed testing and given that the Devil was new as was the lovely Alicia, Tim had input all their details to set the program in motion. The program matched each individual to the qualifications they had listed once they had accepted the job role. A short algorithm later and any gaps evidenced were automatically highlighted for the HR team. Apparently, Alicia's was noneventful but the same could not be said about the Devil. The new system worked well and was to be rolled out in the near future giving the organisation peace of mind that they were employing highly qualified, competent, and honest individuals.

In essence, Tim and Cleo had a hand in the Devil's downfall, but they didn't know it at the time. That old adage 'What goes around, comes around' came to mind.

Chapter 71- Two Fingers Shortbread

Soldier, soldier, won't you marry me, Arthur thought as he drew up a chair in the café. He thought of the place as 'The Two Shortbreads Café'. He often found himself in there with Carol sipping tea and dunking shortbread, hence his waistline. How he loved his wife; as a young soldier he had fallen head over heels for her literally, chasing after her with a red rose before his return to duty begging her to wait for him. It was love at first sight and Arthur never forgot that. Carol kept him going; the mere thought of her kept his spirits high, keeping him vigilant and determined. She was with him in spirit as he longed for peace.

The brass cowbell chimed taking Arthur away from his thought process. He looked up to see Mr Improper heading towards him, nodding his recognition of Arthur as he approached. Arthur stood bolt upright, hand extended to welcome the stranger.

"Long time, no see," he said in a deep, thoughtful tone.

Two coffees and four shortbreads later, both men reminisced about their time spent together in the war zone. Derrick was different now, quieter, less evasive with a depth about him that Arthur could not remember him having. Arthur cast his eyes over a very shabby man, a dirty raincoat, scuffed shoes, unkempt hair, and a stubble protruding from his chin that could be mistaken for a truly short grey beard. He looked weather beaten with wrinkles carefully placed around both eyes and across his forehead like a deep trough about to catch the rain. He had a soft voice with a hint of an accent but not so prominent as to be recognisable as Irish. He seemed sad and lonely.

Derrick, although vague, started to chatter on about 'to be improper'. Arthur said, "What do you mean Derrick?"

"Well," said Derrick, "when something is improper, it isn't right is it, Arthur?"

"Erm, I suppose not," said Arthur.

"So, to be improper isn't good, is it, Arthur?"

"No, it isn't," said Arthur.

"Proper is good though, Arthur, isn't it?"

"Yes," said Arthur wondering where all this was going.

"Improper is rude, Arthur, do you agree?"

"Yes, I do," said Arthur.

"Well," said Derrick, "I wrote the book."

"What book?" said Arthur.

To Be Improper Would be Proper if it wasn't Deemed as Rude."

"Oh, I see," said Arthur.

"Do you?" said Derrick.

"Well not really," said Arthur.

"Let me fill you in then, Arthur," said Derrick.

"You were in command that day. You could see the enemy approaching, you could see that my team were in danger, yet you still gave the order to continue. Because of you, three of my men were blown to smithereens on that fateful day. *Now* do you remember?"

"Well of course I do. It was a difficult decision with the enemy so close. A retreat command was not an option; it would have played straight into enemy hands. I made a decision based on all the facts available to me on that day. I didn't make it lightly as you know but I needed to make it. I wasn't to know that their tank would be blown up by a landmine a few yards in front of their vehicle. I know that I gave that command based on an order from army headquarters, which in hindsight I deeply regret now. But Derrick, this was war; we were battling to save our country as well as our lives."

"It was improper Arthur; it wasn't the proper thing to do, and you were rude about it." said Derrick and continued, "I never had the chance to discuss it with you properly. I never got to say goodbye to my men either. You brushed me aside in a sadistic and rude fashion when I requested a meeting to further discuss it with you. Now all these years later, I can honestly say that you still haven't understood the consequences of your fateful decision that day."

"'To be improper would be proper if it wasn't deemed as rude' is all about you, Arthur, your time in the army as a so-called army Lieutenant. It's about *your* improper actions during your command and inability to be kind to people. It might seem like you've turned a corner now, but you have left a wake of destruction trailing behind you. You were always rude and had little or no time for those serving under you. You made my life hell and for that I cannot forgive you. So, as we sit here sipping tea and eating shortbread, may I just remind you that my life is a living hell. I have been diagnosed with PTSD, which give me bad days and very bad days with little respite in between.

"So, in my eyes that's not proper, Arthur, it's all very improper and my life is difficult to manage. People are very rude to me because of how I look; they have little understanding of my condition and therefore treat me with disdain, brushing me off like some imbecile unable to articulate a word never mind a sentence. My life is a complete and utter mess, and do you know what? Yours is about to be."

As if by magic the Browning 9mm automatic pistol appeared from Derrick's pocket and just like that, with one shot ringing out, Arthur slumped to the floor holding half a piece of shortbread in his right hand. Blood began to trickle from his forehead as Derrick carefully pulled back his chair, placed the gun in his pocket, left twenty pounds on the table and headed out of the door.

Never judge a book by its cover, thought Derrick as he headed off down the High Street.

Derrick couldn't think straight; to kill his Lieutenant in cold blood sent shivers down his spine. He knew his time was limited; he knew he'd caused havoc with Arthur's family, and he knew he was on a downward spiral.

The sirens were getting closer; the true outcome of his actions was soon to be discovered. Give up, hide, run away... what should he do? He thought quickly and in the blink of an eye, he sat by the wayside, took a small bite of the shortbread hidden in his pocket. Then he lifted the 9mm to his head and pulled the trigger. *Bye-bye Arthur, bye-bye Derrick, Mr Raincoat Man and Mr Improper.*

As his body slumped forwards, blood began to trickle down his face onto the pages of his precious book, still clutched tightly, a red river started to meander over the letter P for Proper and into the crevices of the R in Rude.

To be improper would be proper if it wasn't deemed as rude was no more.

Derrick remained in that position for quite a while before the police found him. They cordoned off the area and covered Derrick with a white sheet and laid him flat for collection by the undertaker. The bloodied book was taken into custody for evidence, labelled and put on an exhibits shelf. Maybe Derrick had now found his notoriety in death.

Two deaths, two men, same regiment, one callous killer.

Chapter 72 - A Clink of Cups

Millie opened her long-awaited business in the High Street replacing the 'Shortbread Café' with 'Millie's Memories Tea Shop'.

Her work at AA was done; she now had the funds to realise her dream. All kitted out and ready to go, Millie tied her brand-new apron featuring her new logo around her waist. The logo was a ceramic white teapot tilted to one side, with a cluster of purple flowers adorning its side and some hot, steamy tea cascading from the spout was allowed to 'spill out' onto a bright yellow apron. She felt the part; she looked the part and today was to be her first day of trading.

She took a deep breath and opened the double doors. She'd kept the cowbell perched high on the doorframe; it tinkled as the doors opened to let in the warmth of the day. *Today was going to be a good day, today was going to be the beginning of the rest of my life,* Millie thought. Millie turned the sign around to 'Open'.

The street was busy; the fresh air blew into the café followed by the sound of footsteps: one customer, two customers, three, four and many more began to populate the light and bright space. The coffee began to bubble, the teapots clinked with Earl Grey, ginger, liquorice, peppermint, Tetley, Yorkshire and many more tea flavours on offer. The smell of toasted teacakes engulfed the room.

Oh my, here we go, thought Millie.

The Wine O'clock Club had a new name: the Tea O'clock Club, and a brand-new location.

In filed Rene looking resplendent in her orange mini dress and low-slung boots. She had a gorgeous tan and was looking very trim indeed. She had always been an incredibly attractive young woman and today was no exception.

"Hi there Millie," she called as she headed towards her, arms out waiting to embrace.

Millie was beside herself with excitement to see her friend.

"Hi, Rene! You look fabulous; how lovely to see you. How have you been? Life is obviously treating you well."

"Life is great Millie; my boys and I are doing well. I am fully qualified now and loving my life as a midwife. It was the best thing that could ever have happened to me really, making me redundant although I didn't think so at the time. It pushed me to do something that I've always felt a pull towards but, to be honest, I was scared to even contemplate the change. Hindsight, Millie, is indeed a wonderful thing," she said beaming with delight.

"Sit here Rene, I've set the table for this momentous homecoming. I am super excited to host our very first Tea O'clock Club. I do hope that everyone can come."

"I've not heard anything to the contrary, Millie, so fingers crossed this is going to be a great catch-up, which, if I may say so, is long overdue."

Just then, as if by magic, a familiar voice screeched with excitement. It was Mel. She was overwhelmed by the café, the décor, the clinking of china cups and the pure elation of seeing Millie and Rene that she nearly tripped over herself rushing through the door.

"Hi oh hi!" she yelled. "Oh, my goodness! My work family are all coming back together, like old times, eh Rene?"

Both Millie and Rene greeted Mel like a long-lost puppy, hugs, kisses, and more hugs. It was a beautiful moment for all involved.

Mel was no different; she was a beautiful person inside and out. Her work at the hospice was more fulfilling to her than anything else she had ever done, and she loved it, that was most evident. She had changed very little, the few more grey bits straggled in her hair gave her a very alluring and warm glow. She was still very much in love, adored her family and felt that her life was in a great place. She too, although painful at the time, was more than glad to have a left what she now called a toxic organisation and move to her most sensuous, caring role ever. She recalled the experience of her first death and how privileged she felt to have held that young man's hand until his departure. She relayed his story with tears in her eyes and a warmth that was befitting of her.

Millie thought how much everyone loved Mel, her kindness, her calmness, her pure understanding and love for her fellow colleagues, and her absolute resilience when faced with adversity. Her presence once again in their lives laid claim to a fabulous and devoted woman, a rock, an anchor to steady the ship and to keep everyone grounded.

We all love Mel, Millie thought as she cradled her head on her shoulders and felt that love exuding from her.

How lucky Millie was to have as her very first customers, the people she most cared about in the world, the people she had been with when the news of those terrible redundancies were released.

It wasn't long before an exhausted Anne came waddling through the door. Her shoulder bag started slipping gently down and was caught expertly by her protruding belly. She was dressed as usual in her familiar elasticated waisted trousers, lending themselves to be a bit short, given her expanding waistline. All that aerobic stuff gone to waist (literally) as Anne munched her way through several chocolate bars and biscuits as a source of condolence for the loss of Billy and Tigger. It wasn't really the best actions, but to be honest, Anne really didn't give a fuck.

She waved vigorously at those gathered at a table in the corner. Her navy jacket was crumpled with a button or two missing, but Anne didn't seem to care. Her hair was tied up in its usual ponytail and she had chosen glasses as opposed to contact lenses for the meeting. Anne had found herself and was to be no longer bullied by Billy or Fee. She was becoming her own woman, whatever her own woman was.

Of those that had gathered, they didn't know whether to congratulate Anne, console her or just pay homage to her situation, in the hope that she may open up throughout the day. She had been really pleased to get the invitation and was keen to catch up on others' lives.

By now the tearoom was filling up. Millie had taken on another waitress and a barista to help build the business. She was keeping an eye on things from a short distance should anyone need any help.

At that point in walked Cleo, humming *Islands in the Stream*, her go-to tune.

"Hi," she said excitedly. "How lovely to see you all. I am so keen to hear what's been going on in all your lives—oh and Millie, congratulations, looks like you've done an absolute super job!"

Millie blushed and said, "Why thank you, Cleo, that's very nice of you to say."

"Praise due where praise is due, Millie," came the reply. With that, everyone laughed, the same old Cleo, direct, to the point and straight at ya! How everyone had missed Cleo. She was still at the library, part-time of course, loving the mix of her free time and her interest in books, a really good move for her. Millie thought, *this is going well. At least some of the group were happy with the outcome*.

The sun was now streaming in through the door as a large-brimmed hat appeared at the entrance. It was navy in colour and paired with what appeared to be a broderie anglaise dress in a beautiful peach colour. It could be none other than the debonaire Miss Shand.

All stand, thought Anne as Fee made her entrance. She was as gorgeous and as impeccably turned out as ever, navy heels that matched her sombrero hat and a figure to die for, as usual. It was evident that she wasn't stuffing herself with chocolate while watching *Coronation Street*, Anne thought.

"Well, hello my lovelies," she said as she delicately lowered her elegant frame in a seat by the window. "Oh my God, I have so much to tell you all, I don't know where to begin!" she exclaimed.

Anne couldn't bear it; the woman was years older, looked absolutely fabulous and most definitely had a huge spring in her step.

Had she come into money, Anne wondered? *Those clothes, that hat and those heels looked remarkably expensive. She was always well turned out but today she looked even better than ever.*

"You're not still doing the sex thing are you?" Anne asked rather hesitantly.

"Indeed, I am Anne. It's liberating and I've made a lot of money at it. The best thing is you don't even have to meet the punters. You should try it sometime, Anne."

Fee looked her up and down and thought, *Erm, maybe not, that said, the punters can't even see you, so maybe you could get away with it.*

The tearoom was now full of chatter, an excitement filled the air, a buzz like there had never been before. Next thing, in walked Tim. He was tidier, he was smarter, he'd pulled himself up to his full five-foot-six by straightening his shoulders. His jeans were good quality denim, and they fitted him perfectly. They were a super length for the black Skechers poking out beneath them. His light grey jacket was of a cotton mix, single-breasted and styled as in Man at Marks and Spencer's. This new look really suited him. He was wearing a dark grey polo shirt, if one could believe it, a polo shirt! Tim in a polo shirt and, by gum, did it suit him. He really did look very smart indeed. His hair was nicely cut; gone was his nostril and ear hair. He had replaced his dowdy bottle-top glasses with some really smart specs currently perched on his head allowing his manicured eyebrows to frame his now very bright and sparkly eyes.

"Hi," he said with an air of confidence. "How is everyone?"

Somewhat aghast, Fee remarked, "Erm what have you done with Tim?"

"Very funny, Fee."

To take up the challenge, Tim started to recall his life now and the journey it took for him to get there. Cleo was more than impressed and had truly believed in Tim for some quite considerable time. Tim felt good; he was really glad that

Stanley had managed his diary well enough for him to attend the Tea O'clock Club. In days gone by, he would have shied away at a moment's notice.

Life has a habit of working itself out no matter what. There they all were nearly two years later and how things had changed for this group of people! Millie had always wanted her own business, and a tearoom was exactly what she was looking for, the chance to buy the Shortbread Café couldn't have come at a better time albeit that unfortunate circumstances had led her to this point.

As she pontificated on her life, the sun cast a shadow in the doorway. As she and her old colleagues turned to look, a pair of familiar shiny brogues stepped inside.

A large frame was carrying a medium-sized cardboard box in very big hands. A black shirt with the text 'Next Day Delivery (NDD)' in red was emblazoned on the front.

"Parcel for Millie's Tearooms," he said in a hearty Yorkshire accent.

Within a few seconds two rather tall, slim men – one quite a bit older than the other – pushed past the delivery man and rushed towards the seven ex-colleagues now standing around the table to secure a better view. For a second, it was unbelievable, but there in full view of the group were Denzil Drum and Rupert Hope. How could this be? Where had they miraculously appeared from? Wasn't Denzil dead and Rupert struggling to survive having contracted sepsis? Well, apparently not, because, if their eyes didn't deceive them, standing right in front of them now were the two men! Rupert was somewhat greyer now and much thinner and Denzil still, as ever, sharply dressed and smelling every bit the debonaire man about town.

"Pinch me now," Fee said as she tried to comprehend what was going on. As they took their place in the fold, fit, healthy and well, all nine turned to face the doorway.

Dreams are nothing more than wishes and a wish is just a dream you wish to come true, thought Millie. *Had this all been a figment of her imagination?*

A lovely ginger cat took its place on the tearoom windowsill, preening its whiskers with its paw. Was it, surely not... *was* it?

Anne let out an almighty scream. "Tigger, Tigger, my Tigger, you've come home to me!" she cried.

As Millie took a deep breath, she turned to her colleagues and said, "Revenge is sweet but be careful what you wish for." With that, she took the package from the remarkably familiar carrier and said, "Forget me Knott, Devil, Forget me Knott."

THE END

About the Author

Kym grew up in Northern Ireland. She has a Master's Degree in Strategic Human Resource Management. Her passion is poetry, and she loves writing.

As a great observer of people, places and situations her work, although fictional, often contains some realism. Kym is a published poet and as such decided to embark on her first ever novel. She lives in the beautiful Scottish Borders with her husband and dog.

Kym has been writing for a few years now and has successfully published some poetry. She is very interested in words and their meaning. Inspired by people, events, relationships and life, she decided to embark on her first-ever novel. It has been several years in the making, but she is now immensely proud to present *Nine Lives, No Cat*.

The story is based on the lives, loves and careers of the characters, as it follows a group of people brought together through a set of very unfortunate circumstances.

Kym is married to David, and she credits him with the drive and enthusiasm to enable her to write this novel. Without his love, support and total dedication to read, listen and advise, this novel would never have been completed.

Appendix

__Reference to songs/writers:__

Abide with Me – Henry Francis Lyte

All the People So many People – Dave Rowntree, Alex James, Graham Coxon,

Damon Albarn (Parklife)

All you need is Love – John Lennon

Annie get your Gun – Irving Berlin

As Time goes By – Herman Humfeld

Billy don't be a Hero – Mitch Murray

Blue is the Colour – Rod McQueen and Daniel Boone

Brothers in Arms – Mark Knopfler

Bye, bye Baby – Bob Crewe and Bob Gaudio

Climb every mountain – Oscar Hammerstein

Cry me a River – Arthur Hamilton

Dancing with the Devil – Demi Lovato and Mitch Allan

Don't Look back in Anger – Noel Gallagher

Giant Steps are what we take - Sting

Going to the Chapel – Jeff Barrie, Ellie Greenwich and Phil Spector

He ain't Heavy – Bob Russell

Help me if you can – John Farnham

I am Sailing- Gavin Sutherland

I who have Nothing – Ben E King

Isn't she Lovely – Stevie Wonder

Let's get Physical- Terry Shaddick

Life of Brian – Eric Idel, Michael Palin and Geoffrey Burgon

Love Hurts – Boudleaux Bryant and Felice Bryant

Loving Angels Instead – Robbie Williams

Monday, Monday – John Phillips

Money, Money, Money – Benny Andersson and Bjorn Ulvaeus

Mother of Mine – Bill Parkinson

Oh baby, baby – Smokey Robinson and Pete Moore

Oranges and Lemons – Benjamin Till

People are People – Martin Gore

Pussy Cat, Pussy Cat – Hal David

Raindrops keep failing on my Head- Hal David and Burt Bacharach

Red, Red Wine – Neil Daimond

Ring, ring, why don't you give me a call – Bjorn Ulvaeus, Benny Andersson, Stig Andersson

Savage Garden – Australian Pop Duo, Darren Hayes, Daniel Jones

Sending out an SOS – Alan Landon and Douglas Lenier

So long, Farewell – Oscar Hammerstein II

Take me Home – Taffy Nivert and Bill Danoff

The Bells are Ringing – Jule Styne

When you are a King – John and Roger Hill

You got a Friend – Carole King

Printed in Dunstable, United Kingdom

63761189R00178

CW01622398

ДИТЯЧА
БІБЛІЯ

Об’єднаниі Біблійні Товариства

2022

ДИТЯЧА
БІБЛІЯ

ДИТЯЧА БІБЛІЯ

БІБЛІЙНІ ОПОВІДАННЯ В МАЛЮНКАХ

Борислав Арапович
та
Віра Маттелмяки

Переклад Оксани Галицької і Валентини Новомирової
Редактор: Федір Млинченко

Перше видання, 1992
Видання чотирнадцяте, 2022

Видавець: Об’єднанії Біблійні Товариства,
надруковано з дозволу Інституту перекладу Біблії,
Стокгольм

IBT Children’s Bible in Ukrainian
ISBN 978-0-56-401652-5
BSRL/2022/30M Printed in Poland

© Інститут перекладу Біблії, 1992, 2012 Стокгольм

Ілюстрації використані з дозволу:
© Classic Bible Art LLC, Colorado Springs, Colorado; IFB; Palphot; Pictorial Archives of Near Eastern History Est.; SLT; UBS; БоАр; БрКа; АнОл.

ПРО БІБЛІЮ

Любий друже!

Чи знаєш ти, що це за книга — Біблія? Біблія — це Слово Боже. Вона розкриває нам таємницю походження світу, людини та змісту буття. Біблія — це зібрання Святих Писань, в укладанні яких брали участь близько сорока авторів, сповнених Духом Святим; писалася Вона протягом півтора тисячоліття.

Біблія поділяється на дві частини — Старий Заповіт та Новий Заповіт. Старий Заповіт було написано до Різдва Христового, а Новий Заповіт упродовж першого століття після Різдва Христового. Наше літочислення ведеться від року народження Ісуса Христа.

Старий Заповіт написано давньоєврейською мовою, а Новий Заповіт — давньогрецькою, тобто мовами культур тих часів.

У Старому Заповіті розповідається про те, як Бог створив усесвіт, як згрішили перші люди, якою була історія обраного Богом народу Ізраїлю, як Бог обирав Собі пророків, і що вони пророкували; сюди входять Книга Псалмів (давніх божественних гімнів та молитов до Бога), Книга Еклезіястова, Книга Йова та інші.

У Новому Заповіті йдеться про народження й життя нашого Спасителя — Господа Ісуса Христа, про Його вчення, про Його смерть задля спасіння грішного людства, про Його воскресіння та про життя перших християн. У Новому Заповіті є також послання апостолів Христа — звернення їх до перших християн та до всіх людей на землі; останньою книгою Біблії є «Об'явлення», — опис подій, що станутьcя перед другим пришестям Ісуса Христа.

Учення Ісуса Христа називають «Євангелією». Слово «Євангелія» у перекладі з давньогрецької мови означає «Блага звістка». Про що ця звістка? Про те, що так «Бог полюбив світ, що дав Сина жертву спокути, прийнявши смерть за гріхи людей та вказавши їм істинний шлях у житті.

Центральна тема Біблії — це Особа Господа Ісуса Христа, Сина Божого, Спасителя та Володаря світу.

Біблія — перша у світі друкована книга («Біблія Гутенберга» була надрукована у 1452–1455 роках). Завдячуючи повсюдному підвищенню рівня грамотності та поширенню християнства по всій землі, Біблію читає все більше й більше людей. Біблія стає настільною книгою як у родинах робочого люду, так і в колах інтелігенції. Особливе розповсюдження Біблії спостерігається у наші часи.

За кількістю перекладів різними мовами Біблія займає перше місце у світі. Більш аніж 500 років тому, до моменту винаходу друкарського верстату, Біблія чи її окремі книги були перекладені лише 33 мовами. Але вже у 1804 році, початку зародження Біблійних товариств, переклад Біблії існував 67 мовами. Протягом усього XIX століття книги Біблії виходили вже більш аніж 400 мовами, а за роки XX століття Біблію чи її окремі книги переклали 1500 мовами. До кінця 2010 року Біблію було вже перекладено 2527 мовами. Виявилося, що повна Біблія перекладена 469 мовами, а Новий Заповіт — 1231 мовами; додамо, що 827 мовами перекладено одну чи декілька книг Біблії. Сьогодні лише близько 2% населення земної кулі не має жодної книги Біблії своєю рідною мовою. У наш час Біблія перекладається більш аніж 1000 мов малих народів. Велика робота ведеться над перекладами Біблії мовами, якими спілкуються між собою лише декілька тисяч, сотень або навіть десятків людей.

Варто додати, що окремі книги Біблії, записані на компакт-дисках та аудіокасетах, є посібниками для неписьменних та незрячих людей. Крім того, Біблія видається для сліпих шрифтом Брайля.

За тиражем Біблія посідає перше місце у світі. Давайте порівняємо: 1900 року було видано 5 млн. примірників Біблії та 7 млн. примірників Нового Заповіту, 1980 року — біля 36 млн. Біблії, 57 млн. Нового Заповіту, 2010 року — 28 млн. Біблії, 10 млн. Нового Заповіту.

Таким чином Біблія є найрозповсюдженішою книгою у світі.

ПЕРЕДМОВА

«Дитяча Біблія» підготована для юних читачів. Великі за обсягом розповіді скорочені й спрощені. Уривки тексту, взяті в лапки («…»), дослівно наведені з українського перекладу Біблії професора І. Огієнка, вперше виданого в 1962 році.

Зважаючи на те, що не тільки діти, але й дорослі читатимуть цю книгу, ми включили деякі тексти, призначені, головним чином, для дорослого читача. Кожна розповідь супроводжується кольоровим малюнком, на якому художник зобразив своє бачення того, про що йде мова.

Біблія — це Слово Боже, і всі спроби переказувати чи перекладати її, нехай навіть і найкращими тлумачами й майстрами слова, не можуть відобразити усю глибину і багатство цієї Книги книг.

Читайте цю книгу з любов'ю, згадуйте описані у ній події, бережіть євангельське вчення у серцях ваших. Почніть читати Біблію. Господь хоче, щоб і ви могли сказати:

«Для моєї ноги Твоє слово — світильник, то світло для стежки моєї» (Пс. 118:105).

З дружнім привітанням,

Інститут перекладу Біблії, 1992

СТАРИЙ ЗАПОВІТ

СТАРИЙ ЗАПОВІТ

СТВОРЕННЯ СВІТУ. ПОЧАТОК

Вам добре відомо, як усе поринає в морок у темряві ночі, коли вимкнене освітлення. У такій темряві колись знаходився всесвіт. Тоді не було ні трави, ні дерев, ні чудових квітів, ні птахів, ані навіть неба й землі, але увесь всесвіт був суцільний морок і хаос. Однак Бог не хотів, щоб все так залишалося, і Він створив цей чудовий світ. Ми знаємо, що саме по собі ніщо не створюється. Навколишній світ, сповнений гармонії і краси, свідчить про його великого і мудрого Творця.

У Священній книзі Біблії описане створення світу по волі Божій, за Словом Його:

«На початку Бог створив Небо та землю.

А земля була пуста та порожня, і темрява *була* над безоднею, і Дух Божий ширяв над поверхнею води.

І сказав Бог: «Хай станеться світло!» І сталося світло.

І побачив Бог світло, що добре *воно*, — і Бог відділив світло від темряви.

І Бог назвав світло: «День», а темряву назвав: «Ніч». І був вечір, і був ранок, — день перший.

І сказав Бог: «Нехай станеться твердь посеред води, і нехай відділяє вона між водою й водою».

І Бог твердь учинив, і відділив воду, що під твердю вона, і воду, що над твердю вона. І сталося так.

І назвав Бог твердь: «Небо». І був вечір, і був ранок — день другий.

І сказав Бог: «Нехай збереться вода з-попід неба до місця одного, і нехай суходіл стане видний». І сталося так.

І назвав Бог суходіл: «Земля», а місце зібрання води назвав: «Море». І Бог побачив, що добре *воно*.

І сказав Бог: «Нехай земля вродить траву, ярину, що насіння вона розсіває, дерево овочеве, що за родом своїм плід приносить, що в ньому насіння його на землі». І сталося так.

І земля траву видала, ярину, що насіння розсіває за родом її, і дерево, що приносить плід, що насіння його в нім за родом його. І Бог побачив, що добре воно.

І був вечір, і був ранок, — день третій».

1 М. 1:1–13

СТВОРЕННЯ СВІТУ. ПРОДОВЖЕННЯ

«І сказав Бог: «Нехай будуть світила на тверді небесній для відділення дня від ночі, і нехай вони стануть знаками, і часами умовленими, і днями, і роками.

І нехай вони стануть на тверді небесній світилами, щоб світити над землею». І сталося так.

І вчинив Бог обидва світила великі, — світило велике, щоб воно керувало днем, і світило мале, щоб керувало ніччю, також зорі.

І Бог умістив їх на тверді небесній, щоб світили вони над землею, і щоб керували днем та ніччю, і щоб відділювали світло від темряви. І Бог побачив, що *це* добре.

І був вечір, і був ранок, — день четвертий.

І сказав Бог: «Нехай вода вироїть дрібні істоти, душу живу, і птаство, що літає над землею під небесною твердю».

І створив Бог риби великі, і всяку душу живу плазуючу, що її вода вироїла за їх родом, і всяку пташину крилату за родом її. І Бог побачив, що добре *воно*.

І поблагословив їх Бог, кажучи: «Плодіться й розмножуйтеся, і наповнюйте воду в морях, а птаство нехай розмножується на землі!»

І був вечір, і був ранок, — день п'ятий.

І сказав Бог: «Нехай видасть земля живу душу за родом її, худобу й плазуюче, і земну звірину за родом її». І сталося так.

І вчинив Бог земну звірину за родом її, і худобу за родом її, і все земне плазуюче за родом його. І бачив Бог, що добре *воно*».

Уся земля, створена Словом всемогутнього Творця, осяяна промінням ласкавого сонця, дихала спокоєм і дивною красою. Але це ще не був кінець творення. Бог вирішив створити людей, щоб вони жили у цьому прекрасному світі, насолоджувалися ним і мали спілкування зі своїм Творцем, прославляючи Його.

1 М. 1:14–25

O. Stemler

СТВОРЕННЯ ПЕРШИХ ЛЮДЕЙ

«І сказав Бог: «Створімо* людину за образом Нашим, за подобою Нашою, і хай панують над морською рибою, і над птаством небесним, і над худобою, і над усею землею, і над усім плазуючим, що плазує по землі».

І Бог на Свій образ людину створив, на образ Божий її Він створив, як чоловіка та жінку створив їх.

І поблагословив їх Бог, і сказав Бог до них: «Плодіться й розмножуйтеся, і наповнюйте землю, оволодійте нею, і пануйте над морськими рибами, і над птаством небесним, і над кожним плазуючим живим на землі!»

І сказав Бог: «Оце дав Я вам усю ярину, що розсіває насіння, що на всій землі, і кожне дерево, що на ньому плід деревний, що воно розсіває насіння, — нехай буде на їжу *це* вам! І земній усій звірині і всьому птаству небесному, і кожному, що плазує по землі, що душа в ньому жива, — уся зелень яринна на їжу *для них*». І сталося так.

І побачив Бог усе, що вчинив. І ото, — вельми добре *воно*! І був вечір, і був ранок, — день шостий.

І були скінчені небо й земля, і все воїнство їхнє.

І скінчив Бог дня сьомого працю Свою, яку Він чинив. І Він відпочив у дні сьомім від усієї праці Своєї, яку був чинив».

Ім'я чоловіка було Адам, а жінки — Єва. Господь створив їх вродливими й щасливими. Вони дуже любили свого Творця, і Бог любив їх.

Господь віддав їм усю створену твар, щоб вони піклувалися про неї. Потім «…насадив Господь Бог рай ув Едені на сході, і там осадив людину, що її Він створив. І взяв Господь Бог людину, і в еденському раї вмістив був її, щоб порала його та його доглядала».

Адам і Єва постійно перебували у спілкуванні зі своїм Творцем. На малюнку ви бачите, що їхні очі звернені до Бога — вони щасливі.

1 М. 1:26–2:15

---

* *Чому Бог сказав: «Створімо»? Тому що Бог — єдиний у трьох іпостасях: Бог Отець, Бог Син та Бог Дух Святий. Тому у першій книзі Мойсеєвій, при створенні людини, Бог говорить у множині: «Створімо».*

ВИГНАННЯ АДАМА І ЄВИ З РАЮ

Але одного разу Адам та Єва виявили непослух Богові. Через це Бог був вимушений вигнати їх з раю. А сталося це так. Господь дозволив їм їсти плоди від усіх дерев раю, окрім плодів від дерева, яке звалося деревом пізнання добра й зла. Бог сказав, що в разі порушення цієї заповіді вони помруть.

Але сатана — ворог Бога й людей — вирішив згубити Адама та Єву. Якось він підійшов до Єви у вигляді змія і сказав: «Чи Бог наказав: «Не їжте з усякого дерева раю?» І відповіла жінка змієві: «З плодів дерева раю ми можемо їсти, але з плодів дерева, що в середині раю, — Бог сказав: «Не їжте із нього, і не доторкайтесь до нього, — щоб вам не померти».

Тоді змій, бажаючи посіяти сумнів у серці Єви щодо щирості Божої любові, почав обманювати її, говорячи: «Умерти — не вмрете! Бо відає Бог, що дня того, коли будете з нього ви їсти, ваші очі розкриються, і станете ви, немов Боги, знаючі добро й зло».

Коли Єва після слів змія подивилася на дерево, воно видалось їй гарним для їжі, принадним для очей і бажаним, тому що давало знання. Вона зірвала з дерева плід і з'їла його, і дала також покуштувати чоловікові своєму, Адамові. І сказав Бог Адамові: «За те, що ти послухав голосу жінки своєї та їв з того дерева, що Я наказав був тобі, говорячи: «Від нього не їж», — проклята через тебе земля! Ти в скорботі будеш їсти від неї всі дні свого життя... У поті свого лиця ти їстимеш хліб, аж поки не вернешся в землю, бо з неї ти взятий. Бо ти порох, — і до пороху вернешся».

Господь вигнав Адама та Єву з чудового саду, і вони не змогли більше повернутися туди. Тому вони такі сумні на цьому малюнку.

1 М. 3:1–23

Doré

КАЇН ТА АВЕЛЬ

Щі два юнаки — діти Адама і Єви. Один з них, Авель, випасав вівці, а брат його, Каїн, був землеробом.
Одного разу Каїн приніс від плодів землі дарунок Господу. І Авель також приніс від первородних овець своїх та від лою їхнього. І зглянувся Господь на Авеля і на дарунок його, а на Каїна і на дарунок його не зглянувся. Каїн дуже розгнівався, і сум огорнув обличчя його. Тоді сказав Господь Каїнові: «Чого ти розгнівався, і чого похилилось обличчя твоє? Отож, коли ти добре робитимеш, то підіймеш *обличчя своє*, а коли недобре, то в дверях гріх підстерігає. І до тебе його пожадання, а ти мусиш над ним панувати».

Однак Каїн не зміг здолати свій гріх і надалі продовжував заздрити братові. Одного дня, коли обоє братів були у полі, Каїн напав на Авеля і вбив його. І пролилася на землю кров першої вбитої людини.

Господь покарав Каїна за гріх і зробив його вигнанцем та неприкаяним на землі.

1 М. 4:2–12

W. CRANE

ПОТОП. НОЙ БУДУЄ КОВЧЕГ

Минуло багато сторіч, і на землі з'явилося дуже багато людей — нащадків Адама і Єви. Спочатку більшість із них пам'ятали про Бога і служили Йому, але з часом усе більше вони чинити не по волі Божій. Лише один чоловік, якого звали Ной, залишався вірним своєму Творцю. Апостол Петро назвав Ноя «проповідником праведности» (2 Петр. 2:5). Дух Божий сповнював серце Ноя. Він дуже любив Бога.

Господь побачив, що завелика розпуста поміж людей на землі, і що думки та наміри їхніх сердець увесь час були сповнені злом і нечестям; кожен спотворив свій шлях на землі. Тоді Бог сказав: «Зітру Я людину, яку Я створив, з поверхні землі, — від людини аж до скотини, аж до плазунів, і аж до птаства небесного. Бо жалкую, що їх Я вчинив».

Але Ной отримав благодать перед лицем Господа. Бог звернувся до нього і сказав: «Прийшов кінець кожному тілу перед лицем Моїм, бо наповнилась земля насильством від них. І ось Я винищу їх із землі.

Зроби собі ковчега з дерева ґофер. З перегородками зробиш ковчега, і смолою осмолиш його ізсередини та ізнадвору…

А Я ось наведу потоп, воду на землю, щоб з-під неба винищити кожне тіло, що в ньому дух життя. Помре все, що на землі!

І складу Я заповіта Свого з тобою, і ввійдеш до ковчегу ти, і сини твої, і жінка твоя, і жінки твоїх синів із тобою». Почувши таке повеління Боже, Ной почав будувати ковчег. (Ковчег — це великий корабель). Він часто говорив оточуючим людям, що незабаром розпочнеться потоп і знищить увесь світ, закликав їх покаятися у гріхах своїх та навернутися до Бога. Але ніхто не хотів слухати Ноя.

1 М. 6:7–18

ПОЧАТОК ПОТОПУ НА ЗЕМЛІ

Довгий час будувався ковчег, і коли Ной виконав усі повеління Божі, і ковчег був готовий, то Господь сказав йому: «Увійди ти й увесь дім твій до ковчегу, бо Я бачив тебе праведним перед лицем Своїм в оцім роді. Із усякої чистої худоби візьмеш собі по семеро, самця та самицю її, а з худоби нечистої — двоє: самця та самицю її. Також із птаства небесного по семеро, самця та самицю, щоб насіння сховати живим на поверхні всієї землі. Ось-бо по семи днях Я литиму на землю дощ сорок день і сорок ночей, — і всяку істоту, яку Я вчинив, зітру з-над поверхні землі!»

Ной зробив так, як Господь звелів йому. Він увійшов до ковчегу разом із дружиною, синами та їхніми дружинами; туди ж Ной узяв по сім пар чистих та по дві пари нечистих тварин. Коли всі ввійшли, Сам Господь причинив за ними двері ковчегу.

Через сім днів розпочався потоп і не припинявся сорок днів та сорок ночей. Вода все прибувала і підняла ковчег так, що він плавав на її поверхні. Повінь була такою сильною, що зникли усі високі гори, і все, що мало дихання життя, загинуло на землі. «І винищив *Бог* усяку істоту на поверхні землі, від людини аж до скотини, аж до плазуна, і аж до птаства небесного, — вони стерлись з землі. І зостався тільки Ной та те, що з ним у ковчезі *було*».

1 М. 7:1–23

КІНЕЦЬ ПОТОПУ

Через сто п'ятдесят днів закінчилась повінь, і вода стала поступово спадати. Ковчег Ноя зупинився на горі Арарат. Через сорок днів Ной відчинив вікно ковчегу і випустив крука, щоб довідатись, чи зникла вода. Крук, вилетівши, відлітав та повертався доти, поки земля не просохла.

Потім Ной випустив голуба. Але голуб не знайшов місця спокою для ніг своїх і повернувся до ковчегу, оскільки вода була ще на поверхні усієї землі. Через сім днів Ной знову випустив голуба з ковчегу. Увечері голуб повернувся до нього, тримаючи у дзьобі свіжий лист із оливи. Так Ной дізнався, що вода зійшла з поверхні землі.

Ной зачекав ще сім днів і потім знову випустив голуба, і той голуб вже не повернувся до нього. Тоді Ной відчинив ляду ковчегу і побачив, що поверхня землі висохла.

Бог сказав Ною: «Вийди з ковчегу ти, а з тобою жінка твоя, і сини твої, і невістки твої. Кожну звірину, що з тобою вона, від кожного тіла з-посеред птаства, і з-посеред скотини, і з-посеред усіх плазунів, що плазують по землі, повиводь із собою. І хай рояться вони на землі, і нехай на землі вони плодяться та розмножуються…»

1 М. 8:1–17

D. STEMLER

ВЕСЕЛКА ЯК ЗНАК ЗАПОВІТУ МІЖ БОГОМ ТА ЛЮДИНОЮ

І вийшов Ной з усією своєю родиною із ковчегу. Також усі тварини і птахи вийшли з ковчегу.

Ной склав із каміння жертовник. Потім він узяв із кожної чистої худоби і кожного птаха і приніс у жертву Богові. Господу сподобалася ця жертва, і Він сказав: «Я вже більше не буду землі проклинати за людину, бо нахил людського серця лихий від віку його молодого. І вже більше не вбиватиму всього живого, як то Я вчинив був. Надалі, по всі дні землі, сівба та жнива, і холоднеча та спека, і літо й зима, і день та ніч — не припиняться!»

Бог благословив Ноя та синів його і сказав: «…Ось Свого заповіта укладаю Я з вами та з вашим потомством по вас… жодне тіло не буде вже знищене водою потопу, і більш не буде потопу, щоб землю нищити… Я веселку Свою дав у хмарі, і стане вона за знака заповіту між Мною та між землею. І станеться, коли над землею Я хмару захмарю, то буде виднітися в хмарі веселка. І згадаю про Свого заповіта, що між Мною й між вами, і між кожною живою душею в кожному тілі. І більш не буде вода для потопу, щоб вигубляти кожне тіло… Це знак заповіту, що Я встановив поміж Мною й поміж кожним тілом, що воно на землі».

1 М. 8:18–22; 9:8–17

ВАВИЛОНСЬКА ВЕЖА

У синів Ноя було багато дітей, і від них знов пішли усі народи на землі. Та незабаром виявилося, що люди після потопу були не кращі, ніж до потопу. Тоді на всій землі була одна мова для спілкування людей поміж собою.

І от усі жителі землі зібралися разом і сказали один одному: «Тож місто збудуймо собі, та башту, а вершина її аж до неба. І вчинімо для себе ймення, щоб ми не розпорошилися по поверхні всієї землі». З погордою і бажанням прославити себе люди ревно занялися будівництвом. Але не гідно було це перед Господом. Він подивився на місто та на вежу, яку вони будували, і промовив: «Один це народ, і мова одна для всіх них… Не буде тепер нічого для них неможливого, що вони замишляли чинити. Тож зійдімо, і змішаймо там їхні мови, щоб не розуміли вони мови один одного». (Ви пам'ятаєте, що раніше Бог також сказав у множині: «Створімо людину…»).

Господь змішав мови людей так, що вони не розуміли одне одного і не могли продовжувати будівництво вежі. Ось чому те місце стало зватися Вавилон, тобто «змішання». А потім Бог розсіяв людей з Вавилону по всій землі.

1 М. 11:1–9

АВРААМ

На цьому малюнку зображено визначну людину — Аврама. Пізніше Бог назве його Авраамом, що у перекладі означає: «батько багатьох народів». Авраам дуже любив Господа, був відданим Йому і слухняним. Сам Бог назвав його Своїм другом. Господь і нам говорить у Святому Писанні: «Ви друзі Мої, якщо чините все, що Я вам заповідую».

Одного разу Господь сказав Авраамові: «Вийди зі своєї землі, і від родини своєї, і з дому батька свого до Краю, який Я тобі покажу. І народом великим тебе Я вчиню, і поблагословлю Я тебе, і звеличу ймення твоє, — і будеш ти благословенням.

І поблагословлю, хто тебе благословить, хто ж тебе проклинає, того прокляну. І благословляться в тобі всі племена землі!»

Авраам учинив так, як наказав йому Господь. Він узяв із собою Сару — дружину свою, Лота — сина брата свого, усе майно, яке було у них, та всіх людей, котрих мали на батьківщині, у Харані, і вийшли, щоб іти у вказану Господом землю Ханаанську. Йдучи своїм шляхом, вони прийшли до місця, яке звалося «діброва Мамре». Там Господь явився Авраамові і сказав: «Я дам оцей Край потомству твоєму».

1 М. 12:1–7; Ів. 15:14

АВРААМ І ЛОТ

Авраам і всі, хто був з ним, йшли по Ханаанській землі, яку вказав їм Господь, поки не прийшли до околиць Бет-Елу (Вефілу) і не зупинилися там.

Авраам був дуже багатий. Він мав золото, срібло й чимало різної худоби. У його племінника Лота також було багато наметів, малої та великої худоби. З часом їм стало тісно жити разом, оскільки у обох було забагато майна. Незабаром розпочалася суперечка між їхніми пастухами. І тоді Авраам сказав Лоту: «Нехай сварки не буде між мною та між тобою, і поміж пастухами моїми та поміж пастухами твоїми, бо близька ми рідня. Хіба не ввесь Край перед обличчям твоїм? Відділися від мене! Коли підеш ліворуч, — то я піду праворуч, а як ти праворуч, — то піду я ліворуч».

Лот почав оглядати землю навкруги. Він помітив, що околиця Йордану дуже родюча й добре зрошується водою. Він обрав собі це місце, відокремившись від Авраама, і розкинув свої намети аж до міста Содома. Жителі цього міста були дуже злими та грішними перед Господом. Однак Лот спокусився чудовими ланами і гарними пасовиськами для своєї худоби й розпочав жити серед нечестивого люду. За це його спіткало велике лихо.

Авраам же зупинився біля діброви Мамре і збудував там жертовника Господу.

1 М. 13:1–18

ОБІТНИЦЯ БОЖА АВРААМОВІ

Господь сказав Аврааму після того, як Лот відокремився від нього: «Зведи очі свої, та поглянь із місця, де ти, на північ, і на південь, і на схід, і на захід, бо всю цю землю, яку бачиш, Я її дам навіки тобі та потомству твоєму. І вчиню Я потомство твоє, як той порох землі, так, що коли хто потрапить злічити порох земний, то теж і потомство твоє перелічене буде».

Через деякий час Бог знову у видінні сказав Аврааму: «…Я тобі щит, нагорода твоя вельми велика». Але Авраам, зажурений, що вже старий, а дітей в нього все ще нема, сказав Господу: «Господи, Господи, — що даси Ти мені, коли я бездітний ходжу, а керівник мого господарства… — спадкоємець мені». На це Господь відповів йому: «Він не буде спадкоємець тобі, але той, хто вийде з твойого нутра, — він буде спадкоємець тобі». Потім Він вивів надвір Авраама і сказав йому: «Подивися на небо, та зорі злічи, коли тільки потрапиш ти їх полічити… Таким буде потомство твоє!»

І сказав Бог Аврааму: «Сара, жінка твоя, нехай свого ймення не кличе *вже*: Сара, бо ім'я їй: Сарра. І поблагословлю Я її… з неї дам сина тобі».

Авраам повірив Господу, і Творець залічив це йому за праведність.

1 М. 13:14–16; 15:1–6; 17:15–16

ТРИ ПОСЛАНЦІ БОЖІ У АВРААМА

Якось Авраам сидів під час полуденної спеки біля входу до свого намету. Раптом він побачив трьох людей, що стояли навпроти нього. Авраам, побачивши подорожніх, прийняв їх і приготував їм частування. Коли вони скінчили обідати, один з них сказав Аврааму: «Я напевно вернуся до тебе за рік цього самого часу. І ось буде син у Сарри, жінки твоєї…» Сарра почула ці слова і розсміялася у душі своїй, промовивши: «Коли я зів'яла, то *як* станеться розкіш мені?»

Але Господь звернувся до Авраама зі словами: «Чого то сміялася Сарра?.. Чи для Господа є річ занадто трудна? На означений час Я вернуся до тебе за рік цього самого часу, — Сарра ж *тоді* матиме сина».

У призначений час Господь виконав своє обіцяння, оскільки Він завжди вірний Своїм обітницям, і немає для Нього нічого неможливого!

1 М. 18:1–19; 21:1–3

ЗАГИБЕЛЬ МІСТ СОДОМА ТА ГОМОРРИ

Чотири міста: Содом, Гоморра, Адма та Севоїм були знищені вогнем з неба та стерті з лиця землі. Гнів Господній був викликаний нечестям та жахливими гріхами жителів цих міст. Бог попередив Авраама, що Содом буде знищений. Авраам молився за це грішне місто, і Господь обіцяв йому, що не знищить Содом, якщо там знайдеться хоча б десять праведників. Але їх там не вдалося відшукати.

І ось що трапилося. У Содомі жив Лот, праведна людина, зі своєю жінкою й двома дочками. Бог послав у це місто двох Ангелів у людській подобі. Було це увечері. Гостинний Лот прийняв їх у своєму домі, не відаючи, що це — Ангели.

«Ще вони не полягали, а люди того міста, люди Содому — від малого аж до старого, увесь народ звідусюди оточили той дім. І вони закричали до Лота, і сказали йому: «Де ті мужі, що ночі цієї до тебе прийшли? Виведи їх до нас, — щоб нам їх пізнати!» І Лот вийшов до входу до них, а двері замкнув за собою, і сказав: «Браття мої, — не чиніть лихого!.. Мужам оцим не робіть нічого, бо на те вони прийшли під тінь даху мого». А вони закричали: «Іди *собі* геть!» І сказали: «Цей один був прийшов, щоб пожити чужинцем, а він став *тут* суддею! Тепер ми зло гірше тобі заподієм, ніж їм!» І сильно вони налягали на мужа, на Лота, і підійшли, щоб висадити двері. Тоді вистромили свою руку ті мужі (ангели), і впровадили Лота до себе до дому, а двері замкнули. А людей, що при вході до дому *зібрались*, вони вдарили сліпотою, — від малого аж до великого». І сказали ті мужі до Лота: «...Ми знищимо це місце, бо збільшився їхній крик перед Господом...» Потім взяли за руку його, і дружину його, і обох дочок його, і вивели, і поставили поза містом... І один з них сказав: «...Не оглядайся позад себе ...Ховайся на гору, щоб тобі не загинути».

Сонце зійшло над землю, і Лот прийшов до Цоару. І наслав Господь на Содом і Гоморру дощ із сірки й вогонь від Господа з неба. І зруйнував ті міста, і всю околицю ту, і всіх мешканців міст отих, і всю рослинність землі. Дружина ж Лотова озирнулася і стала соляним стовпом.

Припускають, що ці знищені міста знаходилися у південній частині Мертвого моря. Вираз «содом та гомора» використовується і сьогодні для визначення розпусти. Сюди входить і той гріх, за який Бог так сильно розгнівався на людей, і який в останні часи все більше шириться по землі.

1 М. 19

АВРААМ ПРИНОСИТЬ У ЖЕРТВУ ІСАКА

Пройшов рік відтоді, як Авраама відвідали три посланці Божі, і Сарра народила сина. Авраам назвав його Ісаком. Коли Ісак підріс, то Господь вирішив випробувати віру Авраама та його любов до Себе. Бог звернувся до нього зі словами: «Візьми свого сина, свого одинака, що його полюбив ти, Ісака, та й піди собі до краю Морія, і принеси там його в цілопалення на одній із тих гір, що про неї скажу тобі».

Серце Авраама стискалося від болю і жалю, але він любив Господа понад усе і не міг перечити Творцеві. Він нарубав хмизу, поклав його на осла, узяв із собою двох слуг та Ісака і пішов у вказане Господом місце.

Ісак, не відаючи, кого саме Авраам мусить принести у жертву, запитав у нього: «Батьку мій!.. Ось огонь та дрова, а де ж ягня на цілопалення?» Авраам відповів йому: «Бог нагледить ягня Собі на цілопалення, сину мій!»

Коли вони прийшли до вказаного місця, Авраам наказав слугам чекати їх унизу, а сам із сином піднявся на гору і зробив жертовника; він розклав дрова, зв’язав Ісака і поклав його на жертовник. Але раптом Ангел Божий озвався до нього з неба: «Аврааме, Аврааме!.. Не витягай своєї руки до хлопця, і нічого йому не чини, бо тепер Я довідався, що ти богобійний, і не пожалів для Мене сина свого, одинака свого… Благословляючи, Я поблагословлю тебе…»

1 М. 22:1–18

РЕВЕКА

Минув час, Авраам дуже постарів, а син його Ісак став дорослим юнаком. Якось Авраам покликав до себе вірного слугу і звелів йому вирушити на свою батьківщину, у Месопотамію, і привести звідти дружину для Ісака. І пішов слуга до Месопотамії, до міста Нахора, де жив брат Авраама.

І коли він прийшов туди, то став молитися, щоб Господь послав йому назустріч дівчину, призначену Ісакові. «Господи, Боже пана мого Авраама, — подай же сьогодні мені *це*, і милість вчини з паном моїм Авраамом! Ось я стою над водним джерелом, а дочки мешканців міста виходять воду брати. І станеться, що дівчина, до якої скажу: Нахили-но глека свого, я нап'юся, — а вона відповість: Пий, і так само верблюди твої я понапуваю, — її Ти призначив для раба Свого, для Ісака. І з цього пізнаю, що Ти милість учинив з моїм паном».

Ледве він скінчив молитися, як з'явилася біля джерела чарівна дівчина, яку звали Ревека. Вона наповнила водою свій глек і пішла додому. Слуга Авраамів підбіг до неї і промовив: «Дай-но напитись води з твого глека!» Дівчина відповіла: «Напийся, мій пане!» А коли вона напоїла слугу, то сказала: «Також для верблюдів твоїх наберу я води, аж поки вони не нап'ються». Вражений слуга мовчки дивився, як вона набирала воду для його верблюдів. А потім він спитав її: «Чия ти дочка? Скажи ж мені, чи в домі батька твойого є місце для нас ночувати?» Ревека відповіла, що вона — дочка Бетуїла, сина Нахора, брата Авраама. Почувши це, слуга вклонився Господеві і прославив Його за те, що Він привів його до дому брата Авраама.

Слуга прийшов у дім Бетуїла і розповів усім присутнім про те, як Авраам послав його на свою батьківщину, до родичів, щоб привести дружину для його сина, Ісака.

Батьки покликали свою дочку і спитали її: «Чи ти підеш з оцим чоловіком?» Ревека погодилась. Уся родина її також погодилась, і вони відпустили її з благословенням, бо знали, у цьому є воля Божа.

1 М. 24:1–60

O. Stemler

ІСАК ТА РЕВЕКА

Ревека та слуга Авраамів довго їхали на верблюдах і, нарешті, прибули до країни, де на них чекав Ісак.

Якось увечері Ісак вийшов у поле. Раптом побачив він караван верблюдів, що наближався до нього. На одному з верблюдів їхала його наречена. Він ніколи раніше не бачив Ревеки, а Ревека також не бачила Ісака. Але Ісак та Ревека одразу ж покохали один одного і були дуже щасливі, оскільки Сам Бог обрав їх один для одного.

Господь дарував їм двох синів, яких звали Ісав та Яків. Вони були близнюками, але Ісав народився раніше від Якова, і тому вважався первородним.

Діти виросли. «І став Ісав чоловіком, що знався на вловах, чоловіком поля, а Яків — чоловіком мирним, що в наметах сидів. І полюбив Ісак Ісава, бо здобич мисливська його йому смакувала, а Ревека любила Якова».

1 М. 24:63–67; 25:24–28

ЯКІВ ОТРИМУЄ БЛАГОСЛОВЕННЯ БАТЬКА

Зістарівшись, Ісак почав втрачати зір. Перед смертю він побажав благословити свого сина — первістка Ісава, і, покликавши його до себе, наказав йому приготувати улюблену їжу із дичини. Після цього батько пообіцяв благословити сина.

Коли Ревека почула це, то покликала до себе Якова і переповіла йому все. Вона дуже хотіла, щоб саме Яків отримав батьківське благословення. Тому вона вирішила обдурити Ісака, щоб домогтися своєї мети. На той час Ісав пішов у поле вполювати якусь дичину. Ревека наказала Якову принести з отари двох козенят і приготувала з них улюблену страву Ісака. Потім вона узяла багатий одяг Ісава й надягла його на Якова. Оскільки тіло Ісава було вкрите волоссям, то вона обклала руки та шию Якова шкірою козеняти на той випадок, якщо напівсліпий батько забажає обмацати його.

Яків узяв приготовану їжу, підійшов до батька і запропонував йому покуштувати її. Батько відповів синові: «Підійди-но, і нехай я обмацаю тебе, сину мій, чи ти — це син мій Ісав, чи ні».

Яків підійшов до нього. Ісак обмацав його і сказав: «Голос — голос Яковів, а руки — руки Ісавові». І не впізнав Ісак Якова, бо обкладені шкірою козеняти руки Якова були схожі на руки брата його, Ісава. Після цього батько звелів подати йому їжу. Поївши, Ісак промовив над Яковом слова благословення.

Ось таким облудним шляхом Яків отримав благословення, яке мало належати Ісавові. За це Ісав зненавидів брата свого і пообіцяв убити його.

1 М. 27:1–41

СОН ЯКОВА

Ревека почула, що Ісав загрожує вбити її улюбленого Якова. Вона розповіла йому про це й порадила втекти до її брата Лавана у Месопотамію та пожити у нього деякий час, доки не втихне гнів Ісава.

Ісак, прощаючись з Яковом, заповідав йому не обирати собі дружину з дочок ханаанських, серед яких вони жили, але одружитися у Месопотамії, на батьківщині його матері. Потім він благословив його, проказавши: «…Бог Всемогутній поблагословить тебе… І дасть тобі благословення Авраамове, тобі та потомству твоєму з тобою, щоб віддати тобі землю твого тимчасового замешкання, що Бог дав був її Авраамові». Яків вирушив до Месопотамії.

Подорож Якова тривала багато днів. Одного разу він зупинився ночувати просто неба і ліг, підклавши під голову камінь. І Бог дав йому побачити чарівний сон. Яків бачив уві сні сходи, що сягали аж до неба, і Ангели Божі піднімалися й спускалися ними. Потім Господь звернувся до нього й сказав: «Я Господь, Бог Авраама, батька твого, і Бог Ісака. Земля, на якій ти лежиш, — Я дам її тобі та нащадкам твоїм… І ось Я з тобою, і буду тебе пильнувати скрізь, куди підеш».

І прокинувся Яків зі сну, і сказав: «Дійсно, Господь пробуває на цьому місці, *а того* я й не знав!» Потому він узяв камінь, що вночі був у нього під головою, поставив його як пам'ятник і дав обітницю Господу, мовивши: «Коли Бог буде зо мною, і буде мене пильнувати на цій дорозі, якою ходжу, і дасть мені хліба їсти та одежу вдягнутись, і я з миром вернуся до дому батька свого, то Господь буде мені Богом, і цей камінь, що я поставив за пам'ятника, буде домом Божим. І зо всього, що даси Ти мені… — дам десятину Тобі!»

1 М. 27:41–46; 28:1–22

Doré

ЗУСТРІЧ ЯКОВА ТА РАХІЛІ

Продовжуючи свій довгий шлях до Месопотамії, Яків нарешті прийшов до того місця, де було багато чудових пасовиськ. Він зупинився біля криниці, цямрина якої була прикрита великим каменем. Коли отари під наглядом кількох пастухів збиралися до водопою, то цей камінь відкочували від цямрини, а потім знов прикривали її.

Яків звернувся до пастухів, що знаходились неподалік: «Чи ви знаєте Лавана, сина Нахорового?» Вони відповіли: «Знаємо… А ось Рахіль, дочка його, приходить з отарою». Рахіль наближалася до криниці з отарою овець свого батька, яких вона випасала.

Коли Яків побачив Рахіль, то відкотив камінь від цямрини й напоїв вівці свого дядька Лавана. Потім він поцілував Рахіль й від радощів заплакав, сказавши, що він її двоюрідний брат. Почувши про це, Рахіль мерщій побігла додому й розповіла все батькові. А Лаван, почувши про Якова, вибіг до нього назустріч, обійняв його, поцілував і повів до свого дому.

Яків зостався жити у свого дядька й слугував у нього пастухом. Він став служити Лаванові, щоб той дозволив йому оженитися на Рахілі; і служив йому сім років. Ці роки промайнули для Якова непомітно, так щиро кохав він Рахіль. Лаван віддав Якову обох своїх дочок — Лію та Рахіль. У ті далекі часи можна було одружуватися із родичкою й мати кількох дружин. Тут, у Месопотамії, у Якова народилося аж одинадцять синів і одна дочка, а пізніше, в Ханаані, ще один син.

Яків став заможною людиною. Він жив у наметах зі своїми дружинами та дітьми. У нього було багато рабів і рабинь, а також чимало худоби: овець, верблюдів та ослів.

1 М. 29:1–28

ЯКІВ «БОРЕТЬСЯ» З БОГОМ

Господь наказав Якову, аби він повернувся до себе на батьківщину. Яків узяв своїх дружин та дітей, зібрав усе своє майно й вирушив до країни Ханаанської. Не відаючи, чи згас гнів Ісава на нього, Яків вирішив послати йому багато дарунків, щоб умилостивити його.

Прямуючи до землі батьків, Яків опинився якось перед потоком. Яків перевів усіх родичів через нього, а сам лишився на протилежному боці. Там зустрівся йому Хтось і боровся з ним до світання й пошкодив йому суглоб стегна. На світанку Той сказав Якову: «Пусти Мене, бо зійшла досвітня зоря». Яків же відказав: «Не пущу Тебе, коли не поблагословиш мене». Той запитав: «Як твоє ймення?» Він відповів: «Яків». Той, Хто боровся з ним, сказав: «Не Яків буде називатися вже ймення твоє, але Ізраїль, бо ти боровся з Богом та з людьми, — і подужав».

Також і Яків запитав: «Скажи ж Ім’я Своє». Але відповідь була: «Пощо питаєш про Ймення Моє?» І благословив Він Якова.

1 М. 32:13–30

Schnorr.

ПРИМИРЕННЯ ЯКОВА ТА ІСАВА

Наближаючись до землі Ханаанської, Яків побачив, що назустріч йому йде Ісав, а з ним — чотириста чоловік. Тоді він вийшов наперед і, підходячи до брата, вклонився йому сім разів аж до землі. Ісав підбіг до нього, обійняв його, і вони обидва заплакали. А потім підійшли дружини, діти й служниці й вклонилися Ісавові.

Ісав запитав Якова: «Для чого стільки дарунків, що ти послав їх мені?» Яків відповів: «Щоб знайти милість в очах мого пана». Ісав дружньо промовив: «Я маю багато, мій брате, — твоє нехай буде тобі». На це Яків заперечив йому: «Ні ж бо! Коли я знайшов милість в очах твоїх, то візьми дарунка мого з моєї руки… Візьми ж благословення моє, що припроваджене тобі, бо Бог був милостивий до мене, та й маю я все». І умовив він Ісава прийняти його дари».

Після цього Ісав повернувся до себе додому, а Яків оселився на землі Ханаанській біля міста Сихем. Він купив частину поля і поставив на ньому намет. Він влаштував там жертовник і призвав ім'я Господа Бога.

Так виповнився дивовижний сон, який бачив він колись, в тяжкі часи своєї самотності й нелегких мандрівок. Господь послав йому все, що обіцяв, і Яків не забув віддати хвалу Господеві за все.

1 М. 33:1–20

ЙОСИП — УЛЮБЛЕНИЙ СИН ЯКОВА

Ї от Яків знов оселився на землі Ханаанській. Тут у Рахілі народився ще один син, Веніямин. Таким чином, у Якова було вже дванадцять синів і одна дочка: Рувим, Симеон, Левій, Юда, Дан, Нефталим, Гад, Асир, Іссахар, Завулон, Діна, Йосип та наймолодший, Веніямин. Та найбільше з усіх своїх синів Яків любив Йосипа, «тому що він був сином старості його».

«Йосип, віку сімнадцяти літ, пас, як юнак, отару з братами своїми… І доносив недобрі звістки про них до їхнього батька». Одного разу Яків подарував Йосипові дуже красиве барвисте вбрання. «І бачили його браття, що їх батько полюбив його над усіх братів його, — і зненавиділи його, і не могли говорити з ним спокійно».

Йосип не міг передбачити, до чого призведе зненависть та заздрість його братів. Йосип любив Бога і жив за заповідями Його. А тому усі нещастя й скорботи, що випадуть в майбутньому на його долю, стануть, за допомогою Божою, благословенням для нього та його сім'ї.

1 М. 37:1–4

WM.E.PAY

СНИ ЙОСИПА

«І снився був Йосипові сон, і він розповів своїм браттям, а вони ще збільшили ненависть до нього.

І сказав він до них: «Послухайте-но про той сон, що снився мені. А ото ми в'яжемо снопи серед поля, і ось мій сніп зачав уставати, та й став. І ось оточують ваші снопи, — та й вклоняються снопові моєму».

І сказали йому його браття: «Чи справді ти будеш царювати над нами, чи теж справді ти будеш панувати над нами?» І вони збільшили ненависть до нього через сни його та через слова його.

І снився йому ще сон інший, і він оповів його братам своїм, та й сказав: «Оце снився мені ще сон, — і ось сонце та місяць та одинадцять зір вклоняються мені».

І він розповів *це* батькові своєму та браттям своїм. І докорив йому батько його, та й промовив до нього: «Що то за сон, що снився тобі? Чи справді прийдемо ми, я, та мати твоя, та брати твої, щоб уклонитися тобі до землі?»

І заздрили йому брати його, а батько його запам'ятав ці слова».

Якось, коли брати Йосипа пасли скотину далеко від своєї оселі, Яків вирядив Йосипа відвідати їх, дізнатися про їхнє здоров'я й принести йому звістку від них. Йосип з радістю вирушив у путь.

Довго блукав він полем, аж поки знайшов своїх братів. Вони ж, побачивши його здалеку, злісно сказали один одному: «Ось іде той сновидець…»

І коли Йосип наближався до них у полі, вони радились між собою, щоб вбити його: «А тепер давайте вбиймо його, і вкиньмо його до однієї з ям, та й скажемо: Дикий звір з'їв його!» А потім зловтішно додали: «І побачимо, що буде з його снами».

1 М. 37:5–20

БРАТИ ПРОДАЮТЬ ЙОСИПА

Найстарший брат, Рувим, був милосерднiший вiд iнших братiв. Коли вiн почув про змову проти Йосипа, то вирiшив будь-якою цiною звiльнити його й повернути до батька. Тому Рувим став умовляти братiв не вбивати Йосипа, а лише вкинути його до ями. Брати послухались Рувима i, схопивши Йосипа, здерли з нього барвисту одiж, а самого кинули до рову.

Раптом вони помiтили караван купцiв, що везли товари iз Галааду до Єгипту. Тодi один iз братiв, Юда, запропонував продати Йосипа тим купцям. Усi погодилися, i коли караван проходив повз них, вони продали свого брата «за двадцять срiбнякiв».

Купцi повели Йосипа до Єгипту, а брати закололи козла й замастили його кров'ю вбрання Йосипа. Вони принесли це вбрання батьковi iз такими словами: «Оце ми знайшли. Пiзнай-но, чи це вбрання — твого сина воно, чи нi?» Якiв упiзнав його i в невимовному горi вигукнув: «Вбрання мого сина… Дикий звiр його з'їв… Справдi розшарпаний Йосип!» Невтiшно й гiрко оплакував вiн втрату улюбленого сина, не вiдаючи, що злi сини обдурили його.

Але вiд Всевидячого i Всемогутнього Бога нiщо не можна приховати. Вiн бачив заздрiсть в серцях братiв, яка довела їх до ненавистi, злочину та брехнi.

1 М. 37:21–35

Schnorr

ЙОСИП — УПРАВИТЕЛЬ У ДОМІ ЦАРЕДВОРЦЯ

Коли купці прийшли до Єгипту, то продали Йосипа у невільництво царедворцеві, начальнику охоронців фараона. Господь у всьому допомагав Йосипові, котрий завжди звертався до Нього. Тому Йосип і у неволі мав успіх у всіх ділах, які доводилось йому виконувати.

Його господар, на ім'я Потіфар, помітив, що Господь благословляє усі справи, які робить Йосип. Тому він ще більше полюбив Йосипа і призначив його управителем свого дому, довіривши його нагляду все, що мав. І заради Йосипа Бог благословив дім царедворця. Йосип мудро керував усім домом, і у його господаря не було ніяких турбот.

Йосип був привабливим юнаком. Сталося так, що дружина Потіфара закохалася в нього. Оскільки вона була поганкою і не знала Господа, то стала схиляти Йосипа до перелюбу. Але Йосип, який любив Бога, відмовився від її пропозицій і сказав: «Як же я вчиню це велике зло, і згрішу перед Богом?»

І коли дружина Потіфара зрозуміла, що Йосип ніколи не погодиться виконати її бажання, вона вирішила помститися йому. Вона набрехала своєму чоловікові і обмовила Йосипа: «До мене прийшов був оцей раб єврей, що ти його привів до нас, щоб забавлятися мною. І сталося, як підняла я свій голос і закричала, то він позоставив свою одежу при мені, та й утік надвір». Коли господар його почув слова дружини своєї, що вона оповідала йому, кажучи: «Отакі-то речі вчинив мені твій раб», то запалився гнівом; і взяв Йосипа господар його і віддав його до в'язниці, де були царські в'язні. І перебував він у в'язниці.

1 М. 39:1–20

O.A. Stemler

ЙОСИП У В'ЯЗНИЦІ

Але й у в'язниці Господь був завжди з Йосипом і допомагав йому. Бог прихилив серце начальника в'язниці до Йосипа, і той назначив його розпорядником над усіма в'язнями. Сам же начальник в'язниці ні в що не втручався, бо повністю довіряв Йосипові.

Йосип повністю покладався на Бога й чекав від Нього допомоги.

До в'язниці, де знаходився Йосип, кинули двох слуг царевих. Один з них був начальником чашників і прислужував цареві за столом, наливаючи у царську чашу вино. Інший був начальником пекарів. Завинивши перед царем, вони потрапили до в'язниці.

Якось їм наснилися сни, які вони не могли розтлумачити, відгадати. А Йосип і сказав їм: «Чи ж не в Бога відгадки? Розповіджте-но мені». Начальник чашників першим розповів свій сон. Йому приснився виноградний кущ, на якому було три гілки. А потім цей кущ розцвів, виросли й дозріли грона ягід. Він зібрав ці ягоди, вичавив із них сік у чашу фараона й подав її йому.

І Йосип відразу ж розгадав йому сон, сказавши: «Оце відгадка його: три виноградні галузки — це три дні. Ще за три дні підійме фараон твою голову, і верне тебе на твоє становище, і ти даси чашу фараона до руки його за першим звичаєм, як був ти чашником його». А потім начальник пекарів розповів йому свій сон. Снилося йому, що на голові у нього стояло три кошика з різним печивом. Аж ось птах дзьобав з горішнього кошика у нього над головою.

Вислухавши його, Йосип сказав: «Оце відгадка його: три коші — то три дні. Ще за три дні підійме фараон голову твою з тебе, і повісить тебе на дереві, — і птах поїсть тіло твоє з тебе».

Через три дні з ними сталося саме так, як передбачив їм Йосип.

1 М. 39:21–23; 40:1–22

ЙОСИП ВІДГАДУЄ СНИ ФАРАОНОВІ

Одного разу єгипетський фараон побачив дивний сон. Йому наснилося, що він стоїть біля річки. Раптом з річки вийшло семеро гладких корів й почали пастися в очереті. А за ними вийшло семеро худих корів. І ці худі корови з'їли гладких. Після цього фараон прокинувся. Знов заснувши, він побачив інший сон. На одному стеблі піднялося сім повних і гарних колосків. Та ось поруч з ними виросло сім висушених вітром й тонких колосків, які й проковтнули гарні колоски.

Прокинувшись, фараон дуже збентежився від цих снів. Він покликав усіх мудреців Єгипту й розповів їм про це. Але ніхто не міг розгадати сни фараона.

І тоді чашник сказав фараонові, що він знає одного молодого єврея, Йосипа, який у в'язниці відгадував йому і начальнику пекарів їхні сни, і все збулося, як він їм сказав. Фараон одразу ж послав за Йосипом, і коли його привели, він сказав йому: «Я чув про тебе таке: ти вислухуєш сон, щоб відгадати його». На це Йосип відповів: «Не я, — Бог дасть у відповідь мир фараонові». І фараон розповів йому обидва сни. Йосип відповів: «Що Бог робить, те Він звістив фараонові. Семеро корів добрих — то сім літ, і семеро колосків добрих — сім літ вони… А сім корів худих і бридких, що вийшли за ними, — сім літ вони, і сім колосків порожніх і спалених східнім вітром — то будуть сім літ голодних… Ось приходять сім літ, — великий достаток у всім краї єгипетськім. А по них настануть сім літ голодних, — і буде забутий увесь той достаток в єгипетській землі, і голод винищить край».

А далі Йосип порадив фараонові поставити над Єгиптом мудрого управителя, щоб він робив запаси зерна протягом семи років достатку.

1 М. 41:1–36

O. Stemler

ЙОСИП — УПРАВИТЕЛЬ УСЬОГО ЄГИПТУ

Фараон був дуже задоволений з того, як Йосип розгадав його сни. Він сказав своїм слугам: «Чи знайдеться чоловік, як оцей, що Дух Божий у нім?» А потім він звернувся до Йосипа зі словами: «Що Бог відкрив тобі це все, то немає такого розумного й мудрого, як ти. Ти будеш над домом моїм, а *слів* твоїх уст буде слухатися ввесь народ мій. Тільки троном я буду вищий від тебе».

І фараон зняв зі своєї руки перстень й прикрасив ним руку Йосипа. Він відзначив його золотим ланцюгом довкола шиї і вбрав його у дорогоцінні вісонні шати. Фараон звелів провезти Йосипа по усьому Єгипту на другій із своїх колісниць, сповіщаючи перед ним: «Вклоняйтеся!»

Так був звеличений Йосип. Одразу ж він розпочав виконувати свої обов’язки. Протягом семи років достатку він збирав у засіки запаси зерна, щоб тоді, коли настануть неврожайні роки, народ Єгипту не згинув від голоду.

1 М. 41:37–48

СІМ РОКІВ ГОЛОДУ

А через сім років по всій землі настав голод. З багатьох країн до Єгипту почали приходити люди, аби придбати хліб у Йосипа, бо він зробив великі накопичення зерна у всіх містах Єгипту.

Коли Яків довідався, що у Єгипті є хліб, він послав туди десятьох своїх синів купити хліба, лишивши при собі молодшого сина, Веніямина.

Йосип був начальником землі Єгипетської, і він продавав хліб усьому народові. Брати його підійшли й вклонилися йому до землі, просячи продати хліба і їм. Йосип упізнав своїх братів, але вони не впізнали його. З того часу, як вони продали свого брата, вони нічого не чули про нього й не знали, як він піднісся.

А Йосип вдав, що не впізнав їх, і сказав їм, що вони — вивідувачі, що прийшли розвідати про таємниці Єгипту. Брати казали, що вони люди чесні, діти одного батька, і їхній молодший брат лишився вдома. Та Йосип все ж наказав охороні взяти їх під варту. Третього дня він сказав братам: «Один брат ваш буде ув'язнений, …а ви йдіть, принесіть хліба *для заспокоєння* голоду ваших домів. А свого наймолодшого брата приведіть до мене, — і будуть потверджені ваші слова». Брати, почувши це, сказали один одному: «Справді, винні ми за нашого брата, бо ми бачили недолю душі його, коли він благав нас, а ми не послухали… Тому-то прийшло це нещастя на нас!» Вони не знали, що Йосип розуміє їхню мову, бо з ним був перекладач. А Йосип, почувши ці слова, вийшов до сусіднього помешкання і заплакав. Повернувшись, він наказав затримати лише одного з них, Симеона, а іншим наповнити мішки хлібом і відпустити їх додому.

1 М. 41:54–57; 42:1–25

ЙОСИП ВІДКРИВАЄТЬСЯ БРАТАМ

Коли брати Йосипа повернулися додому й розповіли про все батькові, то Яків рішуче відмовився відпустити до Єгипту наймолодшого сина, Веніямина, «останню втіху його старості».

Коли скінчився той хліб, що брати привезли з Єгипту, Яків знову став збирати їх у дорогу: «Верніться, купіть нам трохи їжі!» На це сини відповіли йому, що правитель Єгипетської землі наказав їм не з'являтися без молодшого брата. Довго ще Яків не бажав відпускати з ними Веніямина, але голод змусив його відіслати синів до Єгипту. Яків благословив їх в дорогу такими словами: «Бог Всемогутній нехай дасть вам милосердя перед лицем того мужа, і нехай він відпустить вам другого вашого брата й Веніямина…»

Отож, брати разом з Веніямином прийшли до Єгипту. Коли ж Йосип побачив Веніямина, то вийшов з кімнати й заплакав. А потім, вмивши лице, Йосип наказав слугам подати братам гарне частування. Брати знітились, не розуміючи, чому він виказує їм таку шану.

Нарешті Йосип вже не міг стримуватися. Він голосно заридав і сказав братам: «Я Йосип… Чи живий ще мій батько?.. Підійдіть же до мене!» І вони підійшли, а він проказав: «Я Йосип, ваш брат, якого ви продали були до Єгипту… А тепер не сумуйте, і нехай не буде жалю в ваших очах, що ви продали мене сюди, бо то Бог послав мене перед вами для виживлення…. І Він зробив мене батьком фараоновим і паном усього дому його, і володарем усього краю єгипетського. Поспішіть, і йдіть до батька мого, та й скажіть йому: Отак сказав син твій Йосип: Бог зробив мене володарем усього Єгипту. Зійди ж до мене, не гайся… І прогодую тебе, …бо голод *буде* ще п'ять років, щоб не збіднів ти, і дім твій, і все, що твоє».

Після цих слів Йосип упав на шию Веніяминові й заплакав. А потім він обіймав і цілував усіх братів. Він любив їх і щиро пробачив їм все зло, яке вони заподіяли йому.

1 М. 42:36–38; 43:1–34; 45:1–15

ЗУСТРІЧ ЙОСИПА З БАТЬКОМ

Коли ж фараон почув про те, що Йосипа відвідали брати, то наказав дати їм у дорогу їжі, одяг та ще й колісниці для них, їхніх дітей та для батька. Він запросив їх усіх приїхати до Єгипту.

Яків, почувши про те, що його улюблений син Йосип живий і він матиме змогу побачити його, зрадів серцем усім і сказав: «Ще живий Йосип, син мій! Піду та побачу його…» Після цього Бог сказав Якову уві сні: «Яків, Я — Бог, Бог батька твого; не бійся йти до Єгипту, бо там породжу від тебе народ великий. Я піду з тобою до Єгипту; і Я виведу тебе назад».

Зібрався Яків з усіма своїми дітьми, онуками та з усім своїм скарбом, та й вирушив до Єгипту. А Йосип запряг свою колісницю і виїхав назустріч їм. Побачивши свого батька, він кинувся йому на шию й довго плакав від щастя.

Коли ж фараон почув, що всі уже прибули, він покликав до себе Йосипа й сказав йому: «Ну от, батько твій та брати твої прибули до тебе. Єгипетський край — увесь перед тобою. У найліпшім місці цього краю осели батька та братів своїх».

І Йосип дав усім своїм рідним у володіння найкращу частину землі Єгипетської і постійно забезпечував їх хлібом та усім необхідним.

Яків не повернувся до землі Ханаанської, а лишився у Єгипті. Перед смертю він благословив двох синів Йосипа: Манасію та Єфрема, а потім і усіх своїх дванадцять синів. Як і заповідав Яків, сини віднесли його тіло до печери на полі Махпела, де вже були поховані Авраам та Сарра, Ісак та Ревека.

1 М. 45–50

РАБСТВО ІЗРАЇЛЬСЬКОГО НАРОДУ В ЄГИПТІ

Минуло безліч років. Помер Яків та всі його сини. Коли Яків боровся із Богом, Господь, благословивши його, дав йому нове ім'я — Ізраїль, яке в перекладі означає: «той, що боровся із Богом». Ось чому нащадки Якова до цього часу називаються ізраїльським народом, а також єврейським народом та народом Божим.

Після смерті Йосипа у Єгипті став царювати інший фараон, який не знав мудрого Йосипа та його добрих справ. Цей фараон побачив, що народ ізраїльський став дуже чисельним і сильнішим від народу єгипетського. Тоді він сказав своєму народу: «Станьмо ж мудріші за нього, щоб він не множився! Бо буде, коли нам трапиться війна, то прилучиться й він до ворогів наших, — і буде воювати проти нас, і вийде з цього краю».

І наказав фараон поставити над народом ізраїльським таких управителів, що виснажували б ізраїльтян непосильною працею. Та чим більше їх пригноблювали, тим більше вони умножувалися й тим більше підносилися, так що єгиптяни жахалися їх. Тому єгиптяни з іще більшою жорстокістю примушували ізраїльтян працювати, намагаючись зробити їхнє життя невимовно тяжким.

Але Бог бачив усе довге страждання народу, який покладав сподівання лише на Нього, і Він послав йому рятівника.

2 М. 1:6–14

НЕМОВЛЯ МОЙСЕЙ У КОШИКУ

І дізнався фараон, що народ ізраїльський не хиріє від непосильної праці, а все міцнішає. Тоді він наказав, щоб кожного новонародженого сина ізраїльтян кидали у річку.

У однієї ізраїльтянки народився син. Ця жінка знала, що лише Бог може врятувати її немовля, і тому вона з молитвою віддала його під опіку Божу. Три місяці переховувала вона свого сина, а коли вже була не в змозі далі таїтися, вона взяла кошик, обсмолила його, поклала в нього дитину, а потім віднесла в очерет на березі річки Нілу.

Сам Бог обрав його у поміч Своєму народові, і тому Він вселив у серце його матері тверду впевненість у тому, що Господь потурбується про нього. І послала вона свою дочку спостерігати за тим, що станеться із малюком.

2 М. 2:1–4

ДОЧКА ФАРАОНА ЗНАХОДИТЬ МОЙСЕЯ

Дочка фараона разом зі своїми служницями вийшла скупатись у річці. Раптом вона помітила між очерету кошик і почула дитячий плач. Вона наказала своїй рабині принести його.

Зазирнувши до кошика, дочка фараона побачила чудове немовля, яке гірко плакало. Вона змилосердилася над ним й вирішила узяти його до себе і всиновити.

Одразу ж підійшла до неї сестра хлопчика та й спитала, чи не хоче принцеса знайти годувальницю для нього. Дочка фараонова погодилась, і коли дівчинка привела свою матір, дочка фараона сказала їй: «На тобі цю дитину, та й годуй її для мене. А я дам тобі заплату». Матір з радістю взяла свого сина, дякуючи Господеві за те, що Він почув її молитви. Коли Мойсей підріс, мати привела його до дочки фараона, і він жив у її палаці як син.

І хоча Мойсей зростав у палаці фараона, він знав, що він — єврей. Коли ж Мойсей став зовсім дорослим, то вирішив подивитися, як живе його рідний народ. І він побачив, що той жорстоко пригнічується. Якось Мойсей помітив, як єгиптянин бив одного еврея. Він хотів захистити свого одноплемінника, та й убив єгиптянина, а його тіло сховав у пісок.

Наступного дня Мойсей спостеріг, як сварилися двоє євреїв. Він запитав у одного з них: «Нащо ти б'єш свого ближнього?» На що той відповів: «Хто тебе настановив за начальника та за суддю над нами? Чи ти думаєш убити мене, як ти вбив був єгиптянина?» Тоді Мойсей злякався й подумав: «Справді, та справа стала відома!» Коли ж фараонові розповіли про цю подію, він захотів убити Мойсея.

Мойсей утік від фараона у землю Мідіянську. Там він познайомився із священиком Їтром та з його сім'єю і залишився жити у них. Священик Їтор видав за Мойсея свою дочку Ціппору.

2 М. 2

ПАЛАЮЧИЙ ТЕРНОВИЙ КУЩ

Життя Мойсея різко змінилося. Перші сорок років свого життя він провів у Єгипті, виховувався у сім'ї фараона. Після цього, наступні сорок років, Мойсей був пастухом у Їтра, свого тестя.

Та ось помер цар єгипетський (тобто фараон). І стогнали сини Ізраїлеві від роботи і волали до Бога.

«А Мойсей пас отару тестя свого Їтра, жерця мідіянського. І провадив він цю отару за пустиню, і прийшов був до Божої гори, до Хориву. І явився йому Ангол Господній у полум'ї огняному з-посеред тернового куща. І побачив він, що та тернина горить огнем, але не згорає кущ. І сказав Мойсей: «Зійду-но, і побачу це велике видіння, — чому не згорає та тернина?»

І побачив Господь, що він зійшов подивитися. І кликнув до нього Бог з-посеред тієї тернини і сказав: «Мойсею, Мойсею!.. Не зближайся сюди! Здійми взуття своє з ніг своїх, бо те місце, на якому стоїш ти, — земля це свята!.. Я Бог батька твого, Бог Авраама, Бог Ісака й Бог Якова!» І сховав Мойсей обличчя своє, бо боявся споглянуть на Бога!

І промовив Господь: «Я справді бачив біду Свого народу, що в Єгипті, і почув його зойк перед його гнобителями, бо пізнав Я болі його. І Я зійшов, щоб визволити його з єгипетської руки, та щоб вивести його з цього краю до Краю доброго й широкого, до Краю, що тече молоком та медом… Ось зойк Ізраїлевих синів дійшов до Мене, і Я також побачив той утиск, що ним єгиптяни їх тиснуть. А тепер іди ж, і Я пошлю тебе до фараона, і виведи з Єгипту народ Мій, синів Ізраїлевих!»

Але Мойсей вагався. Він вважав себе не гідним такого великого призначення. Він сказав Богові: «Хто я, що піду до фараона, і що виведу з Єгипту синів Ізраїлевих?» На що Бог відповів йому: «Я буду з тобою!»

2 М. 3:1–22

МОЙСЕЙ ТА ААРОН ПЕРЕД ФАРАОНОМ

Коли Господь сказав Мойсею, що Він посилає його до фараона, щоб той відпустив народ Божий, то Мойсей відповів на це: «О Господи, — я не промовець ні від учора, ні від позавчора, …бо я тяжкоустий… Молю Тебе, Господи, — пошли *іншого*, кого маєш послати».

Тоді Господь вказав Мойсеєві на його брата Аарона і сказав: «Чи ж не Аарон твій брат, Левит? Я знаю, що він добре буде говорити… Я буду з устами твоїми й з устами його, і буду навчати вас, що маєте робити. І він буде говорити за тебе до народу. І станеться, — він буде тобі устами, а ти будеш йому *замість* Бога».

Після цього Мойсей та Аарон прийшли до фараона й сказали йому: «Так сказав Господь, Бог Ізраїлів: Відпусти народ Мій, — і нехай вони святкують Мені на пустині!» Але фараон відказав на це: «Хто Господь, що послухаюсь слова Його, щоб відпустити Ізраїля? Не знаю Господа, і також Ізраїля не відпущу!.. Чому ви, Мойсею та Аароне, відриваєте народ від його робіт? Ідіть до своїх діл!» І з того дня фараон став поводитися з ізраїльтянами із ще більшою жорстокістю і звелів наглядачам помножити роботу для них.

Чимало різних чудес здійснив Господь на очах фараона, але серце у того було жорстоким, і не хотів він відпустити народ Божий.

Десять жахливих покарань Господніх спіткало увесь народ єгипетський: вода у річці Нілі перетворилася на кров; жаби вкрили всю землю Єгипетську; чисельні рої мух заполонили увесь Єгипет; моровиця впала на худобу, людей та скотину вкрили виразки, з яких ішов гній; град, сарана й темрява по всій Єгипетській землі… Та все жорстокішим робилося серце фараона, хоча й сам страждав від покарань Божих. Однак народові ізраїльському він не дозволяв вийти з Єгипту. І тоді Мойсей та Аарон стали погрожувати йому останньою, десятою карою.

2 М. 4–10

КРОВ ПАСХАЛЬНОГО АГНЦЯ

Отож, серце фараона не стало лагіднішим, хоча він бачив усі великі чудеса і Божу кару. І сказав Мойсей: «Так сказав Господь! Коло півночі Я вийду посеред Єгипту. І помре кожен перворідний єгипетської землі від перворідного фараона, що сидить на своїм престолі, до перворідного невільниці, що за жорнами, і все перворідне з худоби».

Усьому народу ізраїльському Господь звелів через Мойсея, щоб кожна сім'я у цю ніч заколола агнця, здорового й без усякої вади, запекла його, і щоб кожен член родини їв його. Кров'ю заколотого агнця Бог наказав усім ізраїльтянам помазати одвірки й перекладини дверей дому свого. Господь сказав: «І буде та кров вам знаком на тих домах, що там ви, — і побачу ту кров, і обмину вас. І не буде між вами згубної поразки, коли Я вбиватиму в єгипетськім краї».

Сини Ізраїлеві виконали повеління Боже. А єгиптяни, як завжди, лягли спати. Опівночі померли всі їхні первістки. «І встав фараон уночі, він та всі раби його, та ввесь Єгипет. І знявся великий зойк в Єгипті, бо не було дому, щоб не було там померлого!»

З цього часу Господь встановив для ізраїльтян свято, яке має назву «Пасха». Слово «пасха» означає «проходження повз», «перехід»*. Кожного року ізраїльтяни повинні їсти на це свято ягня з прісним хлібом, пригадуючи свій порятунок.

2 М. 11; 12:1–17, 30

* *Це слово має подвійний зміст:*
1. *Господь пройшов повз будинки синів Ізраїлевих та зберіг їхніх первістків.*
2. *Ізраїль, керований Богом, переходить Червоне море.*

ГОСПОДЬ ВИВОДИТЬ ІЗРАЇЛЬТЯН З ЄГИПТУ

Покликав фараон Мойсея та Аарона до себе вночі й сказав: «Устаньте, вийдіть з-посеред народу мого, — і ви, і сини Ізраїлеві. І йдіть, служіть Господеві, як ви казали! І дрібну вашу худобу, і худобу вашу велику візьміть, як ви казали, та й ідіть. І поблагословіть і мене!»

І силували єгиптяни народ ізраїльський швидше вийти із землі тієї, бо жах оволодів ними. Тому вони говорили: «Усі ми помремо!»

І вирушили сини Ізраїлеві з Рамесесу до Суккоту, близько шестисот тисяч чоловік піших, окрім дітей. І багато різноплемінних людей вийшло з ними, і дрібна й велика худоба, череда вельми велика.

І спекли вони із тіста, яке винесли з Єгипту, прісні коржі, бо воно ще не закисло, а вони вигнані були з Єгипту й не могли баритися, і навіть їжі не приготували собі на дорогу.

А часу, що перебували сини Ізраїлеві в Єгипті, було чотириста тридцять років.

Бог повів ізраїльський народ пустельним шляхом, який тягнувся до Червоного моря. Лише один Господь відав, куди повести Свій народ. Тому Він ішов попереду них: вдень у стовпі хмари, а вночі — у стовпі вогню, освітлюючи їм шлях. Коли хмара зупинялась, ізраїльтяни встановлювали свої намети й відпочивали, а коли ж хмара знов рухалась уперед, вони знову продовжували свій шлях. Ніколи не зникав стовп хмари вдень, а стовп вогненний — уночі.

2 М. 12:31–40; 13:20–22

G. STEMLER

ПЕРЕХІД ІЗРАЇЛЬТЯН ЧЕРЕЗ ЧЕРВОНЕ МОРЕ

Дізнався фараон, що ізраїльтяни вийшли з Єгипту не тільки для того, щоб принести жертву своєму Богові, але й аби зовсім не повертатися туди. І погнався за ними з усіма своїми вершниками, колісницями та усім військом, прагнучи повернути їх назад.

Незабаром, коли ізраїльтяни зупинилися на березі Червоного моря і їм нікуди було вже тікати, з'явилися єгиптяни, які швидко наздоганяли їх. Побачивши море попереду себе, а єгиптян — позаду, народ Божий почав нарікати на Мойсея за те, що він вивів їх з Єгипту на загибель в пустелі. Але Мойсей сказав їм: «Не бійтеся! Стійте, і побачите спасіння Господа, що вчинить вам сьогодні. Бо єгиптян, яких бачите сьогодні, більше не побачите їх уже повіки! Господь буде воювати за вас, а ви мовчіть!»

І звелів Бог Мойсею простягнути руку до моря. Коли ж Мойсей простягнув свою руку, Господь погнав морські хвилі сильним східним вітром, так що протягом ночі частина моря перед ізраїльтянами зробилась сушею, вода немовби розступилася перед ними. І пішли усі нащадки Ізраїлеві серед моря по суші, а вода була їм стіною праворуч та ліворуч від них.

2 М. 14:5–22

ЗАГИБЕЛЬ ЄГИПЕТСЬКОГО ВІЙСЬКА У ЧЕРВОНОМУ МОРІ

А єгиптяни продовжували гнатися за ізраїльським народом і також увійшли у море, що розступилося. Вранці Господь привів у замішання увесь єгипетський табір, відібравши колеса у колісниць, так що вони ледве тягли їх за собою. Побачивши це, єгиптяни сказали один одному: «Утікаймо від ізраїльтян, бо Господь воює за них з Єгиптом!»

Коли ж увесь народ Божий пройшов по суші серед моря, Господь сказав Мойсею: «Простягни свою руку на море, і нехай вернеться вода на єгиптян, на їхні колесниці й на комонників їхніх». Мойсей зробив, як звелів йому Господь, і вода у морі повернулася на своє місце і поглинула усіх єгиптян.

Так визволив Господь у той день Свій народ. І побачили ізраїльтяни руку величну, яку Бог явив над єгиптянами, і убоявся народ Господа, і повірив Господеві та Мойсею, рабу Його. Тоді заспівав Мойсей з усім народом урочисту пісню на славу великого Рятівника:

«Моя сила та пісня — Господь, і Він став на спасіння мені! Це мій Бог, — і прославлю Його… Права рука Твоя, Господи, вславлена силою, правиця Твоя трощить ворога, Господи! А Своєю безмірною величчю Ти розбиваєш Своїх заколотників… Хто подібний Тобі, Препрославлений святістю? Ти в славі грізний, Чудотворче!.. Господь зацарює навіки-віків!»

2 М. 14:23–31; 15:1–18

МАННА НЕБЕСНА

А народ ізраїльський продовжував свій шлях, і Господь вів його. Коли вони прийшли до пустелі Сін, то всі почали ремствувати на Мойсея та Аарона, кажучи, що у Єгипті було краще, бо у пустелі нема чого їсти.

Мойсей сказав народу: «Почув Господь ремствування ваші, що ви ремствуєте на Нього. А ми що? Не на нас ремствування ваше, а на Господа!» По тому Господь сказав Мойсею: «Я почув ремствування Ізраїлевих синів. Промовляй до них, кажучи: Під вечір будете їсти м'ясо, а рано насититесь хлібом, — і познаєте, що Я — Господь, Бог ваш!»

А ввечері з'явилися перепелиці й покрили увесь табір, так що народ зміг приготувати собі різноманітні страви із цього смачного м'яса. Вранці ж усі побачили росу навколо стану. Коли ця роса випарувалась, то на поверхні пустелі залишилась крупа, схожа на іній. Це був небесний хліб від Господа для всього народу. Ізраїльтяни назвали цей хліб «манною». За смаком він був схожий на корж із медом. Господь наказав назбирати манни стільки, скільки було необхідно на один день. Якщо ж хтось збирав більше, то залишок псувався протягом ночі. У п'ятницю Бог звелів назбирати манни на два дні, оскільки субота була днем спокою, встановленим Господом для ізраїльського народу, і у цей день ніхто нічого не робив. І лише у п'ятницю зібрана на два дні манна не псувалася.

2 М. 16:1–31

МОЙСЕЙ ЗДОБУВАЄ ВОДУ ЗІ СКЕЛІ

І от ізраїльтяни прийшли до місця Рефідім і з'ясувалося, що немає там питної води. Народ почав докоряти Мойсею: «Дайте нам води, і ми будемо пити!» Мойсей же відповів їм: «Чого ви сваритеся зо мною? Нащо випробовуєте Господа?» І почав він молитися, щоб Бог допоміг йому. Тоді Господь звелів йому вдарити по скелі. Мойсей зробив так, як сказав йому Бог, і вода потекла зі скелі; тоді весь народ вгамував спрагу.

А Мойсей назвав те місце «Масса та Мерива», що означає в перекладі «випробування й сварка», бо саме там ізраїльтяни сварилися і спокушували Господа, коли казали: «Чи є Господь серед нас, чи нема?»

2 М. 17:1–7

ДЕСЯТЬ ЗАПОВІДЕЙ БОЖИХ

Мойсей був дуже смиренною людиною, обранцем Божим, вірним і слухняним Йому. Тому Господь звертався до народу через Мойсея.

Одного разу, коли ізраїльський народ розташувався табором біля гори Сінай, Мойсей зійшов на гору. Там Господь дав йому кам'яні скрижалі. На них було записано десять Заповідей, яких мав дотримуватись народ. На скрижалях були записані такі слова, сказані Богом Мойсею:

«Я — Господь, Бог твій, що вивів тебе з єгипетського краю з дому рабства. Хай не буде тобі інших богів передо Мною!

Не роби собі різьби і всякої подоби *з того*, що на небі вгорі, і що на землі долі, і що в воді під землею. Не вклоняйся їм і не служи їм…

Не призивай Імення Господа, Бога твого, надаремно, бо не помилує Господь того, хто призиватиме Його Імення надаремно.

Пам'ятай день суботній, щоб святити його! Шість день працюй і роби всю працю свою, а день сьомий — субота для Господа, Бога твого…

Шануй свого батька та матір свою, щоб довгі були твої дні на землі, яку Господь, Бог твій, дає тобі!

Не вбивай!

Не чини перелюбу!

Не кради!

Не свідкуй неправдиво на свого ближнього!

Не жадай дому ближнього свого, не жадай жони ближнього свого, ані раба його, ані невільниці його, ані вола його, ані осла його, ані всього, що ближнього твого!»

2 М. 20

ЗОЛОТИЙ ТЕЛЕЦЬ

Господь довго розмовляв з Мойсеєм на горі. А народ, не дочекавшись Мойсея, прийшов до Аарона й сказав: «Зроби нам бога, який би ішов перед нами, бо не знаємо, що сталося з Мойсеєм, який вивів нас із Єгипту». Тоді Аарон відповів їм: «Познімайте золоті сережки із вух ваших і принесіть до мене». Вони принесли йому сережки, а він узяв їх і зробив із них лите теля (тельця), обробивши його різцем. Ізраїльтяни побачили тельця й вигукнули: «Оце Бог твій, Ізраїлю, який вивів тебе із Єгипту!» Наступного ранку вони встали й принесли жертву тельцю, називаючи його своїм господом. Потім люди почали їсти, пити й розважатися досхочу.

Господь же сказав Мойсею на горі: «Іди, та поквапся, бо зіпсувався народ твій, якого ти вивів із землі Єгипетської. Скоро збочили вони зі шляху, що Я заповідав їм…» Бог вирішив знищити цей жорстокий і невгамовний народ, але Мойсей почав благати Його, говорячи: «Хай не буде, Господи, гніву Твого на народ Твій, який вивів Ти із землі Єгипетської силою великою та рукою міцною, щоб не казали єгиптяни: «На загибель Він вивів їх, щоб повбивати їх у горах, та щоб винищити їх з поверхні землі». Відверни полум'яний гнів Твій і відміни нищення народу Твого…»

І почув Господь це прохання й відвернув те, що хотів зробити.

А сам Мойсей запалився страшенним гнівом і розбив кам'яні скрижалі, кинувши їх на землю. Потім він узяв золотого тельця, спалив його у вогні, стер у порох й розсипав по воді.

2 М. 32:1–20

СКИНІЯ ЗАПОВІТУ

Незабаром Мойсей поставив намет подалі від табору ізраїльського й назвав його скинією заповіту. І кожен, хто шукав Господа, приходив сюди.

«І бувало, коли виходив Мойсей до скинії, то підводився ввесь народ, і ставали кожен при вході свого намету, і дивилися за Мойсеєм, аж поки він не входив до скинії. І бувало, коли входив Мойсей до скинії, то сходив стовп хмари, і ставав при вході скинії, та й говорив *Бог* із Мойсеєм. І ввесь народ бачив стовпа хмари, що стояв при вході скинії. І ввесь народ підводився, та й вклонялися, кожен при вході намету свого. І говорив Господь до Мойсея лице в лице, як говорить хто до друга свого. І вертався він до табору, а слуга його, юнак Ісус, син Навинів, не виходив із середини скинії».

2 М. 33:7–11

ЖЕРТВОПРИНОШЕННЯ НА БУДІВНИЦТВО НОВОЇ СКИНІЇ

Якось Господь через Мойсея наказав Своєму народові збудувати іншу скинію, куди люди могли б приносити жертви Богові, і де присутність Його була б постійною.

«І сказав Мойсей до всієї громади Ізраїлевих синів, кажучи: «Оце та річ, що Господь наказав, говорячи: Візьміть від себе приношення для Господа. Кожен за щедрим серцем своїм принесе його, приношення Господеві: золото, і срібло, і мідь, і блакить, і пурпур, і червень, і вісон, і вовну козину, і начервоно пофарбовані баранячі шкурки, і шкурки тахашеві, і акаційні дерева, і оливу на освітлення, і пахощі на оливу помазання, та пахощів на кадило, і каміння оніксове, і каміння на оправу до ефоду й до нагрудника. А кожен із вас мудросердий прийде та зробить, що наказав був Господь».

І пішла вся громада синів Ізраїлевих від Мойсея. І приходили згодом ті, кому підказувало серце, і всі, кого дух до цього схиляв, і приносили пожертви Господу для влаштування скинії заповіту і для всіх потреб її, а також на священні шати. І приходили чоловіки з жінками, і за бажанням серця приносили каблучки, сережки, персні й підвіски, усякі золоті речі, кожен, хто тільки хотів щось принести Господу. І кожен, у кого була вовна блакитного, пурпурового й червоного кольору, вісон і вовна козина, бараняча шкіра червоного й синього кольору, приносили їх. Кожен, хто жертвував срібло або мідь, приносив це в дарунок Господу; а хто мав дерево акацієве, також приносив для всіляких робіт у скинії.

2 М. 35:4–29

ОСВЯЧЕННЯ НОВОЇ СКИНІЇ

Навколо скинії розкинувся двір, довжиною, приблизно, в п'ятдесят метрів, а шириною в двадцять п'ять метрів. Двір був оточений завісами, що висіли на стовпах, обкладених міддю. Сама ж скинія мала форму прямокутника, приблизно, п'ятнадцять метрів довжиною, п'ять метрів шириною та п'ять метрів у висоту. Вхід до неї був зі східного боку.

Усередині скинії було два відділення. Перше відділення, яке назвали «Святиня», мало більші розміри, і в ньому знаходився золотий жертовник кадіння. Поруч з цим жертовником стояв золотий стіл, на якому лежало дванадцять хлібин; ці хлібини називалися «показними хлібами», або «священними хлібами». У цьому ж приміщенні знаходився золотий свічник із сімома лампадами. Друге, найсвятіше місце, або ж «Святеє Святих», відділялося від першого завісою. Там стояв золотий «ковчег заповіту», скриня, зроблена з дерева акації, обкладена щирим золотом із зображеннями двох Ангелів. У ковчезі знаходилися скрижалі заповіту, на яких було записано десять заповідей Божих. Оскільки це місце було сповнене славою й присутністю Божою, воно називалося «Святеє Святих».

У Святиню дозволялося заходити лише священикам, а у Святеє Святих — лише первосвященику один раз на рік.

Коли нову скинію зібрання побудували, Мойсей освятив її і священиків, які мали служити в ній. Після цього хмара огорнула скинію і слава Божа сповнила її. «І не міг Мойсей увійти до скинії заповіту, бо хмара спочивала над нею, а слава Господня наповнила скинію».

Інколи ця хмара високо підіймалася над скинією. Це був знак від Бога. За цим знаком народ вирушав у путь до землі Ханаанської, куди Господь вів їх з Єгипту.

2 М. 40:17–38

РОЗВІДНИКИ В ХАНААНІ

Нарешті ізраїльтяни наблизились до Ханаанської землі. Вони розташувались у пустелі Паран. Звідти Мойсей послав дванадцять мужів достойних зі стану, сказавши їм: «Підіть тут на південь, …та й побачите той Край — який він, і народ, що сидить у ньому, — чи сильний він, чи слабий, чи малий він, чи численний? І який той Край, що він сидить у ньому, — чи він добрий, чи злий? І які ті міста, що він сидить у них… і яка та земля… І будьте відважні, і візьміть з плоду землі».

Дванадцять розвідників вирушили у путь. Сорок днів оглядали вони землю Ханаанську. Вони знайшли там чудові сади, луки й поля і натрапили на великі укріплені міста.

Повернувшись назад, вони принесли із собою гранати, фіґи та інші фрукти, а також гроно винограду, яке мало такі розміри, що могли його нести тільки двоє на жердині. Розвідники описали ту чарівну країну, де «тече молоко та мед», і повідомили, що народ там дуже сильний і живе у великих укріплених містах. «Ми не зможемо ввійти до того народу, бо він сильніший за нас», — говорили вони.

Розвідники поширювали недобрі чутки і сповнювали почуттям страху народ, забуваючи, що Бог обіцяв допомогти їм. Лише двоє з них, Ісус Навин та Калев, були вірними Господу й не хотіли залякувати народ. Вони говорили: «Не бунтуйтесь проти Господа, — і не бійтеся народу того Краю… З нами Господь, — не бійтеся їх!» Але народ не бажав слухати їх. Усі здійняли галас і почали дорікати Мойсею та Аарону за те, що вони вивели їх із Єгипту. А потім вони сказали один одному: «Оберімо *собі* голову, та й вертаймось до Єгипту!» Мойсей та Аарон, почувши бунтівні слова народу, засумували і аж з лиця змінилися. Боляче їм було спостерігати впертість і зневіру свого народу. Тоді Господь сказав Мойсеєві: «Аж доки буде цей народ зневажати Мене, і аж доки не будуть вони вірувати в Мене, у всі ті ознаки, що Я учинив був серед нього?» А ще Господь сказав, що готовий винищити їх усіх та породити новий народ від самого Мойсея, але Мойсей вблагав Його пробачити народові цей тяжкий гріх. І Бог лише заради Мойсея знову вибачив народові, але сказав, що в кару їм буде, що тільки їхні нащадки увійдуть і будуть жити на обітованій Ханаанській землі. А ще Ісус Навин та Калев увійдуть туди за їхню віру у Господа.

4 М. 13:1–33; 14:1–30

Schnorr

ПОКАРАННЯ КОРЕЯ, ДАТАНА І АВІРОНА

І звелів Господь усьому ізраїльському народу слухатись Мойсея і робити так, як він наказує їм, тому що Сам Бог обрав його і настановив мудрим керівником народу. Але якось у ізраїльському таборі відбулося повстання. Двісті п'ятдесят чоловік, яких очолили Корей, Датан та Авірон, збунтувалися проти Мойсея. Вони не хотіли більше слухатись Мойсея й дорікали йому за те, що він підносить себе над усіма.

Почувши про це, Мойсей скликав увесь народ ізраїльський і за наказом Господа звелів їм відійти від наметів Корея, Датана та Авірона і не торкатися навіть до їхніх речей. «І сказав Мойсей: «Оцим пізнаєте, що Господь послав мене зробити всі діла ці, що вони не з моєї вигадки. Якщо вони повмирають, як умирає кожна людина, і їх спіткає доля кожної людини, то не Господь послав мене! А коли Господь створить щось нове, і земля відкриє уста свої та й поглине їх та все, що їхнє, і вони зійдуть живі до шеолу, то пізнаєте, що люди образили Господа». І сталося, як скінчив він говорити всі ці слова, то розступилася та земля, що під ними! А земля відкрила свої уста, та й поглинула їх, і доми їхні, і кожну людину, що Кореєва, та ввесь *їх* маєток. І зійшли вони та все, що їхнє, живі до шеолу, і накрила їх земля, і вони погинули з-посеред збору! А ввесь Ізраїль, що *був* навколо них, повтікав на їхній крик, бо казали: «Щоб земля не поглинула *й* нас!» А решту двісті п'ятдесят чоловік, які повстали разом з ними, побив вогонь з неба, і вони померли.

Так Бог показав усім, що чекає на тих, хто повстає проти Його волі.

4 М. 16:1–3, 23–35

МІДНИЙ ЗМІЙ

Продовжуючи свій шлях по пустелі, народ знову вдався до малодушності й ремствував на Бога та на Мойсея. «Нащо ви вивели нас із Єгипту, щоб ми повмирали в пустині? Бо ж нема *тут* хліба й нема води, а душі нашій обридла ця непридатна їжа». За це ремствування Господь наслав на ізраїльтян отруйних зміїв, які жалили людей, і вони вмирали. Тоді прийшли до Мойсея люди й сказали: «Згрішили ми, бо говорили проти Господа та проти тебе. Молися до Господа, і нехай Він забере від нас цих зміїв». І молився Мойсей за народ.

І Господь наказав Мойсею зробити мідяного змія і виставити його на жердині, і додав: «І станеться, — кожен покусаний, як погляне на нього, то буде жити». І зробив Мойсей мідяного змія… І сталося, якщо змій покусав кого, то той дивився на мідяного змія — і жив!»

4 М. 21:4–9

ПРОРОК ВАЛААМ І АНГЕЛ

Моавитяни були ворогами ізраїльського народу і зичили йому лиха. Одного разу вони принесли великі дарунки пророку Валааму і попросили прийти до них і проклясти народ Божий. Господь сказав пророкові: «Якщо ці люди прийшли покликати тебе, — устань, іди з ними. Але тільки те, що Я промовлятиму до тебе, — те ти зробиш».

Уранці Валаам вирушив до моавитян. Аби отримати щедрі дарунки Валаам був готовий порушити Божий наказ і проклясти Божий народ. Він їхав на своїй ослиці, і з ним було ще двоє слуг. Раптом ослиця побачила Ангела, що стояв на дорозі з оголеним мечем у руці, і звернула з дороги. Валаам двічі вдарив ослицю, щоб повернути її. Але вона знову, побачивши Ангела, зійшла з дороги, потім сіла, а пророк ще раз вдарив її.

І тоді Господь відкрив вуста ослиці, і вона заговорила людським голосом: «Що я зробила тобі, що ти оце тричі вдарив мене?» Господь відкрив очі Валаамові, і він теж побачив Ангела з мечем. Валаам схилився і впав долілиць перед ним. Ангел сказав: «Нащо ти вдарив ослицю свою оце тричі? Ось я вийшов за перешкоду… І побачила мене ця ослиця, і збочила перед лицем моїм ось власне тричі». А Валаам відповів на це Ангелові: «Я згрішив, бо не знав, що ти стоїш на дорозі навпроти мене. А тепер, якщо *це* зле в очах твоїх, то я вернуся собі». І сказав Ангол Господній до Валаама: «Іди з цими людьми, і те слово, що скажу тобі, — його *тільки* будеш говорити».

Моавитяни, побачивши Валаама, який прибув до них, двічі просили його: «Прокляни… проречи зло на Ізраїль». Але Валаам замість проклясти двічі поблагословив Божий народ і додав: «Оце — я одержав наказа — поблагословити… і я того не відверну!»

4 М. 22:3–35; 23:7–20

102

ІСУС НАВИН — СПАДКОЄМЕЦЬ МОЙСЕЯ

Одного дня Бог сказав Мойсею, що він незабаром помре. Але перед смертю Мойсей помолився, щоб Господь дав йому спадкоємця для керування народом Божим, аби вони не були тими вівцями, що не мають свого пастиря.

І тоді Господь сказав йому: «Візьми собі Ісуса, Навинового сина, мужа, що в ньому Дух, і покладеш свою руку на нього. І поставиш його перед священиком Елеазаром та перед усією громадою, і накажеш йому на їхніх очах. І даси на нього з влади своєї, щоб чула вся громада Ізраїлевих синів. І стане він перед священиком Елеазаром, і він запитає для нього вироку уріму* перед Господнім лицем». Мойсей вчинив так, як звелів йому Господь.

Ви, мабуть, пам'ятаєте оповідання «Розвідники в Ханаані». Ісус Навин був одним з тих двох розвідників, які вірили, що Бог допоможе ізраїльському народові ввійти в Ханаан. Вони підбадьорювали людей, кажучи: «З нами Господь, — не бійтеся їх!» Від тих подій пройшло багато часу. Сорок років подорожували ізраїльтяни по пустелі. За цей час усі дорослі, які вийшли з Єгипту, повмирали, так і не побачивши обітованої землі Ханаан. Все сталося так, як сказав Бог: «У цій пустині попадають ваші трупи, та всі перелічені ваші всім вашим числом від віку двадцяти літ і вище, що нарікали на Мене. *Поправді кажу*, — ви не ввійдете до того Краю, що Я підносив був *на присягу* руку Свою, що будете перебувати в нім, — окрім Калева, сина Єфуннеєвого, та Ісуса, сина Навинового. А діти ваші, що *про них* казали ви: станете здобиччю *ворогові*, то впроваджу Я їх, і пізнають вони цей Край, яким ви обридили.... Числом тих днів, що розвідували ви той Край, сорок день, будете ви нести ваші гріхи по року за день — сорок літ, і пізнаєте, *що значить* бути покинутими Мною!»

4 М. 14:29–31, 34–35; 27:18–23

---

* *Буквально слово «урім» означає «світло» чи «довершеність». Через «урім» первосвященик міг дізнатися оголошення волі Божої, отримати дар передбачення майбутнього.*

ПОВЧАННЯ ДІТЯМ: НЕ ЗАБУВАТИ ГОСПОДА

Бог через Мойсея звелів ізраїльському народу: «І будеш пильнувати виконувати їх, як наказав вам Господь, Бог ваш, — не збочите ні праворуч, ні ліворуч. Усією тією дорогою, що наказав вам Господь, Бог ваш, будете ходити, щоб жили ви й *було* вам добре, і щоб довгі були ваші дні в Краї, що ви оволодієте *ним*… Слухай, Ізраїлю: Господь, Бог наш — Господь один! І люби Господа, Бога твого, усім серцем своїм, і всією душею своєю, і всією силою своєю!»

Мойсей звелів ізраїльтянам розповідати своїм нащадкам про всі великі знамення й чудеса, які Господь явив їм в Єгипті і під час переходу через пустелю. Він також звелів навчати дітей несхитно дотримуватись заповідей та настанов Божих. Мойсей сказав їм: «…стережися *тоді*, щоб ти не забув Господа, що вивів тебе з єгипетського краю, з дому рабства! Бійся Господа, Бога свого, і Йому будеш служити… Не будеш ходити за іншими богами з богів тих народів, що в околицях ваших, бо Господь, Бог твій — Бог заздрісний посеред тебе; щоб не запалився на тебе гнів Господа, Бога твого, і щоб Він не вигубив тебе з поверхні землі… Будете конче пильнувати заповідей Господа, Бога вашого, і свідоцтва Його, і постанови Його, що наказав Він тобі. І будеш робити справедливе та добре в Господніх очах…»

5 М. 5:32–33; 6:4–25

אנכי יהוה
לא יהיה
לא תשא
זכור את
כבד את
לא תרצח
לא תנאף
לא תגנב
לא תענה
לא תחמד
CLEVELAND
WOODWARD

ЖЕРТВОПРИНОШЕННЯ

Кожному ізраїльтянинові Господь сказав через Мойсея: «Коли ти ввійдеш до того Краю, що Господь, Бог твій, дає тобі *як* спадок, і посядеш його, і осядеш у ньому, то візьмеш із початків усякого плоду землі… і покладеш *їх* у кіш, та й підеш до місця, яке вибере Господь, Бог твій, щоб там пробувало Ім'я Його. І прийдеш ти до священика, що буде тими днями, та й скажеш йому: «Засвідчую *це* сьогодні Господеві, Богові твоєму, що я ввійшов до Краю, що Господь заприсягнув був батькам нашим, щоб дати нам»… А тепер оце приніс я початок плоду тієї землі, яку Ти дав мені, Господи». І покладеш його перед лицем Господа, Бога свого…

І будеш радіти всім добром, що дав тобі Господь, Бог твій, тобі та домові твоєму, ти, і Левит*, і приходько, що посеред тебе. А коли ти скінчиш десятинити всю десятину врожаю свого року третього, року десятини, і даси Левиту, приходькові, сироті та вдові, і будуть вони їсти в брамах твоїх і наситяться…

Цього дня Господь, Бог твій, наказує тобі виконувати ці постанови та закони, а ти будеш додержувати, та будеш виконувати їх усім серцем своїм та всією душею своєю. Ти сьогодні засвідчив Господеві, що Він буде тобі Богом, і що ти будеш ходити дорогами Його, і що будеш виконувати постанови Його, і заповіді Його, і закони Його, і що будеш слухатися голосу Його. А Господь сьогодні засвідчив тобі, що ти будеш Йому народом вибраним, як Він наказав був тобі, і що ти виконуватимеш усі заповіді Його, і що Він ставить тебе найвищим понад усі народи, яких Господь учинив, на хвалу, і на ім'я, і на славу, і що будеш ти для Господа, Бога свого, народом святим, як Він говорив вам».

5 М. 26:1–19

* *Левити були нащадками Левія, одного із дванадцяти синів Якова. Вони були обрані Богом для служіння біля Його Святині.*

СМЕРТЬ МОЙСЕЯ

І зійшов Мойсей з рівнини Моавської на гору Нево, на верхів'я Пісгі, що проти Єрихона, і показав йому Господь усю землю Ґілеад до самого Дану, і всю землю Нефталимову, і весь край Єфрема та Манасії, і всю землю Юдину, аж до західного моря, і південну країну, і рівнину долини Єрихона, пальмового міста, аж до Сигору. І сказав йому Господь: «Оце той Край, що Я присягнув Авраамові, Ісакові та Якову, говорячи: Насінню твоєму Я дам його. Я вчинив, що ти бачиш його власними очима, та туди не перейдеш».

«І впокоївся там Мойсей, Господній раб, у моавському краї на приказ Господа. І похований він у долині в моавському краї навпроти Бет-Пеору, і ніхто не знає гробу його аж до цього дня. А Мойсей був віку ста й двадцяти літ, коли він помер, *та* не затемнилось око його, і вологість* його не зменшилась. І оплакували Мойсея Ізраїлеві сини в моавських степах тридцять день, та й покінчилися дні оплакування жалоби за Мойсеєм…

І не появився вже в Ізраїлі пророк, як Мойсей, що знав його Господь обличчя в обличчя, щодо всіх ознак та чуд, що Господь послав його чинити в єгипетськім краї фараонові й усім рабам його та всьому його краєві, і щодо всієї тієї сильної руки, і щодо всього того страху великого, що Мойсей чинив на очах усього Ізраїля».

5 М. 34:1–12

* *Вологість — життєві соки, міць.*

O. STEMLER.

РАХАВ РЯТУЄ РОЗВІДНИКІВ

Після смерті Мойсея Господь сказав Ісусу Навину: «Мойсей, раб Мій, помер. А тепер уставай, перейди цей Йордан ти та ввесь народ цей до того Краю, що Я даю їм, Ізраїлевим синам. Кожне місце, що стопа ноги вашої ступить на ньому, Я дав вам, як Я говорив був Мойсеєві… Не встоїть ніхто перед тобою по всі дні життя твого. Як був Я з Мойсеєм, *так* буду з тобою, — не залишу тебе й не покину тебе… Тільки будь дуже сильний та відважний, щоб додержувати чинити за всім тим Законом, що наказав був тобі Мойсей, Мій раб, — не відхилишся від нього ні праворуч, ні ліворуч, щоб щастило тобі в усьому, де ти будеш ходити».

Все ближче й ближче підходили ізраїльтяни до землі Ханаанської і невдовзі мали вони розпочати бій з її нечестивими жителями. Уже було видно стіни великого укріпленого міста Єрихона. Ісус Навин відрядив двох ізраїльтян у розвідку. Прийшовши туди, вони зупинилися переночувати у домі жінки, на ім'я Рахав. Хтось повідомив єрихонського царя, що до міста прийшли розвідники з ізраїльського табору і зупинилися у домі Рахав; цар наказав слугам піти й схопити їх.

Але Рахав чула про чудеса, які творив Бог для ізраїльтян, і вірила, що Господь дасть їм Єрихон, бо він лежав в обітованій землі. Тому, з вірою у Бога, вона сховала спостерігачів, а царським слугам сказала, що вони увечері пішли від неї. Тоді слуги кинулися за ними шляхом, що вів з Єрихона до Йордану. Коли ж настала ніч, Рахав спустила ізраїльтян на мотузці з вікна свого дому, що знаходився у міській стіні. Вона звеліла їм іти на гору й переховуватися там три дні, щоб не зустрітися зі слугами, які переслідували їх.

Єг. 1:1–7; 2:1–16

CLEVELAND
WOODWARD

ПЕРЕХІД ЧЕРЕЗ ЙОРДАН

На шляху до Єрихона ізраїльському народу необхідно було перейти річку Йордан.

«Цього дня розпічну Я звеличувати тебе на очах усього Ізраїля, який буде бачити, що як був Я з Мойсеєм, *так* буду з тобою. А ти накажеш священикам, що носять ковчега заповіту, говорячи: Коли ви ввійдете до краю води Йордану, станете в Йордані». І сказав Ісус до Ізраїлевих синів: «…По цьому пізнаєте, що Бог Живий поміж вами, і конче Він вижене перед вами ханаанеянина, і хіттеянина, і хівveянина, і періззеянина, і ґірґашеянина, і євусеянина. Оце ковчег заповіту Владики всієї землі переходить перед вами через Йордан… І станеться, коли спиняться стопи ніг священиків, що носять ковчега Господа, Владики всієї землі, у воді Йордану, буде спинена вода, що тече зверху, і стане одним валом… І коли носії ковчегу прийшли до Йордану, а ноги священиків, що несли ковчега, занурилися в воду скраю, а Йордан *був* повний по всі береги свої всі дні жнив, то спинилась вода, що зверху текла, стала одним валом, дуже далеко від міста Адама, що збоку Цортану, а та, що текла до степу, *до* Солоного моря, стекла зовсім…»

Тоді увесь ізраїльський народ почав переходити Йордан по сухому дну. Під час їхнього переходу священики стояли посеред пересохлої річки, тримаючи на руках ковчег заповіту. З того місця, де вони стояли, Ісус Навин звелів дванадцятьом чоловікам взяти дванадцять каменів на знак про це чудо. Нарешті весь народ перейшов Йордан. І сказав Господь Ісусу Навину: «Накажи священикам, що носять ковчега заповіту, і нехай вони вийдуть з Йордану». Священики вийшли з річки, і вода потекла по своєму руслу. Дванадцять каменів, узятих з Йордану, Ісус Навин встановив на місці, що звалося Ґілґал.

Єг. 3:7–17; 4:1–24

ВЗЯТТЯ ЄРИХОНА

Коли ізраїльтяни підійшли до Єрихона, єрихонський цар наказав зачинити усі ворота міста. Але Господь сказав Ісусу Навину: «Ось, Я дав у твою руку Єрихон та царя його, сильних вояків. І обійдете навколо це місто, всі вояки, — обхід навколо міста один раз. Так зробиш шість день. А сім священиків будуть нести сім *сурем із* баранячих рогів перед ковчегом. А сьомого дня обійдете навколо те місто сім раз, а священики засурмлять у роги. І станеться, коли засурмить баранячий ріг, коли ви почуєте голос тієї сурми, *а* ввесь народ крикне гучним криком, *то* мур цього міста впаде на своєму місці, а народ увійде кожен перед себе».

«А озброєні йшли перед священиками, що сурмили в роги, а військо заднє йшло за ковчегом. *І* все сурмили в сурми. А народові Ісус наказав, говорячи: «Не будете кричати, і не дасте почути вашого голосу, і не вийде слово з ваших уст аж до дня, коли я скажу вам: Закричіть! І ви закричите». І Господній ковчег пішов навколо міста, — обійшов один раз. І ввійшли до табору, та й ночували в таборі». Так чинили шість днів… Коли на сьомий день… сьомого разу засурмили священики у сурми, то Ісус сказав народу: «Закричіть, бо Господь віддав вам це місто!» І як вигукнув народ, то впали мури Єрихону, а народ увійшов до міста, кожен зі свого боку. І здобули вони те місто.

Двоє спостерігачів, котрі приходили раніше у розвідку до Єрихона, обіцяли врятувати Рахав та її родичів за те, що вона переховувала їх від переслідувачів. За наказом Ісуса вони врятували її разом з усіма рідними. Після цього місто Єрихон було спалене.

Єг. 6:1–24

БИТВА З АМОРЕЯМИ

Одного разу відбулася велика битва ізраїльтян з їхніми ворогами амореями. «І сказав Господь до Ісуса: «Не бійся їх, бо Я віддав їх у твою руку, — ніхто з них не встоїть перед тобою». І прибув до них Ісус зненацька, — цілу ніч ішов із Ґілґалу. І Господь навів на них замішання перед Ізраїлем, і побив їх великою поразкою в Ґів'оні. І він гнав їх дорогою входу до Бет-Хорону, і бив їх аж до Азеки та аж до Маккеди».

Але сталося так, що битва затяглася. Ісус Навин помолився Господу, щоб сонце не зайшло, і щоб подовжився день. Він сказав перед ізраїльтянами: «Стань, сонце, в Ґів'оні, а ти, місяцю, ув айялонській долині!» Бог почув його молитву. «І сонце затрималося, а місяць спинився, аж поки народ відімстився своїм ворогам… І сонце стало на половині неба, і не поспішалося заходити майже цілий день.

І не було *такого*, як день той, ані перед ним, ані по ньому, щоб Господь *так* слухав людського голосу, — бо Господь воював для Ізраїля».

По закінченні битви військо Ісуса Навина повернулося у свій табір, здобувши перемогу.

Бог сказав Ісусу Навину такі слова, які Він говорить кожному, хто вірує в Нього: «Чи ж не наказав Я тобі: будь сильний та відважний? Не бійся й не лякайся, бо з тобою Господь, Бог твій, у всьому, де ти будеш ходити».

Єг. 10:6–15; 1:9

ІЗРАЇЛЬСЬКІ СУДДІ

Раніше, ще до приходу ізраїльтян з Єгипту у Ханаан, там жили різні поганські народи: хіввеї, хіттеї, ґірґашеї, амореї, хананеї, періззеї та євусеї. Іноді ми називаємо їх усіх ханаанеями. За їх численні гріхи Господь вирішив знищити ханаанеїв. Головними богами ханаанеїв були Ваал та його дружина Астарта. Поклоніння Ваалові супроводжувалось безсоромними оргіями. На так званих «висотах» здійснювались жертвоприношення, там приносили в жертву й людей.

Ізраїльтяни оселились на території Ханаану, кордони якого проходили, приблизно, від середини сьогоднішнього Лівану на півночі до півострова Сінай на півдні, а також на схід від річки Йордан. Мойсей розділив землю на одинадцять частин для дванадцяти колін Ізраїлевих — нащадків дванадцяти синів Якова: Рувима, Симеона, Левія, Юди, Дана, Нефталима, Гада, Асира, Іссахара, Завулона, Йосипа (коліно Йосипа, у свою чергу, поділялось на два коліна від двох його синів — Ефраїма та Манасії) і Веніямина.

А коліно Левієве не отримало своєї частки землі. Левити були обрані Богом для служіння у Його Святині, а жили в певних містах, що належали іншим колінам.

Перші 300–400 років після приходу до Ханаану у дванадцяти ізраїльських колін не було центрального управління. Їх поєднувала, головним чином, віра в єдиного Бога, Творця неба і землі. І разом з тим, вони все ж таки скотилися до ідолослужіння, воювали поміж себе і з іншими племенами, які прагнули знищити ізраїльтян. За злочини та ідолослужіння Господь дуже гнівався на Ізраїль і карав його. Господь допускав, аби вороги народу Божого — моавітяни, аммонеї, амаликитяни, филистимляни, ханаанеї, мідіянітяни і сидоняни — поневолювали його. Під ярмом цих народів ізраїльський народ часто перебував у стані виснаження та апатії. Але, щоб допомогти Своєму народові, Господь милостиво висував із їхнього середовища «суддів», які рятували його від рук ворогів. Після смерті суддів народ знову впадав у ідолослужіння і нерідко чинив навіть гірше за батьків, накликаючи на себе гнів Господній. Ізраїльськими суддями були: Отніїл, Егуд, Самегар, Девора, Варак, Гедеон, Авімелех, Тола, Яір, Іфтах, Івцар, Елон, Авдон, Самсон, та Самуїл. У цій книзі ми розповімо лише про деяких з них.

«Того часу не було царя в Ізраїлі, — кожен робив, що здавалося правдивим в його очах!»

Суд. 21:25

ГЕДЕОН

Після смерті Ісуса Навина народ ізраїльський почав ображати Бога і служити ідолам. За це Господь попустив, щоб мідіянітяни перемогли ізраїльський народ.

Через сім років ізраїльтяни знову навернулися і з благанням заголосили до свого Господа. Бог почув їхній плач і призначив їм нового вождя — Гедеона.

Гедеон вважав себе слабосилим, але Бог сказав йому: «Я буду з тобою, і ти поб'єш мідіянітян, як одного чоловіка».

Ще до поразки мідіянітян Господь наказав Гедеонові зруйнувати жертовники ідолам, які були у його батька. Гедеон узяв десять чоловік із рабів своїх, і разом вони зруйнували жертовник Ваалів та зрубали «священне дерево», яке було при ньому.

Після цього Дух Господній обійняв Гедеона, і він став збирати численне військо проти ворогів Ізраїлю. Але ще до початку битви Гедеон попросив у Бога знамення на те, що Він обрав його для спасіння ізраїльтян. І Господь дав йому таке знамення: вовна, яку Гедеон розстелив на току на ніч, стала мокрою від роси, а земля навколо залишилася сухою; а наступної ночі відбулося навпаки: земля навколо вовни була вкрита росою, а вовна — зовсім сухою.

Тоді Гедеон наступного дня розташувався зі своїм військом навпроти мідіянітянського табору. Але Господь сказав Гедеону: «Численний той народ, що з тобою, щоб Я дав мідіянітян в його руку, — щоб не запишався надо Мною Ізраїль, говорячи: Рука моя спасла мене. А тепер поклич до ушей люду, говорячи: Хто боїться й тремтить, нехай вернеться й відійде від гори Ґілеад». І вернулося з народу двадцять і дві тисячі, а десять тисяч позосталось. І сказав Господь до Гедеона: «Ще численний цей народ. Зведи їх до води, і Я там переберу його тобі. І буде, як Я скажу тобі: Цей піде з тобою, — той піде з тобою, а кожен, що скажу тобі: Цей не піде з тобою, той не піде». І привів він народ до води… І було число тих, що хлептали, *носячи* рукою своєю до уст своїх, три сотні чоловік, а вся решта народу припали на коліна свої, щоб пити воду. І сказав Господь до Гедеона: «Трьома сотнями мужів, що хлептали, спасу тебе, і дам мідіянітян у твою руку, а ввесь народ піде кожен на своє місце».

Саме так і сталося. Господь здійснив велике чудо: триста ізраїльтян перемогли мідіянітян і амаликитян, яких було «як сарани».

Суд. 6, 7

CLEVELAND
WOODWARD

БОГАТИР САМСОН

Незважаючи на чудеса, милість і допомогу Божу, ізраїльтяни продовжували відпадати від Господа і чинити негоже в очах Його. За це вони знов потрапили до полону і сорок років знаходились під владою филистимлян. У поневоленні Господь наставив над ними суддю, на ім'я Самсон. Це була людина надзвичайної сили. Ще до його народження Бог сказав батькам, щоб вони не стригли йому волосся, тому що він називатиметься назореєм* Божим й почне рятувати Ізраїль від филистимлян.

Сила Самсонова була настільки великою, що одного разу він роздер, немов козеня, дужого лева, який зустрівся йому на дорозі. Іншого разу він убив протягом одного дня тисячу филистимлян, маючи в руках лише віслюкову щелепу. Цілком вільно він розривав найміцніші мотузки й кайдани.

Якось Самсон прийшов до міста Гази й залишився там ночувати. І филистимляни вирішили вбити його там. Вони зачинили міську браму й стали чатувати на нього. Але опівночі Самсон прокинувся і вирішив піти з міста. Підійшовши до воріт, він побачив, що вони замкнені. Тоді він схопив міську браму разом з косяками і засувами, поклав її на плечі собі й відніс на гору.

Суд. 13:1–5; 14:5, 6; 15:14, 15; 16:3

---

* *Слово «назорей» походить від єврейського «нази», що означає «посвячений». Назореї не пили вина та п'янкого напою, не їли нічого нечистого, лезо не торкалося їхньої голови. Вони присвячували своє життя Богові.*

ЗАГИБЕЛЬ САМСОНА

Протягом двадцяти років Самсон був суддею в Ізраїлі. Дуже непокоїв він ворогів народу ізраїльського, филистимлян. Вони прагнули вбити його, але нічого не могли вдіяти.

Одного разу вони попросили жінку на ім'я Деліла, яку покохав Самсон, вивідати таємницю його надзвичайної сили. Багато разів вона питала його про це, але Самсон не відкривав їй правду. І тоді Деліла почала благати, щодня присікуючись до нього зі своїм проханням. Від цього тяжко ставало Самсонові на душі, і він, врешті-решт, відкрив їй таємницю, сказавши: «Бритва не торкалась моєї голови, бо я Божий назорей від утроби своєї матері. Якщо я буду оголений, то відступить від мене сила моя, і я ослабну, та й стану, як кожна людина».

Почувши це, Деліла приспала його та й покликала филистимлян. Вони прийшли й обстригли йому волосся. І Господь відступив від нього, і сила покинула його.

Филистимляни закували його у мідні кайдани, викололи йому очі та примусили молоти зерно у домі ув'язнених.

Якось филистимляни зібралися, щоб принести жертву своєму богові-ідолу, прославляючи його й кажучи при цьому: «Наш бог передав у нашу руку нашого ворога та спустошителя нашого краю, який наші трупи намножив». І коли вони розвеселилися, то сказали: «Покличте Самсона, і нехай він посмішить нас». Самсона привели й поставили між двома середніми стовпами, на яких тримався весь дім. І тоді Самсон заволав до Бога: «Владико Господи, згадай же про мене, та зміцни мене тільки цього разу, Боже, і нехай я пімщу филистимлянам одну пімсту за двоє очей своїх!.. Нехай помру я разом із филистимлянами!» Самсон з великою силою уперся у стовпи і упав той дім, і тих, хто загинув разом із Самсоном, було більше ніж тих, що він повбивав за все своє життя.

Суд. 16:15–30

Schnorr

РУТ І НООМІ

У ті дні, коли ізраїльським народом керували судді, настав голод у Юдиному краї. Тому один ізраїльтянин разом зі своєю дружиною та двома синами вийшов із міста Віфлеєм, де вони жили, й оселився далеко, в іншій країні. Там жили моавітяни, біля Мертвого моря. «А ім'я тому чоловікові Елімелех, а ім'я жінці його Ноомі; і ім'я двох синів його — Махлон і Кілйон… І помер Елімелех, муж Ноомі, і зосталася вона та два їхні сини. І взяли вони собі за жінок моавітянок, — ім'я одній Орпа, а ім'я другій Рут. І сиділи вони там близько десяти літ. І повмирали й вони обоє, Махлон та Кілйон. І позосталася та жінка по двох дітях своїх та по чоловікові своєму».

Ноомі вирішила повернутися до рідного краю Юдейського, бо почула, що голоду там немає і що Бог дав народові гарний врожай.

«І вийшла вона з того місця, де була там, та обидві невістки з нею, та й пішли дорогою, щоб вернутися до Юдиного краю. І сказала Ноомі до двох своїх невісток: «Ідіть, верніться кожна до дому своєї матері. І нехай Господь зробить із вами милість, як ви зробили з померлими та зо мною. Нехай Господь дасть вам, — і ви знайдете відпочинок кожна в домі свого мужа!» І вона поцілувала їх, а вони підняли свій голос та плакали. І вони сказали до неї: «*Ні*, — з тобою ми вернемось до народу твого!» Але Ноомі наполягала на своїм: «Ні, дочки мої, бо мені значно гірше, як вам, — бо Господня рука знайшла мене». І підняли вони голос свій, і заплакали ще. І поцілувала Орпа свою свекруху, а Рут пригорнулася до неї… Рут відказала: «Не силуй мене, щоб я покинула тебе, щоб я вернулася від тебе, бо куди підеш ти, туди піду *й* я, а де житимеш ти, *там* житиму *й* я. Народ твій буде мій народ, а Бог твій — мій Бог. Де помреш ти, *там* помру *й* я, і там буду похована. Нехай Господь зробить мені так, і так нехай додасть, і *тільки* смерть розлучить мене з тобою».

Рут дуже любила свою свекруху і не хотіла залишати її самотньою.

Рут. 1:1–17

РУТ НА ПОЛІ БОАЗА

Ноомі та Рут йшли довго, аж поки не прийшли до Віфлеєма. «Коли вони входили до Віфлеєму, то зашуміло все місто про них, і говорили: «Чи це Ноомі?» А вона сказала їм: «Не кличте мене: Ноомі, — кличте мене: Мара*, бо велику гіркоту зробив мені Всемогутній. Я заможною пішла була, та порожньою вернув мене Господь».

Одного разу Рут пішла у поле, господарем якого був родич Ноомі, на ім'я Боаз, і стала збирати колоски, що попадали й лишилися після женців.

Господар поля почув, що це невістка Ноомі, яка залишила своїх рідних й прийшла на чужину, щоб допомагати своїй улюбленій свекрусі. Тоді він покликав її і дав дозвіл приходити на поле щодня. А своїм слугам він наказав залишати на полі колоски для неї й не ображати її.

А згодом Боаз сказав Рут: «…Нехай Господь заплатить за чин твій, і нехай буде нагорода твоя повна від Господа, Бога Ізраїлевого, що ти прийшла сховатися під крильми Його!»

Добра й лагідна Рут відповіла йому: «Нехай я знайду милість в очах твоїх, пане мій, бо ти потішив мене, і говорив до серця своєї невільниці. А я не є *навіть* як одна з твоїх невільниць!»

А незабаром Боаз одружився з Рут, і вона народила йому сина. «І сказали жінки до Ноомі: «Благословенний Господь, що не позбавив тебе сьогодні родича! І буде славним ім'я його серед Ізраїля. І він буде тобі потішителем душі та на виживлення твоєї сивини, бо породила його твоя невістка, що любить тебе, що ліпша тобі за сімох синів». І взяла Ноомі ту дитину, і поклала її на коліна свої, і була їй за няньку. А сусідки назвали ім'я йому, говорячи: «Народився син для Ноомі!» І назвали ім'я йому: Овед. А він — батько Єссея, Давидового батька».

Давид був видатним Ізраїльським царем. Про нього ми прочитаємо далі.

Рут 1:19–21; 2:1–16; 4:13–17

---

* *Ноомі — приємна, Мара — гірка.*

МОЛИТВА АННИ

Серед народу ізраїльського, у містечку Раматаїм-Цофім, жив чоловік на ім'я Елкана. Його дружину звали Анна. У неї не було дітей, і це дуже засмучувало її. Кожного року, у призначені дні, ходили вони до міста Шіло, щоб вклонитися та принести жертву Господу. У Шіло був невеликий храм Господній. Коли вони приходили до храму, вони там молилися, і Анна завжди плакала й нічого не їла. Елкана сильно кохав свою дружину, і йому було дуже шкода її.

Якось, коли вони знову прибули до храму Господнього у Шіло, і Анна плакала гірко, Елкана сказав їй: «Анно, чого ти плачеш і чому не їси? І чого сумне твоє серце? Чи ж я не ліпший тобі за десятьох синів?»

І ввійшла Анна до храму, дому Господнього, і молилася Господу і плакала розпачливо. «І склала вона обітницю, та й сказала: «Господи Саваоте, якщо дійсно споглянеш на біду Твоєї невільниці, і згадаєш мене, і не забудеш Своєї невільниці, і даси Своїй невільниці нащадка чоловічої статі, то я дам його Господеві на всі дні життя його, а бритва не торкнеться його голови».

А в той час, як вона довго молилась перед Господом, Ілій поглядав на її вуста. Оскільки Анна розмовляла з Господом у серці своїм, а вуста її не рухались, і не було чутно голосу її, то Ілій вважав, що нетвереза вона. «І сказав до неї Ілій: «Аж доки ти будеш п'яною? Витверезись зі свого вина!» А Анна відповіла та й сказала: «Ні, пане мій, — я жінка скорбна духом, а вина та п'янкого напою не пила я. І я вилила душу свою перед Господнім лицем. Не вважай своєї невільниці за негідницю, бо я говорила аж доти з великої своєї скорботи та з туги своєї». І відповів Ілій та й сказав: «Іди з миром! А Бог Ізраїлів дасть тобі бажання твоє, яке ти від Нього жадала». А вона сказала: «Нехай невільниця твоя знайде милість в очах твоїх!» І пішла та жінка своєю дорогою, та й їла, а обличчя її не було вже *сумне*».

Господь почув молитву Анни, і вона народила сина.

1 Сам. 1:1–18

606

АННА ПРИСВЯЧУЄ САМУЇЛА БОГОВІ

Анна назвала свого сина Самуїлом*. Коли хлопчик підріс, вона привела його у храм до священика Ілія і сказала: «Я та жінка, що стояла з тобою отут, щоб молитися Господеві. Я молилася за дитину цю, — і Господь дав мені жадання моє, що я просила від Нього. А тепер я віддаю його Господеві на всі дні».

Промовивши це, Анна вклонилася милосердному Богові, дякуючи Йому й прославляючи Його у молитві: «Звеселилося Господом серце моє, …бо радію з спасіння Твого! Немає святого, подібного Господу, немає нікого, крім Тебе, і скелі немає, як Бог наш! Більше не говоріть зарозуміло, нехай з ваших уст не виходить зухвальство, бо Господь — Бог знання, і Він упляновує вчинки!.. Він ноги святих Своїх стереже, нечестиві ж погинуть у темряві, бо сильним не з сили стає чоловік. Господь — хай поламані будуть Його супротивники!»

Анна залишила маленького Самуїла у храмі зі священиком Ілієм, і там він підростав і здобував ласку у Господа і у людей. Щороку мати приносила до храму новий одяг, і він служив у ньому перед Господом.

1 Сам. 1:25–28; 2:1–10, 18, 19, 26

---

* *Самуїл (євр.) — жадання від Бога.*

ГОЛОС, ЩО КЛИКАВ САМУЇЛА

На той час, коли отрок Самуїл жив у храмі, Слово Боже до обраного народу звучало зрідка, і видіння були нечасті. «І сталося того дня, коли Ілій лежав на своєму місці, а очі його стали затемнятися, він не міг бачити, і поки Божий світильник ще не погас, а Самуїл лежав у Господньому храмі, там, де Божий ковчег, то покликав Господь до Самуїла: «Самуїле, Самуїле!» А він відказав: «Ось я!» І побіг він до Ілія та й сказав: «Ось я, бо ти кликав мене». А той відказав: «Я не кликав. Вернися, лягай». І він пішов і ліг. А Господь далі покликав: «Самуїле, Самуїле!» І встав Самуїл, і пішов до Ілія та й сказав: «Ось я, бо ти кликав мене». А той відказав: «Не кликав я, сину мій. Вернися, лягай». А Самуїл ще не пізнав *голосу* Господа, і ще не відкрилося йому Господнє слово. А Господь далі покликав Самуїла третій раз. І він устав, і пішов до Ілія та й сказав: «Ось я, бо ти кликав мене». І зрозумів Ілій, що то Господь кличе отрока. І сказав Ілій до Самуїла: «Іди, лягай. І якщо *знову* покличе тебе, то скажеш: «Говори, Господи, бо раб Твій слухає Тебе!» І пішов Самуїл, та й ліг на своє місце. І ввійшов Господь, і став, і покликав, як перед тим: «Самуїле, Самуїле!» А Самуїл відказав: «Говори, *Господи*, бо раб Твій слухає!»

І тоді Господь став казати йому про те, що Він зробить із домом Ілія. Він покарає цього священика за те, що той знав, як його сини ганебно поводили себе, але він не зупиняв їх.

1 Сам. 3:1–14

O. STEMLER.

СМЕРТЬ СВЯЩЕНИКА ІЛІЯ

Господь знову покарав ізраїльський народ за його нечестиві вчинки. Він допустив поневолення ізраїльтян филистимлянами.

«І вишикувались филистимляни навпроти Ізраїля, а коли бій став тяжкий, то Ізраїль був побитий перед филистимлянами. І вони побили в боєвому шикові на полі близько чотирьох тисяч чоловік. І прийшов народ до табору, а Ізраїлеві старші сказали: «Чому вдарив нас Господь сьогодні перед филистимлянами? Візьмімо собі з Шіло ковчега Господнього заповіту, і нехай ввійде поміж нас, і нехай спасе нас із рук наших ворогів». І послав народ до Шіло, і понесли звідти ковчега заповіту Господа Саваота… а там *були* двоє Ілієвих синів, Хофні та Пінхас… І воювали филистимляни. І був побитий Ізраїль, і кожен утікав до свого намету. І та поразка була дуже велика. І впало з Ізраїля тридцять тисяч піхоти.

А Божий ковчег був узятий, і два Ілієві сини, Хофні та Пінхас, полягли…»

З поля бою прибіг один гонець до міста Шіло, де жив тоді Ілій, і повідомив про жахливу поразку свого народу. Мешканці міста, почувши цю звістку, вельми заголосили. У той час священик Ілій сидів при дорозі, біля міської брами. Він спитав у гінця: «Що це за голос того натовпу?» Та людина відповіла йому: «Ізраїль побіг перед филистимлянами, і сталась велика поразка в народі. І обидва сини твої, Хофні та Пінхас, полягли. А ковчег Божий узятий!»

Коли гонець згадав про ковчег Божий, то Ілій впав навзнак і помер. Сорок років Ілій був суддею в Ізраїлі, і помер він, маючи дев'яносто вісім років.

Із родиною Ілія сталося саме те, про що Господь казав Самуїлові у храмі.

1 Сам. 4:1–18

САУЛ — ПЕРШИЙ ЦАР ІЗРАЇЛЮ

Самуїл став істинним пророком Божим серед народу Ізраїля. Він постійно закликав свій народ полишити чужих богів-ідолів і навернутися до живого Бога. Коли ж Самуїл зістарівся, він поставив своїх синів суддями над Ізраїлем. Але вони не пішли шляхом батька свого — шляхом праведності, вдалися вони до хабарництва: брали подарунки, несправедливо судили народ.

Тоді старійшини Ізраїлю прийшли до Самуїла й сказали йому: «Ось ти постарівся, а сини твої не йдуть дорогами твоїми. Тепер настанови нам царя, щоб судив нас, як *у* всіх народів». Самуїл знав, що їх прохання суперечить волі Господа, і він помолився Йому. Господь відповів йому: «Послухай голосу того народу щодо всього, про що він сказав тобі, бо не тобою вони погордували, але Мною погордували, щоб Я не царював над ними. Як усі ті діла, що вони чинили від дня, коли Я вивів їх з Єгипту, і аж до цього дня, і як вони кидали Мене й служили іншим богам, так вони чинять і тобі. А тепер послухай їхнього голосу, тільки конче остережеш їх, і розповіси їм право того царя, що буде царювати над ними».

Самуїл передав народові слова Божі і сказав, що як оберуть вони царя, то він поневолить їх, і вони заплачуть від нього, але Господь не буде чути їх. Та народ не прислухався до порад Самуїла й далі вимагав обрати царя.

Якось Господь послав до Самуїла стрункого й сильного юнака, на ім'я Саул. Коли Самуїл зустрів його, Господь сказав йому: «Оце той чоловік, що Я казав тобі, — він володітиме народом Моїм». Самуїл узяв кухлик з єлеєм і вилляв єлей на голову Саула. Потім він поцілував його й сказав: «Помазав тебе Господь над спадком Своїм на володаря». Після цього Саул став царем Ізраїлю.

1 Сам. 8:1–22; 9:17; 10:1

Jos. Benj. Constant.

ПАСТУШОК ДАВИД — МАЙБУТНІЙ ЦАР ІЗРАЇЛЮ

Серце Саула, помазаного у царі Ізраїлю Самуїлом, виявилося нестійким перед Господом. Під час свого царювання він нерідко порушував повеління Божі. Тому якось Самуїл сказав йому: «Ти зробив нерозумне! Не послухав ти наказів Господа, Бога свого, що наказав був тобі, бо тепер Господь міцно поставив би аж навіки твоє царство над Ізраїлем. А тепер царство твоє не буде стояти, — Господь пошукав Собі мужа за серцем Своїм, і Господь наказав йому *бути* володарем над народом Своїм, бо ти не виконав, що наказав був тобі Господь».

Невдовзі Господь вказав Самуїлові на вродливого й сильного юнака, ім'я якого Давид. Давид пас вівці свого батька. Він був добрим пастухом, і коли траплялося, що лев нападав на вівцю із отари, то він наздоганяв його і виривав вівцю із пащі лева.

За велінням Господа Самуїл помазав єлеєм Давида на царя ізраїльського народу. З тих пір Дух Божий постійно перебував з Давидом. А від Саула Дух Господній відступив, і став непокоїти його злий дух. Тоді Саул наказав своїм слугам знайти йому музиканта, який добре грає на гуслях, щоби він заспокоював його своєю грою. Слуги привели до нього Давида, який став служити у палаці царя. Давид дуже сподобався Саулові, і Саул призначив його своїм зброєносцем. Коли злий дух непокоїв Саула, Давид, узявши гуслі, грав для нього. І тоді душа Саула заспокоювалася, і злий дух покидав його.

1 Сам. 13:13–14; 16:11–22

ДАВИД І ҐОЛІЯТ

Якось филистимляни зібрали своє військо проти ізраїльського народу. Ізраїльтяни, очолювані царем Саулом, теж приготувалися до війни, розташувавшись на горі, навпроти филистимлянських військ.

Троє старших братів Давидових пішли з військом Саула. Через деякий час батько послав Давида до ізраїльського стану віднести хліб для братів і дізнатися про їх здоров'я та потреби.

Прийшовши у табір ізраїльтян, він побачив на полі велетня-филистимлянина на ім'я Ґоліят, одягненого у мідну броню, шолом, та з величезним списом і щитом у руках. Ґоліят насміхався з народу Божого, неславив живого Бога і говорив, що коли хто-небудь з ізраїльтян переможе його, то филистимляни будуть їхніми рабами. Однак ніхто із табору ізраїльтян не зважувався вийти на двобій з Ґоліятом, лякаючись і жахаючись його вигляду.

Давид, почувши як Ґоліят паплюжить ім'я Боже та військо ізраїльтян, підійшов до Саула і попросив дозволити йому вийти на бій з Ґоліятом. Саул відповів йому: «…Ти малий, а він вояк від своєї молодости». Але Давид розповів Саулові, як Бог допомагав йому у боротьбі з левами й ведмедями, коли він пас вівці. І тоді Саул дозволив Давидові битися з Ґоліятом і зодягнув його у броню й мідний шолом. Але Давид не звик до такого озброєння. Він зняв його з себе, узяв свій посох у руку, знайшов п'ять гладких камінців у струмку, поклав їх до сумки і виступив проти филистимлянина.

Ґоліят, побачивши Давида, який прямував до нього, став насміхатися з нього, говорячи: «Чи я пес, що ти вийшов на мене з києм?» Давид відповів йому на це: «Ти йдеш на мене з мечем і списом та ратищем, а я йду на тебе в Ім'я Господа Саваота, Бога військ Ізраїлевих, які ти зневажив». А потім Давид опустив руку у свою сумку, дістав звідти камінь, кинув його із пращі і вразив Ґоліята так, що камінь влучив тому прямо в лоба, і той мертвим впав на землю.

Филистимляни, побачивши, що Ґоліят загинув, стали розбігатися, а ізраїльське військо здобуло над ними перемогу.

1 Сам. 17:1–53

CLEVELAND
WOODWARD

ЙОНАТАН

Коли Давид приніс Саулові голову переможеного ним Ґоліята, Саул запитав його: «Чий ти син, хлопче?» А Давид відказав: «Я син раба твого віфлеємлянина Єссея». При розмові був присутній Йонатан, син царя Саула. Він був дорослий та мужній юнак. Йонатан від усього серця полюбив Давида і вони поклялися один одному в дружбі. На знак цього союзу Йонатан подарував Давидові свій одяг, пояс, меч та лук. Давид також полюбив Йонатана.

Однак Саулові не сподобалася їхня дружба. Коли Давид убив Ґоліята, то народ прославив його словами: «Саул повбивав свої тисячі, а Давид — десятки тисяч свої!» Почувши ці пісні, Саул дуже занепокоївся, бо він жадав слави тільки для себе. З того часу він почав заздрити Давидові й вирішив убити його.

Якось, коли злий дух непокоїв Саула, і Давид грав перед ним на гуслях, Саул кинув у нього списа, але Давид, відхилившись убік, врятувався. Кілька разів Йонатан переховував Давида від гніву свого батька і дорікав Саулові за його злі наміри, говорячи: «Нехай не згрішить цар проти раба свого, проти Давида, бо не згрішив він проти тебе, а вчинки його дуже добрі для тебе. І наражав він на небезпеку життя своє, і вбив филистимлянина, — і Господь учинив велике спасіння для всього Ізраїля. Ти *це* бачив та радів. І для чого згрішиш ти проти невинної крови, *бажаючи* вбити Давида безпричинно?» Попервах Саул слухав свого сина й клявся не вбивати Давида.

1 Сам. 17:57–58; 18:1–11; 19:1–6

ДАВИД ПЕРЕД СПЛЯЧИМ САУЛОМ

Зненависть Саула до Давида зростала в його серці з кожним днем. Нарешті він остаточно вирішив вбити Давида. Йонатан дізнався про це й повідомив свого улюбленого друга. Тоді Давид втік від Саула і, зібравши військо з відданих йому людей, сховався з ним у горах. Саул постійно переслідував його зі своїм військом, але, оскільки Бог оберігав Давида, Саул не зміг його спіймати. Давид же мав змогу вбити Саула, однак він не хотів заподіяти йому ніякого зла, бо дуже любив і боявся Бога.

Якось Саул зібрав військо із трьох тисяч найкращих воїнів Ізраїлю й вирушив на пошуки Давида у гори. Давид дізнався, що Саул із військом своїм зупинився на відпочинок на одному з пагорбів. Тоді Давид взяв свого друга Авішая і вночі спустився з ним у табір Саула, де всі спали. Вони підійшли до сплячого Саула й побачили в головах його списа, встромленого у землю. Авішай сказав Давидові: «Дозволь мені взяти цього списа й вбити ним Саула». Але Давид не дозволив йому вбити помазаника Божого, сказавши, що настане такий день, коли Господь Сам покарає його. Вони взяли списа Саула, його кухоль з водою й пішли геть.

Наступного дня Давид зійшов на гору, яка знаходилася навпроти стану Саулова, і покликав Саула гучним голосом, показуючи йому його речі. Тоді Саул, побачивши, що Давид не помстився йому за все зло, яке він вчинив йому, сказав: «Прогрішив я! Вернися, сину мій, Давиде, бо не вчиню вже тобі зла за те, що дороге було моє життя в очах твоїх цього дня. Оце був я нерозумний, і дуже багато помилявся». Саул обіцяв Давидові більше не переслідувати його, але все ж не позбувся зненависті до нього, тому що не просив Бога вибачити його й дати йому доброти й сумирності.

1 Сам. 20:1–42; 26:2–21

ДАВИД СТАЄ ЦАРЕМ НАД УСІМ ІЗРАЇЛЕМ

Якось завітав до Давида посланець із царського війська й розповів йому, що у битві з филистимлянами загинув Саул та його син, Йонатан. Та людина думала, що Давид дуже зрадіє, почувши про смерть свого ворога, Саула. Але Давид не тримав зла на Саула. У скорботі він склав псалом жалоби на пам'ять про Саула та Йонатана: «Саул та Йонатан, ці улюблені й милі за свого життя, — і в смерті своїй нерозлучні, прудкіші були від орлів та сильніші від левів! Дочки Ізраїлеві, — за Саулом заплачте, що вас зодягав у багряницю з прикрасами, що оздоблював золотом вашу одежу! Ой, попадали лицарі посеред бою!.. Скорблю по тобі, Йонатане, мій брате! Ти для мене був вельми улюблений, — кохання твоє розкішніше для мене було від кохання жіночого!»

Ось так оплакував Давид їхню смерть. Після цього він, за велінням Господа, переїхав й оселився у місті Хевроні. Незабаром туди прийшло й декілька чоловіків — юдеїв, і помазали Давида на царя Юдеї, тобто південної частини Ізраїлю. Згодом Давид став царем над усім Ізраїлем. Бог виконав те, що обіцяв йому через пророка Самуїла.

2 Сам. 1:1–4, 23–27; 2:1–4

КОВЧЕГ ЗАПОВІТУ БОЖОГО В ЄРУСАЛИМІ

Коли Давид став царем над усім Ізраїлем, він заснував свій престол у місті Єрусалимі. Бог дарував Давидові благословення, мудрість і силу перемагати усіх ворогів Ізраїлю.

Давид дуже любив Бога і бажав мати поблизу себе, у своєму місті, святий ковчег заповіту Божого. Цей ковчег під час однієї з битв був захоплений филистимлянами. Пізніше вони повернули його ізраїльтянам, і він знаходився у домі Авінадава у місті Ґів'ї. І ось Давид вирішив перенести його звідти у святе місто Єрусалим.

Якось він зібрав багато людей і вирушив за ковчегом. Який був щасливий Давид, коли внесли цей ковчег у Єрусалим і підняли його на гору Сіон! Він прославляв милосердного Бога грою на арфі і танцював від радості перед Господом. І увесь народ прославляв Бога захопленими вигуками й трубними звуками. Ковчег був встановлений посеред скинії, яку збудував для нього Давид. А потім Давид приніс Господу жертву цілопалення й мирну жертву. Коли він закінчив жертвоприношення, тоді благословив він народ іменем Господа Саваота і роздав усім ізраїльтянам хліб, калачі та печеню.

Після цього Господь пообіцяв Давидові зміцнити його царський дім, сказавши про його нащадка: «Я буду йому за Батька, а він буде Мені за сина. Коли він скривить *дорогу свою*, то Я покараю його людською палицею та поразами людських синів. Та милість Моя не відхилиться від нього, як відхилив Я *її* від Саула, якого Я відкинув перед тобою. І буде певним твій дім та царство твоє аж навіки перед тобою. Престол твій буде міцно стояти аж навіки!» Ці слова Божі передав Давидові пророк Натан. Почувши про це, Давид впав перед Господом і почав молитися: «Хто я, Господи Боже, і що мій дім, що Ти привів мене аж сюди?.. Тому Ти великий, Господи Боже, бо немає *такого*, як Ти, і немає Бога, окрім Тебе… А тепер, Господи Боже, затверди аж навіки те слово, що Ти говорив про Свого раба та про дім його, і вчини, як Ти говорив!»

2 Сам. 6:2–19; 7:3–16, 18–29

ДАВИДОВІ ПСАЛМИ

Коли Давид ще був пастухом овець, то дуже полюбляв грати на арфі і співати псалми, складені ним. І коли він став великим царем, також продовжував складати пісні, які виконувались повсюдно народом на славу Господу.

У Священній книзі Біблії записано чимало псалмів Давида. Вони надихані великою любов'ю до Бога й прославляють Його ім'я.

Давид дуже добре знав, як потрібен вівцям добрий пастух — пастир, бо ще в юності він сам піклувався про свої вівці. Тому в одному зі своїх псалмів він так прославляє Господа:

«Господь — то мій Пастир, *тому* в недостатку не буду, —
на пасовиськах зелених оселить мене,
на тихую воду мене запровадить!
Він душу мою віджибляє,
провадить мене ради Ймення Свого
по стежках справедливости.
Коли я піду хоча б навіть долиною *смертної* темряви,
то не буду боятися злого, бо Ти при мені, —
Твоє жезло й Твій посох — вони мене втішать!
Ти передо мною трапезу зготовив
при моїх ворогах,
мою голову Ти намастив був оливою,
моя чаша — то надмір пиття!
Тільки добро й милосердя мене супроводити будуть
по всі дні мого життя,
а я пробуватиму в домі Господньому довгі часи!»

Пс. 22

O. Stemler

ПРОРОК НАТАН ПЕРЕД ЦАРЕМ ДАВИДОМ

Давид дуже любив Господа і намагався бути слухняним Йому. Але одного разу Давид вчинив великий гріх перед Господом. Якось увечері він вийшов перепочити на покрівлю свого дому. Звідти він побачив жінку на ім'я Вірсавія і закохався у неї з першого погляду. Але Давид не міг одружитися з нею, тому що у неї був чоловік. Сатана став навіювати Давидові грішні думки, і Давид піддався на спокусу. Він наказав послати чоловіка Вірсавії, Урію, у найнебезпечніше місце в ході бою, де той був убитий. Згодом Давид узяв Вірсавію собі за дружину.

Тоді Господь послав до Давида пророка Натана, який розповів йому таку історію:

«Два чоловіки були в одному місті, — один заможний, а один убогий. У заможного було дуже багато худоби дрібної та худоби великої. А вбогий нічого не мав, окрім однієї малої овечки, яку він набув та утримував при житті. І росла вона з ним та з синами його разом, — із кавалка хліба його їла й з келіха його пила, та на лоні його лежала, і була йому як дочка.

І прийшов до багатого чоловіка подорожній, та той жалував узяти з худоби своєї дрібної чи з худоби своєї великої, щоб спорядити *їжу* для подорожнього, ...і він узяв овечку того вбогого чоловіка, і спорядив її для чоловіка, що до нього прийшов».

Давид, почувши цю розповідь, вигукнув з гнівом: «*Як* живий Господь, — вартий смерти той чоловік, що чинить таке. А овечку він оплатить чотирикратно, за те, що зробив таку річ, і за те, що не змилосердився».

І сказав Натан до Давида: «Ти той чоловік!» Таким чином пророк викрив негідний вчинок царя Давида. Давид розкаявся у цьому й сказав: «Згрішив я перед Господом!» Після покаяння Натан сказав Давидові: «І Господь зняв твій гріх, — не помреш! Та що ти спонукав зневаження Господа цією річчю, то син твій, народжений тобі, конче помре». Ось так гріх Давидів був прощений, але не лишився непокараним.

Пізніше Давид написав з цього приводу скорботний псалом, де є такі рядки: «...Обмий Ти мене — і я стану біліший від снігу... Серце чисте створи мені, Боже, і тривалого духа в моєму нутрі віднови».

2 Сам. 11:2–17; 12:1–14; Пс. 50:9, 12

ЗАГИБЕЛЬ АВЕСАЛОМА

Авесалом був одним із синів Давида. Це був вродливий і надзвичайно гордий юнак; він мав дуже гарне й довге волосся. Але він не боявся Бога, мав зле, нещире й пихате серце. Авесалом не любив батька свого, Давида, і мріяв заволодіти його царським престолом. Однак ізраїльтяни дуже любили й поважали Авесалома, тому що він брехнею й лицемірством, нещирою добротою та турботою про них навернув їхні серця до себе. Невдовзі Давидові довелося зібрати військо та покинути палац у Єрусалимі, щоб уникнути переслідувань рідного сина.

Авесалом дізнався, де знаходиться його батько, і пішов проти нього з великим військом. Давид довідався, що його рідний син надумав битися з ним, і послав проти нього свій загін, але наказав не чинити Авесаломові лиха й зберегти йому життя. Давид і надалі продовжував любити його, не дивлячись на те, що син стільки заподіяв йому горя і страждань.

Битва відбулася у лісі. Бог допоміг військам Давида, і вони перемогли. Воїни ж Авесалома намагалися врятуватися й кинулися тікати. Сам Авесалом втікав на мулі. Але сталося так, що проїжджаючи повз великого дуба, він зачепився своїм волоссям за гілля дерева. Мул побіг далі, а Авесалом лишився висіти на дереві, і його ноги не сягали землі.

Найстарший за чином у війську Давида, побачивши це, випустив у царського сина декілька стріл, вціливши прямо у серце, і вбив його.

Давид, дізнавшись про те, що сталося, дуже засумував і довго плакав. «Сину мій, Авесаломе, сину мій! Сину мій, Авесаломе! О, якби я був помер замість тебе, Авесаломе! Сину мій, сину мій!»

Отак Бог покарав Авесалома у розквіті його життя. У Біблії сказано: «Хто кляне свого батька та матір свою — погасне світильник йому серед темряви».

2 Сам. 14:25–26; 15:1–6; 18:2–14, 32; 19:1

МУДРИЙ ЦАР СОЛОМОН

По смерті Давида Господь обрав царем Ізраїлю його доброго сина, Соломона. Одного разу Бог явився Соломону уві сні й сказав: «Проси, що Я маю дати тобі!» І тоді Соломон, знаючи, як важко бути добрим й справедливим царем, попросив «розумного серця», щоб як належить керувати своїм численним народом. Господь так відповів йому: «За те, що просив ти цю річ, а не просив для себе днів довгих та багатства, і не просив душ ворогів своїх, а просив собі розуму, щоб уміти судити, то ось зроблю Я за словом твоїм, — ось Я даю тобі серце мудре та розумне… А також те, чого не просив ти, Я даю тобі: і багатство, і славу таку, що такого, як ти, не було перед тобою *й не буде* нікого серед царів усе життя твоє. А якщо ти ходитимеш Моїми дорогами, щоб дотримувати постанови Мої та заповіді Мої, як ходив був батько твій Давид, то продовжу дні твої!»

Одного разу прийшли до Соломона дві жінки, що сперечалися між собою, і принесли немовля. Кожна з них стверджувала, що ця дитина належить їй. Для того, щоб дізнатися, хто з них говорить неправду, а хто — правду, Соломон наказав розрубати дитину навпіл й віддати кожній із жінок по половині. Ясна річ, він не думав убивати дитину, але сказав це, щоб випробувати їх. І тоді одна з жінок сказала: «Хай не буде ні мені, ні тобі, — розтинайте!» Інша ж закричала: «Прошу, пане мій, дайте їй немовлятко живим, а забити — не забивайте його!»

Так Соломон дізнався, котра з жінок справжня мати цієї дитини, тому що матір скоріше віддасть своє дитя іншому, аби воно лишилося живим.

1 Цар. 3:5–28

Wilbur G. Adam

ХРАМ БОЖИЙ

Бог сказав Давидові, що син його, Соломон, збудує Дім Господній, який буде називатися Храмом. Слава й Присутність Божі мали знаходитися там.

«І збудував Соломон той храм, та й скінчив його». Соломон виконав волю Господню. Внутрішні стіни Храму були вкриті золотом, і при світлі лампад все сяяло і мінилося барвами. Навколо Храму Соломон зробив двір, оточений кам'яною стіною. У дворі стояло десять величезних мідних умивальників, в яких омивали тварин і готували їх до жертви цілопалення. Один з цих умивальників був найбільшим і стояв на дванадцятьох мідних зображеннях волів. Він був наповнений водою для омивання священиків. У дворі знаходився також великий мідний жертовник.

Усередині Храму було місце, зване «девір», обкладене щирим золотом і призначене для ковчега заповіту. Перед девіром стояв золотий жертовник, і на ньому курили фіміам. У девірі стояли два великих Ангела-херувима з оливкового дерева, і вкриті щирим золотом. Ці херувими були настільки великими, що крило одного з них торкалося однієї стіни Храму, а крило іншого — другої. Інші крила херувимів сходилися одне з одним посеред Храму.

На всіх стінах Храму були різні зображення херувимів, пальмових дерев, чудових квітів. Підлога Храму також була вкрита щирим золотом.

1 Цар. 6:14–36

СОЛОМОН МОЛИТЬСЯ В ХРАМІ

Коли Храм було збудовано, священики принесли ковчег заповіту Божого і поставили його в девірі — у місці, яке називалося «Святеє Святих», куди не міг входити ніхто, окрім первосвященика. Він входив раз у рік, щоб принести жертву за себе і за гріхи народу ізраїльського перед Богом. Велика завіса прикривала вхід у Святеє Святих.

Як тільки ковчег заповіту було принесено до Храму і священики зі співаками прославили Творця, Сам Господь з'явився у хмарі, і весь Храм наповнився Його великою Славою. І тоді Соломон став перед жертовником, попереду усього народу, що зібрався тут, звів у молитві руки свої до неба й сказав:

«Господи, Боже Ізраїлів! Нема подібного Тобі Бога на небесах угорі та на землі долі. Ти стережеш заповіта та милість для Своїх рабів, що ходять перед Твоїм лицем усім своїм серцем… Бо чи ж справді Бог сидить на землі? Ось небо та небо небес не обіймають Тебе, — що ж тоді храм той, що я збудував? Та ти зглянешся на молитву Свого раба та на його благання, Господи, Боже мій, щоб почути спів та молитву, якою раб твій молиться перед лицем Твоїм сьогодні, щоб очі Твої були відкриті на цей храм уночі та вдень, на те місце, про яке Ти сказав: Нехай буде Ймення Моє там, щоб почути молитву, якою буде молитися Твій раб на цьому місці! І Ти будеш прислухатися до благання Свого раба, та Свого народу, Ізраїля, що будуть молитися на цьому місці».

1 Цар. 8:3–11, 22–52

СОЛОМОН І ЦАРИЦЯ ШЕВИ

Цей текст з Біблії розповідає про царицю Шеви та про царя Соломона. Вважається, що її царство було у південно-західній Аравії, приблизно на території теперішнього Йємену.

«А цариця Шеви, коли почула була про славу Соломона, щодо Господнього Імени, то прийшла випробувати його загадками. І прийшла вона до Єрусалиму з дуже великим багатством, — з верблюдами, що несли пахощі, і з дуже численним золотом, і з дорогим камінням. І прийшла вона до Соломона, і говорила йому все, що було на серці її. І Соломон вияснив їй усі її слова, — не було речі, незнаної цареві, якої не порішив би він їй. І побачила цариця Шеви всю Соломонову мудрість, та дім, що він збудував, і їжу столу його, і мешкання рабів його, і поставу слуг його та їхні одежі, і напої його, і цілопалення, що він приносить у Господньому домі, — і не могла вона з дива вийти! І сказала вона до царя: «Правдою було те, що я чула в своїм краї про твої діла та про твою мудрість. І не повірила я тим словам, аж поки не прийшла та не побачили мої очі, — і ось не була представлена мені *й* половина: ти перевищив мудрість та добро тієї слави, про яку я чула! Щасливі люди твої, щасливі оці твої слуги, що завжди стоять перед обличчям твоїм, що слухають твою мудрість! Нехай буде благословенний Господь, Бог твій, що вподобав тебе, щоб посадити тебе на Ізраїлів трон, через Господню любов до Ізраїля навіки. І Він настановив тебе царем, щоб чинити право та справедливість». І дала вона цареві сто й двадцять талантів золота, і дуже багато пахощів та дорогого каміння. *Більш* уже *ніколи* не приходило так багато, як оці пахощі, що цариця Шеви дала цареві Соломонові!.. А цар Соломон дав цариці Шеви *на* жадання її все, чого вона бажала, окрім того, що дав їй як царський дарунок Соломонів. І обернулася вона, та й пішла до свого краю, вона та слуги її».

1 Цар. 10:1–13

СОЛОМОН ВІДПАДАЄ ВІД БОГА

Коли будували храм Господній, Бог сказав Соломонові: «Якщо ти ходитимеш Моїми уставами, й постанови Мої будеш виконувати, і будеш дотримувати всі Мої заповіді, щоб ними ходити, то Я виповню на тобі Своє слово, яке Я говорив був батькові твоєму Давидові. І пробуватиму посеред Ізраїлевих синів, і не покину Свого Ізраїлевого народу». Спочатку Соломон від щирого серця дотримувався усіх заповідей Божих.

Але пройшло багато років, і, маючи похилий вік, Соломон став шукати слави не Божої, а людської. Він довго жив, і було в нього багато дружин з поганських племен, а усі вони вклонялися ідолам й не знали живого Бога. І ось жінки-поганки схилили й Соломона до ідолослужіння, і він збудував жертовник їхнім ідолам.

«І розгнівався Господь на Соломона, бо його серце відхилилося від Господа, Бога Ізраїлевого, що двічі йому являвся, і наказував йому про цю річ, — щоб не ходити за іншими богами. Та не виконував він *того*, що наказав був Господь. І сказав Господь до Соломона: «Тому, що було це з тобою, і не виконував ти Мого заповіту та постанов Моїх, що Я наказав був тобі, Я конче відберу царство твоє, та й дам його твоєму рабові. Тільки за твоїх днів не зроблю того ради батька твого Давида, — з руки сина твого відберу його!»

Саме так і сталося. Завдяки великим гріхам царя Соломона країна розділилася на дві частини, і розпочалася в ній міжусобна війна.

1 Цар. 6:12–13; 11:1–13

РОЗПОДІЛ ІЗРАЇЛЮ НА ДВА ЦАРСТВА

Славетне Ізраїльське царство проіснувало лише сто двадцять років: у ньому протягом сорока років царював Саул, а також стільки ж років Давид та Соломон.

Після смерті царя Соломона царство розділилося на Ізраїль та Юдею. Ось як це сталося. У місті Сихемі зібралися всі ізраїльтяни, щоб посадити на престол Рехав'ама, сина померлого царя Соломона. Тоді Єровоам та всі старші Ізраїля прийшли до Рехав'ама й сказали: «Твій батько вчинив був тяжким наше ярмо, а ти тепер полегши жорстоку роботу батька свого та тяжке його ярмо, що наклав він був на нас, і ми будемо служити тобі».

Цар Рехав'ам порадився зі старійшинами, що служили при дворі ще за життя його батька, Соломона, і старійшини так відповіли йому: «Якщо ти сьогодні будеш рабом цьому народові, і будеш служити їм, і відповіси їм, і говоритимеш їм добрі слова, то вони будуть тобі рабами по всі дні». Та він відкинув пораду старших… і радився з молодиками, що виросли разом із ним, що стояли перед ним». Вони дали йому дуже погану пораду: «Так скажеш народові тому: «Мій мізинець грубший за стегна мого батька! А тепер: мій батько наклав був на вас тяжке ярмо, а я додам до вашого ярма! Батько мій карав вас бичами, а я каратиму вас скорпіонами!» …І побачив увесь Ізраїль, що цар не послухався їх».

Як нам відомо, Ізраїль складався з дванадцяти колін, чи племен, родоначальники яких були сини патріарха Якова. Почувши слова нового царя, Рехав'ама, десять племен повстали проти нього, відокремились й обрали собі царя — Єровоама. У Святому Писанні це царство називається «царством Ізраїля». Ми називаємо його також Північним царством, бо знаходилося воно у північній частині Ізраїлю. Спочатку його столицею було місто Сихем, потім — Ренуїл і, нарешті, Самарія. Ізраїльське царство проіснувало більше аніж двісті років і було знищене царем Ассирії Шалманасером у 721 р. до Різдва Христового.

Рехав'аму, сину Соломона, лишилися вірними лише плем'я Юди та частина племені Веніямина, які й утворили «царство Юди», або ж Юдею. Оскільки воно знаходилося на півдні Землі Обітованої, то ми називаємо його Південним царством. Столицею його був Єрусалим. Юдейське царство проіснувало приблизно триста п'ятдесят років і було знищене Вавилоном у 586 р. до Різдва Христового.

1 Цар. 12

ЮДЕЯ — ПІВДЕННЕ ЦАРСТВО

Юдея, або Південне царство, існувало, приблизно, триста п'ятдесят років. Воно розпалося через сто тридцять п'ять років після падіння Північного царства. У Південному царстві царювало двадцять царів: Рехав'ам, Авійя, Аса*, Йосафат*, Єгорам, Ахазія, Аталія, Йоаш*, Амація*, Уззійя*, Йотам*, Ахаз, Єзекія*, Манасія, Амон, Йосія*, Єгоахаз, Єгояким, Єгояхін та Седекія.

І хоча більшість південних царів відступилося від Бога, вклонялися ідолам і вели гріховне життя, все ж деякі з них продовжували служити живому Богові. Під час царювання царів-праведників, наприклад, Єзекії та Йосії, у Південному царстві відбувалося велике пробудження. Тоді царі руйнували храми ідолів, наказували народові читати Слово Боже, не робити нечестивих вчинків і дотримуватись усіх законів, заповідей, та обрядів, які Господь їм заповідав.

Населення царства Юдеї було, приблизно, у шість разів меншим, аніж царства Ізраїлю. У порівнянні з іншими народами-сусідами чисельність царств Юдеї та Ізраїлю була невеликою. Хоча вони й воювали і між собою, головними їх ворогами, однак, лишалися поганські народи: на півночі — Сирія (Арам), на сході — сильні держави Ассирія та Вавилон, на південному заході — филистимляни, а на південному сході — Моав.

Доки Юдея та Ізраїль були вірними Господу Богу, вони перемагали в боях, а коли їхній народ та царі жили в беззаконні, Господь карав їх, передаючи ізраїльтян у руки їхніх ворогів. Все-таки око Господнє постійно спостерігало за цим народом, аж до сьогоднішнього дня: «Знайшов Він його на пустинній землі та в степу завивання пустельних *гієн, та й* його оточив, уважав Він за ним, зберігав Він його, як зіницю *оту* свого ока» (5 М. 32:10).

* *Імена благочестивих царів ми позначили зірочками.*

ІЗРАЇЛЬ — ПІВНІЧНЕ ЦАРСТВО

Ізраїльське царство проіснувало більше двохсот років. Дев'ятнадцять царів змінювали один одного на престолі царства: Єровоам, Надав, Баша, Ела, Зімрі, Омрі, Ахав, Ахазія, Йорам, Єгу, Єгоахав, Йоаш, Єровоам II, Захарія, Шаллум, Менахем, Пекахія, Пеках, Осія.

Історія Ізраїльського царства дуже кривава. Воно постійно воювало з Юдейським царством та з іншими народами. Царів убивали їхні сини та прибічники, щоб самим стати царями; а коли вони сідали на престолі, то їх також вбивали, і все повторювалося спочатку… Так змінилося на престолі Північного царства аж шість династій, тобто родинних ліній. А в Південному царстві династія завжди була одна — від царя Давида.

Ізраїльський народ дуже постраждав як матеріально, так і духовно. Царі Ізраїлю робили «негідне перед очима Господніми». Вони зійшли зі шляхів Божих, чинили розпусту, відреклися від Бога; в їхньому царстві буяли рясним цвітом ідолослужіння і безчестя. Нечестиві ізраїльські царі довели до гріха й увесь свій народ. Вже при першім царі, Єровоамі, народ почав вклонятися ідолам. Ось як це сталося: «І сказав Єровоам у своєму серці: «Тепер вернеться царство до Давидового дому! Якщо народ цей буде ходити до Єрусалиму, щоб приносити жертви в Господньому домі, то вернеться серце цього народу до їхнього пана, до Рехав'ама, царя Юдиного. І вони заб'ють мене, та й вернуться до Рехав'ама, царя Юдиного». І порадився цар, і зробив два золоті тельці, і сказав до *народу*: «Досить вам ходити до Єрусалиму! Оце, Ізраїлю, боги твої, що вивели тебе з єгипетського краю». І поставив він одного в Бет-Елі, а одного в Дані. І була та річ на гріх». Окрім золотого тельця, народ Ізраїлю почав також вклонятися ще й ідолові Ваалу.

На той час в Ізраїлі жив пророк Божий Ахійя. Він пророкував про великі кари, що чекають Єровоама та його царство: «Так сказав Господь, Бог Ізраїлів: «…Робив ти гірше за всіх, хто був перед тобою, і ти пішов і наробив собі інших богів та литих бовванів, щоб гнівити Мене, а Мене ти відкинув геть, тому ось Я наводжу лихо на Єровоамів дім…» Саме так і сталося.

1 Цар. 12, 14

ПРОРОК ІЛЛЯ

Минали роки. Змінювали один одного царі, і ось на престолі Ізраїлю сів Ахав — найбільш нечестивий з царів Ізраїлю, які були до нього. У нього була дружина з поганського роду, на ім'я Єзавель. Вона умовила Ахава вклонятися ідолові Ваалу, а також збудувати йому храм, і намагалася знищити усіх вірних істинному Богові.

На той час в Ізраїлі жив Ілля, істинний пророк Божий, який закликав усіх навернутися до живого Бога.

Ахав та Єзавель ненавиділи та переслідували Іллю за те, що він намагався пробудити каяття в серцях багатьох людей. Саме тоді народ Ізраїлю зійшов зі шляху праведності й став служити ідолам. За це, як пророкував Ілля, Господь наслав на ізраїльтян Своє покарання. Протягом трьох з половиною років на землі Ізраїлю не було дощу. Настала сильна засуха. Господь звелів Іллі сховатися від переслідування Ахава в пустельній місцевості біля джерельця. За наказом Бога ворони приносили пророкові кожного ранку і вечора хліб та м'ясо, а спрагу він вгамовував водою із джерела.

1 Цар. 17:1–6

ВОСКРЕСІННЯ СИНА УДОВИ

З часом вода у струмку, з якого пив Ілля, висохла. І тоді Бог звелів йому піти до міста Сарепти Сидонської та й оселитися там у домі однієї вдови. Ілля, прийшовши до цього дому, попросив у жінки води й шматок хліба. Удова жила із сином і дуже бідувала. У неї нічого не було, окрім жменьки борошна та трішки олії у глечику. Коли вона сказала про це Іллі, то він відповів їй: «Не бійся!.. Бо так сказав Господь, Бог Ізраїлів: Дзбанок муки не скінчиться, і не забракне в горняті олії аж до дня, як Господь дасть дощу на поверхню землі».

Пророк Ілля оселився у домі вдови, і Господь здійснив чудо: щодня вони пекли хліб, але борошна та олії не зменшувалося, як і сказав був Ілля.

Але незабаром син удови захворів та помер. У скорботі мати подумала, що Бог покарав її за минулі гріхи, і зі сльозами прийшла до пророка Іллі з мертвим дитям на руках. Ілля сказав їй: «Дай мені сина свого!» Він узяв з її рук мертвого хлопчика і відніс його до своєї кімнати. Поклавши його на свою постіль, він звернувся до Господа з молитвою: «Господи, Боже мій, чи й цій удові, що я в неї мешкаю, учиниш зло, щоб убити її сина?» Він простерся тричі над дитиною і сказав до Бога: «Господи, Боже мій, нехай вернеться душа цієї дитини в неї!» І вислухав Господь голоса Іллі, і вернулася душа дитини в неї, — і вона ожила… І взяв Ілля дитину, і зніс її з горниці додолу, і віддав її матері її. І сказав Ілля: «Дивися, — твій син живий!» І сказала та жінка до Іллі: «Тепер-то я знаю, що ти Божий чоловік, а Господнє слово в устах твоїх — правда!»

1 Цар. 17:7–24

O. Stemler

ІЛЛЯ ТА ПРОРОКИ ВААЛА

Одного разу Господь звелів Іллі піти до царя Ахава і попросити його, щоб він скликав пророків ідола Ваала та дібровних пророків, а також увесь народ Ізраїля на гору Кармел. Коли цар зібрав усіх на горі, Ілля звернувся до них із такими словами: «Чи довго ви будете скакати на двох галузках? Якщо Господь — Бог, ідіть за Ним, а якщо Ваал — ідіть за ним!» Та не відповів йому народ *ані* слова. І сказав Ілля до народу: «Я сам позостався Господній пророк, а пророків Ваалових — чотири сотні й п'ятдесят чоловік. І нехай дадуть нам двох бичків, і нехай вони виберуть собі одного бичка, і нехай заріжуть його, і нехай покладуть на дрова, а огню не покладуть. І я приготую одного бичка, і дам на дрова, а огню не покладу. І ви покличете ім'я бога вашого, а я покличу Ім'я Господа. І станеться, той Бог, що відповість огнем, — Він Бог!» І відповів той народ та й сказав: «Це добре слово!»

Пророки Ваала поклали тельця на дрова й стали кричати: «Ваале, почуй нас!» Так майже день вони кричали до нестями своєї, але ніякої відповіді не було. Тоді Ілля сказав до всього народу: «Підійдіть до мене!» І підійшов увесь народ до нього. І взяв Ілля дванадцять каменів, за числом племен, синів Якова, і збудував із того каміння жертовника в ім'я Господнє, і наклав дрова, і зарізав бичка та й поклав на дровах. Потім він звелів вилити на жертовник тричі по чотири відра води, так, щоб викопаний навколо нього рів наповнився водою, а потім почав молитися: «Господи, Боже Авраамів, Ісаків та Ізраїлів! Сьогодні пізнають, що Ти Ізраїлів Бог, а я Твій раб, і що все оце я зробив Твоїм словом. Вислухай мене, Господи, вислухай мене, і нехай пізнає цей народ, що Ти — Господь, Бог, і Ти обернеш їхнє серце назад!» Господь почув молитву пророка Свого, і упав вогонь з неба та спалив жертвоприношення, дрова і навіть каміння довкола.

«І побачили *це* всі люди, та й попадали на обличчя свої й говорили: «Господь, — Він Бог, Господь, — Він Бог!»

Так Господь показав усім, що Він — єдиний живий Бог, а пророки ідола Ваала виявилися нечестивими пройдисвітами.

1 Цар. 18:18–39

ЧУДЕСА З ВОДОЮ ТА З ОЛІЄЮ

Бог зробив Єлисея великим пророком і здійснив через нього багато чудес. Одного разу, коли він знаходився у місті Єрихоні, прийшли до нього жителі міста й сказали: «Ось положення цього міста хороше… та вода нехороша, а земля неплідна». Тоді Єлисей попросив дати йому нову чашу і покласти до неї дрібку солі. Коли йому дали це, він прийшов до джерела води, кинув у нього сіль та й сказав: «Так сказав Господь: Уздоровив Я цю воду». Після слів Єлисея вода у джерелі стала напрочуд смачною.

Іншого разу прийшла до Єлисея вдова і з плачем розповіла йому про своє горе. По смерті чоловіка ця жінка не могла розплатитися з боргами. Тоді чоловік, якому вона заборгувала, прийшов, щоб забрати обох її синів за рабів собі. Єлисей, бажаючи допомогти їй, сказав їй: «Розкажи мені, що є в тебе в домі». Жінка відповіла: «Нічого нема в домі твоєї невільниці, — є тільки горня оливи». Пророк сказав їй: «Іди, позич собі на стороні посуд від усіх сусідок твоїх, посуд порожній. Не бери мало! І ввійдеш, і замкнеш двері за собою та за синами своїми, і поналиваєш у всі ті посудини, а повні повідставляй».

Вона пішла і зробила так, як сказав їй Єлисей. Вона позичила у сусідів різних жбанів і чаш, причинила за собою двері свого дому та разом із синами почала розливати у них олію з того горня, у якому вона була. Наповнивши усі посудини, вона побачила, що олія не кінчається у горнятку, з якого вона наливала. Вона сказала синові: «Подай мені ще посуду!» Але він відповів їй: «Нема вже посуду». Тоді вдова помітила, що й олія в горнятку закінчилася.

Отож, коли усі позичені нею посудини були наповнені, жінка пішла до Єлисея й розповіла про те чудо, що сталося з нею. Єлисей відповів їй на це: «Іди, продай ту оливу, та й заплати своєму позичальникові. А ти та сини твої будете жити на позостале».

2 Цар. 2:19–22; 4:1–7

O. Stemmler

СИРІЙСЬКИЙ ВОЄНАЧАЛЬНИК НААМАН

У царя сирійського був чудовий воєначальник на ім'я Нааман. Він був відомою людиною, яку всі поважали, але мав жахливу хворобу — проказу.

Після однієї з битв сирійці взяли у полон маленьку дівчинку-ізраїльтянку, яка стала служницею дружини Наамана. Ця дівчинка вірила в живого Бога і знала про чудеса, які Господь здійснював через Єлисея. Якось вона сказала своїй пані: «Ох, коли б пан мій *побував* у того пророка, що в Самарії, то він вилікував би його від прокази його!» Нааман, почувши про це, прийшов до свого царя й розповів йому про дівчинку-ізраїльтянку. Сирійський цар відказав тоді Наамановi: «Тож піди, а я пошлю свого листа до Ізраїлевого царя».

Нааман, попрощавшись із дружиною своєю, вирушив до Ізраїлю. Прийшовши до царя, він передав йому листа, в якому мовилось: «Ось тепер, як прийде оцей лист до тебе, *то знай*: ото послав я до тебе свого раба Наамана, а ти вилікуєш його від прокази його». Цар Ізраїлю прочитав листа, роздер на собі одяг й сказав: «Чи я Бог, щоб убивати чи лишати при житті, що той посилає до мене, щоб я вилікував чоловіка від прокази його? Тож знайте й дивіться — це він шукає проти мене зачіпки».

Коли Єлисей довідався про це, то послав слугу свого сказати цареві: «Нащо роздер ти шати свої? Нехай той прийде до мене, і пізнає, що є пророк ув Ізраїлі!»

2 Цар. 5:1–8

WM. E. FAY

ЧУДЕСНЕ ЗЦІЛЕННЯ НААМАНА

Нааман приїхав на колісниці до будинку Єлисея й зупинився біля входу. Єлисей послав до нього слугу сказати: «Іди, і вимиєшся сім раз у Йордані, і вигоїться тіло твоє тобі, — й очистишся». Нааман, почувши такі слова, дуже розгнівався і сказав: «Ось я подумав був: він вийде до мене, і стане, і закличе Ім'я Господа, Бога свого, і покладе свою руку на те місце, і вилікує прокаженого… Чи ж не ліпші Авана та Парпар, дамаські річки, від усіх Ізраїлевих вод? Чи не міг я вимитися в них, і стати чистим?» І повернувся він, і пішов у гніві.

І підійшли його раби, і говорили до нього, і сказали: «Батьку мій, *коли б* велику річ говорив тобі той пророк, чи ж ти не зробив би? А що ж, коли він сказав тобі *тільки*: Умийся — і будеш чистий!» І зійшов він, і занурився в Йордані сім раз, за словом Божого чоловіка. І сталося тіло його, як тіло малого хлопця, — і став він чистий!»

Тоді повернувся він до чоловіка Божого й сказав йому: «Оце пізнав я, що на всій землі нема Бога, а тільки в Ізраїлі! А тепер візьми дарунка від свого раба». Але Єлисей відмовився прийняти від нього дарунки, хоча Нааман силував його взяти. Прощаючись, Нааман сказав пророкові, що він ніколи не буде більше приносити цілопалення й жертви іншим богам, крім Господа.

Так просте свідоцтво маленької дівчинки привело Наамана до живого, істинного Бога і він перестав вклонятися ідолам.

2 Цар. 5:9–17

ОСЛІПЛЕНІ ЗАВОЙОВНИКИ

Під час війни Сирії з Ізраїлем Єлисей розкривав царю Ізраїлю місце знаходження сирійських військ, бо Господь вказував Своєму пророкові на це, і тому Ізраїль отримував перемогу за перемогою.

Сирійський цар дуже занепокоївся, гадаючи, що серед його воїнів з'явився зрадник, який видає військові таємниці ізраїльтянам. Але один зі слуг царя сказав йому: «Ні, пане мій царю, *це не наш*, а це Єлисей, той пророк, що в Ізраїлі, доносить Ізраїлевому цареві ті слова, що ти говориш у спальні своїй!»

І сирійський цар наказав дізнатися, в якому місті живе пророк Єлисей, аби захопити його у полон. Коли цар Сирії довідався про це, він послав туди велике військо, яке прийшло вночі й оточило місто. «І зійшли *сирійці* до нього, а Єлисей помолився до Господа й сказав: «Удар цей люд сліпотою!» І Він ударив їх сліпотою за Єлисеєвим словом».

Пророк Єлисей відвів осліплених сирійців від свого міста і привів їх до міста Самарії, яка була тоді столицею Північного царства — Ізраїлю. І як прийшли вони до Самарії, то Єлисей сказав: «Господи, відкрий оці очі, і нехай вони побачать!» І відкрив Господь їхні очі, і вони побачили — аж ось вони в середині Самарії!.. І сказав цар Ізраїлю до Єлисея, коли побачив їх: «Чи побити *їх*, чи побити, мій батьку?» А той відказав: «Не вбивай!.. Поклади хліб та воду перед ними, і нехай вони їдять та п'ють, і нехай ідуть до свого пана». І справив цар для них велику гостину, і вони їли й пили. І він відпустив їх, і пішли вони до володаря свого. І не ходили орди сирійські на землю Ізраїлеву.

Слово Боже вчить нас не помсти, а милосердю й любові до своїх ворогів: «Якщо голодує ворог твій — нагодуй його хлібом, а як спраглий він — напої водою його. Любіть ворогів своїх, благословляйте тих, хто вас проклинає, творіть добро тим, хто ненавидить вас, і моліться за тих, хто вас переслідує… Перемагай зло добром».

2 Цар. 6:8–23

КОРОНУВАННЯ ЙОАША

Ахазія був одним з юдейських царів. Він мав дуже злу й нечестиву матір, Аталію. Коли її син, Ахазія, помер, вона вирішила знищити всіх членів царського роду, щоб самій успадкувати престол Юдейського царства. Але Єгошева, сестра Ахазії, взяла Йоаша, сина Ахазії, й сховала його від Аталії, зберігши, таким чином, йому життя. Шість років Єгошева переховувала Йоаша у Домі Господнім. Протягом цього часу Аталія царювала в Ізраїлі.

Коли Йоашу виповнилося сім років, священик Єгояда скликав у Дім Господній усіх воїнів, сотників, скороходів та царських охоронців. Він показав їм царського сина і домовився з ними про коронування його на престол, щоб Йоаш став царем. Воїни оточили з усіх боків Храм Господній, охороняючи його, а священик Єгояда вивів Йоаша та увінчав його царською короною з прикрасами. «І зробили вони його царем, і помазали його, і вдарили в долоні та й крикнули: «Нехай живе цар!» І весь народ Ізраїлю, почувши про це, дуже зрадів. А Аталія була вбита у царському домі.

Йоаш дуже любив Бога і намагався жити за заповідями Божими до тих пір, доки поруч із ним був священик Єгояда і навчав його мудрості Господній.

Коли Йоаш підріс, то наказав відновити Храм Божий, оскільки на той час Храм був занедбаний. Однак, після смерті Єгояди, цар Йоаш став прислухатися до поганих порад своїх нечестивих радників і, забувши про живого Бога, вдався до ідолослужіння. Він став діяти проти волі Господа. Одного разу син Єгояди, Захарія, викривав нечестя народу. Йоаш, почувши про це, наказав вбити його у дворі Храму Господнього. Після цього нещастя впало на країну: сирійці спустошили Юдею і, як здобич, вивезли усі багатства Храму. Сам цар Йоаш лежав хворий, і в цей час двоє слуг його прийшли і вбили його. «…І поховали його в Давидовому Місті, та не поховали його в гробах царських».

2 Цар. 11, 12; 2 Хр. 24:17–25

ПОКАРАННЯ ПИХАТОГО ЦАРЯ УЗЗІЙЇ

Уззійя був десятим царем царства Юдеї. Він став царем, коли йому виповнилося лише шістнадцять років, і царював він п'ятдесят два роки в Єрусалимі. «І робив він угодне в Господніх очах… І став він звертатися до Бога за днів Захарія, що розумів Божі видіння. А за днів, коли він звертався до Господа, Бог давав йому успіх… Ім'я його пронеслося аж туди, де йдеться до Єгипту, бо він сильно зміцнився. І збудував Уззійя башту в Єрусалимі… і побудував він башти в пустині, і повисікував багато ям *для води*, бо мав великі череди і на долині, і на рівнині, рільників, і виноградарів у горах, і садки, бо він любив хліборобство. І було в Уззійї військо… три сотні тисяч і сім тисяч і п'ять сотень тих, що провадять війну великою силою… і наготовив для них Уззійя для всього війська щити малі й ратища, і шоломи, і панцери, і луки, і пращного каміння. І наробив він в Єрусалимі військових машин, майстерно придуманих, щоб були вони на баштах і на рогах на стріляння стрілами та великим камінням. І пронеслося ім'я його аж надто далеко, бо він дивно зробив, щоб допомогти собі, так що став сильним.

А як він зміцнів, запишалося його серце аж до зіпсуття, і він спроневірився Господеві, Богові своєму. І ввійшов він до храму Господнього, щоб кадити на кадильному жертовнику. А за ним пішов священик Азарія, а з ним Господні священики, вісімдесят хоробрих мужів. І стали вони проти царя Уззійї та й сказали йому: «Не тобі, Уззійє, кадити для Господа, а священикам, синам Аароновим, посвяченим на кадіння… Вийди зі святині, бо ти спроневірився, і не за честь *це буде* тобі від Господа Бога!» І розгнівався Уззійя, — а в руці його *була* кадильниця на кадіння. А коли він розгнівався на священиків, то на чолі його показалася проказа, перед священиками в Господньому домі, при кадильному жертівнику… І глянув на нього первосвященик Азарія та всі священики, аж ось він прокажений на чолі своїм! І вони поспішно вигнали його звідти, та й сам він поспішив вийти, бо вразив його Господь! І був цар Уззійя прокажений аж до дня своєї смерти, і сидів в осібному домі прокажений, бо був вилучений від Господнього дому. А над царським домом *був* син його Йотам, — він судив народ Краю».

Слово Боже вчить нас смиренню: «Минається і світ, і його пожадливість, а хто Божу волю виконує, той повік пробуває!»

2 Хр. 26; 1 Ів. 2:17

ІЗРАЇЛЬ ВІДХОДИТЬ ВІД ГОСПОДА

Сини Ізраїлеві стали грішити перед Господом, Богом своїм, що вивів їх з полону єгипетського, з-під руки фараона, царя Єгипту; і стали вони шанувати інших богів, і чинили за звичаями тих народів, що Господь повиганяв їх перед синами Ізраїлевими; і за звичаями царів ізраїльських, як чинили вони, стали робити й сини Ізраїлеві діла негідні перед Господом, Богом їхнім. І будували собі пагірки у всіх містах своїх від вартової башти аж до фортець, і ставили собі статуї різних божків, Ваала й Астарти, на кожному пагорбі та під усяким зеленим деревом, і кадили там на всіх пагорбах, як ті народи, що Господь вигнав від них, і робили злі речі, що гнівили Господа. Так вони служили бовванам, про яких говорив Господь їм: «Не будете робити цієї речі».

Тоді Господь через пророків Своїх в Ізраїлі та в Юдеї, через прозорливців Своїх попереджав їх: «Верніться з ваших злих доріг, і додержуйте Моїх заповідей, уставів Моїх, згідно зо всім Законом, якого Я наказав був вашим батькам, і якого послав до вас через Моїх рабів пророків». Але вони не слухали і зробили жорстокими серця свої, як серця батьків їхніх, що не вірили в Господа, Бога свого. І нехтували вони настановами Його, і Заповітом Його, що уклав з батьками їхніми, і свідоцтвами Його, що Він ними застерігав їх, і пішли за марнославством і гидотою й поринули у них, та за народами довколишніми, про яких Господь заповідав їм, щоб не наслідували їх. І полишили Заповіді Господа, Бога свого, і зробили собі литого боввана, двох тельців, і влаштували діброву, і вклонялися всьому воїнству небесному, і служили Ваалові; і переводили синів своїх і дочок своїх через вогонь, і чарували чарами, і ворожили, і віддавалися тому, аби чинити зло в очах Господніх, щоб гнівити Його.

«І сильно розгнівався Господь на Ізраїля, і відкинув їх від Свого лиця, — не позостало *нікого*, тільки саме Юдине плем'я».

2 Цар. 17:7–18

CLEVELAND
WOODWARD.

АССИРІЯ ЗАВОЙОВУЄ ІЗРАЇЛЬ

Осія був останнім з царів Північного царства — Ізраїлю. Він царював дев’ять років, з 730 по 721 рік до Р. Х. «І робив він зле в Господніх очах». На північному сході від Ізраїлю знаходилося величезне царство Ассирійське зі столицею Ніневією. Усі народи в ті часи були грабіжниками, а ассирійці були найбрутальнішими й найжорстокішими серед них. У 724 році до Р. Х. могутнє ассирійське військо під керівництвом царя Салманасара вдерлося до Ізраїлю. Ізраїльський цар Осія підпав під владу Салманасара і давав йому данину. Та Салманасар довідався, що Осія готує змову проти нього, бо той послав послів своїх до Со, царя Єгипту, і не поставляв йому данини, як рік у рік робив те раніше; і узяв його цар ассирійський під варту, і зачинив його у домі в’язничному. І пішов цар ассирійський проти всієї землі, і приступив до Самарії, і тримав її в облозі три роки. Дев’ятого року царювання Осії здобув цар ассирійський Самарію, і погнав ізраїльтян до Ассирії, і осадив їх у Халаху і в Хаворі, над річкою Ґозан, і в містах Мідії. Це було занепадом Північного царства.

Так Господь покарав Свій народ за беззаконня. Це сталося у 721 році до Р. Х. Лише через два сторіччя деякі ізраїльтяни з Північного царства повернулися із Ассирії до Ізраїлю.

2 Цар. 17:2–6

НОВІ МЕШКАНЦІ САМАРІЇ

Коли ізраїльтяни Північного царства були захоплені у полон та переселені у далеку Ассирію, їхня країна стала майже безлюдною. Головним містом Північного царства була Самарія. Через певний час там оселилися інші народи, з яких і походять «самаряни». Ось що написано про це у Біблії:

«І спровадив асирійський цар *людей* з Вавилону, і з Кути, і з Авви, і з Гамоту, і з Сефарваїму, й оселив по містах Самарії замість Ізраїлевих синів. І посіли вони Самарію, й осілися по містах її. І сталося, на початку пробування їх там не боялися вони Господа, — і Господь послав на них левів, і вони нищили їх. І сказали вони до асирійського царя, говорячи: «Ті люди, яких ти вигнав та оселив по містах Самарії, не знають прав Бога цього Краю, і Він послав на них оцих левів, і ось вони нищать їх, бо вони не знають права Бога цього Краю». І наказав асирійський цар, говорячи: «Відведіть туди одного зі священиків, яких вигнали звідти, і підуть, і осядуть там, і він навчатиме їх права Бога цього краю». І прибув один із священиків, яких вигнали з Самарії, і осівся в Бет-Елі, і він навчав їх, як мають боятися Господа. Та *крім того* кожен народ робив свого бога, і ставили *їх* у пагірковому місці, що робили *попередні* самаряни, кожен народ по своїх містах, де вони сиділи… Вони боялися Господа, і богам своїм служили за правом тих народів, звідки повиганяли їх».

Щоправда, пізніше вони перестали шанувати інших «богів» і вклонялися лише єдиному Господу. Але ізраїльтянами вони так ніколи й не стали. У них були власні священики й вони дотримувалися своїх звичаїв. (Вони навіть побудували собі храм на горі Ґарізім, який пізніше був зруйнований ізраїльтянами).

2 Цар. 17:24–33

CLEVELAND
WOODWARD

МОЛИТВА ЦАРЯ ЄЗЕКІЇ

Після того як в 721 році до Р. Х. ассирійці захопили Північне царство та переселили ізраїльтян до Ассирії, маленьке Південне царство, з Божою допомогою, ще продовжувало існувати понад сто тридцять років.

Єзекія був одним із царів Юдеї. Він царював у Єрусалимі. Він був найкращим з усіх юдейських царів, бо любив Господа, не відступав від Нього, дотримувався всіх заповідей, які Бог дав через Мойсея. Єзекія почав боротьбу з ідолослужінням. Він понищив усі місця й стовпи на них для поклоніння ідолам і закликав народ до покладання на живого Бога. Єзекія вийшов з-під влади царя ассирійського і не підкорявся йому.

Після цього цар Ассирії, Санхерів, почав погрожувати Єзекії, вимагаючи здатися. Він надіслав Єзекії листа, в якому з погордою висміював покладання царя Юдеї на живого Бога і вимагав безумовного підпорядкування йому, бо усі сусідні царства вже знаходилися під його владою, і ніякі боги не допомогли їм встояти перед міццю ассирійців.

Єзекія, отримавши такого листа, пішов до Храму Господнього. Там він розгорнув листа перед Господом і почав молитися: «Господи, Боже Ізраїлів, що сидиш на херувимах! Ти Той єдиний Бог для всіх царств землі, Ти створив небеса та землю! Нахили, Господи, ухо Своє та й почуй! Відкрий, Господи, очі Свої та й побач, і почуй слова Санхеріва, що прислав ображати Живого Бога! Справді, Господи, асирійські царі попустошили ті народи та їхній край. І кинули вони їхніх богів на огонь, бо не боги вони, а тільки чин людських рук, дерево та камінь, і понищили їх. А тепер, Господи, Боже наш, спаси нас від руки його, і нехай знають усі царства землі, що Ти Господь, Бог єдиний!»

Господь почув молитву царя-праведника й покарав ассирійців поразкою у бою за їх зухвальство проти Святого Імені Його.

2 Цар. 18:1–7; 19:9–19

ЗАПОВІТ ЦАРЯ ЙОСІЇ

Йосія також був одним із царів Юдеї. «Йосія *був* віку восьми літ, коли він зацарював, і царював в Єрусалимі тридцять і один рік. І робив він угодне в Господніх очах, і ходив дорогами свого батька Давида, і не вступався ані праворуч, ані ліворуч».

У шістнадцять років Йосія навернувся до Господа усім серцем, і дванадцятого року свого царювання він розпочав очищати Юду та Єрусалим від ідолів та їх жертовників. По всій землі Юдейській він зруйнував ідолів та бовванів і порозбивав їх вщент. На вісімнадцятий рік свого царювання Йосія дав наказ розпочати роботи в Домі Господньому, щоб оновити його. Для цієї мети народ пожертвував багато срібла.

Серед срібла, що було принесене в Дім Господній, священик Хілкійя знайшов книгу Закону Божого, даного через Мойсея. Хілкійя віддав цю книгу писареві Шафанові, який відніс її цареві. Цар Йосія наказав прочитати її. Коли він почув слова, записані в знайденій книзі, його охопив жах, тому що то були слова Закону Божого, від якого відступив народ Юдеї. «І сталося, як цар почув слова книги Закону, то роздер свої шати…» І сказав Йосія наближеним своїм такі слова: «Ідіть, зверніться до Господа про мене та про позосталих в Ізраїлі та в Юдеї… Великий-бо гнів Господній, що вилився на нас за те, що батьки наші не дотримували Господнього слова, щоб робити все, як написано в цій книзі».

Згодом він прийшов до Храму, скликав весь народ і прочитав їм уголос книгу Заповіту, знайдену в Домі Господнім. «І став цар на своєму місці, і склав заповіта перед Господнім лицем, щоб ходити за Господом та додержувати заповіді Його, і свідчення Його, і устави Його всім серцем своїм та всім життям своїм, щоб виконувати слова того заповіту, що написані в тій книзі». А також і народові всьому звелів він підтвердити цей Заповіт з Богом.

2 Хр. 34:1–8, 14–21, 29–33

ПРОРОК ЄРЕМІЯ

Пророк Єремія постійно свідчив про Бога і багато страждав разом з нещасливим ізраїльським народом. Якось він пристрасно викривав нечестя жителів міст Тофета та Єрусалима за те, що вони вклонялися й приносили жертви чужим богам-ідолам. Єремія виголосив пророцтво про них у Тофеті. Згодом він прийшов до Єрусалима, став серед двору дому Божого і сказав усьому народові, який знаходився там: «Так говорить Господь Саваот, Бог Ізраїлю: «Ось спроваджу до міста цього та до всіх його міст усе те лихо, що Я говорив був на нього, бо вчинили вони свою шию твердою, щоб не слухатися Моїх слів!»

Коли священик у Храмі почув це пророцтво, він дуже розгнівався, вдарив пророка Єремію, зв'язав його і заточив його до в'язниці. Наступного дня він випустив його, і Єремія знову виголосив пророцтво про долю міст Ізраїлю й усього народу та про нечестивого священика. А потому Єремія звернувся до Бога зі словами: «Намовляв мене, Господи, — і був я намовлений, Ти взяв міцно мене — й переміг! Я став цілий день посміховищем, кожен глузує із мене… Бо коли тільки я говорю, то кричу, кличу: «Ґвалт!» та «Грабіж!» і так сталося слово Господнє мені цілий день за ганьбу й посміховище… І я був сказав: Не буду Його споминати, і не буду вже Йменням Його говорити! І стало *це* в серці моїм, як огонь той палючий, замкнений у костях моїх, — і я змучивсь тримати *його* й *більш* не можу!»

Багато було тих, хто гнав і проклинав пророка Божого, але Бог зміцнював і підтримував його вірою. Тому Єремія сказав: «Та зо мною Господь, як потужний силач, тому ті, хто женеться за мною, спіткнуться та не переможуть! Будуть сильно вони посоромлені, бо робили без розуму, — вічний сором *їм буде*, який не забудеться! А Господь Саваот випробовує праведного, бачить нирки та серце… Співайте *пісні* Господеві, *усі* хваліть Господа, бо спасає Він душу убогого від руки лиходіїв!»

Єр. 19:13–15; 20:1–13

БАРУХ ЗАПИСУЄ ПРОРОЦТВА ЄРЕМІЇ

Якось Господь сказав Єремії: «Візьми собі книжкового звоя, і напиши на ньому всі ті слова, що Я говорив тобі про Ізраїля й про Юду, та про всі народи від дня, *коли* Я *почав* говорити тобі, від днів Йосії та аж до цього дня. Може, почує дім Юдин усе те зло, що Я думаю вчинити їм, щоб вернулися кожен зі своєї злої дороги, а Я прощу їхню провину та їхній гріх».

І покликав Єремія Баруха, Нерійїного сина, і Барух написав з уст Єремії всі Господні слова, що Він говорив йому, на книжковий звій. І наказав Єремія Барухові, кажучи: «Я задержаний, — не можу ввійти до Господнього дому. Тому піди сам, прочитай зі звою, що написав ти з моїх уст, Господні слова в вуха народу в Господньому домі в дні посту, а також у вуха всього Юди, що приходить зі своїх міст, відчитаєш їх. Може, впаде їхнє благання перед Господнє лице, і вони вернуться кожен зі своєї злої дороги, бо великий гнів та лютість, що Господь говорив проти народу цього!»

І зробив Барух… усе, що наказав був йому пророк Єремія, щоб прочитати з книги Господні слова в Господньому домі. І сталося п'ятого року Єгоякима, Йосіїного сина, царя Юдиного, дев'ятого місяця, оголосили піст перед Господнім лицем для всього народу в Єрусалимі та для всього того народу, що поприходив з Юдиних міст до Єрусалиму. І прочитав Барух з книги Єреміїні слова в домі Господньому…»

Єр. 36:1–10

CLEVELAND
WOODWARD

ЦАР ЄГОЯКИМ СПАЛЮЄ СУВІЙ ІЗ ПРОРОЦТВАМИ

Коли Барух прочитав у домі Господнім всі слова пророка Єремії, записані у сувої, князів Юдеї охопив жах, і вони негайно віднесли цей сувій царському писарю Єгудію, щоб він прочитав його цареві Єгоякимові. «А цар сидів у зимовому домі… і перед ним був розпалений коминок. І сталося, коли Єгудій перечитував три чи чотири стовпці, *то цар* відрізував це писарським ножем та й кидав до огню, що в коминку, аж поки не згорів увесь звій на огні, що в коминку…». Цар Єгояким та його слуги не злякалися, почувши ці пророцтва. Вони не повірили словам Бога, що за непокірність Йому, юдеї, за пророцтвом Єремії, скоро мусять потрапити у полон до вавилонського царя. Цар наказав схопити писаря Баруха та Єремію, але Господь сховав їх від переслідувачів.

«І було Господнє слово до Єремії потому, як цар спалив був звоя та ті слова, що Барух написав з Єреміїних уст, говорячи: «Візьми собі знову іншого звоя, і напиши на ньому всі перші слова, що були на першому звої, якого спалив Єгояким, цар Юдин. А про Єгоякима, царя Юдиного, скажеш: Так говорить Господь: Ти спалив цього звоя, говорячи: Нащо написав ти на ньому таке: Конче прийде цар вавилонський і знищить оцей Край, і вигубить в ньому людину й скотину. Тому так говорить Господь про Єгоякима, Юдиного царя: Не буде від нього сидячого на Давидовому троні, а його труп буде кинений на спекоту вдень та на холод вночі… І навіщу його та насіння його, і його рабів за їхні провини, і спроваджу на них та на мешканців Єрусалиму й на юдеянина все те зло, що Я говорив до них, та вони не послухали».

І Єремія взяв іншого звоя, і дав його писареві Барухові… і той написав на ньому з Єреміїних уст усі слова тієї книги, яку спалив був Єгояким, цар Юдин, в огні, і до них було додано ще багато подібних слів».

Єр. 36:14–32

ВАВИЛОН ЗАВОЙОВУЄ ЮДЕЮ

Як передрік Господь через пророка Єремію, так воно й сталося: юдеїв узяли у полон вавилонські війська. Ця кара Господня впала на Юдею за те, що народ не покаявся перед Богом, незважаючи на численні попередження й викриття; і тому, що не відійшов від служіння ідолам, від зла та гріха. І це при тому, що Південне царство було свідком того, як Господь покарав Північне царство — Ізраїль. Юдеяни і надалі продовжували жити нечестиво. Тоді Господь вирішив зруйнувати і це царство, як за сто тридцять років перед тим покарав Північне царство, Ізраїль, наславши на нього ассирійців. «Єгояхін *був* віку вісімнадцяти літ, коли він зацарював, і царював в Єрусалимі три місяці… І робив він зло в Господніх очах, усе так, як робив його батько. Того часу прийшли до Єрусалиму раби Навуходоносора, царя вавилонського, і місто попало в облогу. І прийшов Навуходоносор, вавилонський цар, на місто, а його раби облягали його. І вийшов Єгояхін, цар Юдин, до вавилонського царя, він та мати його, і слуги його, і князі його, і евнухи його, — і вавилонський цар узяв його восьмого року свого царювання. І позабирав він звідти всі скарби Господнього дому та скарби дому царевого, і повідрубував всі золоті речі, які поробив був Соломон, цар Ізраїлів, у Господньому храмі, як говорив Господь. І повиводив він увесь Єрусалим, і всіх князів, і всіх лицарів військових, — десять тисяч пішло до неволі, — і всіх теслів та ковалів. Не позоставив *нікого*, окрім нужденного народу Краю». Завойовники переселили їх до Вавилону.

«А царем настановив вавилонський цар Маттанію, дядька *Єгояхіна*, замість нього, і перемінив ім'я його на Седекію. Седекія був віку двадцяти й одного року, коли він зацарював, і він царював в Єрусалимі одинадцять років… І робив він зло в Господніх очах, усе так, як робив був Єгояким. Бо за Господній гнів сталося *це* на Єрусалим та на Юду, і Він відкинув їх від Свого лиця…»

2 Цар. 24:8–20

ЗНИЩЕННЯ ЄРУСАЛИМА ТА ХРАМУ ГОСПОДНЬОГО

Раніше ми вже читали, як цар Ізраїлю, Соломон, за велінням Господа збудував чудовий храм в Єрусалимі. Але коли завойовники удруге, через одинадцять років, захопили Єрусалим, вони знищили також і цей дивовижний храм Божий. Ось що написано про це в Біблії:

«І сталося… прийшов Навуходоносор, цар вавилонський, він та все військо його, на Єрусалим, і розтаборився проти нього, і побудували проти нього вала навколо. І було місто в облозі аж до одинадцятого року царя Седекії. Дев'ятого *дня* місяця настав сильний голод у місті, і не було хліба для народу Краю. І пробитий був пролом у мурі міста, і всі вояки *повтікали* вночі дорогою брами між двома мурами, що при царському садку, бо халдеї були при місті навколо. А *цар* утік дорогою в степ. А халдейське військо погналося за царем, та й догнали його в єрихонських степах, а все його військо розпорошилося від нього. І схопили царя, і відвели його до вавилонського царя до Рівли, і *там* його той засудив. А синів Седекії зарізали на його очах, а очі Седекії він вибрав, і скував його двома мідяними кайданами, та й відвів його до Вавилону…

Прийшов до Єрусалиму Невузар'адан, начальник царської сторожі, слуга вавилонського царя. І він спалив дім Господній та дім царевий, і всі доми в Єрусалимі, і кожен великий дім спалив огнем. І мури навколо Єрусалиму порозбивало все халдейське військо, що *було* з начальником царської сторожі. А решту народу, що позостався в місті, і тих, що перебігли до вавилонського царя, і решту простого люду повиганяв Невузар'адан, начальник царської сторожі. А з бідноти Краю начальник царської сторожі позоставив *декого* за винярів та за рільників. А мідяні стовпи, що в Господньому домі, і підстави, і мідяне море, що в Господньому домі, халдеї поламали, і віднесли їхню мідь до Вавилону. І горнята, і лопатки, і ножі, і ложки, і ввесь мідяний посуд, що вживається при службі, позабирали. І кадильниці, і чаші, *усе*, що *було* золоте — *забрав* золото, а що було срібне — срібло взяв начальник царської сторожі». Це трапилося у 587–586 роках до Р. Х. Храм Соломона простояв більш аніж чотириста років.

Пізніше ізраїльтяни відбудували Храм у Єрусалимі, але їм так і не вдавалося створити такого чудового храму, який був збудований за часів царя Соломона.

2 Цар. 25:1–15

ДАНИЇЛ І ТРОЄ ЙОГО ДРУЗІВ

Вавилонський цар Навуходоносор, який захопив у полон жителів Єрусалима, звелів начальнику царедворців відібрати серед полонених ізраїльтян молодих юнаків царського й княжого роду, «…юнаків, що нема в них жодної вади, і вони вродливого вигляду та розумні в усякій мудрості, і здібні до знання, і розуміють науку, і щоб у них *була* моторність служити в царському палаці, і щоб навчати їх книг та мови халдеїв. І призначив їм цар щоденну поживу, з царської їжі та з вина, що сам його пив, а на їхнє виховання — три роки, а по закінченні їх стануть вони перед царським обличчям».

І були серед них з Юдиних синів Даниїл, Ананія, Мисаїл та Азарія. У палаці вавилонському їх стали називати: Даниїла — Валтасаром, Ананія — Шадрахом, Мисаїла — Мешахом, Азарія — Авед-Неґо. Ці юнаки зберігали в серці велику любов до Бога й щиру віру у Нього. Даниїл вирішив не ганьбити себе їжею та вином з царського столу, можливо, тому, що ця їжа була приготована з м'яса тварин та птахів, яких ізраїльтянам, за законом Мойсея, не дозволялося їсти і, можливо, ще й тому, що вони приносили їх у жертву вавилонським божкам. Він попросив начальника царедворців дати йому та його друзям для їжі овочів та воду для пиття. Начальник спочатку не наважувався виконати його прохання, побоюючись, що юнаки схуднуть, а це може накликати на нього гнів царя. Але Даниїл умовив його, запропонувавши таке випробовування для себе й своїх друзів: давати їм лише воду та овочі протягом десяти днів. Через десять днів обличчя чотирьох віруючих юнаків виявилися ще вродливішими, і тілом вони були повніші, аніж юнаки, які споживали їжу із царського столу.

Бог дав Даниїлові, Ананії, Мисаїлу та Азарії знання та мудрість, а Даниїлові Він дав ще й вміння розуміти всілякі видіння та сни.

Через три роки цар Вавилону наказав привести до нього усіх відібраних ізраїльських юнаків. Після того, як цар порозмовляв з кожним із них окремо, він дійшов висновку, що досі не було подібних Даниїлу, Ананії, Мисаїлу та Азарії. «А всяку справу мудрости та розуму, що шукав від них цар, то він знайшов їх удесятеро *мудрішими* від усіх чарівників та заклиначів, що *були* в усьому його царстві». Тому їх лишили для служби при цареві.

Дан. 1:3–20

ЗОЛОТИЙ БОВВАН І ТРОЄ СМІЛИВИХ ЮНАКІВ

Цар Вавилону, Навуходоносор, звелів відлити золотого боввана заввишки у шістдесят ліктів, завширшки у шість ліктів і встановити його в долині Дура, що у вавилонській місцевості. І цар Навуходоносор проголосив через своїх оповісників: «До вас говориться, народи, люди та язики! …Поклонітся золотому бовванові… А той, хто не впаде й не поклониться, тієї хвилі буде вкинений до середини палахкотючої огненної печі».

Хтось із халдеїв доніс цареві: «Є юдейські мужі… Шадрах, Мешах та Авед-Неґо, — ці мужі не звернули на тебе, царю, уваги: богам твоїм не служать, і золотому бовванові… не вклоняються». Тоді Навуходоносор у гніві та люті звелів привести Шадраха, Мешаха та Авед-Неґо і сказав їм: «…якщо ви не поклонитеся, тієї години будете вкинені до середини палахкотючої огненної печі, і хто той Бог, що врятує вас від моїх рук?» Вони відповіли царю так: «Якщо наш Бог, Якому ми служимо, може врятувати нас з палахкотючої огненної печі, то Він урятує *й* з твоєї руки, о царю!..» Почувши це, Навуходоносор розлютувався й наказав воїнам своїм зв'язати й кинути непокірних юдеїв до розпеченої печі.

Оскільки повеління царя було дуже суворим, а піч була сильно розпечена, то тих людей, які кидали юнаків у піч, вбило полум'я.

Ті ж троє, яких кинули до печі, були зв'язаними. Придивившись до вогню, Навуходоносор дуже здивувався, швидко встав і сказав вельможам своїм: «Чи ж не трьох зв'язаних мужів ми кинули до середини огню?.. Таж я бачу чотирьох мужів непов'язаних, що ходять посеред огню, і шкоди їм нема, а вигляд того четвертого подібний до Божого сина!»

«Тоді Навуходоносор наблизився до челюстів палахкотючої огненної печі, заговорив та й сказав: «Шадраху, Мешаху та Авед-Неґо, раби Його, Бога Всевишнього, — вийдіть і прийдіть!» Тоді Шадрах, Мешах та Авед-Неґо вийшли з середини огню. І зібралися сатрапи, заступники, і підсатрапи, і цареві радники, *та й* побачили тих мужів, що огонь не мав сили над їхнім тілом, і не опалився волос їхньої голови, і їхні плащі не змінилися, і запах огню не ввійшов у них. Навуходоносор заговорив та й сказав: «Благословенний Бог Шадраха, Мешаха та Авед-Неґо, що послав Свого Ангола, і врятував Своїх рабів, які надіялися на Нього…» І звеличив цар Шадраха, Мешаха й Авед-Неґо в країні Вавилонській.

Дан. 3

ДАНИЇЛ РОЗ'ЯСНЮЄ ТАЄМНИЧІ ЗНАКИ НА СТІНІ

Після Навуходоносора царем Вавилону став його син, Валтасар. Одного разу він влаштував великий бенкет для тисячі своїх вельмож. Для цього він наказав слугам принести золоті й срібні чаші, які батько його, Навуходоносор, виніс із Храму в Єрусалимі. Коли були принесені чаші, узяті зі святого дому Божого в Єрусалимі, цар, його вельможі та їхні дружини стали пити з них вино й прославляти своїх богів — золотих, срібних, мідяних, залізних, дерев'яних та камінних.

Та раптом у царському покої, де йшла гулянка, з'явилася людська рука й стала писати на стіні навпроти світильника. Цар, побачивши це, з лиця змінився від переляку. Він раптом заслаб, і коліна його стали тремтіти. Цар голосно закричав і звелів привести мудреців Вавилону, які б могли пояснити написане. Він пообіцяв зробити третім володарем у своєму царстві того, хто пояснить значення незрозумілих слів. Але ніхто з мудреців Вавилону не зміг пояснити цареві зміст таємничих знаків.

Цариця почула про це, ввійшла до зали, де йшов бенкет, й розповіла цареві про Даниїла, сказавши, що у ньому живе Дух Святого Бога, знання, розум, здатність пояснювати сни, а також тлумачити загадкові явища. Привели Даниїла, і цар попросив його прочитати й пояснити значення незрозумілих слів.

Даниїл сказав Валтасарові, що Бог гнівається на нього за пихатість його і за те, що він взяв священні чаші, аби пити з них вино, прославляючи при цьому своїх ідолів. Згодом він сказав, що значить написане на стіні «МЕНЕ, МЕНЕ, ТЕКЕЛ, УПАРСІН».

«Ось розв'язка цієї речі: «Мене» — порахував Бог царство твоє, і покінчив його. «Текел» — ти зважений на вазі, і знайдений легеньким. «Перес» — поділене царство твоє, і віддане мідянам та персам». Тоді наказав Валтасар, і надягли на Даниїла пурпуру, а золотого ланцюга — на шию його, і розголосили про нього, що він буде третім пануючим у царстві. Тієї ж ночі був забитий Валтасар, цар халдейський. А мідянин Дарій одержав царство…»

Дан. 5:1–30; 6:1

ДАНИЇЛ МОЛИТЬСЯ ГОСПОДУ

Цар Дарій, який заволодів престолом Вавилону після Валтасара, був людиною гордою і вклонявся ідолам. Але він дуже полюбив Даниїла за його мудрість й високий дух.

Вирішив був Дарій поставити над царством своїм сто двадцять сатрапів, щоб вони керували усім царством, а над ними поставив ще трьох найвищих князів: один з них і був Даниїл. Сатрапи звітували перед ними, щоб не турбувати царя. Даниїл перевершував інших князів та сатрапів висотою свого розуму й духу, і цар вже мав намір поставити його над усім царством.

«Тоді найвищі урядники та сатрапи стали шукати причини оскаржити Даниїла в справі царства, але жодної причини чи вади знайти не могли, бо той *був* вірний, і жодна помилка чи вада не була знайдена на нього».

Нарешті царедворці вигадали хитрий план, щоб заплямувати Даниїла перед царем. Вони знали, що Даниїл часто молиться своєму Богові. Тому вони звернулися до царя з проханням видати наказ, що забороняв би протягом тридцяти днів будь-що просити у якого-небудь бога чи людини, окрім царя Дарія. Якщо хто-небудь зважиться порушити цей закон, то його вкинуть до рову з левами.

Цар не знав дійсної причини цього прохання і підписав цей наказ.

Даниїл, почувши про новий наказ, не перестав молитися своєму Господу. Він, як і раніше, тричі у день схилявся на свої коліна й молився у світлиці. Вікна його світлиці були відчинені у бік його рідного міста Єрусалима, де, ще до зруйнування його, Слава Божа з'являлася у Храмі. У своїй молитві Даниїл мав від Господа духовну підтримку й благословення.

Злі люди, що ненавиділи Даниїла, «…поспішили *до нього*, і знайшли Даниїла, що він просив та благав свого Бога». Тоді вони пішли й розповіли все цареві.

Дан. 6:1–13

O.Stemler

ДАНИЇЛ У ЛЕВ'ЯЧОМУ РОВІ

Прийшовши до царя Дарія, прибічники, які ненавиділи Даниїла, розповіли йому, що Даниїл не звертає ніякої уваги ні на царя, ні на підписаний ним наказ і тричі у день молиться своєму Богові. Почувши про це, цар дуже засмутився й вирішив врятувати Даниїла. Але придворні сказали йому, що за законом жоден царський наказ не можна змінити. Тоді цар звелів кинути Даниїла до рову з левами. Але він знав, що Бог Даниїла був всемогутнім Богом, і тому він сказав: «Твій Бог, що ти Йому служиш, Він завжди врятує тебе!» Потім цар повернувся до свого палацу, відмовився від вечері і протягом всієї ночі не міг заснути. На світанку цар поспішив до рову з левами, і, підійшовши, жалібним голосом покликав Даниїла: «Даниїле, рабе Бога Живого, чи твій Бог, Якому ти завжди служиш, міг урятувати тебе від левів?» А Даниїл відповів йому: «Мій Бог послав Свого Ангола, і позамикав пащі левів, і вони не пошкодили мені, бо перед Ним знайдено було мене невинним, а також перед тобою, царю, я не зробив шкоди».

Дарій надзвичайно зрадів, що Даниїл живий, і звелів підняти його з лев'ячого рову. І коли його підняли, виявилось, що леви не заподіяли йому ніякої шкоди. «І сказав цар, і привели тих мужів, що донесли на Даниїла, і повкидали до лев'ячої ями їх… І вони не сягнули *ще* до дна ями, як леви *вже* похапали їх, і потрощили всі їхні кості».

Після цього випадку цар Дарій написав листа і розіслав його по всьому своєму царству. У цьому листі він звелів усім народам шанувати Бога Даниїла, тому що він — Бог живий, вічний, а владарювання Його — нескінченне. «Він рятує та визволяє, і чинить знаки та чуда на небі та на землі, Він урятував Даниїла від лев'ячої сили».

Дан. 6:12–28

ПОВЕРНЕННЯ ЮДЕЇВ З ПОЛОНУ ВАВИЛОНСЬКОГО

Як нам вже відомо, війська ассирійців завоювали Північне царство, Ізраїль, та забрали із собою всіх ізраїльтян. (Це трапилося у сьомому сторіччі до Р. Х.). Через сто років об'єднані війська мідійців та вавилонян після дворічної облоги знищили столицю Ассирії, Ніневію. Отож, Вавилон став дуже сильною державою й грабував усі сусідні народи. Захопив він також і Південне царство, Юдею, разом з Єрусалимом, і забрав юдеїв у вавилонський полон.

Але й сильному Вавилону настав кінець. Вавилонську імперію завоювали мідійці та перси. Незабаром цар Персії, Кір, дозволив ізраїльтянам повернутися у рідні місця: «Так говорить Кір, цар перський: Усі земні царства дав мені Господь, Бог Небесний, і Він наказав мені збудувати Йому храма в Єрусалимі, що в Юдеї. Хто між вами з усього Його народу, — *нехай* буде Бог його з ним, і нехай він іде до Єрусалиму, що в Юдеї, і нехай будує дім Господа, Бога Ізраїлевого». На батьківщину повернулися більше сорока тисяч євреїв; головним чином це були юдеї, тобто євреї з коліна Юдиного. Вважається також, що повернулися на батьківщину люди з інших колін Ізраїля. Але чимало євреїв лишилося жити у країнах Перської імперії.

Пройшов рік після повернення на батьківщину, і ізраїльтяни, зібравшись в Єрусалимі, вирішили відбудувати зруйнований храм Господа. Було закладено фундамент нового храму. «А багато хто зі священиків і Левитів та з голів батьківських *родів*, старші, що бачили перший храм, при заснуванні його, того храму, своїми очима, плакали ревним голосом, а багато хто покликували піднесеним голосом у радості…» Зоровавель керував будівництвом цього храму. Але народи, які оселилися за цей час там, де раніше жили ізраїльтяни, ненавиділи їх і усіляко перешкоджали їм у будівництві храму; вони залякували ізраїльтян і звинувачували їх перед царем Персії Артаксерксом. Їм вдалося затримати роботу по відновленню храму Господнього на п'ятнадцять років — до царювання нового царя Персії, Дарія (це інший Дарій, а не той, про якого ми читали раніше, і який завоював Вавилон).

Цар Дарій підтвердив повеління царя Кіра, яке було дане Кіром раніше, і послав до Єрусалима листа з наказом закінчити будівництво храму. «І закінчений був цей храм до третього місяця адара, що він *місяць дванадцятий*, шостого року царювання царя Дарія».

Езд. 1–6

ЦАРИЦЯ ЕСТЕР

Цар Персії Ахашверош вирішив одружитися. Щоб знайти собі найвродливішу у Перськім царстві дружину, цар розіслав гінців у різні кінці свого царства, щоб зібрати вродливих дівчат у свою столицю, Сузи. Там протягом дванадцяти місяців їх готували до прийому у царя. На цей час у Персії було багато нащадків ізраїльтян, яких ассирійці та вавилоняни колись узяли у полон. «А в замку Сузи був один юдеянин, а ім'я йому Мордехай… І він виховував Гадассу, вона ж Естер, дочку свого дядька, бо не мала вона ні батька, ні матері. А ця дівчина була хорошої постави та вродливого вигляду, а коли помер її батько та мати її, Мордехай узяв її собі за дочку. І сталося, коли був оголошений царський наказ… взята була *й* Естер до царського дому… І цар покохав Естер понад усіх жінок… і він поклав царську корону на її голову, і зробив її царицею… І справив цар велику гостину для всіх своїх князів та своїх слуг, гостину *для* Естери, і зробив полегшення для округ, і дав дарунка за царською спроможністю… Естер *же* не виявляла місця свого народження та народу свого, як наказав був їй Мордехай…»

Після цього звеличив цар одного з князів своїх, Гамана, вище від усіх князів перських. «А всі цареві раби, що *були* в царській брамі, падали на коліна та вклонялися Гаманові, бо так про нього наказав цар. А Мордехай не падав на коліна й не вклонявся… і Гаман переповнився лютістю… і шукав *випадку* вигубити всіх юдеян, що *були* в усьому Ахашверошевому царстві…

І сказав Гаман до царя Ахашвероша: «Є один народ, розпорошений та поділений між народами в усіх округах твого царства, а закони їх різняться від *законів* усіх народів і законів царських вони не виконують, — і цареві не варто позоставляти їх…» І сказав цар до Гамана: «…*Дається тобі*… той народ, щоб робити з ним, як угодно в очах твоїх!» І були послані листи через гінців до всіх царських областей, щоб були повирубувані, побиті та понищені всі юдеї від малого й до старого, діти та жінки в один день, тринадцятий день дванадцятого місяця адара, а майно їх пограбувати… А в кожній окрузі та місці, куди доходило слово царя та його наказ, було велике лихо в юдеїв, і піст, і плач, і голосіння…»

Продовження далі

O. STEMLER.

ЦАРИЦЯ ЕСТЕР

Продовження

Коли Мордехай дізнався про все, що робиться навколо, то повідомив царицю Естер про царський наказ і наказував їй піти до царя благати його про милість та просити за народ свій. А Естер відповіла Мордехаю: «Кожен чоловік та жінка, що прийде до царя до внутрішнього подвір'я непокликаний, один йому закон, — убити *його*, окрім того, кому цар простягне золоте берло, — і буде він жити. А мене не кличуть входити до царя от уже тридцять день…» І сказав Мордехай у відповідь Естер: «Не думай в душі своїй, що втечеш до царського дому *одна* з усіх юдеїв… А хто знає, чи не на час, як оцей, досягла ти царства!» І сказала Естер у відповідь Мордехаю: «Іди, збери всіх юдеїв, що знаходяться в Сузах, і постіть за мене, і не їжте й не пийте три дні, ніч та день. Також я та дівчата мої будемо постити так, і так прийду до царя, хоч *це* не *буде* за законом. А якщо я загину, *то* загину…»

Між тим злий Гаман приготував «дерево заввишки у п'ятдесят ліктів… щоб повісити Мордехая на ньому». На третій день Естер вдяглася по-царськи й пішла до входу у дім царя Ахашвероша. «І цар простягнув Естері золоте берло, що в руці його, а Естер підійшла й доторкнулася до кінця берла», і запросила царя з Гаманом того ж дня на бенкет і вони прийшли. Під час бенкету Естер запросила їх прийти і наступного дня. Наступного дня «сказав до неї цар: «Що тобі, царице Естер? І яке прохання твоє?»… І відповідала Естер: «Нехай буде дане мені життя моє на жадання моє, а народ мій — на прохання моє! Бо продані ми, я та народ мій, на вигублення, на забій та на погибіль…» Так цар дізнався про підступні наміри Гамана. Тоді, за наказом царя, Гамана повісили на дереві, яке той приготував для Мордехая.

І були написані нові листи про те, «що цар дав *право* юдеям, які *живуть* у кожному місті, зібратися й стати за своє життя, вигубити, забити та погубити всяке військо народу та округи, що ненавидять їх, дітей та жінок… Гінці, що поїхали верхи на швидких конях, вийшли, приспішені та пігнані царським словом», щоб передати ці листи управителям ста двадцяти семи царських областей від Індії аж до Ефіопії.

На спомин про врятування ізраїльтян Мордехай встановив щорічне свято, яке зветься «Пурім», що й досі святкується євреями на 14-й та 15-й день єврейського місяця адар (у березні місяці).

КНИГА ЕСТЕР

НЕЕМІЯ ЗВОДИТЬ СТІНИ ЄРУСАЛИМА

Неемія був впливовим придворним царя Персії Артаксеркса у престольному місті Сузи.

Якось один ізраїльтянин повернувся з Єрусалима до Персії й розповів Неемії: «Позосталі, що лишилися з полону, там в окрузі, *живуть* у великій біді та в ганьбі, а мур Єрусалиму поруйнований, а брами його попалені огнем…» Почувши ці слова, Неемія «плакав, і був у жалобі *кілька* днів, і постив, і молився перед лицем Небесного Бога». Побачивши плач і жалобу Неемії цар Артаксеркс дозволив Неемії піти до Єрусалима, щоб звести стіни міста.

Повернувшись до Єрусалима, Неемія та ізраїльтяни почали відбудовувати зруйновані стіни й брами Єрусалима. Про це довідалися вороги Ізраїлю й погрозами вирішили перешкодити зведенню стін Єрусалима. Але Неемія озброїв своїх людей. «Будівничі *працювали* на мурі, а носії наладовували тягар, — вони однією рукою робили працю, а однією міцно тримали списа… А в кожного будівничого його меч був прив'язаний на стегнах його, і *так* вони будували». Рука Божа захищала будівельників, і через сто сорок років після того, як вавилонське військо зруйнувало й спалило Єрусалим, стіна була відбудована повністю.

«І зібрався ввесь народ, як один чоловік, на майдан… і сказали учителеві Ездрі принести книги Мойсеєвого Закону, що наказав був Господь Ізраїлеві. І приніс священик Ездра Закона перед збори з чоловіків та аж до жінок, і всіх, хто розумів чуте, першого дня сьомого місяця. І читав він… від світанку аж до полудня, перед чоловіками й жінками та тими, хто розуміє, а уші всього народу *були звернені* до книги Закону…. І поблагословив Ездра Господа, Бога великого, а ввесь народ відповів: «Амінь, Амінь!» *з* піднесенням своїх рук. І *всі* схилялися, і вклонялися Господеві обличчям до землі!»

Неем. 1–8

НАРОД ЗВЕРТАЄТЬСЯ ДО БОГА

Двадцять четвертого дня того місяця зібралися всі сини Ізраїлеві у пості та у веретищах, і попіл був на головах їхніх. І відділилося сім'я Ізраїлеве від усіх чужинців, і поставали й сповідали гріхи свої та провини батьків своїх. І стояли на місці своїм, і чверть дня читали з книги Закону Господа, Бога свого, а чверть — сповідалися і вклонялися Господеві, Богові своєму. «І сказали Левити: Ісус, і Кадміїл, Бані, Хашавнея, Шеревея, Годійя, Шеванія, Петахія: «Устаньте, поблагословіть Господа, Бога свого, відвіку аж довіку! І нехай благословляють Ім'я слави Твоєї, і нехай воно буде звеличене над усяке благословення та славу! Ти Господь єдиний! Ти вчинив небо, небеса небес, і все їхнє військо, землю та все, що на ній, моря та все, що в них, і Ти оживляєш їх усіх, а небесне військо Тобі вклоняється!»

Народ глибоко розкаявся в своїх гріхах і відступництві від Господа і молився: «А тепер, Боже наш, Боже великий, сильний та страшний, що бережеш заповіта та милість, — нехай не буде малою перед лицем Твоїм уся та мука, що спіткала нас, наших царів, наших зверхників, і священиків наших, і пророків наших, і батьків наших, і ввесь Твій народ від днів асирійських царів аж до цього дня! А ти справедливий у всьому, що приходить на нас, бо Ти правду робив, а ми були несправедливі… Через те все ми складаємо певну умову, і підписуємо, а печатки кладуть наші зверхники, наші Левити, наші священики».

І підписали цей заповіт найпочесніші люди й приклали свої печатки «…і решта народу, священики, Левити, придверні, співаки, *храмові* підданці, і кожен, відділений від народів краю до Божого Закону, їхні жінки, їхні сини, та їхні дочки, кожен знаючий *та* розуміючий, зміцняють *присягу* при браттях своїх, при своїх шляхетних, і вступили в клятву та присягу, щоб ходити в Божому Законі, що був даний через Мойсея, Божого раба, і щоб дотримуватися, і щоб виконувати всі заповіді Господа, нашого Бога, і права Його, і постанови Його».

Так прийняття слова Божого і молитви до Господа Бога здійснили й можуть здійснити велике пробудження в житті народу.

Неем. 9:1–6; 9:32–10:30

CLEVELAND
WOODWARD

СТРАЖДАННЯ ЙОВА

У країні Уц жив багатий чоловік на ім'я Йов. «І був чоловік цей невинний та праведний, і він Бога боявся, а від злого втікав». У нього було семеро синів та три дочки.

Йов любив Господа й постійно прославляв його в молитвах. Але сатана, надумавши згубити його, вирішив зробити все, аби змусити Йова відвернутися від Бога й зневажити Його.

Одного разу прийшов сатана до Бога. Господь запитав його: «Звідки ти йдеш?» А сатана відповів Господеві: «Я мандрував по землі та й перейшов її». Господь сказав йому: «Чи звернув ти увагу на раба Мого Йова? Бо немає *такого*, як він, на землі: муж він невинний та праведний, що Бога боїться, а від злого втікає». І відповів сатана Господеві й сказав: «Чи ж Йов дармо боїться Бога? Чи ж Ти не забезпечив його, і дім його, і все, що його? Чин його рук Ти поблагословив, а маєток його поширився по краю. Але простягни тільки руку Свою, і доторкнися до всього, що його, — чи він не зневажить Тебе перед лицем Твоїм?» Тоді Господь дозволив сатані випробувати Йова. Бог сказав сатані: «Ось усе, що його, — у твоїй руці…»

І тоді диявол почав шкодити Йову. Він вигубив усіх його дітей, знищив усе його майно. Але замість того, щоб зневажити Бога, Йов сказав: «Господь дав, — і Господь узяв… Нехай буде благословенне Господнє Ім'я!» А дружині своїй він сказав: «Чи ж ми будем приймати від Бога добре, а злого не приймем?» При цьому Йов не згрішив перед Господом і нічого поганого не сказав на Нього. Тоді сатана наслав на Йова жахливу хворобу — проказу. Страждання Йова були неймовірно тяжкі, і впав він у відчай.

Коли троє його друзів почули про те нещастя, що впало на нього, то прийшли поспівчувати йому та втішити його. Однак, замість того, щоб підтримати його у біді, вони почали викривати його, кажучи: «Пригадай-но, чи гинув невинний, і де праведні вигублені?» Йов мав надію лише на всемогутнього Творця й чекав допомоги лише від Нього.

Йов 1, 2, 4, 5

O. Stemler

ЙОВ ПІСЛЯ ТЯЖКИХ ВИПРОБУВАНЬ

Ніхто не пожалів Йова, крім Господа, Який з любов'ю слідкував за ним. Йов мав надію на Господа і сказав: «Та я знаю, що мій Викупитель живий, і останнього дня Він підійме із пороху цю шкіру мою, яка розпадається, і з тіла свого я Бога побачу…»

Раптом почалася сильна буря, і серед шуму її почувся голос Самого Господа. Бог став задавати питання, на які важко було знайти відповідь, і Йов ще ясніше зрозумів всемогутність і велич Творця.

Після того, як Господь закінчив говорити, Йов сказав Йому: «Я знаю, що можеш Ти все, і не спиняється задум у Тебе!»

Бог, випробувавши Йова, повністю повернув йому все втрачене і ще послав йому вдвоє більше від того, що він мав колись. А друзям Йова, які виявилися слабкі духом й вірою своєю, Господь сказав, що гнів Його впаде на голови їх за невірні слова про Нього, на відміну від Йова. Ось чому Бог наказав їм принести за себе жертву цілопалення і попросити Йова помолитися за них, бо тільки його молитву Він прийме. Друзі Йова вчинили за наказом Господнім, і, після молитви Йова, одержали прощення від Бога.

Після тяжких випробувань до Йова прийшли брати й сестри та всі колишні знайомі й принесли йому подарунки. «А Господь поблагословив останок *днів* Йова більше від початку його… І було в нього семеро синів та три дочки… І таких вродливих жінок, як Йовові дочки, не знайшлося по всій землі».

Йов 19:25–26 і розд. 37–42

КНИГА ПСАЛМІВ

До Книги псалмів, чи Псалтиря, читачі Біблії звертаються найчастіше. Вона складається зі ста п'ятдесяти псалмів, тобто поем, чи пісень, покладених на музику. У псалмах висловлюється все, що так хвилює серця вірних Богові: скорбота з приводу беззаконня на землі, надія на перемогу світла над темрявою, каяття у своїх гріхах і прагнення спасіння… У деяких псалмах знаходимо пророцтва про прихід Месії, Христа.

Як правило, мова йде про «Псалми Давида», бо він написав більшість із них, але серед них є й богодухновенні псалми, написані іншими авторами.

Нижче ми наводимо для прикладу два псалми. Уважно прочитавши їх, ми можемо мати деяке уявлення про решту псалмів. За змістом псалми були настільки довершені, що більшість християнських молитов складалася пізніше за ними.

Псалом 120

«Свої очі я зводжу на гори, звідки прийде мені допомога, — мені допомога від Господа, що вчинив небо й землю! Він не дасть захитатись нозі твоїй, не здрімає твій Сторож: оце не дрімає й не спить Сторож Ізраїлів! Господь — то твій Сторож, Господь — твоя тінь при правиці твоїй, — удень сонце не вдарить тебе, ані місяць вночі! Господь стерегтиме тебе від усякого зла, стерегтиме Він душу твою, — Господь стерегтиме твій вихід та вхід відтепер аж навіки!»

Псалом 150

«Алілуя! Хваліть Бога в святині Його, хваліте Його на могутнім Його небозводі! Хваліте Його за чини могутні Його, хваліте Його за могутню величність Його! Хваліте Його звуком трубним, хваліте Його на арфі та гуслах! Хваліте Його на бубні та танцем, хваліте Його на струнах та флейті! Хваліте Його на цимбалах дзвінких, хваліте Його на цимбалах гучних! Все, що дихає, — хай Господа хвалить! Алілуя!»

ЗАПАМ’ЯТАЄМО ДЕЯКІ ВІРШІ З КНИГИ ПСАЛМІВ

«Блажен муж, що за радою несправедливих не ходить, і не стоїть на дорозі грішних, і не сидить на сидінні злоріків» (1:1).

«І на Тебе надіятись будуть *усі*, що Ім’я Твоє знають, бо не кинув Ти, Господи, тих, хто шукає Тебе!» (9:11).

«Небо звіщає про Божую славу, а про чин Його рук розказує небозвід» (18:2).

«Буде боятися Господа ціла земля, всі мешканці всесвіту будуть лякатись Його…» (32:8).

«Скуштуйте й побачте, який добрий Господь, блаженна людина, що надію на Нього кладе!» (33:9).

«На Господа здай дорогу свою, і на Нього надію клади, і Він зробить…» (36:5).

«І до Мене поклич в день недолі, — Я тебе порятую, ти ж прославиш Мене!» (49:15).

«Серце чисте створи мені, Боже, і тривалого духа в моєму нутрі віднови» (50:12).

«*Мій* народе, — кожного часу надійтесь на Нього, серце своє перед Ним виливайте, Бог для нас — пристановище!» (61:9).

«…Щоб пізнати дорогу Твою на землі, посеред народів усіх — спасіння Твоє!» (66:3).

«Перше ніж гори народжені, і *поки* Ти витворив землю та світ, то відвіку й довіку — Ти Бог!» (89:2).

«І Господь став для мене твердинею, і мій Бог *став* за скелю притулку мого…» (93:22).

«Благослови, душе моя, Господа, і не забувай за всі добродійства Його!» (102:2).

«Бо як високо небо стоїть над землею, — велика така Його милість до тих, хто боїться Його…» (102:11).

«Початок премудрости — страх перед Господом…» (110:10).

«Зо мною Господь — не боюся *нікого*, що зробить людина мені?» (117:6).

«Чим додержить юнак у чистоті свою стежку? — Як держатиметься Твоїх слів!» (118:9).

«Твій я, спаси Ти мене…» (118:94).

«Хто сіє з слізьми, зі співом той жне…» (125:5).

«Господь близький всім, хто взиває до Нього, хто правдою кличе Його!» (144:18).

«Для моєї ноги
Твоє слово —
світильник,
то світло
для стежки моєї»

Пс. 118:105

КНИГА ПРИПОВІСТЕЙ СОЛОМОНОВИХ

Одна з книг Біблії має назву «Книга приповістей Соломонових». Більша частина цих приповістей написана мудрим царем Соломоном. Вона складається з коротких, стислих повчань, призначених, головним чином, для молоді. Теми приповістей — мудрість, праведність, страх Господній, знання, мораль, стриманість, наполегливість, здоровий глузд, покладання на Бога, співчуття до знедолених, любов до ворогів та інше. Ось деякі з них:

«Страх Господній — початок премудрости, — нерозумні погорджують мудрістю та напучуванням. Послухай, мій сину, напучення батька свого, і не відкидай науки матері своєї…» (1:7, 8).

«Мій сину, як грішники будуть тебе намовляти, — *то з ними* не згоджуйся ти!» (1:10).

«Надійся на Господа всім своїм серцем, а на розум свій не покладайся! Пізнавай ти Його на всіх дорогах своїх, і Він випростує твої стежки» (3:5, 6).

«Мій сину, карання Господнього не відкидай, і картання Його не вважай тягарем, — бо кого Господь любить, картає того, і кохає, немов батько сина!» (3:11, 12).

«Прокляття Господнє на домі безбожного, а мешкання праведних Він благословить» (3:33).

«Стережи, сину мій, заповідь батька свого, і не відкидай науки матері своєї!» (6:20).

«Я кохаю *всіх* тих, хто кохає мене, хто ж шукає мене — мене знайде!» (8:17).

«Хто тисне нужденного, той ображає свого Творця, а хто милостивий до вбогого, той поважає Його» (14:31).

«Праведність люд підіймає, а беззаконня — то сором народів» (14:34).

«Розум людини обдумує путь її, але кроки її наставляє Господь» (16:9).

«Хто батька грабує, хто матір жене? — Це син, що застиджує та осоромлює…» (19:26).

«Привчай юнака до дороги його, і він, як постаріється, не уступиться з неї» (22:6).

«Дай мені, сину мій, своє серце, і очі твої хай кохають дороги мої» (23:26).

«Якщо голодує твій ворог — нагодуй його хлібом, а як спрагнений він — водою напій ти його…» (25:21).

КНИГА ПРОПОВІДНИКА

Наступною книгою Біблії, після приповістей Соломонових, є «Книга Еклезіястова», або «Книга Проповідника». Вона складається із дванадцяти розділів і містить у собі чудові й мудрі висловлювання, дуже близькі до повчань з книги приповістей Соломонових. Ось декілька віршів із цієї книги:

«Наймарніша марнота, сказав Проповідник, наймарніша марнота, — марнота усе!» (1:2).

«Кращий смуток від сміху, бо при обличчі сумнім добре серце!» (7:3).

«Мудрість краща від зброї військової, але один грішник погубить багато добра…» (9:18).

«Хто яму копає, той в неї впаде, а хто валить мура, того гадина вкусить» (10:8).

«Хліб свій пускай по воді, бо по багатьох днях *знов* знайдеш його…» (11:1).

«Тішся, юначе, своїм молодецтвом, а серце твоє нехай буде веселе за днів молодощів твоїх! І ходи ти дорогами серця свого й видінням очей своїх, але знай, що за все це впровадить тебе Бог до суду!» (11:9).

«І пам'ятай в днях юнацтва свого про свого Творця, аж поки не прийдуть злі дні й не наступлять літа, про які говорити ти будеш: «Для мене вони неприємні!», аж поки не стемніє сонце, і світло, і місяць, і зорі, і не вернуться хмари густі за дощем, у день, коли затремтять ті, хто дім стереже, і зігнуться мужні, і спинять роботу *свою* млинарі, бо їх стане мало, і потемніють ті, хто в вікно визирає, і двері подвійні на вулицю замкнені будуть, як зменшиться гуркіт млина, і голос пташини замовкне, і затихнуть всі дочки співучі, і будуть боятись високого місця, і жахи в дорозі *їм будуть*, і мигдаль зацвіте, й обтяжіє кобилка, і загине бажання, бо людина відходить до вічного дому свого, а по вулиці будуть ходити довкола голосільники, аж поки не пірветься срібний шнурок, і не зломиться кругла посудина з золота, і при джерелі не розіб'ється глек, і не зламається коло, *й не руне* в криницю… І вернеться порох у землю, як був, а дух вернеться *знову* до Бога, що дав був його!» (12:1–7).

КНИГА ЕКЛЕЗІЯСТОВА

C.L. WOODWARD

ПРОРОКИ БОЖІ

Господь нерідко звертався до народу ізраїльського через людей, особливо наближених до Нього — пророків. Вони не лише передбачали майбутнє народу, але й звіщали волю Божу. Час від часу Господь посилав Своїх пророків, щоб вони за Об'явленням Його звіщали народові волю Його, попереджали, застерігали від гріха та ідолослужіння й свідчили про могутні діла Божі у минулому та майбутньому. Бог обирав пророків серед ізраїльтян, які жили у Північному та у Південному царствах. Часто пророки свідчили людям тоді, коли царі, священики й простий народ сходили зі шляху, вказаному Господом, робили нечестиві вчинки; коли царствам загрожували війна, голод та інші лиха. Нагадуючи про діла Господа у минулому, пророки пробуджували у людях усвідомлення необхідності повної відданості Богові, а не лише виконання завчених ритуалів та обрядів; вони сповіщали про майбутню кару від Господа — напад поганських народів на непокірний Ізраїль; водночас вони свідчили й про помсту Господа тим народам, які чинять лихо Ізраїлю. Пророки прорекли про розсіяння народу Ізраїля по всьому світу, та про Його повернення у землю обітовану; вони передбачали й пришестя Месії, тобто Помазаника Божого, Його смерть задля спасіння Ізраїля і всього світу і Його воскресення; розповідали й про світле майбутнє, коли Месія знову прийде і буде царювати вічно…

Деякі пророки писали пророцькі книги. У Біблії є сімнадцять пророчих книг. За своїм обсягом — це п'ята частина усієї Біблії. Ці книги були записані шістнадцятьма пророками (з них Єремія написав дві книги). Ось імена пророків Старого Заповіту у приблизній хронологічній послідовності: Йоіл, Йона, Амос, Осія, Ісая, Михей, Софонія, Наум, Єремія, Авакум, Овдій, Даниїл, Єзекіїль, Огій, Захарія та Малахія. Пророчі книги Біблії не завжди розташовані відповідно до хронології їх написання. Корисно запам'ятати імена усіх пророків, щоб потім легше було знаходити їхні книги у Біблії.

ПРОРОК ІСАЯ

Пророк Ісая жив в Ізраїлі багато сторіч тому, задовго до нашої ери, тобто до Різдва Христового. Він із щирим серцем захищав Славу Божу, викривав лицемірну побожність ізраїльського народу, який відпадав від Господа, та закликав зухвалих грішників до каяття. Він пророкував про долю багатьох міст, і ці пророцтва здійснилися повністю.

Пророк Ісая постійно закликав народ покладатися на Бога. Наведемо один з його закликів: «Хіба ж ти не знаєш, або ти не чув: Бог відвічний — Господь, що кінці землі Він створив? Він не змучується та не втомлюється, і не збагненний розум Його. Він змученому дає силу, а безсилому — міць. І помучаться хлопці й потомляться, і юнаки спотикнутись — спіткнуться, а ті, хто надію складає на Господа, силу відновлять, крила підіймуть, немов ті орли, будуть бігати — і не потомляться, будуть ходити — і не помучаться!»

Ісая пророче передбачив народження Месії — Спасителя людства, Ісуса Христа. У своїй книзі він так ясно виклав історію народження Христа, Його життя, страждання, смерть та воскресення, що можна подумати, що Ісая вже тоді, за декілька сторіч до народження Ісуса Христа, наяву бачив те, що відбудеться у далекому майбутньому і що записане у книгах Нового Заповіту. Це ще раз свідчить про богодухновенність Біблії, в якій зібрані книги, написані різними людьми у різні часи.

«Направду ж Він немочі наші узяв і наші болі поніс, а ми уважали Його за пораненого, ніби Бог Його вдарив *поразами* й мучив… А Він був ранений за наші гріхи, за наші провини Він мучений був, — кара на Ньому *була за* наш мир, Його ж ранами нас уздоровлено! Усі ми блудили, немов ті овечки, розпорошились кожен на власну дорогу, — і на Нього Господь поклав гріх усіх нас! Він гноблений був та понижуваний, але уст Своїх не відкривав. Як ягня був проваджений Він на заколення, і як овечка перед стрижіями своїми мовчить, *так* і Він не відкривав Своїх уст…»

Іс. 40:28–31; 53:4–7

«І МЕЧІ СВОЇ ПЕРЕКУЮТЬ ВОНИ НА ЛЕМЕШІ...»

У книзі пророка Ісаї серед багатьох пророцтв ми читаємо про останні часи та про царство Месії, Якого всі чекають, Богом обіцяного Спасителя та Володаря світу:

«І станеться на кінці днів,
міцно поставлена буде гора
дому Господнього на шпилі гір,
і піднята буде вона понад згір'я, —
і полинуть до неї всі люди.
І підуть численні народи та й скажуть:
«Ходіть та зберімось на гору Господню,
до дому Бога Якового,
і доріг Своїх Він нас навчить,
і ми підемо стежками Його!
Бо вийде з Сіону Закон,
і слово Господнє — з Єрусалиму».
І Він буде судити між людьми,
і буде численні народи розсуджувати.
І мечі свої перекують вони на лемеші,
а списи свої — на серпи.
Не підійме меча народ проти народу,
і більше не будуть навчатись війни!»

Іс. 2:2–4

C.L. WOODWARD.

І ЗЛА НЕ БУДЕ НА ЗЕМЛІ…

Господь відкрив пророку Ісаї, що настане у майбутньому царство Месії — Ісуса Христа, Сина Божого. Тоді на землі не буде ані зла, ані лиха.

«Його уподобання — в страху Господньому,
і Він не на погляд очей Своїх буде судити,
і не на послух ушей Своїх буде рішати,
але буде судити убогих за правдою,
і правосуддя чинитиме слушно сумирним землі.
І вдарить Він землю жезлом Своїх уст,
а віддихом губ Своїх смерть заподіє безбожному.
І станеться поясом клубів Його справедливість,
вірність же — поясом стегон Його!
І замешкає вовк із вівцею,
і буде лежати пантера з козлям,
і *будуть* разом телятко й левчук, та теля відгодоване,
а дитина мала їх водитиме!
А корова й ведмідь будуть пастися *разом*,
разом будуть лежати їхні діти,
і лев буде їсти солому, немов та худоба!
І буде бавитися немовлятко над діркою гада,
і відняте від перс *дитинча* простягне свою руку
над нору гадюки, —
не вчинять лихого та шкоди не зроблять
на всій святій Моїй горі,
бо земля буде повна пізнання Господнього *так*,
як море вода покриває!»

Іс. 11:3–9

ПРОРОК ОСІЯ

Ми вже читали про те, як Ізраїль, чи Північне царство, відвернувся від Господа, про його беззаконня, нечестя та поклоніння ідолам. Господь посилав Своїх пророків, неодноразово карав народ Ізраїлю, щоб навернути його на шлях праведності, але все було марним. Царі й народ продовжували чинити беззаконня і вклонятися ідолам. Тому Господь вирішив зруйнувати це царство і віддати його народ у руки загарбників.

Невдовзі до падіння Північного царства у ньому жили пророки Осія*, Ісая та Михей. У книзі пророка Осії відносини Бога з Ізраїлем показані у вигляді шлюбу, а відступлення Ізраїля від Господа — як зрада дружини чоловікові. Ось як пророк Осія говорить про зрадливість народу Ізраїлю:

«Послухайте слова Господнього, Ізраїлеві сини, *бо* Господь має прю із мешканцями земними, бо нема на землі ані правди, ні милости, ані богопізнання. Клянуть та неправду говорять, і вбивають та крадуть, і чинять перелюб, поставали насильниками, а кров доторкається крови… Погине народ Мій за те, що не має знання: тому, що знання ти відкинув, відкину *й* тебе, щоб не був ти для Мене священиком. А тому, що забув ти Закон свого Бога, забуду синів твоїх і Я!.. Не тішся, Ізраїлю, радістю, як ті народи, бо ти чиниш блуд, *відступаючи* від свого Бога, дар блудодійний кохаєш на всіх токах збіжжевих…»

Але пророк Божий каже й про те, як Господь благословить народ Свій, коли Ізраїль навернеться до Господа й покається в гріхах своїх: «Вернися, Ізраїлю, до Господа, Бога свого, бо спіткнувся ти через провину свою! Візьміть із собою слова, та й зверніться до Господа… «Ворохобність їхню вилікую, добровільно любитиму їх, бо Мій гнів відвернувся від нього. Я буду Ізраїлеві, як роса, розцвіте він, неначе лілея, і пустить коріння своє, мов Ливан».

Ось що Осія пророкує щодо далекого майбутнього Ізраїлю, який розкається у гріхах своїх: «І буде число Ізраїлевих синів, як морський пісок, що його не можна ані зміряти, ані злічити. І станеться, замість того, що говориться їм: «Ви не народ Мій», буде їм сказано: «*Ви* сини Бога Живого».

Ос. 4:1–2, 6; 9:1; 14:2–6; 2:1

---

* *Останнього царя Північного царства також звали Осія.*

C.L. WOODWARD.

ПРОРОК ЙОІЛ

Невідомо, коли саме жив пророк Йоіл, але вважається, що він був одним з перших пророків Юдеї. У книзі Йоіла є багато пророцтв про далеке майбутнє, про грядущий День Господній:

«Горе дневі тому! Бо близький день Господній, і прийде він від Всемогутнього… Засурміть на Сіоні в сурму, здійміть крик на святій горі Моїй! Затремтіть, всі мешканці землі, бо прийшов день Господній, бо близько *вже він*… І буде потому, — виллю Я Духа Свого на кожне тіло, і пророкуватимуть ваші сини й ваші дочки, а вашим старим будуть снитися сни, юнаки ваші бачити будуть видіння. І також на рабів та невільниць за тих днів виллю Духа Свого. І дам Я ознаки на небі й землі, — кров та огонь, та стовпи диму. Заміниться сонце на темність, а місяць — на кров перед приходом Господнього дня, великого та страшного! І станеться, — кожен, хто кликати буде Господнє Ім'я, *той* спасеться, бо на Сіонській горі та в Єрусалимі буде спасіння, як Господь говорив, та для тих позосталих, що Господь їх покличе». Через багато сторіч після того святий апостол Петро наводив народові Ізраїлю деякі з цих слів, коли свідчив їм про Господа Ісуса Христа.

Є у книзі пророка Йоіла місце, де він говорить про поновлення Ізраїлю:

«Бо ось тими днями та часу того, коли долю Юді та Єрусалиму верну, то зберу всі народи, зведу їх у долину Йосафатову, і там буду судитися з ними за народ Мій і спадщину Мою, за Ізраїля, що його розпорошили поміж народами, а Мій Край поділили. І за народ Мій вони кидали жереба… І Господь загримить із Сіону, та з Єрусалиму Свій голос подасть, і небо й земля затремтять, та Господь — охорона Своєму народові, і твердиня синам Ізраїлевим! І пізнаєте ви, що Я — Господь, Бог ваш, Який пробуває в Сіоні, на святій Своїй горі. І станеться Єрусалим за святиню…»

КНИГА ПРОРОКА ЙОІЛА

ПРОРОК ЙОНА

Якось Господь сказав Йоні: «Устань, іди до Ніневії, великого міста, і проповідуй проти нього, бо їхнє зло прийшло перед лице Моє». Йона, не бажаючи послухатись, вирішив утекти від лиця Господнього. Він дійшов до Яфи, а там сів на корабель, що плив до міста Таршіш.

Але Господь наслав сильний вітер, на морі здійнялася буря страшна, і корабель ледве не розбився. Моряки дуже злякалися, кожен став молитися до свого бога і викидати у море вантаж, щоб полегшити судно. Йона ж, зійшовши у трюм, міцно спав. Коли моряки розбудили його, Йона розповів їм, що біжить від лиця Господнього. А тоді він сказав їм: «Візьміть мене, і киньте мене до моря, і втихомириться море перед вами; бо я знаю, що через мене оця велика буря на вас». Йону кинули в море, і воно відразу ж заспокоїлося. Тоді всі на кораблі вжахнулися жахом великим перед Господом, принесли Йому жертви і дали обітницю. Бог же звелів великій рибі проковтнути Йону. І той, перебуваючи три дні і три ночі в череві її, молився Господу, Богу своєму. І тоді Господь звелів рибі вивергнути Йону на суходіл.

Господь звернувся до Йони вдруге: «Устань, іди до Ніневії, великого міста, і проповідуй на нього те слово, що Я говорив був тобі!» Цього разу Йона не ослухався Господа і пішов до Ніневії. Коли він прийшов туди, то став проповідувати на вулицях і казати: «Ще сорок день, — і Ніневія буде зруйнована!» Цар же Ніневії, довідавшись про це, вийшов зі свого палацу, скинув із себе царські шати, вбрався у веретище (жалобну одежу) і звелів, щоб усі люди, і навіть худоба, були вкриті веретищем, щоб вони постилися, і щоб народ весь час закликав до Бога, і молив Його про прощення усіх своїх гріхів, злих вчинків, нечестивих думок і хибних шляхів. Усі жителі Ніневії повірили Богові й пророку Його.

Господь побачив, що жителі Ніневії відвернулися від злих діянь, змилосердився над ними і не наслав на них того лиха, яким хотів їх покарати. Милосердний Господь не хоче загибелі грішників, але хоче, щоб усі люди отримали спасіння каяттям у гріхах своїх і наверненням до Нього.

КНИГА ПРОРОКА ЙОНИ

ПРОРОК МИХЕЙ

Пророк Михей народився у місті Назареті, яке розташоване, приблизно, у п'ятдесяти кілометрах на південний захід від Єрусалима. Він пророкував у 740–700 роках до Р. Х., коли на престолі Юдеї сиділи царі Йотам, Ахаз та Єзекія, а на престолі Ізраїлю — царі Менахем, Пекахія, Пеках та Осія.

Пророк Михей жив у темну добу духовного занепаду ізраїльтян. Він яскравими та вдумливими прикладами викривав зіпсованість духовенства та всі злодіяння, запозичені від поганських народів. Михей пророкував про відхід народу від Бога, про майбутню кару від Господа та суд над керівниками народу, про знищення Самарії, Єрусалима та Храму Господнього… Він пророкував також і про майбутнього Царя Сіону та про Його Всесвітнє Царство, про Месію — Ісуса Христа.

«Та буде наприкінці днів, гора дому Господнього міцно поставлена буде вершиною гір, і піднесена буде вона понад узгір'я, і будуть народи до неї пливсти. І підуть численні народи та й скажуть: Ходімо, і вийдім на гору Господню та до дому Якового, і Він буде навчати доріг Своїх нас, і ми будемо ходити стежками Його. Бо вийде Закон із Сіону, а слово Господнє — із Єрусалиму. І Він буде судити численні племена, і розсуджувати буде народи міцні аж у далечині. І вони перекують мечі свої на лемеші, а списи свої — на серпи. Не підійме меча народ на народ, і більше не будуть навчатись війни! І буде кожен сидіти під своїм виноградником, і під своєю фіґовницею, і не буде того, хто б страшив, бо уста Господа Саваота *оце* прорекли. Усі-бо народи ходитимуть кожен ім'ям свого бога, а ми будем ходити Ім'ям Господа, нашого Бога, навіки-віків! Того дня — промовляє Господь — позбираю кульгаве й зґромаджу розігнане, і те, що на нього навів *коли* лихо. І зроблю Я кульгаве останком, а віддалене — потужним народом, і зацарює над ними Господь на Сіонській горі відтепер й аж навіки! А ти, башто Черідна, підгірку Сіонської доньки, прийде до тебе і дійде старе панування, царювання для донечки Єрусалиму…»

«І Яковів залишок буде посеред численних народів, як роса та від Господа, як той дощ на траві…»

КНИГА ПРОРОКА МИХЕЯ

ПРОРОЦТВО ПРО ПЕРШЕ ПРИШЕСТЯ МЕСІЇ

На початку цієї книги розповідалось, як Бог створив людину за образом Своїм та за подобою Своєю. Господь бажав, щоб людина була такою, як Він Сам: милосердною, справедливою та безгрішною. Але вже перші люди — Адам і Єва — не встояли перед спокусою гріха. Їх перший син Каїн убив свого брата Авеля. І земля згодом настільки просякла гріхом, що Господь сказав: «Усе повідступало, разом стали бридкими вони, нема доброчинця, нема ні одного!..» А розплата за гріх — довічна загибель. Господь Бог обрав Собі один народ на землі, щоб той зберігав віру у Нього, істинного Бога, та жив би за заповідями Його. І обрав Він синів Ізраїлевих. Бог нерідко через пророків Своїх казав ізраїльському народові, що незабаром прийде Спаситель світу — Месія (Помазаник), або грецькою мовою — Христос. Так, у передбаченні майбутнього, пророк Ісая за сімсот років до народження Ісуса Христа передрік: «Бо Дитя народилося нам, даний нам Син, і влада на раменах Його, і кликнуть ім'я Йому: Дивний Порадник, Бог сильний, Отець вічности, Князь миру».

Пророк Михей вказав навіть на те місце, де народиться Месія: «А ти, Віфлеєме-Єфрате, хоч малий ти у тисячах Юди, — із тебе Мені вийде Той, що буде Владика в Ізраїлі, і віддавна постання Його, від днів віковічних».

Ми дізнаємося також і про основну мету пришестя Месії: відвернути людство від гріха, навернути до Бога і врятувати всіх людей, прийнявши Самому смерть за їхні гріхи. Ось що написано про це у п'ятдесят третьому розділі книги пророка Ісаї: «Направду ж Він немочі наші узяв і наші болі поніс, а ми уважали Його за пораненого, ніби Бог Його вдарив *поразами* й мучив… А Він був ранений за наші гріхи, за наші провини Він мучений був, — кара на Ньому *була за* наш мир, Його ж ранами нас уздоровлено! Усі ми блудили, немов ті овечки, розпорошились кожен на власну дорогу, — і на Нього Господь поклав гріх усіх нас! Він гноблений був та понижуваний, але уст Своїх не відкривав».

І все, написане у пророчих книгах Біблії, збулось! Бо Слово Боже істинне. Усі ці пророцтва здійснилися через пришестя на землю Ісуса Христа. У другій частині нашої книги розповідається про народження Ісуса Христа, про Його життя та вчення, про Його смерть і воскресення із мертвих.

Пс. 13:3; Іс. 9:5, 53:4–7; Мих. 5:1

O.A. STEMLER

НОВИЙ ЗАПОВІТ

НОВИЙ ЗАПОВІТ

Новий Заповіт складається з 27 книжок, або частин. До Нового Заповіту входять чотири Євангелії (від Матвія, Марка, Луки та Івана), Дії апостолів, 21 послання та «Об'явлення святого Івана Богослова». Грецьке слово «Євангелія» означає «Блага звістка».

У всіх Євангеліях викладається одне і те ж вчення, хоча і написані вони чотирма різними авторами під впливом Духа Святого. У них описується, головним чином, життя і вчення Спасителя світу, Господа Ісуса Христа. Чотири Євангелії — це майже половина Нового Заповіту.

«Дії святих апостолів» відтворюють події, що сталися після вознесення Ісуса Христа. Ця книга, як і «Євангелія від святого Луки», написана лікарем Лукою.

Усі послання, тобто листи, святих апостолів написані учнями та послідовниками Ісуса Христа. Яків та Юда написали по одному посланню, Петро — два, Іван — три, а Павло — тринадцять послань. Хто був автором «Послання до Євреїв» точно не відомо, хоч є припущення, що воно належить Павлу. У посланнях пропонуються настанови як треба жити християнинові, пояснюється євангельське вчення, а також, частково, описуються події, пов'язані із життям перших християн.

«Об'явлення святого Івана Богослова» було написане апостолом Іваном, тим самим учнем Ісуса Христа, який є автором «Євангелії від святого Івана». Ця книга — об'явлення майбутнього, книга про те, що Господь відкрив «рабові Своєму Івану» і «що незабаром має статися».

НОВИЙ ЗАПОВІТ

ЗАХАРІЙ ТА АНГЕЛ У ХРАМІ

Коли почалися події, описані у Новому Заповіті, тобто дві тисячі років тому, єврейський народ був у дуже важкому становищі. Вже декілька століть ізраїльтяни не мали власного царя. Ізраїлем володіли ассирійці, вавилоняни, греки… і, нарешті, римські завойовники. Бог вже не звертався до народу Свого через пророків, як у давні часи. Останній з пророків Божих, Малахія, жив у п'ятому сторіччі до народження Ісуса Христа.

Отож, народ, тяжко страждаючи, з нетерпінням чекав пришестя обіцяного Месії, Який звільнив би його від іноземного ярма та навернув людські серця до Бога. Але перш ніж з'явився Месія, Ісус Христос, Бог почав готувати народ Ізраїлю до Його пришестя через проповідника Івана.

Народження Івана Христителя було незвичайним. Батько його, Захарій, був священиком. Жив він разом із дружиною своєю Єлисаветою в горах Юдеї. Подружжя було праведним і жило за всіма заповідями та настановами Божими. Були вони похилого віку, але дітей не мали. Одного разу, коли Захарій служив у храмі в Єрусалимі, а безліч людей молилося у дворі храму, під час кадіння з'явився йому Ангел Господній, Гавриїл. Захарій дуже злякався. Ангел же промовив до нього: «Не бійся, Захаріє, бо почута молитва твоя, і дружина твоя Єлисавета сина породить тобі, ти ж даси йому ймення Іван. І він буде на радість та втіху тобі, і з його народження багато хто втішаться. Бо він буде великий у Господа, «ні вина, ні п'янкого напою не питиме», і наповниться Духом Святим ще з утроби своєї матері. І багато синів із Ізраїля він наверне до їхнього Господа Бога».

Але Захарій засумнівався у словах Ангела і відповів: «Із чого пізнаю я це? Я ж старий, та й дружина моя *вже* похилого віку».

Ангел почав докоряти священику Захарію за його зневіру і сказав: «…І замовкнеш ось ти, і говорити не зможеш аж до дня, коли станеться це, за те, що ти віри не йняв був словам моїм, які збудуться часу свого!»

Між тим, народ чекав, коли Захарій вийде з храму Господнього, і всі дивувались, чого він не з'являється.

Лк. 1:5–25

НАРОДЖЕННЯ ІВАНА ХРИСТИТЕЛЯ

Сталося саме так, як напророкував Ангел Гавриїл. Не пройшло і року, як у Захарія та Єлисавети народився син. Вони дуже зраділи, а разом з ними і їхні родичі. У ті давні часи у родинах було значно більше дітей, аніж сьогодні. Якщо ж у когось не було дітей, як у Захарія та Єлисавети, то це вважалося великим нещастям. Дітям давали імена батьків чи родичів.

«І сталося восьмого дня, прийшли, щоб обрізати дитя, і хотіли назвати його йменням батька його — Захарій. І озвалася мати його та й сказала: «Ні, — нехай названий буде Іван!» А до неї сказали: «Таж у родині твоїй нема жадного, який названий був тим ім'ям!» І кивали до батька його, — як хотів би назвати його? Попросивши ж табличку, написав він слова: «Іван імення йому». І всі дивувались. І в тій хвилі уста та язик розв'язались йому, — і він став говорити, благословляючи Бога! І страх обгорнув усіх їхніх сусідів, і по всіх верховинах юдейських пронеслася чутка про це все… А всі, що почули, розважали у серці своїм та казали: «Чим то буде дитина оця?»… І Господня рука була з нею.

Його ж батько Захарій наповнився Духом Святим, та й став пророкувати й казати: «Благословенний Господь, Бог Ізраїлів, що зглянувся й визволив люд Свій! Він ріг спасіння підніс нам у домі Давида, Свого слуги, як був заповів відвіку устами святих пророків Своїх… Ти ж, дитино, станеш пророком Всевишнього, бо будеш ходити перед Господом, щоб дорогу Йому приготувати, щоб народу Його дати пізнати спасіння у відпущенні їхніх гріхів, через велике милосердя нашого Бога, що ним Схід із висоти нас відвідав, щоб світити *всім* тим, хто перебуває в темряві й тіні смертельній, щоб спрямувати наші ноги на дорогу миру!»

Про юнацькі роки Івана написано дуже мало. У Євангелії від святого Луки можна лише прочитати: «А дитина росла, і скріплялась на дусі, і перебувала в пустинях до дня свого з'явлення перед Ізраїлем».

Лк. 1:57–80

БЛАГОВІЩЕННЯ ПРО НАРОДЖЕННЯ ІСУСА ХРИСТА

Послав Бог у цей гріховний світ Свого Сина, Ісуса Христа, щоб врятувати людство від гріхів та вічної загибелі. З Його народженням на землі настала нова ера. Навіть наше літочислення починається від року народження Христа. Дивовижною є сама історія народження Ісуса. Уявіть-но тільки собі: Йому, Синові Творця всесвіту, довелося народитися у хліві для худоби. Незабаром цар тієї країни вирішив убити Його.

Але почнемо спочатку. У маленькому місті Назареті, на півночі Ізраїлю, жила дівчина, яку звали Марія. Вона дуже любила Господа і мала чисте серце. Одного разу їй з'явився Ангел Гавриїл, посланий Богом, і промовив: «Радій, благодатная, Господь із тобою! Ти благословенна між жонами!» Марія, побачивши Його, дуже збентежилася. Але Ангел сказав їй: «Не бійся, Маріє, — бо в Бога благодать ти знайшла! І ось ти в утробі зачнеш, і Сина породиш, і даси Йому ймення Ісус. Він же буде Великий, і Сином Всевишнього званий, і Господь Бог дасть Йому престола Його батька Давида. І повік царюватиме Він у домі Якова, і царюванню Його не буде кінця».

Марія не була одруженою, вона була заручена із благочестивим чоловіком, якого звали Йосип. «Вона запитала Ангела: «Як же станеться це, коли мужа не знаю?» І Ангел промовив у відповідь їй: «Дух Святий злине на тебе, і Всевишнього сила обгорне тебе, через те то й Святе, що народиться, буде Син Божий!»… Марія відповіла: «Я ж Господня раба: нехай буде мені згідно з словом твоїм!» І відійшов Ангел від неї».

Дізнавшись, що Марія чекає дитину, Йосип хотів таємно відпустити її. Але Ангел Господній з'явився йому уві сні й сказав: «Йосипе, сину Давидів, не бійся прийняти Марію, дружину свою, бо зачате в ній — то від Духа Святого. І вона вродить Сина, ти ж даси Йому ймення Ісус, бо спасе Він людей Своїх від їхніх гріхів».

Лк. 1:26–35, 38; Мт. 1:19–21

НАРОДЖЕННЯ ІСУСА ХРИСТА

Коли Марія була вже вагітною, то довелося їй та Йосипові вирушити у далеку дорогу, бо римський кесар Август наказав зробити перепис населення по всій імперії. Кожному треба було піти до міста своїх предків. Йосип та Марія походили із дому та роду царя Давида, який правив Ізраїлем за тисячу років до народження Ісуса. Рідним містом Давида був Віфлеєм.

Отож, Йосип та Марія вирушили до Віфлеєма, міста свого предка Давида. Від Назарета до Віфлеєма — більше ста кілометрів. На той час ще не існувало ні поїздів, ні автомобілів, і така подорож тривала декілька днів. Назарет знаходиться на півночі Ізраїлю, у Галілеї, а Віфлеєм — на півдні, в Юдеї. Йдучи з Галілеї до Юдеї, треба було пройти й через Самарію. А Самарія та Юдея — гірські місцевості.

Коли, нарешті, Йосип та Марія дійшли до Віфлеєма, вільних місць у гостиному дворі не виявилося. Чимало людей прийшло до Віфлеєма для перепису. Марії ж настав час родити. «І породила вона свого Первенця Сина, і Його сповила, і до ясел поклала Його…» — читаємо у Євангелії. Це значить, що вони заночували в загоні для худоби. Давні перекази стверджують, що цей хлів знаходився у печері. І до сьогоднішнього дня пастухи у Палестині використовують для своїх овець такі печери.

Лк. 2:1–7

АНГЕЛИ ЗВІЩАЮТЬ ПАСТУХАМ ПРО НАРОДЖЕННЯ ІСУСА ХРИСТА

У ті часи навколо містечка Віфлеєм знаходилось багато пасовиськ. У ніч, коли народився Ісус, деякі пастухи не спали, бо стерегли свою отару.

«Аж ось Ангол Господній з'явивсь коло них, і слава Господня осяяла їх. І вони перестрашились страхом великим… Та Ангол промовив до них: «Не лякайтесь, бо я ось благовіщу вам радість велику, що станеться людям усім. Бо сьогодні в Давидовім місті народився для вас Спаситель, Який є Христос Господь. А ось вам ознака: Дитину сповиту ви знайдете, що в яслах лежатиме». І ось раптом з'явилася з Анголом сила велика небесного війська, що Бога хвалили й казали: «Слава Богу на висоті, і на землі мир, у людях добра воля!»

Як бачите, для народження Ісуса Христа, Спасителя світу, Бог обрав не палац, а печеру. І першими сповістив про народження Його не багачів, а простих пастухів, які прийшли першими вклонитися Спасителю людства.

Лк. 2:9–14

HHofmann

ПАСТУХИ ПРИХОДЯТЬ ДО ІСУСА

Ми можемо лише уявити собі, як злякалися пастухи, побачивши Ангелів, як вони здивувались, почувши про народження Спасителя, Господа Христа. Тому й зрозуміло, що вони залишили свою отару й попрямували до Віфлеєма. Ось як про це написано в Євангелії: «І сталось, коли Анголи відійшли від них в небо, пастухи зачали говорити один одному: «Ходім до Віфлеєму й побачмо, що сталося там, про що сповістив нас Господь». І прийшли, поспішаючи, і знайшли *там* Марію та Йосипа, та Дитинку, що в яслах лежала. А побачивши, розповіли про *все* те, що про Цю Дитину було їм звіщено. І всі, хто почув, дивувались тому, що їм пастухи говорили… А Марія оці всі слова зберігала, розважаючи, у серці своїм. Пастухи ж повернулись, прославляючи й хвалячи Бога за все, що почули й побачили, так як їм було сказано».

Лк. 2:15–20

ПРАВЕДНИЙ СТАРЕЦЬ СЕМЕН

Коли Божественному Немовляті виповнилося вісім днів, священик здійснив над Ним обряд обрізання, і дано було Йому ім'я Ісус. Це ім'я, наречене Йому Ангелом Господнім ще до Його народження, означає: «Бог рятує».

За законом Господа кожний первісток, тобто перший син у сім'ї, повинен бути присвячений Богові. Тому, коли Ісусові сповнилося шість тижнів, Його принесли до чудового Єрусалимського храму, щоб поставити Його перед Господом і щоб принести у жертву, як написано у Законі Господнім, «пару горличат або двоє голубенят».

Тоді в Єрусалимі жив старець, на ім'я Семен. Він був людиною праведною та благочестивою і чекав пришестя Месії для спасіння людей, і Дух Святий був на ньому. «І від Духа Святого йому було звіщено смерти не бачити, перше ніж побачить Христа Господнього». За велінням Духа Святого Семен прийшов до храму саме тоді, коли батьки принесли туди Немовля Ісуса, щоб здійснити над Ним законний обряд. Він узяв на руки Христа, благословив Бога й сказав: «Нині відпускаєш раба Свого, Владико, за словом Твоїм із миром, бо побачили очі мої Спасіння Твоє, яке Ти приготував перед всіма народами, Світло на просвіту поганам і на славу народу Твого Ізраїля!» І дивувалися батько Його й мати тим, що про Нього було розповіджене».

Потім Семен благословив їх і сказав Марії: «…І меч душу прошиє самій же тобі, — щоб відкрились думки сердець багатьох!»

Лк. 2:21–35

Hofmann.

ПОКЛОНІННЯ МУДРЕЦІВ

Коли Ісус народився у Віфлеємі Юдейському, в часи царювання Ірода, прийшли до Єрусалима мудреці зі Сходу і говорять: «Де народжений Цар Юдейський? Бо на сході ми бачили зорю Його, і прибули поклонитись Йому».

Почувши це, цар Ірод дуже занепокоївся, і весь Єрусалим разом із ним. І, зібравши всіх первосвящеників і книжників народних, він випитував у них, де має народитись Христос? Вони ж відказали йому: «У Віфлеємі Юдейськім, бо в пророка написано так: «І ти, Віфлеєме, земле Юдина, не менший нічим між осадами Юдиними, бо з тебе з'явиться Вождь, що буде Він пасти народ Мій ізраїльський». Тоді Ірод покликав таємно *отих* мудреців, і докладно випитував їх про час, коли з'явилась зоря. І він відіслав їх до Віфлеєму, говорячи: «Ідіть, і пильно розвідайтеся про Дитятко; а як знайдете, сповістіть мене, щоб і я міг піти й поклонитись Йому».

Насправді ж цар вирішив вбити Немовля, бо дуже боявся, що Він у майбутньому може зайняти його престол.

Мудреці, вислухавши царя, пішли собі. «І ось зоря, що на сході вони її бачили, ішла перед ними, аж прийшла й стала зверху, де Дитятко було. А бачивши зорю, вони надзвичайно зраділи».

Мт. 2:1–10

Rolfsen

ДАРУНКИ МУДРЕЦІВ І ПОБИТТЯ НЕМОВЛЯТ

Прийшовши до Віфлеєма, мудреці увійшли до того дому, над яким зупинилася зоря.

Побачивши там Немовля з Марією, Матір'ю Його, вони вклонились Йому і, відчинивши скарбниці свої, піднесли Йому свої дари: золото, ладан та смирну.

«А вві сні остережені, щоб не вертатись до Ірода, відійшли вони іншим шляхом до своєї землі».

Дізнавшись про це, цар Ірод дуже розгнівався і послав своїх воїнів до Віфлеєма, щоб вони повбивали там всіх немовлят від двох років і молодших — «за часом, що його в мудреців він був випитав». Воїни прийшли до Віфлеєма і вбили безвинних дітей. Так справдилися слова пророка Єремії: «Чути голос у Рамі, плач *та* ридання гірке: Рахиль плаче за дітьми своїми, не хоче потішена бути за діти свої, — бо нема їх».

Мт. 2:1–12, 16; Єр. 31:15

ВТЕЧА ДО ЄГИПТУ

Ірод гадав, що серед вбитих немовлят буде саме Той, про Якого говорили мудреці й священики як про майбутнього царя Ізраїлю. Але цього не сталося. Коли мудреці пішли, Ангел Господній з'явився вві сні Йосипові і сказав: «Уставай, візьми Дитятко та матір Його, і втікай до Єгипту, і там зоставайся, аж поки скажу тобі, бо Дитятка шукатиме Ірод, щоб Його погубити». І він устав, узяв Дитятко та матір Його вночі, та й пішов до Єгипту. І він там зоставався аж до смерти Іродової, щоб збулося сказане від Господа пророком, який провіщає: «Із Єгипту покликав Я Сина Свого».

Від Віфлеєма до Єгипту — довгий шлях, сотні кілометрів, Йосипові і Марії нелегко було втікати із маленькою дитиною.

Мт. 2:13–15

CLEVELAND
WOODWARD

ХЛОПЧИК ІСУС У НАЗАРЕТІ

Йосип, Марія та маленький Ісус залишалися у Єгипті аж до смерті царя Юдеї Ірода. Коли Ірод помер, Ангел Господній знову з'явився Йосипові вві сні й сказав: «Уставай, візьми Дитятко та матір Його, та йди в землю Ізраїлеву, бо вимерли ті, хто шукав був душу Дитини».

Йосип вчинив так, як звелів йому Ангел, і прийшов до Ізраїлю. Почувши, що в Юдеї править син Ірода Архелай, він не наважився туди йти. І тоді Йосип знову отримав остереження вві сні про те, що йому слід іти з Немовлям у місто Назарет.

Ми дуже мало знаємо про життя Ісуса в Назареті. Оскільки Йосип був теслею, то Ісус допомагав йому у цій роботі. В Євангеліях дуже мало написано про хлопчика та юнака Ісуса. Але те, що ми читаємо, говорить нам: «А Дитина росла та зміцнялася духом, набираючись мудрости. І благодать Божа на Ній пробувала».

І далі: «А Ісус зростав мудрістю, і віком та благодаттю, у Бога й людей».

Тут важливо згадати, що Ісус шанував Своїх земних батьків, бо святий євангеліст Лука пише: «…і був їм слухняний». Усім дітям треба коритися батькам своїм. Цього бажає Сам Господь. Одна з десяти заповідей Божих говорить так: «Шануй свого батька та матір свою, щоб довгі були твої дні на землі, яку Господь, Бог твій, дає тобі!»

Мт. 2:19–23; Лк. 2:40, 50–52; 2 М. 20:12

ІСУС У ХРАМІ

Ісус жив і виховувався у місті Назареті. Він зростав, зміцнювався Духом Святим, сповнювався мудрості, і благодать Божа була на Ньому.

Кожного року Його земні батьки ходили до Єрусалима на свято Пасхи. Коли Ісусові виповнилося дванадцять років, вони узяли Його із собою.

Після закінчення свята всі поверталися додому, а хлопчик Ісус залишився в Єрусалимі. Марія та Йосип цього не помітили, бо вважали, що Він іде з іншими родичами. Однак, через деякий час вони почали розшукувати Його серед своїх рідних та знайомих, з якими поверталися із Єрусалима. Не знайшовши Ісуса, Марія та Йосип повернулися назад до Єрусалима і тільки через три дні знайшли Його у храмі, де Він сидів серед вчителів. Він слухав та питав їх, а всі присутні дивувалися Його розумові і Його словам.

Матір Ісуса здивувалась, що її слухняний Син залишився у храмі, не попередивши її. Вона сказала Йому: «Дитино, — чому так Ти зробив нам? Ось Твій батько та я із журбою шукали Тебе»… А Він їм відказав: «Чого ж ви шукали Мене? Хіба ви не знали, що повинно Мені бути в тому, що належить Моєму Отцеві?» Цими словами Ісус хотів сказати, що Йому доручено Його Небесним Отцем велику справу на землі. Але батьки не зрозуміли Його слів. Однак Марія, Матір Його, зберегла їх у серці своїм.

Ісус повернувся зі Своїми батьками до Назарета і залишався завжди слухняним їм.

Лк. 2:40–51

HHofmann

ІВАН ПРОПОВІДУЄ І ХРИСТИТЬ

Іван жив у пустелі. Господь готував його до особливої служби — він повинен був сповістити народові про близьке пришестя Месії, тобто Ісуса Христа, і закликати народ до покаяння. Про те, що Іван має підготувати народ до пришестя Месії, пророки писали ще за сотні років до народження Івана: «Ось перед обличчя Твоє посилаю Свого посланця, який перед Тобою дорогу Твою приготує». І далі: «Голос того, хто кличе: У пустині готуйте дорогу для Господа, рівняйте стежки Йому».

Іван носив одяг з верблюжої вовни і шкіряний пояс, а їв сарану та дикий мед. Іван ходив по усіх околицях річки Йордан і закликав народ Ізраїлю до каяття й хрищення, щоб їхні гріхи були прощені Господом. До нього приходили сповідатися у своїх гріхах люди з усієї Юдеї та з Єрусалима, і Іван христив їх у Йордані.

«А люди питали його й говорили: «Що ж нам робити?» І сказав він у відповідь їм: «У кого дві сорочки, — нехай дасть немаючому; а хто має поживу, — нехай робить так само». І приходили й митники, щоб христитись від нього, і питали його: «Учителю, що ми маємо робити?» А він їм казав: «Не стягайте нічого над те, що вам звелено». Питали ж його й вояки й говорили: «А нам що робити?» І він їм відповів: «Нікого не кривдьте, ані не оскаржайте фальшиво, удовольняйтесь платнею своєю».

Мр. 1:1–8; Лк. 3:2–18

ХРИЩЕННЯ ГОСПОДА ІСУСА

Оскільки народ Ізраїлю чекав пришестя Месії, то багато людей запитувало: «Чи Іван не є обіцяним Богом Месією?» Але Іван відповідав: «Я хрищу вас водою на покаяння, але Той, Хто йде по мені, потужніший від мене: я недостойний понести взуття Йому! Він христитиме вас Святим Духом й огнем». Це він казав про Ісуса Христа.

І от Ісус прийшов до Івана, щоб христитися від нього. Іван же знав, що Ісус не має потреби христитися і каятися у гріхах Своїх, і, стримуючи Його, казав: «Я повинен христитись від Тебе, і чи Тобі йти до мене?» А Ісус відповів і сказав йому: «Допусти *це* тепер, бо так годиться нам виповнити усю правду». Тоді допустив він Його. І охристившись Ісус, зараз вийшов із води. І ось небо розкрилось, і побачив *Іван* Духа Божого, що спускався, як голуб, і сходив на Нього. І ось голос почувся із неба: «Це Син Мій Улюблений, що Його Я вподобав!»

Мт. 3:11–17

СПОКУШУВАННЯ ІСУСА В ПУСТЕЛІ

Після хрищення Дух повів Ісуса в пустелю для спокуси від диявола. Ісус Христос постився там сорок днів та сорок ночей, і вкінці зголоднів. «І *ось* приступив до Нього спокусник, і сказав: «Коли Ти Син Божий, скажи, щоб каміння це стало хлібами!» А Він відповів і промовив: «Написано: Не хлібом самим буде жити людина, але кожним словом, що походить із уст Божих».

Тоді диявол вирішив спокушати Ісуса також словами із Писання. Він підніс Ісуса на дах храму і сказав: «Коли Ти Син Божий, то кинься додолу, бо ж написано: «Він накаже про Тебе Своїм Анголам, і вони на руках понесуть Тебе, щоб об камінь коли не спіткнув Ти Своєї ноги». Ісус відказав йому: «Ще написано: Не спокушуй Господа Бога свого!»

Диявол вирішив ще раз спокусити Ісуса. Він підніс Його на дуже високу гору, показав Йому всі царства світу та славу їх і сказав: «Це все Тобі дам, якщо впадеш і мені Ти поклонишся!» Тоді каже до нього Ісус: «Відійди, сатано! Бо ж написано: Господеві Богові своєму вклоняйся, і служи Одному Йому!» Тоді позоставив диявол Його. І ось Анголи приступили, і служили Йому».

Мт. 4:1–11

ДВАНАДЦЯТЬ УЧНІВ ІСУСА ХРИСТА

«І, покинувши Він Назарета, прийшов й оселився в Капернаумі приморськім, на границі країн Завулонової й Нефталимової, щоб справдилось те, що сказав був Ісая пророк, промовляючи: «Завулонова земле, і Нефталимова земле, за Йорданом при морській дорозі, Галілеє поганська! Народ, що в темноті сидів, світло велике побачив, а тим, хто сидів у країні смертельної тіні, засяяло світло».

З того часу Ісус почав проповідувати і говорити: «Покайтеся, бо наблизилось Царство Небесне!» За Ісусом йшло багато людей з різних міст, і Він навчав їх та зціляв від хвороб.

Ісус обрав Собі дванадцять учнів, щоб вони завжди були з Ним, і навчав їх премудрості Божої. Ось імена цих учнів: Симон (Петро), Яків, Іван, Андрій, Пилип, Варфоломій, Матвій, Хома, Яків Алфієвий, Тадей, Симон Кананіт та Юда Іскаріотський, котрий потім зрадив Його. Усі учні Ісуса були звичайними людьми, але Бог дав їм щастя бути друзями і учнями Ісуса Христа — Сина Божого.

Андрій і його брат Симон-Петро ловили рибу у Галілейському озері. Ісус, побачивши їх, сказав: «Ідіть за Мною, — Я зроблю вас ловцями людей!» Це значило, що Він навчить їх відвертати людей від гріха і приводити їх до Істини. Покинувши свої рибальські човни, Андрій і Петро пішли за Ним. Ідучи далі Ісус побачив у човні братів Якова та Івана з їхнім батьком, Зеведеєм, що лагодили рибальські неводи. Ісус покликав їх, і вони, залишивши човен та батька свого, пішли за Ним.

Так само й інші учні, як тільки їх кликав Ісус, негайно йшли за Ним. Ісус почав посилати їх на проповідь і дав їм владу зціляти хворих та виганяти нечистих духів.

Мт. 4:12–22; Мр. 3:13–19

ПЕРШЕ ЧУДО ІСУСА

Якось Ісуса разом з учнями запросили на весілля до Кани Галілейської. Сталося так, що під час весільного бенкету не вистачило вина. Матір Ісуса також була з Ним. Вона сказала Йому: «Не мають вина!» Але Він відповів їй, що Його час ще не настав. Потім Марія звернулася до служителів, вказуючи на Ісуса: «Зробіть усе *те*, що Він вам скаже!»

«Було тут шість камінних посудин на воду, що стояли для очищення юдейського, що відер по два чи по три вміщали. Ісус каже до *слуг*: «Наповніть водою посудини». І їх поналивали вщерть. І Він каже до них: «Тепер зачерпніть, і занесіть до весільного старости».

Скуштувавши те, що було в посудинах, розпорядник покликав нареченого і сказав йому: «Кожна людина подає перше добре вино, а як понапиваються, тоді гірше; а ти добре вино аж на досі зберіг». Не знав же він, звідки це вино; знали про це лише слуги, які черпали воду.

Саме так у Кані Галілейській Ісус вперше здійснив чудо і явив славу Свою; і увірували в Нього учні Його.

Ів. 2:1–11

ІСУС ВИГАНЯЄ ГЕНДЛЯРІВ З ХРАМУ

Напередодні свята Пасхи* юдейської Ісус прийшов до Єрусалима. Увійшовши до храму, Він побачив, що там продавали «волів, і овець, і голубів, та сиділи міняльники. І, зробивши бича з мотузків, Він вигнав із храму всіх, — вівці й воли, а міняльникам гроші розсипав, і поперевертав *їм* столи. І сказав продавцям голубів: «Заберіть оце звідси, і не робіть із дому Отця Мого дому торгового!» Тоді учні Його згадали, що написано: «Ревність до дому Твого з'їдає Мене!»

На це юдеї сказали Йому: «Яке нам знамено покажеш, що Ти можеш робити таке?» Ісус відповів і промовив до них: «Зруйнуйте цей храм, — і за три дні Я поставлю його!» Відказали ж юдеї: «Сорок шість літ будувався цей храм, а Ти за три дні поставиш його?» А Він говорив про храм тіла Свого. Коли ж Він із мертвих воскрес, то учні Його згадали, що Він говорив це, і ввірували в Писання та в слово, що сказав був Ісус.

А як в Єрусалимі Він був у свято Пасхи, то багато хто ввірували в Його Імення, побачивши чуда Його, що чинив».

Ів. 2:13–23

---

* *Слово «Пасха» (євр.) означає «проходження повз кого-небудь» або «помилування»; свято Пасхи відзначалося ізраїльтянами як пам'ять про їхній вихід з Єгипту.*

БЕСІДА ІСУСА З НИКОДИМОМ

Між фарисеїв був чоловік на ім'я Никодим, один з начальників юдейських.

Він прийшов до Ісуса вночі і сказав: «Учителю, знаємо ми, що прийшов Ти від Бога, як Учитель, — бо не може ніхто таких чуд учинити, які чиниш Ти, коли Бог із ним не буде». Ісус відповів і до нього сказав: «Поправді, поправді кажу Я тобі: Коли хто не народиться згори, то не може побачити Божого Царства». Никодим Йому каже: «Як може людина родитися, бувши старою? Хіба може вона ввійти до утроби своїй матері знову й родитись?» Ісус відповів: «Поправді, поправді кажу Я тобі: Коли хто не родиться з води й Духа, той не може ввійти в Царство Боже. Що вродилося з тіла — є тіло, що ж уродилося з Духа — є дух. Не дивуйся тому, що сказав Я тобі: Вам необхідно родитись згори».

Далі Ісус почав йому пояснювати таємницю пришестя Його на землю та Божий план спасіння людей від гріхів. Він сказав: «І, як Мойсей підніс змія в пустині, так мусить піднесений бути й Син Людський, щоб кожен, хто вірує в Нього, мав вічне життя. Так-бо Бог полюбив світ, що дав Сина Свого Однородженого, щоб кожен, хто вірує в Нього, не згинув, але мав життя вічне. Бо Бог не послав Свого Сина на світ, щоб Він світ засудив, але щоб через Нього світ спасся. Хто вірує в Нього, не буде засуджений; хто ж не вірує, — той вже засуджений, що не повірив в Ім'я Однородженого Сина Божого. Суд же такий, що світло на світ прибуло, люди ж темряву більш полюбили, як світло, — лихі-бо були їхні вчинки! Бо кожен, хто робить лихе, ненавидить світло, і не приходить до світла, щоб не зганено вчинків його. А хто робить за правдою, той до світла йде, щоб діла його виявились, бо зроблені в Бозі вони».

Ів. 3:1–21

ІСУС І САМАРЯНКА

Якось Ісус пішов з Юдеї, південної частини Ізраїлю, до Галілеї, яка знаходилася на півночі цієї країни. Між Юдеєю та Галілеєю лежала Самарія. Самаряни, як і ізраїльтяни, вірили в єдиного Бога, Творця неба та землі, але у них були свої звичаї, свої священики і навіть свій храм. Євреї не бажали спілкуватися з ними.

Коли Ісус зі Своїми учнями прийшов до самарянського міста Сіхара, то, стомившись від довгого шляху, сів біля криниці, а учні Його пішли купити щось поїсти. Було це опівдні. Якась самарянка прийшла до криниці набрати води. «Ісус каже до неї: «Дай напитись Мені!»… Тоді каже Йому самарянка: «Як же Ти, юдеянин бувши, та просиш напитись від мене, самарянки?»… Ісус відповів і промовив до неї: «Коли б знала ти Божий дар, і Хто Той, Хто говорить тобі: «Дай напитись Мені», — ти б у Нього просила, і Він тобі дав би живої води». Каже жінка до Нього: «І черпака в Тебе, Пане, нема, а криниця глибока, — звідки ж маєш Ти воду живу?.. Ісус відповів і сказав їй: «Кожен, хто воду цю п'є, буде прагнути знову. А хто питиме воду, що Я йому дам, прагнути не буде повік, бо вода, що Я йому дам, стане в нім джерелом тієї води, що тече в життя вічне». Потім Ісус почав свідчити про Бога: «Бог є Дух, і ті, що Йому вклоняються, повинні в дусі та в правді вклонятись». Відказує жінка Йому: «Я знаю, що прийде Месія, що зветься Христос, — як Він прийде, то все розповість нам». Промовляє до неї Ісус: «Це Я, що розмовляю з тобою».

Тоді жінка залишила глек свій, побігла до міста і розповіла усім людям про Чоловіка, Якого зустріла вона. І казала людям вона: «Чи Він не Христос?»… З того ж міста багато хто із самарян в Нього ввірували через слово жінки… А коли самаряни до Нього прийшли, то благали Його, щоб у них позостався. І Він перебув там два дні. Значно ж більш вони ввірували через слово Його».

Завдяки свідоцтву однієї бідної самарянки багато людей увірувало у Господа. Ця розповідь учить: перед Господом рівні усі народи, бо усі ми — Його творіння.

Ів. 4:1–42

Hofmann

НЕЗВИЧАЙНИЙ УЛОВ

Часто Ісус учив народ, стоячи на березі озера. Інколи Він входив у човен, що стояв біля берега, і проповідував з нього. Одного разу, коли Він закінчив навчати, то промовив до Симона: «Попливи на глибінь, — і закиньте на полов свій невід». А Симон сказав Йому у відповідь: «Наставнику, — цілу ніч ми працювали, і не вловили нічого, — та за словом Твоїм укину невода». А зробивши оце, вони безліч риби набрали — і їхній невід почав прориватись… І кивали вони до товаришів, що були в другім човні, щоб прийшли помогти їм. Ті прийшли, та й наповнили обидва човни, — аж стали вони потопати. А як Симон Петро *це* побачив, то припав до колін Ісусових, кажучи: «Господи, — вийди від мене, бо я грішна людина!» Бо від полову риби, що зловили вони, обгорнув жах його та й усіх, хто з ним був… І сказав Ісус Симонові: «Не лякайсь, — від цього часу ти будеш ловити людей!»

Минув час, і дійсно, Симон-Петро став проповіддю своєю навертати людей до Ісуса і тим рятувати їх.

Лк. 5:1–10

ЗЦІЛЕННЯ РОЗСЛАБЛЕНОГО

Коли Ісус знаходився у Капернаумі, то прийшло до Нього багато і простих і знатних людей з різних міст Ізраїлю. Він навчав їх, і сила Господа являла себе у зціленні хворих. Якісь люди принесли розслабленого, тобто паралізованого, до дому, де проповідував Ісус, щоб Він зцілив його. Але через багатолюдність вони не змогли пронести його дверима і, розібравши стелю, опустили свого хворого друга на ношах усередину кімнати і поклали перед Ісусом. Ісус, побачивши їхню віру, сказав розслабленому: «Чоловіче, прощаються тобі гріхи твої!» А книжники та фарисеї* почали міркувати й казати: «Хто ж Оцей, що богозневагу говорить? Хто може прощати гріхи, окрім Бога Самого?»… Відчувши ж Ісус думки їхні, промовив у відповідь їм: «Що міркуєте ви в серцях ваших? Що легше: сказати: «Прощаються тобі гріхи твої», чи сказати: «Уставай та й ходи»? Але щоб ви знали, що Син Людський має владу на землі прощати гріхи», — тож каже Він розслабленому: «Кажу Я тобі: Уставай, візьми ложе своє, та й іди у свій дім!» І той зараз устав перед ними, узявши те, на чому лежав, і пішов у свій дім, прославляючи Бога.

І всіх жах обгорнув, — і славили Бога вони. І переповнились страхом, говорячи: «Дивні речі сьогодні ми бачили!»

Лк. 5:17–26

---

* *Фарисейство (відокремленість) було громадсько-релігійним рухом серед євреїв. Основна мета фарисеїв — зберегти суворе дотримання закону Мойсея.*

НАГІРНА ПРОПОВІДЬ
1. ЗАПОВІДІ БЛАЖЕНСТВА

Одного разу Ісус піднявся на гору, сів там і, коли підійшли до Нього учні та народ, став навчати їх заповідям блаженства. Проповідь, яку Ісус сказав до народу, називають також «Нагірною проповіддю». Вона записана у 5, 6 та 7 розділах Євангелії від святого Матвія. «Нагірна проповідь» — основа вчення Ісуса Христа. Разом із «Десятьма заповідями», які Бог дав людям за часів Старого Заповіту, «Нагірна проповідь» є важливим путівником нашого життя. Тому прочитаємо її майже повністю з Євангелії від святого Матвія:

«Блаженні вбогі духом, бо їхнєє Царство Небесне.

Блаженні засмучені, бо вони будуть утішені.

Блаженні лагідні, бо землю вспадкують вони.

Блаженні голодні та спрагнені правди, бо вони нагодовані будуть.

Блаженні милостиві, бо помилувані вони будуть.

Блаженні чисті серцем, бо вони будуть бачити Бога.

Блаженні миротворці, бо вони синами Божими стануть.

Блаженні вигнані за правду, бо їхнє Царство Небесне.

Блаженні ви, як ганьбити та гнати вас будуть, і будуть облудно на вас наговорювати всяке слово лихе ради Мене. Радійте та веселіться, — нагорода-бо ваша велика на небесах! Бо так гнали *й* пророків, що були перед вами.

Ви — сіль землі. Коли сіль ізвітріє, то чим насолити її? Не придасться вона вже нінащо, хіба щоб надвір була висипана та потоптана людьми.

Ви світло для світу. Не може сховатися місто, що стоїть на верховині гори. І не запалюють світильника, щоб поставити його під посудину, але на свічник, — і світить воно всім у домі. Отак ваше світло нехай світить перед людьми, щоб вони бачили ваші добрі діла, та прославляли Отця вашого, що на небі».

Мт. 5:3–16

Продовження далі

НАГІРНА ПРОПОВІДЬ
2. ПРО ЗАКОН, ШОСТУ ЗАПОВІДЬ, ПОДРУЖНЄ ЖИТТЯ ТА КЛЯТВУ

«Не подумайте, ніби Я руйнувати Закон чи Пророків прийшов, — Я не руйнувати прийшов, але виконати. Поправді ж кажу вам: доки небо й земля не минеться, — ані йота єдина, ані жаден значок із Закону не минеться, аж поки не збудеться все. Хто ж порушить одну з найменших цих заповідей, та й людей так навчить, той буде найменшим у Царстві Небеснім; а хто виконає та й навчить, той стане великим у Царстві Небеснім. Кажу-бо Я вам: коли праведність ваша не буде рясніша, як книжників та фарисеїв, то не ввійдете в Царство Небесне!

Ви чули, що було стародавнім наказане: «Не вбивай, а хто вб'є, підпадає він судові». А Я вам кажу, що кожен, хто гнівається на брата свого, підпадає *вже* судові. А хто скаже на брата свого: «рака*», підпадає верховному судові, а хто скаже «дурний», підпадає геєнні огненній. Тому, коли принесеш ти до жертівника свого дара, та тут ізгадаєш, що брат твій щось має на тебе, — залиши отут дара свого перед жертівником, і піди, примирись перше з братом своїм, — і тоді повертайся, і принось свого дара…

Ви чули, що сказано: «Не чини перелюбу». А Я вам кажу, що кожен, хто на жінку подивиться із пожадливістю, той уже вчинив із нею перелюб у серці своїм… Також сказано: «Хто дружину свою відпускає, нехай дасть їй листа розводового». А Я вам кажу, що кожен, хто пускає дружину свою, крім провини розпусти, той доводить її до перелюбу. І хто з відпущеною побереться, той чинить перелюб.

Ще ви чули, що було стародавнім наказане: «Не клянись неправдиво», але «виконуй клятви свої перед Господом». А Я вам кажу не клястися зовсім: ані небом, бо воно престол Божий; ні землею, бо підніжок для ніг Його *це*; ані Єрусалимом, бо він місто Царя Великого; не клянись головою своєю, — бо навіть однієї волосинки ти не можеш учинити білою чи чорною. Ваше ж слово хай буде: «так-так», «ні-ні». А що більше над це, то *те* від лукавого».

Мт. 5:17–37

Продовження далі

* *Рака (євр.) — пуста людина.*

H. Hofmann

НАГІРНА ПРОПОВІДЬ
3. ПРО ЛЮБОВ І МОЛИТВУ

«Ви чули, що сказано: «Око за око, і зуб за зуба». А Я вам кажу не противитись злому. І коли вдарить тебе хто у праву щоку твою, — підстав йому й другу. А хто хоче тебе позивати й забрати сорочку твою, — віддай і плаща йому. А хто силувати тебе буде відбути подорожнє на милю одну, — іди з ним навіть дві. Хто просить у тебе — то дай, а хто хоче позичити в тебе — не відвертайсь *від нього*.

Ви чули, що сказано: «Люби свого ближнього, і ненавидь свого ворога». А Я вам кажу: Любіть ворогів своїх, благословляйте тих, хто вас проклинає, творіть добро тим, хто ненавидить вас, і моліться за тих, хто вас переслідує, щоб вам бути синами Отця вашого, що на небі, що наказує сходити сонцю Своєму над злими й над добрими, і дощ посилає на праведних і на неправедних. Коли-бо ви любите тих, хто вас любить, то яку нагороду ви маєте? Хіба не те саме й митники* роблять? І коли ви вітаєте тільки братів своїх, то що ж особливого робите? Чи й погани не чинять отак? Отож, будьте досконалі, як досконалий Отець ваш Небесний!

Стережіться виставляти свою милостиню перед людьми, щоб бачили вас; а як ні, то не матимете нагороди від Отця вашого, що на небі. Отож, коли чиниш ти милостиню, не сурми перед себе, як то роблять *оті* лицеміри по синагогах та вулицях, щоб хвалили їх люди. Поправді кажу вам: вони мають уже нагороду свою! А як ти чиниш милостиню, — хай не знатиме ліва рука твоя, що робить правиця твоя, щоб таємна була твоя милостиня, а Отець твій, що бачить таємне, віддасть тобі явно.

А як молитеся, то не будьте, як *ті* лицеміри, що люблять ставати й молитися по синагогах та на перехрестях, щоб їх бачили люди. Поправді кажу вам: вони мають уже нагороду свою! А ти, коли молишся, «увійди до своєї комірчини, зачини свої двері, і помолися» Отцеві своєму, що в таїні; а Отець твій, що бачить таємне, віддасть тобі явно.

А як молитеся, не проказуйте зайвого, як *ті* погани, — бо думають, ніби вони будуть вислухані за своє велемовство. Отож, не вподобляйтеся їм, бо знає Отець ваш, чого потребуєте, ще раніше за ваше прохання! Ви ж моліться отак:

Мт. 5:38–48; 6:1–13

---

* *Митники — збирачі податків.*

Продовження далі

ОТЧЕ НАШ

Отче наш, що єси на небесах!
Нехай святиться Ім'я Твоє,
нехай прийде Царство Твоє,
нехай буде воля Твоя,
як на небі, так і на землі.
Хліба нашого насущного
дай нам сьогодні.
І прости нам довги наші,
як і ми прощаємо
винуватцям нашим.
І не введи нас у випробовування,
але визволи нас від лукавого.
Бо Твоє є царство,
і сила, і слава навіки.

Амінь

НАГІРНА ПРОПОВІДЬ
4. ПРО ПІСТ І НАДІЮ НА НЕБЕСНОГО ОТЦЯ

«А як постите, то не будьте сумні, як *оті* лицеміри: вони-бо змінюють обличчя свої, щоб бачили люди, що постять вони. Поправді кажу вам: вони мають уже нагороду свою! А ти, коли постиш, намасти свою голову, і лице своє вмий, щоб ти посту свого не виявив людям, а Отцеві своєму, що в таїні; і Отець твій, що бачить таємне, віддасть тобі явно.

Не складайте скарбів собі на землі, де нищить *їх* міль та іржа, і де злодії підкопуються й викрадають. Складайте ж собі скарби на небі, де ні міль, ні іржа *їх* не нищить, і де злодії *до них* не підкопуються та не крадуть. Бо де скарб твій, — там буде й серце твоє!

Око — то світильник для тіла. Тож як око твоє буде здорове, то й усе тіло твоє буде світле. А коли б твоє око лихе було, то й усе тіло твоє буде темне. Отож, коли світло, що в тобі, є темрява, — то яка ж то велика *та* темрява!

Ніхто двом панам служити не може, — бо або одного зненавидить, а другого буде любити, або буде триматись одного, а другого знехтує. Не можете Богові служити й мамоні*.

Через те вам кажу: Не журіться про життя своє — що будете їсти та що будете пити, ні про тіло своє, — у що зодягнетеся. Чи ж не більше від їжі життя, а від одягу тіло? Погляньте на птахів небесних, що не сіють, не жнуть, не збирають у клуні, та проте ваш Небесний Отець їх годує. Чи ж ви не багато вартніші за них? Хто ж із вас, коли журиться, зможе додати до зросту свого *бодай* ліктя одного? І про одяг чого ви клопочетесь? Погляньте на польові лілеї, як зростають вони, — не працюють, ані не прядуть. А Я вам кажу, що й сам Соломон у всій славі своїй не вдягався отак, як одна з них. І коли польову ту траву, що сьогодні ось є, а взавтра до печі вкидається, Бог отак зодягає, — скільки ж краще *зодягне* Він вас, маловірні! Отож, не журіться, кажучи: Що ми будемо їсти, чи: Що будемо пити, або: У що ми зодягнемось? Бо ж *усього того* погани шукають; але знає Отець ваш Небесний, що всього того вам потрібно. Шукайте ж найперш Царства Божого й правди Його, — а все це вам додасться. Отож, не журіться про завтрашній день, — бо завтра за себе само поклопочеться. Кожний день має досить своєї турботи!»

Мт. 6:16–34

* *Мамона (євр.) — багатство, земні блага.*

Продовження далі

LE JEUNE

НАГІРНА ПРОПОВІДЬ
5. НЕ СУДІТЬ ІНШИХ, НАПОЛЕГЛИВІСТЬ У МОЛИТВІ, ЗОЛОТЕ ПРАВИЛО, ХОДІТЬ ВУЗЬКОЮ СТЕЖКОЮ

«Не судіть, щоб *і* вас не судили; бо яким судом судити будете, *таким же* осудять *і* вас, і якою мірою будете міряти, *такою* відміряють вам. І чого в оці брата свого ти заскалку бачиш, колоди ж у власному оці не чуєш? Або як ти скажеш до брата свого: «Давай вийму я заскалку з ока твого», коли он колода у власному оці? Лицеміре, — вийми перше колоду із власного ока, а потім побачиш, як вийняти заскалку з ока брата твого.

Не давайте святого псам, і не розсипайте перел своїх перед свиньми, щоб вони не потоптали їх ногами своїми, і, обернувшись, щоб не розшматували й вас…

Просіть — і буде вам дано, шукайте — і знайдете, стукайте — і відчинять вам; бо кожен, хто просить — одержує, хто шукає — знаходить, а хто стукає — відчинять йому. Чи ж то серед вас є людина, що подасть своєму синові каменя, коли хліба проситиме він? Або коли риби проситиме, то подасть йому гадину? Тож як ви, бувши злі, потрапите добрі дари своїм дітям давати, — скільки ж більше Отець ваш Небесний подасть добра тим, хто проситиме в Нього!

Тож усе, чого тільки бажаєте, щоб чинили вам люди, те саме чиніть їм і ви. Бо в цьому Закон і Пророки.

Увіходьте тісними ворітьми, бо просторі ворота й широка дорога, що веде до погибелі, — і нею багато хто ходять. Бо тісні ті ворота, і вузька та дорога, що веде до життя, — і мало таких, що знаходять її!»

Мт. 7:1–14

Продовження далі

ЗОЛОТЕ ПРАВИЛО

**«Тож усе,
чого тільки бажаєте,
щоб чинили
вам люди,
те саме чиніть
їм і ви»**

Матвія 7:12

НАГІРНА ПРОПОВІДЬ
6. ПРО ЛЖЕПРОРОКІВ, ПРО ВИКОНАННЯ ВОЛІ БОЖОЇ, ПРО ДВІ ОСНОВИ

«Стережіться фальшивих пророків, що приходять до вас ув одежі овечій, а всередині — хижі вовки. По їхніх плодах ви пізнаєте їх. Бо хіба ж виноград на тернині збирають, або фіґи — із будяків? Так ото родить добрі плоди кожне дерево добре, а дерево зле плоди родить лихі. Не може родить добре дерево плоду лихого, ані дерево зле плодів добрих родити. Усяке ж дерево, що доброго плоду не родить, — зрубується та в огонь укидається. Отож-бо, — по їхніх плодах ви пізнаєте їх!

Не кожен, хто каже до Мене: «Господи, Господи!» увійде в Царство Небесне, але той, хто виконує волю Мого Отця, що на небі. Багато хто скажуть Мені того дня: «Господи, Господи, хіба ми не Ім'ям Твоїм пророкували, хіба не Ім'ям Твоїм демонів ми виганяли, або не Ім'ям Твоїм чуда великі творили?» І їм оголошу Я тоді: «Я ніколи не знав вас… Відійдіть від Мене, хто чинить беззаконня!»

Отож, кожен, хто слухає цих Моїх слів і виконує їх, подібний до чоловіка розумного, що свій дім збудував на камені. І линула злива, і розлилися річки, і буря знялася, і на дім отой кинулась, — та не впав, бо на камені був він заснований. А кожен, хто слухає цих Моїх слів, та їх не виконує, — подібний до чоловіка того необачного, що свій дім збудував на піску. І линула злива, і розлилися річки, і буря знялася й на дім отой кинулась, — і він упав. І велика була та руїна його!»

І ото, як Ісус закінчив ці слова, то народ дивувався з науки Його. Бо навчав Він їх, як можновладний, а не як ті книжники їхні».

Мт. 7:15–29

ВОСКРЕСІННЯ СИНА УДОВИ

Якось Ісус прийшов у місто Наїн. Разом із Ним йшли Його учні та чимало людей.

Коли Він підійшов до міської брами, то побачив людей, що несли ховати померлого — єдиного сина вдови. Побачивши ридаючу матір, Господь змилосердився над нею і сказав їй: «Не плач!» І Він підійшов, і доторкнувся до мар, носії ж зупинились. Тоді Він сказав: «Юначе, кажу тобі: встань!» І мертвий устав, і почав говорити. І його Він віддав його матері. А всіх острах пройняв, і Бога хвалили вони й говорили: «Великий Пророк з'явився між нами, і зглянувся Бог над народом Своїм!»

Для Ісуса Христа немає нічого неможливого, чого б Він не зміг зробити, тому що Він — Син живого та всемогутнього Бога. Вчення Його пройняте любов'ю та мудрістю, а вчинки Його — співчуттям та милосердям до людей. Пророк Ісая за багато століть до народження Христа писав про Нього: «Він очеретини надломленої не доломить, і ґнота тліючого не погасить…» Саме так ставився Ісус Христос до людей.

Лк. 7:11–16; Іс. 42:3

ПРИТЧА ПРО СІЯЧА

Ісус розповів людям таку притчу: «Ось вийшов сіяч, щоб посіяти. І як сіяв він *зерна*, упали одні край дороги, — і пташки налетіли, та їх повидзьобували. Другі ж упали на ґрунт кам'янистий, де не мали багато землі, — і негайно посходили, бо земля неглибока була; а як сонце зійшло, — то зів'яли, і коріння не мавши, — посохли. А інші попадали в терен, — і вигнався терен, і їх поглушив. Інші ж упали на добрую землю — і зродили: одне в сто раз, друге в шістдесят, а те втридцятеро. Хто має вуха, щоб слухати, нехай слухає!»

Потім Ісус роз'яснив учням суть цієї притчі: «До кожного, хто слухає слово про Царство, але не розуміє, приходить лукавий, і краде посіяне в серці його; це те, що посіяне понад дорогою.

А посіяне на кам'янистому ґрунті, — це той, хто слухає слово, і з радістю зараз приймає його; але кореня в ньому нема, тому він непостійний; коли ж утиск або переслідування настають за слово, то він зараз спокушується.

А між терен посіяне, — це той, хто слухає слово, але клопоти віку цього та омана багатства заглушують слово, — і воно зостається без плоду.

А посіяне в добрій землі, — це той, хто слухає слово й *його* розуміє, і плід він приносить, і дає один у сто раз, другий у шістдесят, а той утридцятеро».

Мт. 13:3–9, 18–23

ШІСТЬ ПРИТЧ ПРО ЦАРСТВО НЕБЕСНЕ

Якось Ісус, вийшовши з дому, сів біля моря. І зібралося біля Нього безліч народу, так що Він зайшов до човна та й почав вчити людей, говорячи:

«Царство Небесне подібне до чоловіка, що посіяв був добре насіння на полі своїм. А коли люди спали, прийшов ворог його, і куколю між пшеницю насіяв, та й пішов. А як виросло збіжжя та кинуло колос, тоді показався і кукіль. І прийшли господареві раби, та й кажуть йому: «Пане, чи ж не добре насіння ти сіяв на полі своїм? Звідки ж узявся кукіль?» А він їм відказав: «Чоловік супротивник накоїв оце». А раби відказали йому: «Отож, — чи не хочеш, щоб пішли ми і його повиполювали?» Але він відказав: «Ні, — щоб, виполюючи *той* кукіль, ви не вирвали разом із ним *і* пшеницю. Залишіть, — хай разом обоє ростуть аж до жнив; а в жнива накажу я женцям: Зберіть перше кукіль і його пов'яжіть у снопки, щоб їх попалити; пшеницю ж спровадьте до клуні моєї».

Іншу притчу подав Він їм, кажучи: «Царство Небесне подібне до зерна гірчичного, що взяв чоловік і посіяв на полі своїм. Воно найдрібніше з увсього насіння, але, коли виросте, більше воно за зілля, і стає деревом, так що птаство небесне злітається, і кублиться в віттях його».

Іншу притчу Він їм розповів: «Царство Небесне подібне до розчини, що її бере жінка, і кладе на три міри муки, аж поки все вкисне…

Царство Небесне подібне ще до захованого в полі скарбу, що людина, знайшовши, ховає його, і з радости з того йде, та й усе, що має, продає та купує те поле. Подібне ще Царство Небесне до того купця, що пошукує перел добрих, а як знайде одну дорогоцінну перлину, то йде, і все продає, що має, і купує її.

Подібне ще Царство Небесне до невода, у море закиненого, що зібрав він усячину. Коли він наповниться, тягнуть на берег його, і, сівши, вибирають до посуду добре, непотріб же геть викидають. Так буде й наприкінці віку: Анголи повиходять, і вилучать злих з-поміж праведних, і їх повкидають до печі огненної, — буде там плач і скрегіт зубів!»

Мт. 13:24–50

ІСУС ВГАМОВУЄ БУРЮ НА ОЗЕРІ

Одного разу Ісус та учні Його перепливали в човні Генісаретське (Галілейське) озеро. Тим часом Спаситель заснув. Тоді це озеро називали морем. Раптом на морі знялася сильна буря, і човен стали заливати хвилі. Тоді учні Його, підійшовши до Нього, розбудили Його і сказали: «Рятуй, Господи, — гинемо!» А Він відповів їм: «Чого полохливі ви, маловірні?» Тоді встав, заказав бурі й морю, — і тиша велика настала… А народ дивувався й казав: «Хто ж це такий, що вітри та море слухняні Йому?»

Дійсно, слову Господньому підкоряється весь всесвіт!

Мт. 8:23–27

ВОСКРЕСІННЯ ДОЧКИ ЯІРА

Якось на березі Галілейського моря Ісус учив народ, який прийшов до Нього з різних міст. До Нього підійшов один із старших синагоги, на ім'я Яір. І впавши до ніг Ісуса, почав гаряче просити Його: «Моя дочка кінчається. Прийди ж, поклади *Свої* руки на неї, щоб видужала та жила!»

Ісус пішов із Яіром. За Ним невідступно йшов великий натовп і тиснувсь до Нього з усіх сторін. Тут одна жінка, що дванадцять років страждала від кровотечі і, довго лікуючись у лікарів, не зцілилася, почула про Ісуса. Вона протислась крізь натовп, підійшла ззаду до Ісуса і непомітно доторкнулася до Його одежі. Жінка думала: «Коли хоч доторкнусь до одежі Його, то одужаю…» І відразу вона відчула, що видужала від хвороби!

У той же час Ісус відчув, що із Нього вийшла сила. Він запитав: «Хто доторкнувсь до Моєї одежі?» Учні, не зрозумівши, чому Він запитує про це, відповіли, що це народ тисне з усіх боків. Але Ісус оглядався навколо, щоб побачити ту, що зробила це. Жінка, знаючи, що з нею сталося, з тремтінням і страхом підійшла, впала перед Ним і розповіла Йому все як було. Він же сказав їй: «Твоя віра, о дочко, спасла тебе; іди з миром, і здоровою будь від своєї недуги!»

Коли Він ще говорив це, прийшли до начальника синагоги люди його і сказали: «Дочка твоя вмерла; чого ще турбуєш Учителя?» Але Ісус, почувши це, звернувся до Яіра зі словами: «Не лякайсь, — тільки віруй!» Прийшовши у його дім, Він побачив «метушню та *людей*, що плакали та голосили». Ісус сказав їм: «Чого ви метушитеся та плачете? Не вмерло дівча, але спить!» І сміялися з Нього. Але Ісус взяв Петра, Якова, Івана та батьків померлої дівчини і увійшов до кімнати, де вона лежала. Він наблизився до неї, взяв її за руку і промовив: «Дівчатко, кажу тобі — встань!» І в ту ж мить дівчинка підвелася й почала ходити. Всі, хто бачив це, дивом дивувалися.

Мр. 5:21–42

ІСУС НАГОДОВУЄ П'ЯТЬ ТИСЯЧ ЛЮДЕЙ П'ЯТЬМА ХЛІБИНАМИ

Одного разу Ісус пішов із учнями на другу сторону моря Галілейського. «А за Ним ішла безліч народу, бо бачили чуда Його, що чинив над недужими.

Ісус же на гору зійшов, і сидів там зі Своїми учнями. Наближалася ж Пасха, свято юдейське. А Ісус, звівши очі Свої та побачивши, яка безліч народу до Нього йде, говорить Пилипові: «Де ми купимо хліба, щоб вони поживились?» Він же це говорив, його випробовуючи, бо знав Сам, що Він має робити.

Пилип Йому відповідь дав: «І за двісті динаріїв їм хліба не стане, щоб кожен із них бодай трохи дістав».

Говорить до Нього Андрій, один з учнів Його, брат Симона Петра: «Є тут хлопчина один, що має п'ять ячних хлібів та дві риби, але що то на безліч таку!» А Ісус відказав: «Скажіть людям сідати!» А була на тім місці велика трава. І засіло чоловік числом із п'ять тисяч.

А Ісус узяв хліби, і, подяку вчинивши, роздав тим, хто сидів. Так само і з риб, скільки хотіли вони. І, як наїлись вони, Він говорить до учнів Своїх: «Позбирайте куски позосталі, щоб ніщо не загинуло». І зібрали вони. І дванадцять повних кошів наклали кусків, що лишились їдцям із п'яти ячних хлібів.

А люди, що бачили чудо, яке Ісус учинив, гомоніли: «Це Той справді Пророк, що повинен прибути на світ!»

Ів. 6:2–14

ІСУС ІДЕ ПО ВОДІ

Відразу після здійснення чуда із хлібами та рибою Ісус звелів учням Своїм сісти у човен і дістатися іншого берега, доки Він відпустить народ. «Відпустивши ж народ, Він на гору пішов помолитися на самоті; і як вечір настав, був там Сам. А човен вже був на середині моря, і кидали хвилі його, бо вітер зірвавсь супротивний.

А о четвертій сторожі нічній* Ісус підійшов до них, ідучи по морю. Як побачили ж учні, що йде Він по морю, то настрашилися та й казали: «Мара!» І від страху вони закричали… А Ісус до них зараз озвався й сказав: «Заспокойтесь, — це Я, не лякайтесь!»

Петро ж відповів і сказав: «Коли, Господи, Ти це, то звели, щоб прийшов я до Тебе по воді». А Він відказав йому: «Іди». І, вилізши з човна, Петро став іти по воді, і пішов до Ісуса. Але, бачачи велику бурю, злякався, і зачав потопати, і скричав: «Рятуй мене, Господи!»… І зараз Ісус простяг руку й схопив його, і каже до нього: «Маловірний, чого усумнився?» Як до човна ж вони ввійшли, буря вщухнула.

А приявні в човні вклонились Йому та сказали: «Ти справді Син Божий!»

Мт. 14:22–33

---

* *За нашим часом це від трьох до шести годин ранку.*

CLEVELAND
WOODWARD

ПЕРЕОБРАЖЕННЯ ІСУСА

Ісус сказав якось Своїм учням про те, що Йому належить померти в Єрусалимі.

Через декілька днів Ісус разом з Петром, Яковом та Іваном зійшов на високу гору і раптом змінився перед їхніми очима: лице Його засяяло, немов сонце, а одіж зробилася білою, як світло. «І ось з'явились до них Мойсей та Ілля, і розмовляли із Ним. І озвався Петро та й сказав до Ісуса: «Господи, добре бути нам тут! Коли хочеш, поставлю отут три шатра: для Тебе одне, і одне для Мойсея, і одне для Іллі». Як він ще говорив, ось хмара ясна заслонила їх, і ось голос із хмари почувсь, що казав: «Це Син Мій Улюблений, що Його Я вподобав. Його слухайтеся!»

А почувши, попадали учні долілиць, і полякалися сильно… А Ісус підійшов, доторкнувся до них і промовив: «Уставайте й не бійтесь!» Звівши ж очі свої, нікого вони не побачили, окрім Самого Ісуса.

А коли з гори сходили, заповів їм Ісус і сказав: «Не кажіть нікому про цеє видіння, аж поки Син Людський із мертвих воскресне».

Мт. 17:1–9

D.R. STEMLER

ВСЕПРОЩАЮЧА ЛЮБОВ

Якось підійшов Петро до Ісуса і запитав Його: «Господи, — скільки разів брат мій може згрішити проти мене, а я маю прощати йому? Чи до семи раз?» Ісус промовляє до нього: «Не кажу тобі — до семи раз, але аж до семидесяти раз по семи!»

«Тим-то Царство Небесне подібне одному цареві, що захотів обрахунок зробити з своїми рабами. Коли ж він почав обраховувати, то йому привели одного, що винен був десять тисяч талантів*. А що він не мав із чого віддати, наказав пан продати його, і його дружину та діти, і все, що він мав, — і заплатити. Тоді раб той упав до ніг, і вклонявся йому та благав: «Потерпи мені, — я віддам тобі все!» І змилосердився пан над рабом тим, — і звільнив його, і простив йому борг. А як вийшов той раб, то спіткав він одного з своїх співтоваришів, що був винен йому сто динаріїв*. І, схопивши його, він душив та казав: «Віддай, що ти винен!» А товариш його впав у ноги йому, і благав його, кажучи: «Потерпи мені, — і я віддам тобі!» Та той не схотів, а пішов і всадив до в'язниці його, — аж поки він боргу не верне. Як побачили ж товариші його те, що сталося, то засмутилися дуже, і прийшли й розповіли своєму панові все, що було. Тоді пан його кличе його, та й говорить до нього: «Рабе лукавий, — я простив був тобі ввесь той борг, бо просив ти мене. Чи й тобі не належало змилуватись над своїм співтоваришем, як і я над тобою був змилувався?» І прогнівався пан його, — і катам його видав, аж поки йому не віддасть всього боргу. Так само й Отець Мій Небесний учинить із вами, коли кожен із вас не простить своєму братові з серця свого їхніх прогріхів».

У молитві Господній «Отче наш» Ісус вчить нас, як треба звертатися до Бога. Є там і такі слова: «І прости нам довги наші, як і ми прощаємо винуватцям нашим».

Мт. 18:21–35; 6:12

* *Талант дорівнював 6000 динаріїв, динарій — приблизно денний заробіток за тих часів.*

752

ПРИТЧА ПРО МИЛОСЕРДНОГО САМАРЯНИНА

Один законник, випробовуючи Ісуса, запитав Його: «Вчителю, що мені робити, щоб успадкувати життя вічне?» Ісус відповів йому: «Що в Законі написано, як читаєш?» А той відповів: «Возлюби Господа Бога твого усім серцем твоїм, і всією душею твоєю, і всією силою твоєю, і усім твоїм розумом, і ближнього твого, як самого себе». Ісус сказав йому: «Правильно ти відповів; чини так — і будеш жити». Але законник, бажаючи виправдати себе, сказав Ісусові: «А хто мій ближній?» У відповідь Ісус розповів йому таку притчу:

«Один чоловік ішов з Єрусалиму до Єрихону, і попався розбійникам, що обдерли його, і завдали *йому* рани, та й утекли, покинувши ледве живого *його*. Проходив випадком тією дорогою священик один, побачив його, — і проминув. Так само й Левит надійшов на те місце, поглянув, — і *теж* проминув. Проходив же *там* якийсь самарянин, та й натрапив на нього, і, побачивши, змилосердився. І він підійшов, і обв'язав йому рани, наливши оливи й вина. Потому його посадив на худобину власну, і приставив його до гостиниці, та й клопотався про нього. А другого дня, від'їжджавши, вийняв він два динарії, та й дав *їх* господареві й проказав: «Заопікуйся ним, а як більше що витратиш, — заплачу тобі, як вернуся».

Розповівши цю притчу, Ісус запитав законника: «Котрий же з цих трьох — на думку твою — був ближній тому, хто попався розбійникам?» А він відказав: «Той, хто вчинив йому милість». Ісус же сказав йому: «Іди, — і роби так і ти!»

Лк. 10:25–37

ІСУС — ДОБРИЙ ПАСТИР

Ісус Христос, Син Божий, був посланий на землю для спасіння людства. Ісус часто говорив народові і Своїм учням про гріхопадіння людей, про необхідність покаяння і навернення до Бога. Також Він стверджував, що «так-бо Бог полюбив світ, що дав Сина Свого Однородженого, щоб кожен, хто вірує в Нього, не згинув, але мав життя вічне».

Про це Ісус нерідко говорив у Своїх притчах, наводячи образні приклади. Як пастир турбується про своїх овечок, так і Ісус, Спаситель світу, турбується про тих, хто прийме Його у серце своє і буде дотримуватись заповідей Його у своєму житті. Ось слова Господа Ісуса Христа:

«Поправді, поправді кажу вам, що Я — двері вівцям. Усі, скільки їх перше Мене приходило, — то злодії й розбійники, але вівці не слухали їх. Я — двері: коли через Мене хто ввійде, спасеться, і той ввійде та вийде, і пасовисько знайде. Злодій тільки на те закрадається, щоб красти й убивати та нищити. Я прийшов, щоб ви мали життя, і подостатком щоб мали.

Я — Пастир Добрий! Пастир добрий кладе життя власне за вівці. А наймит, і той, хто не вівчар, кому вівці не свої, *коли* бачить, що вовк наближається, то кидає вівці й тікає, а вовк їх хапає й полошить. А наймит утікає тому, що він наймит, і не дбає про вівці.

Я — Пастир Добрий, і знаю Своїх, і Свої Мене знають. Як Отець Мене знає, так і Я Отця знаю, і власне життя Я за вівці кладу. Також маю Я інших овець, які не з цієї кошари, — Я повинен і їх припровадити. І Мій голос почують вони, — і буде отара одна *й* Один Пастир!

Через те Отець любить Мене, що Я власне життя віддаю, щоб ізнову прийняти його. Ніхто в Мене його не бере, але Я Сам від Себе кладу його. Маю владу віддати його, і маю владу прийняти його знову, — Я цю заповідь взяв від Свого Отця».

Ів. 10:7–18

СЕСТРИ МАРТА І МАРІЯ

Народ був вражений глибокою мудрістю і силою Ісуса. Ісус любив людей, а люди любили Його. Але були у Ісуса й вороги, головним чином, серед фарисеїв та книжників (вчителів народу). Вони Його ненавиділи, і, незважаючи на всі ті дива, які Він творив, не вірили, що Він є Син Божий.

Неподалік від Єрусалима знаходилось містечко, яке називалось Віфанія. У ньому жили дві сестри — Марта та Марія, а також брат їхній, Лазар. Усі троє дуже любили Ісуса і запрошували Його до себе.

Якось Ісус прийшов до них, і Марія одразу сіла біля ніг Його, щоб послухати слово Боже. «А Марта великою послугою клопоталась, а спинившись, сказала: «Господи, чи байдуже Тобі, що на мене саму полишила служити сестра моя? Скажи ж їй, щоб мені помогла». Господь же промовив у відповідь їй: «Марто, Марто, — турбуєшся й журишся ти про багато чого, а потрібне одне. Марія ж обрала найкращу частку, яка не відбереться від неї».

Лк. 10:38–42

Hofmann.

ПРИТЧА ПРО НЕРОЗУМНОГО БАГАЧА

Ісус, проповідуючи народові, сказав якось: «Глядіть, остерігайтеся всякої зажерливости, — бо життя чоловіка не залежить від достатку маєтку його». І Він розповів їм притчу, говорячи: «В одного багача гойно нива вродила була. І міркував він про себе й казав: «Що робити, що не маю куди зібрати плодів своїх?» І сказав: «Оце я зроблю, — порозвалюю клуні свої, і просторніші поставлю, і позбираю туди пашню свою всю та свій достаток. І скажу я душі своїй: «Душе, маєш багато добра, на багато років складеного. Спочивай, їж та пий, і веселися!» Бог же до нього прорік: «Нерозумний, — ночі цієї ось душу твою зажадають від тебе, і кому позостанеться те, що ти був наготовив?»… Так *буває і з тим*, хто збирає для себе, та не багатіє в Бога».

Ісус продовжував: «І не шукайте, що будете їсти, чи що будете пити, і не клопочіться. Бо всього цього й люди світу оцього шукають, Отець же ваш знає, що того вам потрібно. Шукайте отож Його Царства, а це вам додасться!

Не лякайся, черідко мала, бо сподобалося Отцю вашому дати вам Царство. Продавайте достатки свої та милостиню подавайте. Робіть калитки собі не старіючі, — невичерпний скарб той у небі, куди не закрадається злодій, і міль де не точить. Бо де скарб ваш, там буде й серце ваше!»

Лк. 12:15–21, 29–34

ПРИТЧА ПРО БАГАЧА І ЛАЗАРЯ

У цій притчі розповідається про двох людей, життя яких дуже різнилося: один жив багато, але неправедно, інший — в бідності, але праведно.

«Один чоловік був багатий, і зодягався в порфіру й вісон, і щоденно розкішно бенкетував. Був і вбогий один, на ім'я *йому* Лазар, що лежав у воріт його, струпами вкритий, і бажав годуватися кришками, що зі столу багатого падали; пси ж приходили й рани лизали йому… Та ось сталось, що вбогий умер, — і на Авраамове лоно віднесли його Анголи. Умер же й багатий, — і його поховали. І, терплячи муки в аду, звів він очі свої, та й побачив здаля Авраама та Лазаря на лоні його. І він закричав та сказав: «Змилуйся, отче Аврааме, надо мною, і пошли *мені* Лазаря, — нехай умочить у воду кінця свого пальця, і мого язика прохолодить, бо я мучуся в полум'ї цім!»… Авраам же промовив: «Згадай, сину, що ти вже прийняв за життя свого добре своє, а Лазар так само — лихе; тепер він тут тішиться, а ти мучишся. А крім того всього, поміж нами та вами велика безодня поставлена, так що ті, що хочуть, переходити не можуть ізвідси до вас, ані не переходять ізвідти до нас». А він відказав: «Отож, отче, благаю тебе, щоб його ти послав у дім батька мого, бо п'ятьох братів маю, — хай він їм засвідчить, щоб і вони не прийшли на це місце страждання!» Авраам же сказав: «Вони мають Мойсея й Пророків, — нехай слухають їх!» А він відказав: «Ні ж бо, отче Аврааме, — але коли прийде хто з мертвих до них, то покаються». Йому ж він відказав: «Як Мойсея й Пророків не слухають, то коли хто й із мертвих воскресне, — не йнятимуть віри!»

Лк. 16:19–31

ПРИТЧА ПРО ЗАГУБЛЕНУ ВІВЦЮ

Ісус Христос так полюбив рід людський, що залишив славу небес і прийшов на землю, щоб віднайти і врятувати людей, які гинуть у своїх гріхах, відступили від Бога й забули про Нього. Він, як той добрий Пастир, завжди шукає загублену вівцю.

В одній із Своїх притч Ісус сказав: «Котрий з вас чоловік, мавши сотню овець і загубивши одну з них, не покине в пустині тих дев'ятидесяти й дев'яти, та й не піде *шукати* загинулої, аж поки не знайде її? А знайшовши, кладе на рамена свої та радіє. І, прийшовши додому, скликає він друзів і сусідів, та й каже до них: «Радійте зо мною, бо знайшов я вівцю свою *тую* загублену». Говорю вам, що так само на небі радітимуть *більш* за одного грішника, що кається, аніж за дев'ятдесятьох і дев'ятьох праведників, що не потребують покаяння!»

Лк. 15:3–7

ПРИТЧА ПРО БЛУДНОГО СИНА

Одного разу Ісус розповів таку притчу: «У чоловіка одного було два сини. І молодший із них сказав батькові: «Дай мені, батьку, належну частину маєтку!» І той поділив поміж ними маєток.

А по небагатьох днях зібрав син молодший усе, та й подавсь до далекого краю, і розтратив маєток свій там, живучи марнотратно. А як він усе прожив, настав голод великий у тім краї, — і він став бідувати. І пішов він тоді і пристав до одного з мешканців тієї землі, а той вислав його на поля свої пасти свиней. І бажав він наповнити шлунка свого *хоч* стручками, що їли їх свині, та ніхто не давав *їх* йому. Тоді він спам'ятався й сказав: «Скільки в батька мого наймитів мають хліба аж надмір, а я отут з голоду гину! Устану, і піду я до батька свого, та й скажу йому: «Прогрішився я, отче, против неба та супроти тебе… Недостойний я вже зватись сином твоїм; прийми ж мене, як одного з своїх наймитів»…

І, вставши, пішов він до батька свого».

Лк. 15:11–20

Продовження далі

Bida

ПОВЕРНЕННЯ БЛУДНОГО СИНА

Христос продовжив притчу про блудного сина: «А коли він далеко ще був, його батько вгледів його, — і переповнився жалем: і побіг він, і кинувсь на шию йому, і зачав цілувати його! І озвався до нього той син: «Прогрішився я, отче, против неба та супроти тебе, і недостойний вже зватися сином твоїм…» А батько рабам своїм каже: «Принесіть негайно одежу найкращу, і його зодягніть, і персня подайте на руку йому, а сандалі на ноги. Приведіть теля відгодоване та заколіть, — будемо їсти й радіти, бо цей син мій був мертвий — і ожив, був пропав — і знайшовся!» І почали веселитись вони.

А син старший його був на полі. І коли він ішов і наближався до дому, почув музики та танці. І покликав одного зі слуг, та й спитав: «Що це таке?» А той каже йому: «То вернувся твій брат, і твій батько звелів заколоти теля відгодоване, — бо ж здоровим його він прийняв». І розгнівався той, — і ввійти не хотів. Тоді вийшов батько його й став просити його. А той відповів і до батька сказав: «Ото, стільки років служу я тобі, і ніколи наказу твого не порушив, — ти ж ніколи мені й козеняти не дав, щоб із приятелями своїми потішився я… Коли ж син твій вернувся оцей, що проїв твій маєток із блудницями, — ти для нього звелів заколоти теля відгодоване»…

І сказав він йому: «Ти завжди зо мною, дитино, і все моє — то твоє! Веселитись та тішитись треба було, бо цей брат твій був мертвий — і ожив, був пропав — і знайшовся!»

Цією притчею Ісус ще раз показав, з якою великою радістю і всепрощенням приймає Небесний Отець усякого грішника, що приходить до Нього з каяттям і смиренним серцем.

Лк. 15:20–32

ІСУС ВОСКРЕШАЄ ЛАЗАРЯ

Якось, знаходячись зі Своїми учнями у відлюдному місці, Ісус отримав сумну звістку про хворобу друга свого, Лазаря, що жив у Віфанії з сестрами Мартою та Марією. Сестри хворого послали сказати Йому: «Ось нездужає, Господи, той, що кохаєш його!» Ісус, почувши це, сказав: «Не на смерть ця недуга, а на Божу славу, — щоб Син Божий прославився нею». Побувши ще два дні там, де знаходився, Він вирушив до Віфанії, знаючи, що Лазар вже помер.

Багато юдеїв прийшло до сестер і втішали їх у їхній журбі за братом. Марта побачила Ісуса й сказала Йому: «Коли б, Господи, був Ти отут, — то не вмер би мій брат… Та й тепер, — знаю я, — що чого тільки в Бога попросиш, то дасть Тобі Бог!» Промовляє до неї Ісус: «Воскресне твій брат… Я воскресення й життя. Хто вірує в Мене, — хоч і вмре, буде жити. І кожен, хто живе та хто вірує в Мене, — повіки не вмре. Чи ти віруєш в це?» Вона каже Йому: «Так, Господи! Я вірую, що Ти Христос, Син Божий, що має прийти на цей світ» Після цього вона пішла й покликала свою сестру Марію.

Коли Ісус побачив Марію у сльозах та юдеїв, що прийшли з нею й гірко плакали, Він Сам затужив духом і сказав: «Де його ви поклали?» Говорять Йому: «Іди, Господи, та подивися!»

Ісус підійшов до печери, у якій був похований Лазар. (У тій країні за тодішнім звичаєм ховали у печері, завалюючи вхід до неї великим каменем). Ісус звелів відсунути камінь, але Марта відказала, що Лазар вже чотири дні як помер. Ісус відповів їй: «Чи тобі не казав Я, що як будеш ти вірувати, — славу Божу побачиш?» Коли камінь відвалили, Ісус звів очі до неба й промовив: «Отче, дяку приношу Тобі, що Мене Ти почув. Та Я знаю, що Ти завжди почуєш Мене, але ради народу, що довкола стоїть, Я сказав, щоб увірували, що послав Ти Мене». І, промовивши це, Він скричав гучним голосом: «Лазарю, — вийди сюди!» І вийшов померлий, по руках і ногах обв'язаний пасами, а обличчя у нього було перев'язане хусткою».

Багато юдеїв, які бачили це диво, увірували в Нього. Однак фарисеї та первосвященики зібрали раду, щоб обговорити, як убити Ісуса Христа.

Ів. 11:1–50

Bida

ДЕСЯТЬ ПРОКАЖЕНИХ

По дорозі до Єрусалима Ісус зайшов до одного селища. Тут Його зустріли десятеро прокажених, які зупинились осторонь і кричали: «Ісусе, Наставнику, — змилуйсь над нами!» І, побачивши *їх*, Він промовив до них: «Підіть і покажіться священикам!» І сталось, коли вони йшли, то очистились…

Один же з них, як побачив, що видужав, то вернувся, і почав гучним голосом славити Бога. І припав він обличчям до ніг Його, складаючи дяку Йому. А то самарянин був…

Ісус же промовив у відповідь: «Чи не десять очистилось, — а дев'ять же де? Чому не вернулись вони хвалу Богові віддати, крім цього чужинця?»

Христос назвав вдячного зціленого чоловіка чужинцем тому, що самаряни та євреї були двома різними народами. Вони відрізнялись і за своїм віросповіданням (див. стор. 214). Потім Ісус звернувся до нього зі словами: «Підведися й іди: твоя віра спасла тебе!»

Лк. 17:11–19

ПРИТЧА ПРО ФАРИСЕЯ ТА МИТНИКА

Ми часто буваємо високої думки про себе і вважаємо себе дуже чесними, праведними та зовсім безгрішними. Але Господь вчить нас не гордувати й завжди бути смиренними перед Ним. Наступну притчу про фарисея та митника розповів Ісус для тих, хто був впевнений у своїй праведності, водночас принижуючи при цьому інших.

«Два чоловіки до храму ввійшли помолитись, — один фарисей, а другий *був* митник. Фарисей, ставши, так молився про себе: «Дякую, Боже, Тобі, що я не такий, як інші люди: здирщики, неправедні, перелюбні, або як цей митник. Я пощу двічі на тиждень, даю десятину з усього, що тільки надбаю!» А митник здалека стояв, та й очей навіть звести до неба не смів, але бив себе в груди й казав: «Боже, будь милостивий до мене грішного!»... Говорю вам, що цей повернувся до дому свого більш виправданий, аніж той. Бо кожен, хто підноситься, — буде понижений, хто ж понижається, — той піднесеться».

У нагірній проповіді Ісус повчав Своїх учнів і народ:

«Не судіть, щоб *і* вас не судили; бо яким судом судити будете, *таким же* осудять *і* вас, і якою мірою будете міряти, *такою* відміряють вам».

Лк. 18:10–14; Мт. 7:1–2

ІСУС БЛАГОСЛОВЛЯЄ ДІТЕЙ

Ісус Христос дуже любить дітей.

Якось до Ісуса привели діточок, щоб Він поклав на них руки і помолився за них. Учні ж Його не підпускали їх до Нього. Але Ісус сказав: «Пустіть діток, і не бороніть їм приходити до Мене, — бо Царство Небесне належить таким». Відтак Він поклав на них руки і благословив їх.

Іншим разом учні запитали Ісуса: «Хто найбільший у Царстві Небеснім?» Він же дитину покликав, і поставив її серед них, та й сказав: «Поправді кажу вам: коли не навернетесь, і не станете, як ті діти, — не ввійдете в Царство Небесне!

Отже, хто впокориться, як дитина оця, той найбільший у Царстві Небеснім.

І хто прийме таку дитину одну в Моє Ймення, той приймає Мене».

Мт. 18:1–5; 19:13–15

ЗЦІЛЕННЯ СЛІПОГО

Якось Ісус прийшов до великого міста Єрихона. Багато народу, як завжди, супроводжувало Його.

Біля входу в місто сидів при дорозі сліпий і просив милостиню. Його звали Вартимеєм. Почувши, що повз нього йде Ісус, про чудеса Якого він чув раніше, сліпий почав кричати: «Сину Давидів, Ісусе, — змилуйся надо мною!» Ісуса називали Сином Давидовим тому, що Його земні батьки були з роду царя Давида. Багато хто сварився на сліпого, щоб він мовчав, але той ще голосніше став кричати: «Сину Давидів, — змилуйся надо мною!»

Ісус зупинився і наказав його покликати. Декілька чоловік підійшли до сліпого й сказали: «Будь бадьорий, устань, — Він кличе тебе». Вартимей скинув плаща, щоб не заважав, скочив з місця і прийшов до Ісуса. Ісус сказав йому: «Що ти хочеш, щоб зробив Я тобі?» Сліпий же Йому відказав: «Учителю, — нехай я прозрю!» Ісус же до нього промовив: «Іди, — твоя віра спасла тебе!» І той зараз прозрів, і пішов за Ісусом дорогою.

Мр. 10:46–52

O. STEMLER

НАВЕРНЕННЯ МИТНИКА ЗАКХЕЯ

І знову Ісус відвідав місто Єрихон, що знаходилося поблизу Мертвого моря. У цьому місті жив митник Закхей. Митники збирали податки і часто займалися здирством, беручи з народу данину більшу, аніж передбачалася законом. Тому прості люди ненавиділи їх.

«І, ввійшовши *Ісус*, переходив через Єрихон. І ось чоловік, що звався Закхей, — він був старший над митниками, і був багатий, — бажав бачити Ісуса, хто Він, але з-за народу не міг, — бо малий був на зріст. І, забігши вперед, він виліз на фіґове дерево, щоб бачити Його, бо Він мав побіч нього проходити. А коли на це місце Ісус підійшов, то поглянув угору до нього й промовив: «Закхею, — зійди зараз додолу, бо сьогодні потрібно Мені бути в домі твоїм!»

І той зараз додолу ізліз, і прийняв Його з радістю. А всі, як побачили *це*, почали нарікати, і казали: «Він до грішного мужа в гостину зайшов!»

І, немов у відповідь на нарікання, Закхей підвівся і промовив до Господа: «Господи, половину маєтку свого я віддам ось убогим, а коли кого скривдив був чим, — верну вчетверо». Ісус же промовив до нього: «Сьогодні на дім цей спасіння прийшло, бо й він син Авраамів. Син-бо Людський прийшов, щоб знайти та спасти, що загинуло!»

Ісус однаково любить як праведних, так і грішних. Його чудодійна любов приводить грішників до каяття.

Лк. 19:1–10

КОМУ БАГАТО ПРОЩАЄТЬСЯ, ТОЙ БАГАТО ЛЮБИТЬ

Один з фарисеїв, Симон, запросив Ісуса до себе на обід. Ісус погодився і прийшов до нього.

«І ось жінка з міста того, котра була грішниця, довідавшись, що Він у фарисеєвім домі… принесла алюбастрову пляшечку з миром* і, припавши до ніг Його ззаду, плачучи, почала обливати слізьми ноги Йому і волоссям своїм витирати, і цілувала ноги Йому, і мастила миром.

Побачивши це, фарисей, що покликав Його, міркував собі подумки: «Коли б Він був пророк, то знав би, хто й яка жінка до Нього доторкується, бо то ж грішниця». Звернувшись до нього, Ісус сказав: «Маю, Симоне, дещо сказати тобі». А той відказав: «Кажи, Вчителю». І промовив Ісус:

«Були два боржники в одного вірителя; один був винен п'ятсот динаріїв, а другий — п'ятдесят. Як вони ж не могли заплатити, простив він обом. Скажи ж, котрий із них більше полюбить його?» Відповів Симон, говорячи: «Думаю, — той, кому більше простив». І сказав Він йому: «Розсудив ти правдиво».

І, обернувшись до жінки, Він промовив до Симона: «Чи ти бачиш цю жінку? Я прибув у твій дім, — ти на ноги Мої не подав і води, а вона окропила слізьми Мої ноги й обтерла волоссям своїм. Поцілунку не дав ти Мені, — а вона, відколи ввійшов Я, Мої ноги цілує невпинно. Голови ти Моєї оливою не намастив, — а вона миром ноги мої намастила… Ось тому говорю Я тобі: «Численні гріхи її прощені, бо багато вона полюбила. Кому ж мало прощається, такий мало любить».

А до неї промовив: «Прощаються тобі гріхи!» А ті, що сиділи з Ним при столі, почали гомоніти про себе: «Хто ж це Такий, що прощає й гріхи?» А до жінки сказав Він: «Твоя віра спасла тебе, — іди з миром *собі*!»

Лк. 7:37–50

---

* *Миро — це дорогоцінна нардова пахуча олія.*

ВХІД ГОСПОДНІЙ В ЄРУСАЛИМ

Ісус по дорозі у Єрусалим прийшов до Вітфагії, що розташована біля гори Оливної. Звідти Він послав двох учнів, сказавши їм: «Ідіть у село, яке перед вами, і знайдете зараз ослицю прив'язану та з нею осля; відв'яжіть, і Мені приведіть *їх*. А як хто вам що скаже, відкажіть, що їх потребує Господь, — і він зараз пошле їх». Посланці пішли і найшли те, про що сказав їм Христос. Коли ж вони відв'язували осла, то господарі запитали їх, для чого вони це роблять. Учні відповіли: «Господь потребує його».

Вони привели до Ісуса ослицю та молодого осла і поклали на них свій одяг. Ісус сів на осла, і коли Він під'їжджав до Єрусалима, багато народу простилали перед Ним свою одіж і пальмове гілля, зустрічаючи Його вигуками: «Осанна* Сину Давидовому! Благословенний, хто йде у Господнє Ім'я! Осанна на висоті!» Ось так збулися слова, які ще задовго до цього сказав пророк Захарія: «Скажіте Сіонській доньці:** Ось до тебе йде Цар твій! Він покірливий, і всів на осла, — на осля, під'яремної сина».

Коли Ісус увійшов до Єрусалима, все місто завирувало, усі почали питати про Нього: «Хто це такий?» А народ говорив: «Це Пророк, — Ісус із Назарету Галілейського!» Багато хто свідчив, що Він воскресив Лазаря й учинив багато дивного. Тоді фарисеї почали говорити між собою: «Ви бачите, що нічого не вдієте: ось пішов *увесь* світ услід за Ним!» Вони звернулися до Ісуса з вимогою, щоб Він заборонив учням прославляти Його, але Ісус відповів їм: «Кажу вам, що коли ці замовкнуть, то каміння кричатиме!»

Мт. 21:1–11; Лк. 19:29–40; Ів. 12:12–19

---

* *Осанна (євр.) — спасіння; слава.*

** *Мається на увазі Єрусалим та його народ.*

Hofmann

ПЛАЧ ІСУСА ЗА ЄРУСАЛИМОМ

Ісус уболівав за Єрусалимом, за тими, хто не прийняв Його і жадав вбити Його. «Єрусалиме, Єрусалиме, що вбиваєш пророків та каменуєш посланих до тебе! Скільки раз Я хотів позбирати дітей твоїх, як *та* квочка збирає під крила курчаток своїх, — та ви не захотіли! Ось «ваш дім зостається порожній для вас!» Говорю-бо Я вам: Ви мене не побачите, аж поки не настане, що скажете: «Благословенний, Хто йде в Господнє Ім'я!»

Іншим разом Ісус наблизився до Єрусалима і, дивлячись на нього, заплакав за ним і сказав: «О, якби й ти хоч цього дня пізнало, що *потрібне* для миру тобі! Та тепер від очей твоїх сховане *це*. Бо прийдуть на тебе *ті* дні, і твої вороги тебе валом оточать, і обляжуть тебе, і стиснуть тебе звідусюди. І зрівняють з землею тебе, і *поб'ють* твої діти в тобі, і не позоставлять у тобі каменя на камені, бо не зрозуміло ти часу відвідин твоїх».

Лк. 13:34, 35; 19:41–44

ПРИТЧА ПРО ЗЛИХ ВИНОГРАДАРІВ

Ісус розповів первосвященикам і фарисеям притчу про їх ставлення до Нього.

«Був господар один. Насадив виноградника він, обгородив його муром, видовбав у ньому чавило, башту поставив, — і віддав його винарям, та й пішов. Коли ж надійшов час плодів, він до винарів послав рабів своїх, щоб прийняти плоди свої. Винарі ж рабів його похапали, — і одного побили, а другого замордували, а того вкаменували. Знов послав він інших рабів, більш як перше, — та й їм учинили те саме. Нарешті послав до них сина свого і сказав: «Посоромляться сина мого». Але винарі, як побачили сина, міркувати собі стали: «Це спадкоємець; ходім, замордуймо його, — і заберемо його спадщину!» І, схопивши його, вони вивели за виноградник його, та й убили. Отож, як прибуде той пан виноградника, що зробить він тим винарям?» Вони кажуть Йому: «Злочинців погубить жорстоко, виноградника ж віддасть іншим винарям, що будуть плоди віддавати йому своєчасно».

Ісус промовляє до них: «Чи ви не читали ніколи в Писанні: «Камінь, що його будівничі відкинули, — той наріжним став каменем; від Господа сталося це, і дивне воно в очах наших!» Тому кажу вам, що від вас Царство Боже відійметься, і дасться народові, що плоди його буде приносити.

І хто впаде на цей камінь — розіб'ється, а на кого він сам упаде, — то розчавить його».

А як первосвященики та фарисеї почули ці притчі Його, то вони зрозуміли, що про них Він говорить. І намагались схопити Його, але побоялись людей, бо вважали Його за Пророка».

Мт. 21:33–46

«БАГАТО ПОКЛИКАНИХ, ТА ВИБРАНИХ МАЛО»

Одного разу Ісус, запрошений у гості до фарисея, сказав господареві: «Коли ти справляєш обід чи вечерю, не клич друзів своїх, ні братів своїх, ані своїх родичів, ні сусідів багатих, щоб так само й вони коли не запросили тебе, — і буде взаємна відплата тобі. Але, як справляєш гостину, клич убогих, калік, кривих та сліпих, і будеш блаженний, бо не мають вони чим віддати тобі, — віддасться ж тобі за воскресіння праведних!»

Як почув це один із отих, що сиділи з Ним при столі, то до Нього сказав: «Блаженний, хто хліб споживатиме в Божому Царстві!»

Він же промовив до нього: «Один чоловік спорядив був велику вечерю, і запросив багатьох. І послав він свого раба часу вечері сказати запрошеним: «Ідіть, бо вже все наготовано». І зараз усі почали відмовлятися. Перший сказав йому: «Поле купив я, і маю потребу піти та оглянути його. Прошу тебе, — вибач мені!» А другий сказав: «Я купив *собі* п'ять пар волів, — і йду спробувати їх. Прошу тебе, — вибач мені!» І знов інший сказав: «Одружився *ось* я, і через те я не можу прибути».

І вернувся той раб, і панові своєму про все розповів. Розгнівавсь господар тоді, та й сказав до свого раба: «Піди швидко на вулиці та на завулки міські, і приведи сюди вбогих, і калік, і сліпих, і кривих». І *згодом* раб повідомив: «Пане, сталося так, як звелів ти, та місця є ще». І сказав пан рабові: «Піди на дороги й на загороди, та й силуй прийти, щоб наповнився дім мій. Кажу-бо я вам, що жаден із запрошених мужів тих не покуштує моєї вечері… Бо багато покликаних, та вибраних мало!»

Лк. 14:12–24

«КЕСАРЕВЕ — КЕСАРЕВІ, А БОГОВІ — БОЖЕ»

Фарисеї дуже лютували на Ісуса за Його слова і діла, повні благодаті Божої. Вони довго радились про те, як спіймати Його на слові, і послали до Нього своїх учнів, які сказали Йому: «Учителю, знаємо ми, що Ти справедливий, і наставляєш на Божу дорогу правдиво, і не зважаєш ні на кого, бо на людське обличчя не дивишся Ти. Скажи ж нам, як здається Тобі: чи годиться давати податок для кесаря, чи ні?» (Кесар — це правитель Римської імперії, під владою якої знаходилася Палестина).

Запитання фарисеїв було дуже підступним. Якби Ісус відповів, що кесарю треба давати податок, то Його звинуватили б у зрадництві і у підтримці влади Риму. Якби Він сказав, що податок платити не можна, то тоді б Його назвали бунтарем.

Ісус, бачачи їхнє лукавство, сказав: «Чого ви, лицеміри, Мене випробовуєте? Покажіть Мені гріш податковий». І принесли динарія Йому. А Він каже до них: «Чий це образ і напис?» Ті відказують: «Кесарів». Тоді каже Він їм: «Тож віддайте кесареве — кесареві, а Богові — Боже». А почувши таке, вони диву далися. І, лишивши Його, відійшли».

Після цього Ісус звернувся до народу та учнів Своїх зі словами: «На сидінні Мойсеєвім усілися книжники та фарисеї. Тож усе, що вони скажуть вам, — робіть і виконуйте; та за вчинками їхніми не робіть, бо говорять вони, — *та* не роблять *того*! Вони ж в'яжуть тяжкі тягарі, і кладуть їх на людські рамена, самі ж *навіть* пальцем своїм не хочуть їх порушити… Усі ж учинки свої вони роблять, щоб їх бачили люди…»

Мт. 22:15–22; 23:1–5

«НАЙБІЛЬША Й НАЙПЕРША ЗАПОВІДЬ»

Якось підійшов до Ісуса один законник. В Євангеліях згадуються законники та книжники. Так називали вчених євреїв, які все своє життя присвятили дослідженню та тлумаченню Святого Писання, особливо Закону Мойсеєвого.

Законник запитав Ісуса: «Учителю, котра заповідь найбільша в Законі?» Він же промовив йому:

«Люби Господа Бога свого всім серцем своїм, і всією душею своєю, і всією своєю думкою».

Це найбільша й найперша заповідь. А друга однакова з нею:

«Люби свого ближнього, як самого себе».

На двох оцих заповідях увесь Закон і Пророки стоять».

Любі діти, збережіть і запам'ятайте ці слова Господа Ісуса Христа у серці своїм.

Мт. 22:36–40

ДВІ ЛЕПТИ БІДНОЇ УДОВИ

Якось Ісус учив народ у храмі, кажучи: «Стережіться тих книжників, що люблять у довгих одежах проходжуватись, і привіти на ринках, і перші лавки в синагогах, і перші місця на прийняттях, що вдовині хати поїдають, і моляться довго напоказ, — вони тяжче осудження приймуть!»

І сів Він навпроти скарбниці, і дививсь, як народ мідяки до скарбниці вкидає. І багато заможних укидали багато. І підійшла одна вбога вдовиця, і поклала дві лепти, цебто гріш.

І покликав Він учнів Своїх та й промовив до них: «Поправді кажу вам, що ця вбога вдовиця поклала найбільше за всіх, хто клав у скарбницю. Бо всі клали від лишка свого, а вона поклала з убозтва свого все, що мала, — свій прожиток увесь».

Мр. 12:38–44

ІСУС ГОВОРИТЬ ПРО МАЙБУТНЄ

У багатьох місцях Біблії є пророцтва про друге пришестя Ісуса. Вдруге Він прийде у всій славі Своїй як Господь усього світу. Перед Його пришестям буде велике лихоліття на землі. Про це Він і Сам свідчив, коли змальовував Своїм учням картину Свого другого пришестя:

«Стережіться, щоб вас хто не звів! Бо багато хто прийде в Ім'я Моє, кажучи: «Я Христос». І зведуть багатьох. Ви ж про війни почуєте, і про воєнні чутки, — глядіть, не лякайтесь, бо «статись належить тому». Але це не кінець ще. Бо «повстане народ на народ, і царство на царство», і голод, мор та землетруси настануть місцями. А все це — початок терпінь *породільних*. На муки тоді видаватимуть вас, і вбиватимуть вас, і вас будуть ненавидіти всі народи за Ймення Моє. І багато хто в той час спокусяться, і видавати один одного будуть, і один одного будуть ненавидіти. Постане багато фальшивих пророків, — і зведуть багатьох. І через розріст беззаконства любов багатьох охолоне. А хто витерпить аж до кінця, — той буде спасений! І проповідана буде ця Євангелія Царства по цілому світові, на свідоцтво народам усім... Постануть христи неправдиві, і неправдиві пророки, і будуть чинити великі ознаки та чуда, що звели б, коли б можна, і вибраних... І зараз, по скорботі тих днів, «сонце затьмиться, і місяць не дасть свого світла», і зорі попадають з неба, і сили небесні порушаться. І того часу на небі з'явиться знак Сина Людського, і тоді «заголосять всі земні племена», і побачать вони «Сина Людського, що йтиме на хмарах небесних» із великою потугою й славою... Небо й земля проминеться, але не минуться слова Мої! А про день той і годину не знає ніхто: ані Анголи небесні, ані Син, — лише Сам Отець... Тож пильнуйте, бо не знаєте, котрого дня прийде Господь ваш».

Мт. 24:4–42

ПРИТЧА ПРО ДЕСЯТЬ ДІВ

Про Своє друге пришестя на землю Ісус розповів і таку притчу:

«Тоді Царство Небесне буде подібне до десяти дів, що побрали каганці свої, та й пішли зустрічати молодого. П'ять же з них нерозумні були, а п'ять мудрі. Нерозумні ж, узявши каганці, не взяли із собою оливи. А мудрі набрали оливи в посудинки разом зі своїми каганцями. А коли забаривсь молодий, то всі задрімали й поснули.

А опівночі крик залунав: «Ось молодий, — виходьте назустріч!» Схопились тоді всі ті діви, і каганці свої наготували. Нерозумні ж сказали до мудрих: «Дайте нам із своєї оливи, бо наші каганці *ось* гаснуть». Мудрі ж відповіли та сказали: «Щоб, бува, нам і вам не забракло, — краще вдайтеся до продавців, і купіть собі». І як вони купувати пішли, то прибув молодий; і готові ввійшли на весілля з ним, — і замкнені двері були.

А потім прийшла й решта дів і казала: «Пане, пане, — відчини нам!» Він же у відповідь їм проказав: «Поправді кажу вам, — не знаю я вас!»

Тож пильнуйте, бо не знаєте ні дня, ні години, коли прийде Син Людський!»

Мт. 25:1–13

«Я — ВИНОГРАДИНА, ВИ — ГАЛУЗЗЯ»

Три роки Ісус Христос навчав народ, зціляв хворих і звіщав Євангелію, Благу Звістку. Він готував Своїх учнів до праці на ниві Господній. Ось приклад того, як Ісус навчав їх:

«Я правдива Виноградина, а Отець Мій — Виноградар. Усяку галузку в Мене, що плоду не приносить, Він відтинає, але всяку, що плід родить, обчищає її, щоб рясніше родила. Через Слово, що Я вам говорив, ви вже чисті. Перебувайте в Мені, а Я в вас! Як та вітка не може вродити плоду сама з себе, коли не позостанеться на виноградині, так і ви, як в Мені перебувати не будете. Я — Виноградина, ви — галуззя! Хто в Мені перебуває, а Я в ньому, той рясно зароджує, бо без Мене нічого чинити не можете ви. Коли хто перебувати не буде в Мені, той буде відкинений геть, як галузка, і всохне. І громадять їх, і кладуть на огонь, — і згорять. Коли ж у Мені перебувати ви будете, а слова Мої позостануться в вас, то просіть, чого хочете, — і станеться вам!..

Як Отець полюбив Мене, так і Я полюбив вас. Перебувайте в любові Моїй! Якщо будете ви зберігати Мої заповіді, то в любові Моїй перебуватимете, як і Я зберіг Заповіді Свого Отця, і перебуваю в любові Його… Це Я вам заповідую, — щоб любили один одного ви!..

Коли вас світ ненавидить, знайте, що Мене він зненавидів перше, як вас. Коли б ви зі світу були, то своє світ любив би. А що ви не зі світу, але Я вас зі світу обрав, тому світ вас ненавидить…. Як Мене переслідували, — то й вас переслідувати будуть; як слово Моє зберігали, — берегтимуть і ваше. Але все це робитимуть вам за Ім’я Моє, бо не знають Того, Хто послав Мене. Коли б Я не прийшов і до них не казав, то не мали б гріха, а тепер вимовки не мають вони за свій гріх. Хто Мене ненавидить, — і Мого Отця той ненавидить».

Ів. 15:1–7, 9, 10, 17–23

ОСТАННЯ ВЕЧЕРЯ

Коли наступило свято Пасхи, Ісус послав Петра та Івана, говорячи: «Підіть, і приготуйте нам пасху, щоб *її* спожили ми». А вони запитали Його: «Де Ти хочеш, щоб ми приготували?» А Він їм відказав: «Ось, як будете входити в місто, стріне вас чоловік, воду несучи у глекові, — ідіть за ним аж до дому, куди він увійде. І скажіть до господаря дому: Учитель питає тебе: «Де кімната, в якій споживу зі Своїми учнями пасху?» І він вам покаже велику горницю вистелену: там приготуйте».

І вони відійшли, і знайшли, як Він їм говорив, — і зачали там готувати пасху.

А коли настав час, сів до столу, і апостоли з Ним. І промовив до них: «Я дуже бажав спожити цю пасху із вами, перш ніж муки прийму. Бо кажу вам, що вже споживати не буду її, поки сповниться в Божому Царстві вона».

Узявши ж чашу, і вчинивши подяку, Він промовив: «Візьміть її, і поділіть між собою. Кажу ж вам, що віднині не питиму Я від оцього плоду виноградного, доки Божеє Царство не прийде».

Узявши ж хліб і вчинивши подяку, поламав і дав їм, проказуючи: «Це тіло Моє, що за вас віддається. Це чиніть на спомин про Мене!»

По вечері так само ж і чашу, говорячи: «Оця чаша — Новий Заповіт у Моїй крові, що за вас проливається».

Лк. 22:8–20

E. ZIMMERMANN

БЕСІДА ПІСЛЯ ВЕЧЕРІ

Під час вечері Ісус устав, оперезався рушником, налив води до умивальниці і почав омивати ноги учням Своїм та обтирати їх рушником. Коли Він підійшов до Симона-Петра, той сказав Йому: «Ти, Господи, митимеш ноги мені?» Ісус відказав і промовив йому: «Що Я роблю, ти не знаєш тепер, але опісля зрозумієш»... Коли ж пообмивав їхні ноги... засів знову за стіл і промовив до них: «Чи знаєте ви, що Я зробив вам? Ви Мене називаєте: Учитель і Господь, — і добре ви кажете, бо Я є. А коли обмив ноги вам Я, Господь і Вчитель, то повинні й ви один одному ноги вмивати. Бо то Я вам приклада дав... Поправді, поправді кажу вам: Раб не більший за пана свого, посланець же не більший від того, хто вислав його. Коли знаєте це, то блаженні ви, якщо таке чините!

Не про всіх вас кажу. Знаю Я, кого вибрав, але щоб збулося Писання: «Хто хліб споживає зо Мною, підняв той на Мене п'яту свою!»...

Затривожився духом Ісус, і освідчив, говорячи: «Поправді, поправді кажу вам, що один із вас видасть Мене!»

Тоді учні, озираючись один на одного, дивувались, не розуміючи, про кого Він говорить. Іван же, припавши до грудей Ісуса, запитав Його: «Хто це, Господи?» Ісус же відказує: «Це той, кому, умочивши, подам Я куска». І, вмочивши куска, подав синові Симона, — Юді Іскаріотському!..»

Юда, прийнявши шматок, одразу ж вийшов; а була ніч. Коли він вийшов, Ісус сказав: «*Мої* дітоньки!.. Нову заповідь Я вам даю: Любіть один одного! Як Я вас полюбив, так любіть один одного й ви! По тому пізнають усі, що ви учні Мої, як будете мати любов між собою».

Згодом Спаситель повідав їм, що цієї ночі усі вони спокусяться щодо Нього. Але Петро відповів: «Якби й усі спокусились про Тебе, — я не спокушуся ніколи». Промовив до нього Ісус: «Поправді кажу тобі, що ночі цієї, перше ніж заспіває півень, — відречешся ти тричі від Мене».

Ів. 13:4–38; Мт. 26:33, 34

МОЛИТВА В ГЕФСИМАНІЇ

Тієї ж ночі після вечері Ісус з одинадцятьма учнями вирушив до місцевості, званої Гефсиманією. Там Ісус сказав учням: «Посидьте ви тут, аж поки піду й помолюся отам». І, взявши Петра й двох синів Зеведеєвих, зачав сумувати й тужити. Тоді промовляє до них: «Обгорнена сумом смертельним душа Моя! Залишіться тут, і попильнуйте зо Мною»… І, трохи далі пройшовши, упав Він долілиць, та молився й благав: «Отче Мій, коли можна, нехай обмине ця чаша Мене… Та проте, — не як Я хочу, а як Ти»… І Ангол із неба з'явився до Нього, — і додавав Йому сили. А як був у смертельній тривозі, ще пильніш Він молився. І піт Його став, немов каплі крови, що спливали на землю… І, підвівшись з молитви, Він до учнів прийшов, і знайшов їх, що спали з журби».

У цій молитві Христос говорив про чашу страждань, яку Він мусив прийняти за гріхи наші. Ніхто не може навіть уявити собі глибини її гіркоти і жаху. Але Син Божий прийняв її покірно. Він знав, що жертвує Собою для того, щоб врятувати кожного з нас. Якби Він не випив цієї чаші страждань, наші гріхи залишилися б і досі неспокутуваними.

Мт. 26:36–44; Лк. 22:39–46

H. Hofmann.

ІСУСА БЕРУТЬ ПІД ВАРТУ

Побачивши сплячих учнів Ісус розбудив зі словами: «Ви ще далі спите й спочиваєте? Ось година наблизилась, — і до рук грішникам виданий буде Син Людський… Уставайте, ходім, — ось наблизився Мій зрадник!»

І коли Він іще говорив, аж ось прийшов Юда, один із Дванадцятьох, а з ним люду багато від первосвящеників і старших народу з мечами та киями. А зрадник Його дав був знака їм, кажучи: «Кого поцілую, то Він, — беріть Його». І зараз Він підійшов до Ісуса й сказав: «Радій, Учителю!» І поцілував Його. Ісус же йому відказав: «Чого, друже, прийшов ти?.. Чи *оце* поцілунком ти, Юдо, видаєш Сина Людського?» Тоді Ісус звернувся до воїнів, які прийшли разом із Юдою, і запитав їх: «Кого ви шукаєте?» Вони відповіли: «Ісуса Назорея». Господь відказав їм: «Це Я». Почувши таке, вони відступили й впали перед Ним на коліна.

Потім Ісус сказав їм: «Немов на розбійника вийшли ви з мечами та киями, щоб узяти Мене! Я щоденно сидів у храмі і навчав, і ви не хапали Мене… але тепер ваш час і влада пітьми…»

Воїни схопили Ісуса і повели Його в дім первосвященика, а учні, залишивши Його, повтікали.

Мт. 26:45–57; Лк. 22:45–53; Ів. 18:1–12

ЗРЕЧЕННЯ ПЕТРА

Петро та ще один учень Ісуса йшли на відстані за Ним аж до двору первосвященика, щоб побачити, чим це все закінчиться.

Первосвященики і старійшини, і весь синедріон шукали на Ісуса неправдивого свідчення, щоб засудити Його до смерті, але не знаходили, хоча багато приходило фальшивих свідків. Нарешті, прийшли двоє свідків та й сказали: «Він говорив: Я можу зруйнувати храм Божий, — і за три дні збудувати його». Тоді первосвященик устав і до Нього сказав: «Ти нічого не відповідаєш *на те*, що свідчать супроти Тебе?» Ісус же мовчав. І первосвященик сказав Йому: «Заприсягаю Тебе Живим Богом, щоб нам Ти сказав, — чи Христос Ти, Син Божий?» Промовляє до нього Ісус: «Ти сказав… А навіть повім вам: відтепер ви побачите Людського Сина, що сидітиме праворуч сили *Божої*, і на хмарах небесних приходитиме!»

Тоді первосвященик роздер одежу* свою та й сказав: «Він богозневажив! Нащо нам іще свідки потрібні? Ось ви чули тепер *Його* богозневагу! Як вам іздається?» Вони ж відповіли та сказали: «Повинен умерти!»

Тоді стали плювати на обличчя Йому, та бити по щоках Його, інші ж киями били, і казали: «Пророкуй нам, Христе, хто то вдарив Тебе?»

Петро ж був на подвір'ї і грівся біля вогню разом з прислужниками. Було холодно. І підійшла до Нього одна служниця й сказала: «І ти був з Ісусом Галілеянином!» А він перед всіма відрікся, сказавши: «Не відаю я, що ти кажеш»… А коли до воріт він підходив, побачила інша його та й сказала приявним там *людям*: «Оцей був з Ісусом Назарянином!» І він знову відрікся та став присягатись: «Не знаю Цього Чоловіка!»… Підійшли ж трохи згодом присутні й сказали Петрові: «І ти справді з отих, та й мова твоя виявляє тебе». Тоді він став клястись та божитись: «Не знаю Цього Чоловіка!» І заспівав півень хвилі тієї…

І згадав Петро сказане слово Ісусове: «Перше ніж заспіває півень, — відречешся ти тричі від Мене». І, вийшовши звідти, він гірко заплакав…»

Мт. 26:58–75

---

* *У євреїв був звичай роздирати одежу свою на знак великого смутку чи обурення.*

ІСУС ПЕРЕД ПИЛАТОМ

А коли настав ранок, усі первосвященики й старійшини зібрали нараду супроти Ісуса, щоб заподіяти Йому смерть. Вони зв'язали Його, відвели та й передали Понтію Пилату». Пилат був римським правителем в Юдеї та в Самарії, бо тоді Свята Земля була завойована римлянами.

«Тоді вийшов Пилат… до них і сказав: «Яку скаргу приносите ви на Цього Чоловіка?» Вони відповіли та й сказали йому: «Коли б Цей злочинцем не був, ми б Його тобі не видавали» (Ів. 18:28–30). «…І зачали оскаржати Його й говорити: «Ми ствердили, що Цей ворохобить народ наш, і забороняє податок давати кесареві, та й говорить, що Він, — Христос Цар» (Лк. 23:2). «Пилат… покликав Ісуса, і до Нього сказав: «Чи Ти Цар Юдейський?» Ісус відповів: «…Моє Царство не із світу цього. Якби із цього світу було Моє Царство, то служба Моя воювала б, щоб не виданий був Я юдеям. Та тепер Моє Царство не звідси»… Сказав же до Нього Пилат: «Так Ти Цар?» Ісус відповів: «Сам ти кажеш, що Цар Я. Я на те народився, і на те прийшов у світ, щоб засвідчити правду. *І* кожен, хто з правди, той чує Мій голос». Говорить до Нього Пилат: «Що є правда?» І сказавши оце, до юдеїв знов вийшов, та й каже до них: «Не знаходжу Я в Ньому провини ніякої» (Ів. 18:33–38).

Коли Пилат довідався, що Ісус походить з Галілеї, вирішив передати Його цареві Галілеї Іроду, бо той саме у ці дні перебував в Єрусалимі. «Коли ж Ірод побачив Ісуса, то дуже зрадів, бо він від давнього часу бажав Його бачити… І багато питався Його, та нічого не відповідав Він йому. І стояли *тут* первосвященики й книжники, та завзято Його оскаржали. Тоді Ірод… ізневажив Його й насміявся, зодягнувши Його в яснобілу одіж, і відіслав до Пилата Його. І того дня стали Ірод із Пилатом за приятелів між собою, бо давніш ворожнеча між ними була.

А Пилат скликав первосвящеників, і старшин, і народ, і промовив до них: «Привели ви мені Чоловіка Цього, як того, що бунтує народ. А ось я перед вами розвідав, — і не знаходжу в Людині Оцій ані однієї провини такої, про що ви оскаржаєте»… Пилату потрібно було відпустити задля свята одного засудженого і він хотів відпустити Ісуса. Але увесь народ став кричати: «Візьми Цього, — відпусти ж нам Варавву!» Варавва був посаджений до в'язниці за заколот, який стався у місті, та за вбивство… І взяв гору крик їхній та первосвящеників» (Лк. 23:7–23).

ШЛЯХ НА ГОЛГОФУ

Тоді Пилат взяв Ісуса та й звелів збичувати Його. Потім воїни, сплівши з терену вінець, поклали Йому на голову, зодягли Його у багряницю, і казали: «Радій, Царю Юдейський!» І били по щоках Його… І знову вийшов до народу Пилат та й сказав їм: «Ось Його я виводжу назовні до вас, щоб ви переконались, що провини ніякої в Нім не знаходжу». І вийшов назовні Ісус, у терновім вінку та в багрянім плащі. А *Пилат* до них каже: «Оце Чоловік!» Як зобачили ж Його первосвященики й служба, то закричали, говорячи: «Розіпни, розіпни!» Пилат каже до них: «То візьміть Його ви й розіпніть, — бо провини я в Нім не знаходжу!» Відказали юдеї йому: «Ми маємо Закона, а за Законом Він мусить умерти, — бо за Божого Сина Себе видавав!» Як зачув же Пилат оце слово, налякався ще більш… і питає Ісуса: «Звідки Ти?» Та Ісус йому відповіді не подав. І каже до Нього Пилат: «Не говориш до мене? Хіба ж Ти не знаєш, що маю я владу розп'ясти Тебе, і маю владу Тебе відпустити?» Ісус відповів: «Надо Мною ти жадної влади не мав би, коли б тобі зверху не дано було; тому більший гріх має той, хто Мене тобі видав»… Після цього Пилат намагався пустити Його, та юдеї кричали, говорячи: «Якщо Його пустиш, то не кесарів приятель ти! Усякий, хто себе за царя видає, противиться кесареві». Як зачув же Пилат оце слово, то вивів назовні Ісуса, і засів на суддеве сидіння, на місці, що зветься літостротон*, по-гебрейському ж гаввата» (Ів. 19:1–13).

«А первосвященики й старші попідмовляли народ, щоб просити за Варавву, а Ісусові смерть заподіяти… Пилат каже до них: «А що ж маю зробити з Ісусом, що зветься Христос?» Усі закричали: «Нехай розп'ятий буде!»… І, як побачив Пилат, що нічого не вдіє, а неспокій ще більший стається, набрав він води, та й перед народом умив *свої* руки й сказав: «Я невинний у крові Його! Самі ви побачите»… А ввесь народ відповів і сказав: «На нас Його кров і на наших дітей!»… Тоді відпустив їм Варавву, а Ісуса… видав, щоб розп'ятий був» (Мт. 27:20–26).

Воїни «взяли Ісуса й повели… І, нісши Свого хреста, Він вийшов на місце, Черепповищем зване, по-гебрейському Голгофа» (Ів. 19:16, 17). «А за Ним ішов натовп великий людей і жінок, які плакали та голосили за Ним». (Лк. 23:27).

* *Кам'яний поміст.*

Doré

РОЗП'ЯТТЯ ІСУСА

«І вели з Ним також двох злочинників інших, щоб убити. А коли прибули на те місце, що звуть «Череповище», розп'яли тут Його та злочинників, — одного праворуч, а одного ліворуч. Ісус же промовив: «Отче, відпусти їм, — бо не знають, що чинять вони!» (Лк. 23:27–34).

«А Пилат написав і написа, та й умістив на хресті. Було ж *там* написано: «Ісус Назарянин, Цар Юдейський»… А було по-гебрейському, по-грецькому *й* по-римському написано… Розп'явши ж Ісуса, вояки взяли одіж Його, та й поділили на чотири частини, по частині для кожного вояка, теж і хітона» (Ів. 19:19–23).

«А люди стояли й дивились… Насміхалися з ними й старшини, говорячи: «Він інших спасав, — нехай Сам Себе визволить, коли Він Христос, Божий Обранець!» І вояки глузували з Нього: приступаючи, оцет Йому подавали, і казали: «Коли Цар Ти Юдейський, — спаси Себе Сам!» … А один із розп'ятих злочинників став зневажати Його й говорити: «Чи Ти не Христос? То спаси Себе й нас!» Обізвався ж той другий, і докоряв йому, кажучи: «Чи не боїшся ти Бога, коли й сам на те саме засуджений? Але ми справедливо *засуджені*, і належну заплату за вчинки свої беремо, — Цей же жадного зла не вчинив». І сказав до Ісуса: «Спогадай мене, Господи, коли прийдеш у Царство Своє!» І промовив до нього Ісус: «Поправді кажу тобі: ти будеш зо Мною сьогодні в раю!» (Лк. 23:35–43).

«А від години шостої аж до години дев'ятої* — темрява сталась по цілій землі! А коло години дев'ятої скрикнув Ісус гучним голосом, кажучи: «Елі, Елі, лама савахтані?» цебто: «Боже Мій, Боже Мій, нащо Мене Ти покинув?»… А один із них зараз побіг і взяв губку та, оцтом її наповнивши, настромив на тростину й давав Йому пити…» (Мт. 27:45–49). «А коли Ісус оцту прийняв, то промовив: «Звершилось!» (Ів. 19:30).

«І, скрикнувши голосом гучним, промовив Ісус: «Отче, у руки Твої віддаю Свого духа!» І це прорікши, Він духа віддав» (Лк. 23:46).

«І ось завіса у храмі роздерлась надвоє — від верху аж додолу, і земля потряслася… А сотник та ті, що Ісуса з ним стерегли, як землетруса побачили, …налякалися дуже й казали: «Він був справді Син Божий!» (Мт. 27:51–54). «І ввесь натовп, який зійшовсь на видовище це, як побачив, що сталось, — бив у груди себе та вертався» (Лк. 23:48).

---

* *За теперішнім обчисленням — з дванадцятої до третьої години.*

Plockhorst

ПОХОВАННЯ ІСУСА

Ісус помер на хресті у п'ятницю. Юдеї пішли до Пилата просити дозволу на те, щоб швидше зняти розп'ятих з хрестів, перебивши їм гомілки, бо не можна було залишати тіла покараних у суботу, тому що в цей день мало бути велике свято… Отримавши дозвіл від правителя, воїни прийшли та перебили гомілки у обох розбійників. Коли вони підійшли до Ісуса, то побачили, що Він вже мертвий і не перебили у Нього гомілок. Але один з воїнів списом своїм простромив Йому ребра, і з рани потекла кров та вода. Все сталося згідно з написаним у Святому Писанні: «…костей його не зламаєте» (2 М. 12:46). А пророк Захарія сказав: «І будуть дивитись на Мене, Кого прокололи» (Зах. 12:10).

Після цього до Пилата прийшла багата та поважна людина, член синедріону, Йосип із Ариматеї. Він також був таємним (оскільки боявся переслідувань) учнем Ісуса. Йосип попросив Пилата дозволити зняти тіло Ісуса з хреста, і Пилат погодився на це. Прийшов також на Голгофу ще один член синедріону, Никодим, який приходив до Ісуса вночі і «смирну приніс, із алоєм помішану, щось літрів із сто*. Отож, узяли вони тіло Ісусове, та й обгорнули його плащаницею із пахощами, як є звичай ховати в юдеїв. На тім місці, де Він був розп'ятий, знаходився сад, а в саду новий гріб, що в ньому ніколи ніхто не лежав». Там вони Його і поховали.

Наступного дня, у суботу, первосвященики та фарисеї прийшли до Пилата і почали висловлювати йому свої побоювання: «Пригадали ми, пане, собі, що обманець отой, як живий іще був, то сказав: «По трьох днях Я воскресну». Звели ж гріб стерегти аж до третього дня, щоб учні Його не прийшли, та й не вкрали Його, і не сказали народові: Він із мертвих воскрес! І буде остання обмана гірша за першу».

Отримавши дозвіл, вони пішли до гроба і поставили там вартових, а сам камінь запечатали.

Ів. 19:31–42; Лк. 23:53; Мт. 27:62–66

---

* *Літра — римська міра ваги за часів Ісуса Христа; вона дорівнює, приблизно, 350 г; 100 літрів — це 35 кг.*

ХРИСТОС ВОСКРЕС!

«Як минула ж субота, на світанку дня першого в тижні… великий ось ставсь землетрус, бо зійшов із неба Ангол Господній, і, приступивши, відвалив від *гробу* каменя, та й сів на ньому.

Його ж постать була, як *та* блискавка, а шати його *були* білі, як сніг. І від страху перед ним затряслася сторожа, та й стала, як мертва». Отямившись, «дехто зі сторожі до міста прийшли та й первосвященикам розповіли все, що сталось. І, зібравшись зі старшими, вони врадили раду, і дали сторожі чимало срібняків, і сказали: «Розповідайте: Його учні вночі прибули, — і вкрали Його, як ми спали. Як почує ж намісник про це, то його ми переконаємо, і від клопоту визволимо вас». І, взявши вони срібняки, зробили, як навчено їх».

На світанку недільного дня Марія Магдалина і Марія Яковова, і Саломія пішли до саду, де була печера, щоб намастити пахощами тіло Ісуса. Поки йшли вони, то з сумом говорили між собою: «Хто відвалить нам каменя від могильних дверей?» А зиркнувши, побачили, що камінь відвалений; був же він дуже великий… І, ввійшовши до гробу, побачили *там* юнака, що праворуч сидів, і був одягнений в білу одежу, — і жахнулись вони… А він промовляє до них: «Не лякайтеся, бо я знаю, що Ісуса розп'ятого *це* ви шукаєте. Нема Його тут, — бо воскрес, як сказав. Підійдіть, — подивіться на місце, де знаходився Він. Ідіть же хутко, і скажіть Його учням, що воскрес Він із мертвих».

Поспішно вийшовши із печери, жінки зі страхом і великою радістю побігли сповістити учням про воскресення Христа.

Мт. 28:1–8, 11–15; Мр. 16:1–7; Лк. 24:1–7

Bouguereau

ІСУС ЖИВИЙ!

Коли жінки йшли сповістити учням дивну звістку про воскресення, Ісус зустрів їх на дорозі й сказав їм: «Радійте!» Вони ж підійшли, обняли Його ноги і вклонились Йому до землі. Промовляє тоді їм Ісус: «Не лякайтесь! Ідіть, повідомте братів Моїх*, — нехай вони йдуть у Галілею, — там побачать Мене!»

Прийшовши до одинадцяти учнів, жінки сповістили їм, що бачили воскреслого Ісуса. Але сумним і розчарованим учням їхні слова здалися пустими й вони не повірили їм.

Та все ж, почувши звістку про воскресення Ісуса, Петро та Іван побігли мерщій до гробу. Їм так хотілося вірити почутому й особисто переконатися в цьому! В їхніх серцях палала гаряча любов до Вчителя, але вони були дуже пригнічені й збентежені тим, що сталося. Вони думали, що Христос буде Царем великого царства на цій землі, і не могли зрозуміти слів Ісуса про те Царство Боже, яке Він прийшов утвердити в серцях людей. Вони не зрозуміли Ісуса, коли Він сказав: «Божеє Царство всередині вас!»

Іван біг швидше від Петра і першим дістався до печери, де був похований Ісус. Нахилившись і зазирнувши до печери, він побачив плащаницю, але не зайшов туди, очікуючи Петра.

«Прибуває і Симон Петро, що слідком за ним біг, і входить до гробу, і плащаницю оглядає, що лежала, і хустка, що була на Його голові, лежить не з плащаницею, але осторонь, згорнена, в іншому місці… Тоді ж увійшов й інший учень, що перший до гробу прибув, і побачив, — і ввірував. Бо ще не розуміли з Писання вони, що Він має воскреснути з мертвих».

Мт. 28:8–10; Лк. 17:21, 24:9–11; Ів. 20:3–9

* *Тут мова йде про апостолів Ісуса Христа.*

Eugene Burnand

ІСУС З'ЯВЛЯЄТЬСЯ УЧНЯМ, ЯКІ ЙДУТЬ В ЕММАУС

Того ж дня двоє з учнів Ісуса пішли до селища Еммаус, що недалеко від Єрусалима. По дорозі вони розмовляли між собою про події останніх днів. І Сам Ісус, наблизившись до них, пішов поруч із ними, але вони не впізнали Його.

Ісус запитав Своїх учнів: «Що за речі такі, що про них між собою в дорозі міркуєте, і чого ви сумні?» І озвався один, йому ймення Клеопа, та й промовив до Нього: «Ти хіба *тут* у Єрусалимі єдиний захожий, що не знає, що сталося в нім цими днями?» І спитався Він їх: «Що таке?» А вони розповіли Йому: «Про Ісуса Назарянина, що Пророк був, могутній у ділі й у слові перед Богом і всім народом. Як первосвященики й наша старшина Його віддали на суд смертний, — і Його розп'яли… А ми сподівались були, що Це Той, що має Ізраїля визволити. І до того, оце третій день вже сьогодні, як усе оте сталося… А дехто з наших жінок, що рано були коло гробу, нас здивували: вони тіла Його не знайшли, та й вернулися й оповідали, що бачили й з'явлення Анголів, які кажуть, що живий Він… І пішли дехто з наших до гробу, і знайшли так, як казали й жінки; та Його не побачили»…

Тоді Він сказав їм: «О, безумні й запеклого серця, щоб повірити всьому, про що сповіщали Пророки! Чи ж Христові не це перетерпіти треба було, і ввійти в Свою славу?» І Він почав від Мойсея, і від Пророків усіх, і виясняв їм зо всього Писання, що про Нього було. І наблизились вони до села, куди йшли. А Він удавав, ніби хоче йти далі. А вони не пускали Його й намовляли: «Зостанься з нами, бо вже вечоріє, і кінчається день». І Він увійшов, щоб із ними побути.

І ото, коли сів Він із ними до столу, то взяв хліб, поблагословив, і, ламаючи, їм подавав… Тоді очі відкрилися їм, — і пізнали Його. Але Він став для них невидимий… І говорили вони один одному: «Чи не палало нам серце обом, коли промовляв Він до нас по дорозі, і коли виясняв нам Писання?»

Лк. 24:13–32

ІСУС З'ЯВЛЯЄТЬСЯ ІНШИМ УЧНЯМ

Коли Ісус став невидимим для двох учнів, яким з'явився по дорозі до Еммауса, вони одразу ж встали й пішли до Єрусалима, знайшли там одинадцять апостолів, які зібралися разом, та й почали розповідати їм про те, що сталося в дорозі, і як вони впізнали Ісуса під час ламання хліба.

Коли вони говорили про це, Сам Ісус став серед них і промовив: «Мир вам!» А вони налякалися та перестрашились, і думали, що бачать духа. Він же промовив до них: «Чого ви стривожились? І пощо ті думки до сердець ваших входять? Погляньте на руки Мої та на ноги Мої, — це ж Я Сам! Доторкніться до Мене й дізнайтесь, — бо не має дух тіла й костей, а Я, бачите, маю». І, промовивши це, показав Він їм руки та ноги.

І, як ще не йняли вони віри з радощів та дивувались, Він сказав їм: «Чи не маєте тут чогось їсти?» Вони ж подали Йому кусника риби печеної та стільника медового. І, взявши, Він їв перед ними. І промовив до них: «Це слова, що казав Я до вас, коли був іще з вами: Потрібно, щоб виконалось усе, що про Мене в Законі Мойсеєвім, та в Пророків, і в Псалмах написане… Так написано є, і так потрібно було постраждати Христові, і воскреснути з мертвих дня третього, і щоб у Ймення Його проповідувалось покаяння, і прощення гріхів між народів усіх, від Єрусалиму почавши. А ви свідки того. І ось Я посилаю на вас обітницю Мого Отця; а ви позостаньтеся в місті, аж поки зодягнетесь силою з висоти».

Лк. 24:33–49

«ЧИ ТИ ЛЮБИШ МЕНЕ?»

Ісус з'явився також учням Своїм у Галілеї біля моря Тіверіядського.

«Укупі були Симон Петро, і Хома, званий Близнюк, і Нафанаїл, із Кани Галілейської, і обидва сини Зеведеєві, і двоє інших із учнів Його. Говорить їм Симон Петро: «Піду риби вловити». Вони кажуть до нього: «І ми підемо з тобою». І пішли вони, і всіли до човна. Та ночі тієї нічого вони не вловили.

А як ранок настав, то Ісус став над берегом, але учні не знали, що то був Ісус. Ісус тоді каже до них: «Чи не маєте, діти, якоїсь поживи?» — «Ні», вони відказали. А Він їм сказав: «Закиньте невода праворуч від човна, то й знайдете!» Вони кинули, — і вже не могли його витягнути із-за безлічі риби… Тоді учень, якого любив був Ісус, говорить Петрові: «Це ж Господь!»… А Симон Петро, як зачув, що Господь то, накинув на себе одежину, — бо він був нагий, — та й кинувся в море… Інші ж учні, що були недалеко від берега — якихсь ліктів із двісті — припливли човником, тягнучи невода з рибою…

Це вже втретє з'явився Ісус Своїм учням, як із мертвих воскрес.

Як вони *вже* поснідали, то Ісус промовляє до Симона Петра: «Симоне, сину Йонин, — чи ти любиш мене більше цих?» Той каже Йому: «Так, Господи, — відаєш Ти, що кохаю Тебе!» Промовляє йому: «Паси ягнята Мої!» І говорить йому Він удруге: «Симоне, сину Йонин, — чи ти любиш Мене?» Той каже Йому: «Так, Господи, — відаєш Ти, що кохаю Тебе!» Промовляє йому: «Паси вівці Мої!» Утретє Він каже йому: «Симоне, сину Йонин, — чи кохаєш Мене?» Засмутився Петро, що спитав його втретє: «Чи кохаєш Мене?» І він каже Йому: «Ти все відаєш, Господи, — відаєш Ти, що кохаю Тебе!» Промовляє до нього Ісус: «Паси вівці Мої!»

Словами «Паси ягнята Мої» і «Паси вівці Мої» Господь Ісус доручає турботу про віруючих Петрові, як і решті учнів. Мабуть, тричі повторене одне й те ж запитання «Чи ти любиш Мене?» повинно було нагадати Петрові про те, що він тричі відрікся від Христа.

Ів. 21:1–17

CLEVELAND
WOODWARD
755

ВОЗНЕСЕННЯ ІСУСА ХРИСТА

Після воскресення Ісус ще впродовж сорока днів з'являвся учням Своїм, розповідаючи їм про Царство Боже. Перед Своїм вознесенням Ісус сказав учням, «щоб вони не відходили з Єрусалиму, а чекали обітниці Отчої, «що про неї, — *казав*, — ви чули від Мене. Іван-бо водою христив, — ви ж охрищені будете Духом Святим через кілька тих днів!» А потім промовив: «Ви приймете силу, як Дух Святий злине на вас, і Моїми ви свідками будете в Єрусалимі, і в усій Юдеї та в Самарії, та аж до останнього краю землі…»

Після цих слів Ісус Христос почав підніматися угору на очах у учнів, і хмара сховала Його від них. І коли дивилися вони на небо під час Його вознесення, раптом постали перед ними два мужі у білому одязі й сказали їм: «Галілейські мужі, — чого стоїте й задивляєтесь на небо? Той Ісус, що вознісся на небо від вас, прийде так, як бачили ви, як ішов Він на небо!»

Дії 1:3–11

Plockhorst

«Я — ДОРОГА, І ПРАВДА, І ЖИТТЯ…»

Від року народження Господа Ісуса починається наше літочислення. У тридцятилітньому віці Ісус почав Своє служіння на землі, яке продовжувалось близько трьох років — до Його розп'яття на хресті. Він проповідував Євангелію, тобто «Благу Звістку», про спасіння і про Царство Боже. Господь Ісус Христос, Спаситель світу, творив і говорив набагато більше, аніж наведено у нашій книзі. Ось деякі дуже важливі повчання Господа Ісуса Христа:

«Я — дорога, і правда, і життя. До Отця не приходить ніхто, якщо не через Мене» (Ів. 14:6).

«Я воскресення й життя. Хто вірує в Мене, — хоч і вмре, буде жити» (Ів. 11:25).

«Доки Я в світі, — Я Світло для світу» (Ів. 9:5).

«Я — хліб життя. Хто до Мене приходить, — не голодуватиме він, а хто вірує в Мене, — ніколи не прагнутиме» (Ів. 6:35).

«Син-бо Людський прийшов, щоб знайти та спасти, що загинуло» (Лк. 19:10).

«Шукайте ж найперш Царства Божого й правди Його…» (Мт. 6:33).

«Зоставляю вам мир, мир Свій вам даю! Я даю вам не так, як дає світ. Серце ваше нехай не тривожиться, ані не лякається» (Ів. 14:27).

«Прийдіть до Мене, усі струджені та обтяжені, — і Я вас заспокою! Візьміть на себе ярмо Моє, і навчіться від Мене, бо Я тихий і серцем покірливий, — і «знайдете спокій душам своїм». Бо ж ярмо Моє любе, а тягар Мій легкий!» (Мт. 11:28–30).

«…Хто слухає слова Мого, і вірує в Того, Хто послав Мене, — життя вічне той має, і на суд не приходить, але перейшов він від смерти в життя» (Ів. 5:24).

«Хто вірує в Сина, той має вічне життя; а хто в Сина не вірує, той життя не побачить — а гнів Божий на нім перебуває» (Ів. 3:36).

«…Коли хоче хто йти вслід за Мною, хай зречеться самого себе, і хай візьме щоденно свого хреста, та й за Мною йде» (Лк. 9:23).

«…Хто Мене визнає перед людьми, того перед Небесним Отцем Моїм визнаю й Я. Хто ж Мене відцурається перед людьми, того й Я відцураюся перед Небесним Отцем Моїм» (Мт. 10:32, 33).

ДІЇ АПОСТОЛІВ

Події від народження до вознесення Ісуса Христа на небо записані в чотирьох книгах Нового Заповіту, що називаються Євангеліями. Ці книги написані чотирма авторами: Матвієм, Марком, Лукою та Іваном.

П'ята книга Нового Заповіту — «Дії святих апостолів». У цій книзі описується, в основному, історія поширення християнства у різних провінціях Риму — на території сьогоднішнього Ізраїлю, Туреччини, Греції та Італії. У «Діях святих апостолів» увага зосереджується, головним чином, на служінні апостолів Петра та Павла і, особливо, на місіонерській діяльності апостола Павла у світі поган (язичників).

Варто також нагадати, що головні теми Старого Заповіту — багатовікова історія єврейського народу, опіка Божа над цим народом і Його задум благословення й спасіння всіх народів світу через Сина Свого, Месію, Ісуса Христа, Який народився серед ізраїльтян.

Отже, в «Діях святих апостолів» ми бачимо вже, що звістка про спасіння, здійснене Ісусом Христом на Голгофському Хресті, починає розповсюджуватися і серед язичників.

Вважається, що «Євангелія від Луки» і «Дії святих апостолів» написані освіченим лікарем Лукою не пізніше 63 року після Різдва Христового.

СХОДЖЕННЯ ДУХА СВЯТОГО НА УЧНІВ

Повернувшись до Єрусалима з Оливної гори, звідки вознісся Христос, учні ввійшли у світлицю і там разом з жінками, Марією — Матір'ю Ісуса Христа та братами Його невпинно молилися. Замість Юди дванадцятим апостолом був обраний Маттій.

Коли настало свято П'ятдесятниці, яке відмічалося на п'ятдесятий день після Пасхи і було днем завершення жнив, усі вони були однодушно разом. «І нагло зчинився шум із неба, ніби буря раптова зірвалася, і переповнила ввесь той дім, де сиділи вони. І з'явилися їм язики поділені, немовби огненні, та й на кожному з них по одному осів. Усі ж вони сповнились Духом Святим, і почали говорити іншими мовами, як їм Дух промовляти давав.

Перебували ж в Єрусалимі юдеї, люди побожні, від усякого народу під небом. А коли оцей гомін зчинився, зібралася безліч народу, — та й диву далися, бо кожен із них *тут* почув, що вони розмовляли їхньою власною мовою!.. Усі ж побентежилися та дивувалися, та й казали один до одного: «Хіба ж не галілеяни всі ці, що говорять? Як же кожен із нас чує свою власну мову, що ми в ній народились?.. *Усі* чуємо ми, що говорять вони про великі діла Божі мовами нашими!»

І всі не виходили з дива, і безрадні були, і говорили один до одного: «Що ж то статися має?» А інші казали глузуючи: «Вони повпивались вином молодим!»

Дії 1:12–26; 2:1–13

ПРОПОВІДЬ ПЕТРА

Петро разом із одинадцятьма апостолами став перед натовпом народу й голосно заговорив: «Мужі юдейські та мешканці Єрусалиму! Нехай вам оце стане відоме, і послухайте слів моїх! Бо не п'яні вони, як ви думаєте, — бо третя* година дня, а це те, що пророк Йоіл передрік: «І буде останніми днями, говорить Господь: Я виллю від Духа Свого на всяке тіло, — і будуть пророкувати сини ваші та ваші доньки, юнаки ж ваші бачити будуть видіння, а старим вашим сни будуть снитися. І на рабів Моїх і на рабинь Моїх за тих днів Я також виллю від Духа Свого, — і пророкувати вони будуть!.. І станеться, що кожен, хто покличе Господнє Ім'я, той спасеться».

Мужі ізраїльські, послухайте ви оцих слів: Ісуса Назарянина, Мужа, що Його Бог прославив вам силою, і чудами, і тими знаменами, що Бог через Нього вчинив серед вас, як самі ви *те* знаєте, Того, що був виданий певною волею та передбаченням Божим, ви руками беззаконників розп'яли та забили. Та Бог воскресив Його, пута смерти усунувши, — вона-бо тримати Його не могла…

Бог Ісуса Цього воскресив, чого свідки всі ми! А отож, як правицею Божою був Він вознесений, і обітницю Духа Святого прийняв від Отця, то й злив Він оте, що ви бачите й чуєте… Отож, нехай ввесь Ізраїлів дім твердо знає, що і Господом, і Христом учинив Бог Його, Того Ісуса, що Його розп'яли ви!»

Як почули ж *оце*, вони серцем розжалобились, та й сказали Петрові та іншим апостолам: «Що ж ми маємо робити, мужі-браття?» А Петро до них *каже*: «Покайтеся, і нехай же охриститься кожен із вас у Ім'я Ісуса Христа на відпущення ваших гріхів, — і дара Духа Святого ви приймете! Бо для вас ця обітниця, і для ваших дітей, і для всіх, що «далеко *знаходяться*, кого б тільки покликав Господь, Бог наш»…

Отож ті, хто прийняв його слово, охристилися. І пристало *до них* того дня душ тисяч зо три!» З того часу «…щоденно до Церкви Господь додавав тих, що спасалися», тобто до зібрання людей, спокутуваних Ісусом Христом.

Дії 2:14–47

---

* *За нашим часом — дев'ята година ранку.*

O.Stemler

ЗЦІЛЕННЯ КУЛЬГАВОГО

Якось Петро та Іван ішли разом до храму в годину молитви. Біля воріт храму, які називалися Красними, сидів кульгавий чоловік, якого щодня приносили й саджали там просити милостиню у перехожих. Побачивши Петра й Івана біля входу у храм, він став просити у них милостиню.

Петро з Іваном, придивившись до нього, сказали: «Подивися на нас!» Жебрак пильно подивився на апостолів, сподіваючись отримати що-небудь від них. Та Петро промовив до нього: «Срібла й золота в мене нема, але що я маю, даю тобі: У Ім'я Ісуса Христа Назарянина — устань та й ходи!» І, узявши його за правицю, він підвів його. І хвилі тієї зміцнилися ноги й суглобці його!.. І, зірвавшись, він устав та й ходив, і з ними у храм увійшов, ходячи та підскакуючи, і хвалячи Бога! Народ же ввесь бачив, як ходив він та Бога хвалив. І пізнали його, що це той, що при Красних воротях храму сидів ради милостині. І вони переповнились жахом та подивом із того, що сталось йому! А тому, що тримався він Петра та Івана, увесь народ зачудований збігся до них на той ґанок, який Соломоновим зветься. І, побачивши *це*, промовив Петро до народу:

«Мужі ізраїльські! Чого ви дивуєтесь цим, та чого ви на нас позираєте так, ніби те, що він ходить, ми зробили своєю силою чи благочестям?.. Бог наших батьків, Сина Свого прославив», Ісуса, Якого ви видали, і відцуралися перед Пилатом, як він присудив був пустити *Його*… Начальника ж життя ви забили, та Його воскресив Бог із мертвих, чого свідками — ми! І через віру в Ім'я Його вздоровило Ім'я Його того, кого бачите й знаєте. І віра, що від Нього, принесла йому вздоровлення це перед вами всіма.

А тепер, браття, знаю, що вчинили ви це з несвідомости, як і ваші начальники. А Бог учинив так, як Він провіщав був устами Своїх усіх пророків, щоб терпіти Христові.

Покайтеся ж та наверніться, щоб Він змилувався над вашими гріхами, щоб часи відпочинку прийшли від обличчя Господнього, і щоб послав заповідженого вам Ісуса Христа, що Його небо мусить прийняти аж до часу відновлення всього, про що провіщав Бог відвіку устами всіх святих пророків Своїх!..

Воскресивши Свого Отрока, Бог послав Його перше до вас, щоб вас поблагословити, щоб кожен із вас відвернувся від злих своїх учинків!»

Дії 3:1–26

АРЕШТ ПЕТРА ТА ІВАНА

Після зцілення кульгавого та проповіді Петра близько п'яти тисяч людей увірували в Ісуса Христа. Але первосвященики та начальники, обурені їхньою проповіддю, наказали схопити й віддати під варту Петра та Івана. Другого дня в Єрусалимі зібралися начальники, старійшини, книжники і первосвященики. Вони покликали апостолів, поставили їх посередині й запитали про зцілення кульгавого: «Якою ви силою чи яким ви ім'ям те робили?» Тоді Петро, переповнений Духом Святим, промовив до них: «Начальники люду та старшини Ізраїлеві! Як сьогодні беруть нас на допит про те добродійство недужій людині, як вона вздоровлена, — нехай буде відомо всім вам, і всім людям Ізраїлевим, що Ім'ям Ісуса Христа Назарянина, що Його розп'яли ви, та Його воскресив Бог із мертвих, — Ним поставлений він перед вами здоровий! Він «камінь, що ви, будівничі, відкинули, *але* каменем став Він наріжним!» І нема ні в кім іншім спасіння. Бо під небом нема іншого Ймення, даного людям, що ним би спастися ми мали».

А бачивши сміливість Петра та Івана, і спостерігши, що то люди обидва невчені та прості, дивувалися, і пізнали їх, що вони з Ісусом були. Та бачивши, що вздоровлений чоловік стоїть з ними, нічого навпроти сказати не могли. І, звелівши їм вийти із синедріону, зачали радитися між собою, говорячи: «Що робити нам із цими людьми? Бо ж усім мешканцям Єрусалиму відомо, що вчинили вони явне чудо, і не можемо *того* заперечити. Та щоб більш не поширювалось *це* в народі, то з погрозою заборонімо їм, щоб нікому з людей вони не говорили про Це Ім'я».

І, закликавши їх, наказали їм не говорити, і взагалі не навчати про Ісусове Ймення. І відповіли їм Петро та Іван, та й сказали: «Розсудіть, чи це справедливе було б перед Богом, щоб слухатись вас більш, як Бога? Бо не можемо ми не казати про те, що ми бачили й чули!» А вони пригрозили їм ще, і відпустили їх, не знайшовши нічого, щоб їх покарати, через людей, бо всі славили Бога за теє, що сталось».

Дії 4:1–21

СМЕРТЬ СТЕПАНА — ПЕРШОГО МУЧЕНИКА ЗА ВІРУ

За пропозицією апостолів Церква обрала сім дияконів, тобто служителів, доручивши їм особливу опіку про бідних та нужденних. Одним із перших дияконів обрали Степана — людину, сповнену Духа Святого, віри та сили Божої. Він творив великі чудеса та знамення в народі. Вороги християнства ненавиділи його за це і вступили з ним у суперечку, але не могли протистояти мудрості й Духу, Яким він говорив. Тоді вони навчили окремих людей звинуватити його в тому, наче він хулив Бога і Мойсея. Підбуривши народ, вони схопили його і привели до синедріону. Коли обвинувачі почали давати фальшиві свідчення, то всі, хто сидів у синедріоні, дивлячись на Степана, побачили, що обличчя його як у Ангела.

Первосвященик вислухав всі обвинувачення і запитав Степана: «Чи це так?» Тоді Степан нагадав їм історію ізраїльського народу, а на закінчення докорив присутнім: «О ви, твердошиї, люди серця й вух необрізаних! Ви завжди противитесь Духові Святому, як ваші батьки, так і ви!..» Як зачули ж оце, вони запалилися гнівом у серцях своїх, і скреготали зубами на нього…

А *Степан*, повний Духа Святого, на небо споглянув, — і побачив Божу славу й Ісуса, що по Божій правиці стояв, і промовив: «Ось я бачу відчинене небо, і Сина Людського, що по Божій правиці стоїть!»… Та вони гучним голосом стали кричати та вуха собі затуляти, та й кинулися однодушно на нього!.. І за місто вони його вивели, і зачали побивати камінням його». Степан же молився: «Не залічи їм, о Господи, цього гріха!» І, промовивши це, він спочив».

Багато тисяч християн за віру в Ісуса Христа померли мученицькою смертю, віддаючи хвалу Богові, і, подібно до Степана, молячись за своїх ворогів. Але помирали вони непереможеними. Їхня смерть була перемогою, бо вона запалювала в багатьох серцях віру в живого Бога.

Дії 6:2–15; 7:1–60

ПИЛИП ТА ЕФІОПСЬКИЙ ВЕЛЬМОЖА

Якось Ангел Господній сказав дияконові Пилипу: «Устань та на південь іди, на дорогу, що від Єрусалиму до Гази спускається, — порожня вона». І, вставши, пішов він. І ось муж етіопський, скопець, вельможа Кандаки, цариці етіопської, що був над усіма її скарбами, що до Єрусалиму прибув поклонитись, вертався, і, сидячи на повозі своїм, читав пророка Ісаю.

А Дух до Пилипа промовив: «Підійди, та й пристань до цього повозу». Пилип же підбіг і почув, що той читає пророка Ісаю, та й спитав: «Чи розумієш, що ти читаєш?» А той відказав: «Як же можу, як ніхто не напутить мене?» І впросив він Пилипа піднятись та сісти з ним. А слово Писання, що його він читав, було це: «Як вівцю на заріз Його ведено, і як ягня супроти стрижія безголосе, так Він не відкрив Своїх уст! У приниженні суд Йому віднятий був, а про рід Його хто розповість? Бо життя Його із землі забирається»…

Відізвався ж скопець до Пилипа й сказав: «Благаю тебе, — це про кого говорить пророк? Чи про себе, чи про іншого кого?» А Пилип відкрив уста свої, і, зачавши від цього Писання, благовістив про Ісуса йому.

І, як шляхом вони їхали, прибули до якоїсь води. І озвався скопець: «Ось вода. Що мені заважає христитись?» А Пилип відказав: «Якщо віруєш із повного серця свого, то можна». А той відповів і сказав: «Я вірую, що Ісус Христос — то Син Божий!» І звелів, щоб повіз спинився. І обидва — Пилип та скопець — увійшли до води, і охристив він його. А коли вони вийшли з води, Дух Господній Пилипа забрав, і скопець уже більше не бачив його. І він їхав, радіючи, шляхом своїм».

Так Господь навернув поганина з Африки, чим підтвердив, що Бог не дивиться на обличчя людини, його країну чи націю, але «кожен, хто покличе Господнє Ім'я, той спасеться».

Дії 8:26–39, 2:21

O. Stemler

ГОНИТЕЛЬ ХРИСТИЯН САВЛ

Юдеї розпочали величезне гоніння на учнів Ісуса Христа. Одним із непримиренних гонителів Єрусалимської Церкви був Савл. Коли Степана побивали камінням, він стеріг одяг тих, хто кидав каміння у Степана. Він уривався в оселі віруючих християн, хапав їх, зв'язував і віддавав до в'язниці.

Савл був фарисеєм. Він одержав гарну релігійну освіту і дуже добре знав Святе Писання. Він був великим поборником батьківських переказів, старанно виконував усі обряди та заповіді. Але, не знаючи істини, Савл не вірив, що Ісус Христос — обіцяний Месія і вважав християн єретиками.

«Савл, іще дишучи грізьбою й убивством на учнів Господніх, приступивши до первосвященика, попросив від нього листи у Дамаск синагогам, щоб, коли знайде яких чоловіків та жінок, що тієї дороги вони, то зв'язати й привести до Єрусалиму».

Дії 7:58; 8:3; 9:1, 2

C.L. WOODWARD.

З'ЯВЛЕННЯ ГОСПОДА САВЛОВІ

Коли Савл наближався до Дамаска, то зненацька осяяло його світло з неба. Він впав на землю й почув голос, що говорив йому: «Савле, Савле, — чому ти Мене переслідуєш?» А він запитав: «Хто Ти, Пане?» А Той: «Я Ісус, що Його переслідуєш ти. [Трудно тобі бити ногою колючку!» А він, затрусившися та налякавшися, каже: «Чого, Господи, хочеш, щоб я вчинив?» А до нього Господь:] «Уставай, та до міста подайся, а *там* тобі скажуть, що маєш робити!»

А люди, що йшли з ним, оніміли стояли, бо вони чули голос, та нікого не бачили. Тоді Савл підвівся з землі, і хоч очі розплющені мав, нікого не бачив… І за руку його повели й привели до Дамаску. І три дні невидющий він був, і не їв, і не пив.

А в Дамаску був учень один, на ймення Ананій. І Господь у видінні промовив до нього: «Ананію!»… Устань, і піди на вулицю, що Простою зветься, і пошукай в домі Юдовім Савла на ймення, тарсянина, ось-бо він молиться, і мужа в видінні він бачив, на ймення Ананія, що *до нього* прийшов і руку на нього поклав, щоб став він видющий».

Відповів же Ананій: «Чув я, Господи, від багатьох про цього чоловіка, скільки зла він учинив в Єрусалимі святим Твоїм! І тут має владу від первосвящеників, щоб в'язати усіх, хто кличе Ім'я Твоє». І промовив до нього Господь: «Іди, бо для Мене — посудина вибрана він, щоб носити Ім'я Моє перед народами, і царями, і синами Ізраїля. Бо Я покажу йому, скільки має він витерпіти за Ім'я Моє».

І Ананій пішов, і до дому ввійшов, і руки поклавши на нього, промовив: «Савле брате, Господь Ісус, що з'явився тобі на дорозі, якою ти йшов, послав *ось* мене, щоб став ти видющий, і наповнився Духа Святого!» І хвилі тієї відпала з очей йому ніби луска, і зараз видющий він став… І, вставши, охристився, і, прийнявши поживу, на силах зміцнів. І він зараз зачав у синагогах звіщати про Ісуса, що Він — Божий Син».

Дії 9:3–20

C.L.WOODWARD.

САВЛ ТІКАЄ З ДАМАСКА

Всі, хто чув проповіді Савла, дивувалися й говорили: «Хіба це не той, що переслідував в Єрусалимі визнавців оцього Ім'я*, та й сюди не на те він прибув, щоб отих пов'язати й привести до первосвящеників?» А Савл іще більше зміцнявся, і непокоїв юдеїв, що в Дамаску жили, удоводнюючи, що Той — то Христос.

А як часу минуло доволі, юдеї змовилися його вбити, та Савлові стала відома їхня змова. А вони день і ніч чатували в воротях, щоб убити його. Тому учні забрали його вночі, та й із муру спустили в коші.

А коли він до Єрусалиму прибув, то силкувався пристати до учнів, та його всі лякалися, не вірячи, що він учень. Варнава тоді взяв його та й привів до апостолів, і їм розповів, як дорогою той бачив Господа, і як Він йому промовляв, і як сміливо навчав у Дамаску в Ісусове Ймення». Тоді апостоли й вся Церква прийняли Савла як брата. Пізніше він став називатися апостолом Павлом. Метою його життя стало проповідування Христа і розповсюдження Світла Христового серед поганських народів.

Апостол Павло написав багато послань (листів) Церквам різних міст. Ці послання вміщені у Новому Заповіті. В одному зі своїх листів він писав: «Але те, що для мене було за надбання, те ради Христа я за втрату вважав. Тож усе я вважаю за втрату ради переважного познання Христа Ісуса, мого Господа, що я ради Нього відмовився всього, і вважаю все за сміття, щоб придбати Христа, щоб знайтися в Нім не з власною праведністю, яка від Закону, але з тією, що з віри в Христа, праведністю від Бога за вірою…» Так Христос змінив серце фарисея Савла, який став Його відданим учнем.

Дії 9:21–28; Фил. 3:7–9

* *Тобто, ім'я Ісуса.*

УЧЕНИЦЯ ТАВІТА

Колись Йоппія була портовим містом Середземного моря. Місто це існує й досі, але називається тепер Яффою. Сучасна Яффа знаходиться на відстані двох кілометрів від Тель-Авіва — найбільшого міста Ізраїлю.

«А в Йоппії була одна учениця, на ймення Тавіта, що в перекладі Сарною зветься. Вона повна була добрих вчинків та милостині, що чинила. І трапилося тими днями, що вона занедужала й умерла. Обмили ж її й поклали в горниці».

Апостол Петро перебував тоді в Лідді. Оскільки Лідда була недалеко від Йоппії, то християни з Йоппії послали до Петра двох чоловіків з проханням, щоб він негайно прийшов до них.

«І, вставши, Петро пішов із ними. А коли він прибув, то ввели його в горницю. І обступили його всі вдовиці, плачучи та показуючи *йому* сукні й плащі, що їх Сарна робила, як із ними була. Петро ж із кімнати всіх випровадив, і, ставши навколішки, помолився, і, звернувшись до тіла, промовив: «Тавіто, вставай!» А вона свої очі розплющила, і сіла, уздрівши Петра… Він же руку подав *їй*, і підвів її, і закликав святих і вдовиць, та й поставив живою її.

А *це* стало відоме по цілій Йоппії, і багато хто в Господа ввірували. І сталось, що він багато днів пробув у Йоппії, в одного гарбарника Симона».

Слово Боже вчить нас творити добрі діла, допомагати ближнім. «А роблячи добре, не знуджуймося, бо часу свого пожнемо, коли не ослабнемо».

Дії 9:36–43; Гал. 6:9

O. STEMLER

СОТНИК КОРНИЛІЙ

За життя Ісуса Христа та Його апостолів не лише вся земля Ізраїлю, а й усі країни Середземномор'я були захоплені Римом. Римляни мали в цих країнах свої полки. «Проживав же один чоловік у Кесарії, на ймення Корнилій, сотник полку, що звавсь Італійським. З усім домом своїм він побожний був та богобійний, подавав людям щедру милостиню, і завжди Богові молився. Явно він у видінні, десь коло години дев'ятої дня, бачив Ангола Божого, що до нього зійшов і промовив йому: «Корнилію!»… Молитви твої й твоя милостиня перед Богом згадалися. Тепер же пошли до Йоппії людей, та й приклич Симона, що зветься Петром… Він скаже тобі, що ти маєш робити». Коли ж Ангол, що йому говорив, відійшов, той закликав двох із своїх слуг домових, і вояка богобійного з тих, що служили при ньому, і розповів їм усе та й послав їх в Йоппію».

Йоппія розташована на відстані шістдесяти кілометрів на південь від Кесарії. Коли воїни прийшли в Йоппію, вони знайшли Петра. Він пригостив їх і наступного дня пішов з ними. «І назавтра прийшли вони до Кесарії. А Корнилій чекав їх, рідню й близьких друзів покликавши…» Тоді Петро звернувся до всіх, що зібралися, і сказав: «Пізнаю я поправді, що «не дивиться Бог на обличчя», але в кожнім народі приємний Йому, хто боїться Його й чинить правду. Він слово послав для Ізраїлевих синів, благовістячи мир через Ісуса Христа, що Господь Він усім…. І ми свідки всьому, що Він учинив у Юдейському краї та в Єрусалимі, — та вбили Його, на дереві повісивши… Але Бог воскресив Його третього дня… І Він нам звелів, щоб народові ми проповідували та засвідчили, що то Він є призначений Богом Суддя для живих і для мертвих. Усі пророки свідкують про Нього, що кожен, хто вірує в Нього, одержить прощення гріхів Його Йменням». Корнилій та весь дім його, а також друзі, увірували в Ісуса Христа, Сина Божого, та охристилися.

Дії 10

O. STEMLER

АНГЕЛ ВИЗВОЛЯЄ ПЕТРА З В'ЯЗНИЦІ

У ті часи перших християн почалося гоніння на Церкву Христову. За наказом царя Ірода був убитий апостол Яків, брат Івана. Бачачи, що це приємно юдеям, Ірод посадив до в'язниці й апостола Петра, маючи намір після свята Пасхи вивести його перед народом на страту. «Отож, у в'язниці Петра стерегли, а Церква ревно молилася Богові за нього.

А як Ірод хотів його вивести, Петро спав тієї ночі між двома вояками, закутий у два ланцюги, і сторожа пильнувала в'язницю при дверях. І ось Ангол Господній з'явився, і у в'язниці засяяло світло. І, доторкнувшись до боку Петрового, він збудив його, кажучи: «Мерщій вставай!» І ланцюги йому з рук поспадали. А Ангол до нього промовив: «Підпережися, і взуй сандалі свої». І він так учинив. І каже йому: «Зодягнися в плаща свого, та й за мною йди». І, вийшовши, він ішов услід за ним, і не знав, чи то правда, що робилось від Ангола, бо думав, що видіння він бачить. Як сторожу минули вони першу й другу, то прийшли до залізної брами, що до міста веде, — і вона відчинилась сама їм. І, вийшовши, пройшли одну вулицю, — і відступив Ангол зараз від нього.

Сказав же Петро, опритомнівши: «Тепер знаю правдиво, що Господь послав Свого Ангола, і видер мене із рук Іродових та від усього чекання народу юдейського». А зміркувавши, він прийшов до садиби Марії, матері Івана, званого Марком, де багато зібралося й молилося». Прийшовши до них, він розповів про те, як Господь вивів його із в'язниці.

Дії 12:1–17

ПЕРША МІСІОНЕРСЬКА ПОДОРОЖ ПАВЛА — НА КІПР І В МАЛУ АЗІЮ

Апостол Павло був одним із найвідданіших місіонерів за всю історію християнства. Він ревно виконував заповідь Господа Ісуса Христа, яка й сьогодні актуальна для усіх християн: «Тож ідіть, і навчіть всі народи, христячи їх в Ім'я Отця, і Сина, і Святого Духа, навчаючи їх зберігати все те, що Я вам заповів…» Три місіонерські подорожі, які, головним чином, проходили по території сучасних Греції та Туреччини, Павло розпочав із міста Антіохії.

У першій подорожі разом із Павлом був і Варнава. Із Антіохії вони пливли на кораблі до Кіпру. У Біблії ми читаємо, що саме тут, на Кіпрі, ім'я цього великого слуги Божого, замість єврейського — Савл, стало римським — Павло. З Кіпру вони знову повернулися до Малої Азії і згодом, пішки і на ослах, дісталися до провінції Галатії, спочатку до міста Іконії, де у Христа увірувало дуже багато народу, потім вирушили до міста Лістри. У Лістрі Господь через Павла зцілив одного кульгавого. Народ подумав, що Павло й Варнава — боги. Жрець ідола Зевса хотів учинити їм жертвоприношення. Але Павло і Варнава не допустили цього: «Що це робите, люди? Таж і ми такі самі смертельні, подібні вам люди, і благовістимо вам, — від оцих ось марнот навернутись до Бога Живого, що створив небо й землю, і море, і все, що в них є. За минулих родів попустив Він усім народам, щоб ходили стежками своїми, але не зоставив Себе Він без свідчення, добро чинячи: подавав нам із неба дощі та врожайні часи, та наповнював їжею й радощами серця наші». І, говорячи це, заледве спинили народ не приносити їм жертов. А з Антіохії та з Іконії посходились юдеї, і, підбуривши натовп, камінням побили Павла, та й за місто геть виволікли, мавши думку, що вмер він… Коли ж учні його оточили, то він устав, та й вернувся до міста. А наступного дня він відбув із Варнавою в Дервію. І як звістили Євангелію тому містові, і учнів багато придбали, вони повернулися в Лістру, та в Іконію, та в Антіохію… перейшли Пісідію, прибули в Памфілію; і, звіставши Господнє Слово в Пергії, вони в Атталію ввійшли, а звідти поплинули в Антіохію, звідки були благодаті Божій віддані на діло, що його й закінчили. А прибувши та скликавши Церкву, вони розповіли, як багато вчинив Бог із ними, і що відкрив двері віри поганам».

Перша місіонерська подорож апостола Павла продовжувалась, приблизно, три роки (з 45 до 48 року після Різдва Христового).

Дії 13–14

O. STEMLER

ДРУГА МІСІОНЕРСЬКА ПОДОРОЖ ПАВЛА — ДО МАКЕДОНІЇ ТА ГРЕЦІЇ

Під час другої місіонерської подорожі апостола Павла супроводжував Сила, один з єврейських християн. З Антіохії вони знову пішли до міст Дервії та Лістри. Тут Павло зустрів молодого чоловіка — Тимофія, який став найвірнішим його помічником.

Вони прибули до Троади — міста на азіатському узбережжі Егейського моря. Вночі Павло побачив видіння: «Якийсь македонянин став перед ним і благав його, кажучи: «Прийди в Македонію, і нам поможи!» Апостол Лука, який, мабуть, приєднався до Павла в Троаді, пише: «Як побачив він це видіння, то ми зараз хотіли піти в Македонію, зрозумівши, що Господь нас покликав звіщати їм Євангелію». Македонія була римською провінцією на північному сході Греції. На кораблі вони перетнули Егейське море і прийшли до міста Филипи. Мабуть, саме у Филипах була заснована перша європейська християнська Церква. У Филипах Павла й Силу вкинули до в'язниці. Про це прочитаємо у наступному оповіданні.

Із Филипів Павло прийшов до Солуня — великого портового міста біля Егейського моря. Тут багато гелленів, а з ними й частина євреїв, увірували в Ісуса Христа. Серед іншої ж частини євреїв зчинилося велике обурення, і тоді Павло й Сила змушені були перебратися до міста Верії.

Із Верії Павло прибув до Атен, головного міста Греції. Греція на той час була вже під владою Риму. Її перейменували на Ахаю. В Атенах Павло проповідував Слово Боже перед філософами і простим людом. І про це ми прочитаємо в одному з наступних оповідань. Із Атен він прийшов у Коринт, одне з найважливіших міст Римської імперії. У Коринті Павло пробув півтора роки, протягом яких тут була заснована велика християнська Церква.

Із Коринту Павло повернувся морем до Малої Азії й прибув у велике місто Ефес. Відтак він продовжив свій шлях, побував у Єрусалимі й повернувся до міста Антіохії.

Друга подорож Павла тривала, приблизно, три роки (з 50 до 53 року після Різдва Христового). За цей час апостол Павло пройшов декілька тисяч кілометрів.

Дії 15:36–18:22

ПАВЛО ТА СИЛА У В'ЯЗНИЦІ

Коли апостол Павло і Сила прийшли до римського міста-колонії Филипи, Павло іменем Ісуса зцілив одну служницю, одержиму віщунським духом. Через віщування, тобто вгадування і передбачення, вона давала великий прибуток своїм панам. Побачивши, що джерело їхніх прибутків щезло, пани схопили Павла і Силу, потягли їх на міський майдан до начальників і сказали їм: «Ці люди, юдеї, наше місто бунтують, і навчають звичаїв, яких нам, римлянам, не годиться приймати, ані виконувати». І натовп піднявся на них. А начальники здерли одежу із них, та звеліли їх різками сікти. І, завдавши багато їм ран, посадили у в'язницю, наказавши в'язничному дозорцеві, щоб їх пильно стеріг. Одержавши такого наказа, той їх повкидав до внутрішньої в'язниці, а їхні ноги забив у колоди. А північної пори Павло й Сила молилися, і Богові співали, а ув'язнені слухали їх.

І ось нагло повстало велике трясіння землі, аж основи в'язничні були захиталися! І повідчинялися зараз усі двері, а кайдани з усіх поспадали… Як прокинувся ж сторож в'язничний, і побачив відчинені двері в'язниці, то витяг меча та й хотів себе вбити, мавши думку, що повтікали ув'язнені. А Павло скрикнув голосом гучним, говорячи: «Не чини собі жодного зла, бо всі ми ось тут!» Зажадавши ж той світла, ускочив, і тремтячий припав до Павла та до Сили. І вивів їх звідти й спитав: «Добродії! Що треба робити мені, щоб спастися?» А вони відказали: «Віруй у Господа Ісуса, — і будеш спасений ти *сам* та твій дім»… І *сторож* забрав їх того ж часу вночі, *їхні* рани обмив, — і охристився негайно він сам та його всі *домашні*…

А коли настав день, то прислали начальники слуг *поліційних*, наказуючи: «Відпусти тих людей!»… А Павло відказав їм: «Нас, римлян, незасуджених, різками сікли прилюдно, і до в'язниці всадили, а тепер нас таємно виводять? Але ні! Хай вони самі прийдуть, та й виведуть нас!» Ці ж слова *поліційні* слуги донесли начальникам. А ті налякались, почувши, що римляни вони. І прийшли, та їх перепросили, а вивівши, благали, щоб із міста пішли».

Дії 16:16–39

ПАВЛО В АТЕНАХ (АФІНАХ)

Під час своєї другої місіонерської подорожі Павло, як ми вже розповідали, прибув до Атен. Сила і Тимофій мали саме приєднатися до Павла. «Як Павло ж їх чекав ув Атенах, у ньому кипів його дух, як бачив це місто, повне ідолів. Тож він розмовляв у синагозі з юдеями та з богобійними, і на ринку щоденно зі стрічними. А дехто з філософів епікуреїв та стоїків сперечалися з ним. Одні говорили: «Що то хоче сказати оцей пустомов?» А інші: «Здається, він проповідник чужих богів», бо він їм звіщав Євангелію про Ісуса й воскресення.

І, взявши його, повели в ареопаг* та й казали: «Чи можемо знати, що то є ця наука нова, яку проповідуєш ти? Бо чудне щось вкладаєш до наших вух. Отже, хочемо знати, що то значити має?»… Тоді Павло став посередині ареопагу й промовив: «Мужі атенські! Із усього я бачу, що ви дуже побожні. Бо, проходячи та оглядаючи святощі ваші, я знайшов також жертівника, що на ньому написано: «Незнаному Богові». Ось Того, Кого навмання ви шануєте, Того я проповідую вам. Бог, що створив світ і все, що в ньому, бувши Господом неба й землі, проживає не в храмах, рукою збудованих, і Він не вимагає служіння рук людських, ніби в чомусь Він мав би потребу, бо Сам дає всім, і життя, і дихання, і все. І ввесь людський рід Він з одного створив, щоб замешкати всю поверхню землі, і призначив окреслені доби й границі замешкання їх, щоб Бога шукали вони, чи Його не відчують і не знайдуть, хоч Він недалеко від кожного з нас. Бо ми в Нім живемо, і рухаємось, і існуємо, як і деякі з ваших поетів казали: «Навіть рід ми Його!» Отож, бувши Божим *тим* родом, не повинні ми думати, що Божество подібне до золота, або срібла, чи до каменю, твору мистецтва чи людської вигадки. Не зважаючи ж Бог на часи невідомости, ось тепер усім людям наказує, щоб скрізь каялися, бо Він визначив день, коли хоче судити поправді ввесь світ через Мужа, що Його наперед Він поставив, і Він подав доказа всім, із мертвих Його воскресивши».

Дії 17:16–31

---

* *Пагорби в Афінах, де збиралися люди. Тут же була й найвища судова установа в Афінах.*

ТРЕТЯ МІСІОНЕРСЬКА ПОДОРОЖ ПАВЛА — ТРИ-ЧОТИРИ РОКИ ШЛЯХУ

Через деякий час Павло вирушив із Антіохії у свою третю місіонерську подорож. Він знову пішов на північ. Пройшовши через провінцію Фріґію, він прибув до Ефеса, портового міста на узбережжі Егейського моря. Ефес був великим містом із населенням у чверть мільйона. У цьому місті Павло трудився біля двох років. А Бог же чинив надзвичайні дива руками Павловими. В Ефесі був чудовий храм богині Артеміди, який будували двісті двадцять років. Цей храм був збудований із мармуру і був одним із семи чудес світу. Золотарі та художники, що виготовляли і продавали срібні храми Артеміди, як сувеніри, підняли у місті великий бунт проти Павла та християнських вождів, оскільки багато колишніх прихильників Артеміди навернулись до живого Господа Бога.

Павлові довелося залишити місто Ефес, вирушити на кораблі через Егейське море і відвідати міста у Македонії та Греції, у тому числі знову Филипи й Коринт. Потім він повернувся до Малої Азії і вдруге проповідував у Троаді. Із Троади він продовжив свій шлях до Асс і звідти на кораблі поплив до Мітілени, Самосу, Мілету. Павло запросив до Мілета пресвітерів великої Церкви з Ефеса, щоб попрощатися з ними, бо він знав, що більше не зустріне їх у цьому житті (див. стор. 480). Проїхавши через порти на островах Кос і Родос та малоазійські порти Патару і Тир, Павло прибув до Птолемаїди. Звідти він продовжив свою подорож пішки до Кесарії і далі до Єрусалима. В Єрусалимі Павло був заарештований.

Третя місіонерська подорож Павла тривала три-чотири роки (з 54 до 57 року після Різдва Христового).

Поширюючи Благу Звістку про Ісуса Христа, Павло зазнав багатьох страждань і небезпек. Сам Павло пише: «Я був… у працях, у ранах над міру, …у в’язницях, часто при смерті. Від євреїв п’ять раз я прийняв був по сорок *ударів* без одного, тричі киями бито мене, один раз мене каменували, тричі розбивсь корабель, ніч і день я пробув у глибочині *морській*; у мандрівках я часто бував, *бував* у небезпеках на річках, у небезпеках розбійничих, у небезпеках свого народу, у небезпеках поган, у небезпеках по містах, у небезпеках на пустині, у небезпеках на морі, у небезпеках між братами фальшивими».

Дії 18:23–21:34; 2 Кор. 11:23–26

ГРІХ ЧАКЛУНСТВА

Нині чимало людей займається чаклунством (окультизмом, спіритизмом, ворожінням, магією, заклинанням та іншими сатанинськими справами). Це — великий гріх, і Бог саме тому звелів нам не мати нічого спільного з цим.

У Старому Заповіті ми читаємо, що Бог дуже суворо наказав своєму народові берегтися чародійства і навіть убивати злочинців: «Не будете ворожити, і не будете чарувати!» (3 М. 19:26). «Нехай не знайдеться між тобою такий, хто переводить свого сина чи дочку свою через огонь, хто ворожить ворожбу, хто ворожить по хмарах, і хто ворожить по птахах, і хто чарівник, і хто чорнокнижник, і хто викликає духа померлого та духа віщого, і хто питає померлих. Бо гидота для Господа кожен, хто чинить таке…» (5 М. 18:10–12). «А чоловік або жінка, коли будуть вони викликати духа мерців або ворожити, — будуть конче забиті, камінням закидають їх, кров їхня на них» (3 М. 20:27).

Ось один випадок, що стався з апостолом Павлом під час його третьої місіонерської подорожі, коли він перебував у місті Ефесі: «І Бог чуда чинив надзвичайні руками Павловими, так що навіть хустки й пояси з його тіла приносили хворим, — і хвороби їх кидали, і духи лукаві виходили з них. Дехто ж із мандрівних ворожбитів юдейських зачали закликати Ім'я Господа Ісуса над тими, хто мав злих духів, проказуючи: «Заклинаємо вас Ісусом, Якого Павло проповідує!» Це ж робили якісь сім синів юдейського первосвященика Скеви. Відповів же злий дух і сказав їм: «Я знаю Ісуса, і знаю Павла, а ви хто такі?» І скочив на них чоловік, що в ньому злий дух був, і, перемігши обох, подужав їх так, що втекли вони з дому нагі та поранені. І це стало відоме юдеям та гелленам, усім, що в Ефесі замешкують, — і острах напав на всіх їх, і славилося Ім'я Господа Ісуса. І багато хто з тих, що ввірували, приходили, визнаваючи та відкриваючи вчинки свої. І багато хто з тих, що займалися чарами, позносили книги *свої* та й перед усіма попалили. І злічили ціну їх, і вийшло *на* срібло п'ятдесят тисяч *драхм*. Так могуче росло та зміцнялося Божеє Слово!»

Дії 19:11–20

ПРОЩАННЯ АПОСТОЛА ПАВЛА З ПРЕСВІТЕРАМИ ЕФЕСЬКОЇ ЦЕРКВИ

Коли пресвітери із Ефеської Церкви прийшли до Павла у Мілет, щоб попрощатися з ним, він сказав їм: «Ви знаєте, як із першого дня, відколи прибув в Азію, я з вами ввесь час перебував, і служив Господеві з усією покорою, і з рясними слізьми та напастями, що спіткали мене від юдейської змови, як нічого корисного я не минув, щоб його вам звістити й навчити вас прилюдно і в домах. І я свідчив юдеям та гелленам, щоб вони перед Богом покаялись, та ввірували в Господа нашого Ісуса Христа. І ось тепер, побуджений Духом, подаюсь я в Єрусалим, не відаючи, що там трапитись має мені, тільки Дух Святий в кожному місті засвідчує, кажучи, що кайдани та муки чекають мене… Але я ні про що не турбуюсь, і свого життя не вважаю для себе цінним, аби-но скінчити дорогу свою та служіння, яке я одержав від Господа Ісуса, — щоб засвідчити Євангелію благодаті Божої. І ось я знаю тепер, що обличчя мого більш не будете бачити всі ви, між якими ходив я, проповідуючи Царство Боже… Бо я знаю, що як я відійду, то ввійдуть між вас вовки люті, що отари щадити не будуть… Із вас самих навіть мужі постануть, що будуть казати перекручене, аби тільки учнів тягнути за собою… А тепер доручаю вас Богові та слову благодаті Його, Який має силу будувати та дати спадщину, серед усіх освячених. Ні срібла, ані золота, ні одежі чиєсь я не побажав… Самі знаєте, що ці руки мої послужили потребам моїм та отих, хто був зо мною. Я вам усе показав, що, працюючи так, треба поміч давати слабим, та пам’ятати слова Господа Ісуса, бо Він Сам проказав: «Блаженніше давати, ніж брати!»

Проказавши ж оце, він навколішки впав, та й із ними всіма помолився. І знявсь між усіма плач великий, і вони припадали на Павлову шию, і його цілували… А найтяжче вони сумували з-за слова, яке він прорік, що не бачитимуть більш обличчя його. І вони провели його до корабля».

Дії 20:17–38

O. STEMLER

ПАВЛО ПЕРЕД ПРАВИТЕЛЕМ ФЕСТОМ

Наступного дня після арешту Павла у Єрусалимі його привели з фортеці до синедріону. На суді справа дійшла до великої колотнечі, і Павла ледь було не роздерли, але римський тисяцький разом зі своїми воїнами врятував його.

Тієї ж ночі з'явився Павлові у фортеці Господь, кажучи: «Будь бадьорий! Бо як в Єрусалимі про Мене ти свідчив, так треба тобі свідкувати й у Римі!» А коли настав день, то дехто з юдеїв зібрались, та клятву склали, говорячи, що ні їсти, ні пити не будуть, аж доки Павла не заб'ють! А тих, що закляття таке поклали, було більш сорока». Дізнавшись про цей задум, тисяцький послав Павла до Кесарії під охороною двох сотень піших воїнів, сімдесяти вершників та двохсот стрільців. Кесарія знаходиться на Середземному морі, на відстані ста кілометрів від Єрусалима. Тоді це місто було резиденцією римських правителів Юдеї. Юдея, як і вся Свята земля, належала римським завойовникам. У Кесарії Павло постав на допит перед римським намісником Феліксом. Той ні в чому не зміг його звинуватити, але все ж залишив на два роки у в'язниці.

Минуло два роки, і на місце Фелікса на посаду правителя було призначено Порція Феста. Через декілька днів цар Агріппа та його дружина Верніка прибули до Кесарії, щоб привітати Феста. І так Фест влаштував, щоб вони могли послухати слова Павла. Коли Агріппа і Верніка прийшли з великою пишністю і знатними громадянами і увійшли до судової палати, привели Павла. Павло розповів про своє життя, навернення до Господа і про Христа, а далі сказав: «…Поміч від Бога одержавши, я стою аж до дня сьогоднішнього та свідкую малому й великому, нічого не розповідаючи, окрім того, що сказали Пророки й Мойсей, що статися має, — що має Христос постраждати, що Він, як перший воскреснувши з мертвих, проповідувати буде світло народові й поганам!»

Коли ж він боронився отак, то Фест проказав гучним голосом: «Дурієш ти, Павле! Велика наука доводить тебе до нерозуму!» А Павло: «Не дурію, — сказав, — о Фесте достойний, але провіщаю слова правди та щирого розуму… Благав би я Бога, щоб… усі, хто чує сьогодні мене, зробились такими, як і я, крім оцих ланцюгів».

Дії 23–26

O STEMLER

ПАВЛО НА ШЛЯХУ ДО РИМА

Апостола Павла посадили до в'язниці за свідоцтво про живого Бога і Спасителя Ісуса Христа. Павло, знаючи, що він нічого поганого не вчинив, вимагав суду кесаря. Тоді його разом з іншими в'язнями відправили кораблем до Рима.

Під час плавання на морі знялася сильна буря, так що корабель кидало з хвилі на хвилю. На третій день люди змушені були викинути свої речі у море. Оскільки буря продовжувалася багато днів, усі втратили будь-яку надію на порятунок. Довго ніхто нічого не їв. Тоді Павло став посеред всіх і сказав: «Ні одна душа з вас не згине, окрім корабля. Бо ночі цієї з'явився мені Ангол Бога, Якому належу й Якому служу, та й прорік: «Не бійся, Павле, бо треба тобі перед кесарем стати, і ось Бог дарував тобі всіх, хто з тобою пливе».

Тому-то тримайтесь на дусі, о мужі, бо я вірую Богові, що станеться так, як було мені сказано. І ми мусимо наткнутись на острів якийсь».

На чотирнадцятий день з корабля помітили затоку, що мала пологий берег, і вирішили, по можливості, причалити до берега. Піднявши якорі й мале вітрило, вони попрямували до берега. Але раптом корабель сів на мілину так, що ніс його загруз і залишився нерухомим, а корму почали розбивати сильні хвилі. Сотник звелів усім, хто вміє плавати, виплисти на берег, а решта мусила рятуватися, тримаючись за дошки чи якісь інші залишки від корабля. Таким чином, усі двісті сімдесят шість чоловік, які знаходилися на кораблі, врятувалися. Жителі того острова виявили до потерпілих неабияке милосердя, і Господь здійснив там чимало чудес через апостола Павла. Через три місяці вони продовжили свою подорож до Рима на одному з олександрійських кораблів. Перед від'їздом жителі острова спорядили їх усім необхідним й віддали належну шану, завдячуючи апостолу Павлу, який багатьох із них зцілив від тяжких хвороб.

Апостол Павло продовжував трудитися для Господа й переніс різні випробування. Він твердо вірив, що кожним кроком його життя керує великий і милосердний Бог. У своєму Посланні до Римлян (8:28) він писав: «І знаємо, що тим, хто любить Бога, хто покликаний *Його* постановою, усе допомагає на добре».

Дії 25:1–12; 27:14–44; 28:1–11

ПАВЛО У РИМІ

«А коли прибули ми до Риму, — пише лікар Лука, — Павлові дозволено жити осібно, уразі із вояком, що його сторожив. І сталось, по трьох днях Павло скликав знатніших з юдеїв… А коли вони визначили йому день, то дуже багато прийшло їх до нього в господу. А він їм від ранку до вечора розповідав, та про Божеє Царство свідоцтва давав, і переконував їх про Ісуса Законом Мойсея й Пророками. І одні вірили в те, про що він говорив, а інші не вірили. Вони між собою незгідні були й повиходили, як промовив Павло одне слово, що добре прорік Дух Святий отцям нашим через пророка Ісаю, промовляючи: «Піди до народу цього та й скажи: Ви вухом почуєте, та розуміти не будете, дивитися будете оком, але не побачите! Затовстіло-бо серце людей цих, тяжко чують на вуха вони, і зажмурили очі свої, щоб якось не побачити очима, і не почути вухами, і не зрозуміти *їм* серцем, і не навернутись, щоб Я їх уздоровив!»

Тож нехай для вас буде відоме, що послано Боже спасіння оце до поган, — і почують вони!»

Як промовив він це, розійшлися юдеї, велику суперечку провадивши поміж собою. І цілих два роки Павло пробув у найнятім домі своїм, і приймав усіх, хто приходив до нього, і проповідував він Боже Царство, та з відвагою повною беззаборонно навчав про Господа Ісуса Христа!»

Цими словами закінчується книга «Дії святих апостолів».

Читачів, мабуть, цікавить, що сталося далі з апостолом Павлом. З Біблії не можна довідатись про це достеменно. Із послань апостола Павла до Церков та до служителів, а також з інших джерел можна дійти до висновку, що Павло був звільнений і трудився на ниві Божій, проповідуючи Євангелію в Італії, Греції та Малій Азії. Згідно з переказом, Павло помер мучеником під час переслідувань християн при імператорі Нероні.

Дії 28:16, 17, 23–31

O. Stemler.

ПОСЛАННЯ АПОСТОЛІВ

Відразу після смерті й воскресення Ісуса Христа Його вчення — Євангелія — почало швидко розповсюджуватись у Палестині, по всій Римській імперії і в країнах Близького Сходу, а згодом і по всьому світу. Апостоли, тобто вибрані учні Ісуса Христа, та інші учні розійшлися по різних містах і країнах проповідувати Слово Боже. Господь підтверджував їхні слова чудесами: коли вони молилися Богові в ім'я Ісуса Христа, хворі одужували, кульгаві зцілялися і навіть мертві поверталися до життя... Тому люди приймали до серця Слово Боже, наверталися на шлях праведності. Християн переслідували, але віра в Ісуса Христа, Сина Божого, була сильнішою від усяких гонінь.

Щоб підкріпити віру в Христа, апостоли писали Церквам листи. Ці листи називалися «посланнями». Деякі послання були коротенькими, приблизно на одну сторінку, а деякі, як, наприклад, «Послання святого апостола Павла до римлян», — дуже довгі. Одні послання (Якова, Петра, Івана та Юди) були написані для всіх християн, а інші (Послання Павла) — окремим Церквам та особам.

Деякі послання апостол Павло написав у в'язниці, куди його кинули за проповідь Слова Божого. «Я терплю муки аж до ув'язнення, як той злочинець. Але Слова Божого не ув'язнити!» — писав Павло до Тимофія (2 Тим. 2:9).

Новий Заповіт має в собі 21 послання. Вони були написані під впливом і проводом Святого Духа Божого, так що вони, разом з іншими книгами Біблії, тобто Святого Писання, є СЛОВОМ БОЖИМ. Перші християни знали це і старанно переписували ці послання, читали їх у Церквах і вдома своїм дітям, показували друзям, дарували їх іншим людям, сприяючи таким чином розповсюдженню Слова Божого.

УЧАСТЬ У ВЕЧЕРІ ГОСПОДНІЙ

Апостол Павло написав Перше послання до коринтян, щоб покласти край усіляким суперечкам та щоб відповісти на ряд суперечливих питань, які виникли у коринтській Церкві. Одне з них стосувалося участі християн в язичницьких бенкетах. Апостол Павло застерігає їх: «Чаша благословення, яку благословляємо, — чи не спільнота *то* крови Христової? Хліб, який ломимо, чи не спільнота він тіла Христового? Тому що один хліб, тіло одне — нас багато, бо ми всі спільники хліба одного. Погляньте на Ізраїля за тілом: чи ж ті, що жертви їдять, не спільники вівтаря? Тож що я кажу? Що ідольська жертва є щось? Чи що ідол є щось? Ні, але те, що в жертву приносять, «демонам, а не Богові в жертву приносять». Я ж не хочу, щоб ви спільниками для демонів стали. Бо не можете пити чаші Господньої та чаші демонської; не можете бути спільниками Господнього столу й столу демонського».

У цьому ж посланні апостол Павло дає настанови коринтянам щодо Вечері Господньої, яка звершується згідно із вказівкою Ісуса Христа: «Бо прийняв я від Господа, що й вам передав, що Господь Ісус ночі *тієї*, як виданий був, узяв хліб, подяку віддав, і переломив, і сказав: «Прийміть, споживайте, це тіло Моє, що за вас ломається. Це робіть на спомин про Мене!» Так само і чашу *взяв* Він по Вечері й сказав: «Ця чаша — Новий Заповіт у Моїй крові. Це робіть, коли тільки будете пити, на спомин про Мене!»

1 Кор. 10:16–21; 11:23–25

F. PHILIPPOTEAUX

ПОСЛАННЯ ЯКОВА

У посланні Якова ми знаходимо багато коротких і глибоких висловлювань, наприклад, таких:

— **про мирське багатство**: «…сонце зійшло зі спекотою, і траву посушило, — і відпав цвіт її, і зникла краса її виду… Так само зів'яне й багатий у дорогах своїх!»

— **про спокусу**: «Блаженна людина, що витерпить пробу, бо, бувши випробувана, дістане вінця життя, якого Господь обіцяв тим, хто любить Його».

— **про гнів**: «Отож, мої брати любі, нехай буде кожна людина швидка послухати, забарна говорити, повільна на гнів. Бо гнів людський не чинить правди Божої».

— **про виконання Слова Божого**: «Будьте ж виконавцями слова, а не слухачами самими, що себе самих обманюють».

— **про мертву віру**: «Так само й віра, коли діл не має, — мертва в собі… Бо як тіло без духа мертве, так і віра без діл — мертва!»

— **про гріх язика**: «Так само й язик, — малий член, але хвалиться вельми! Ось маленький огонь, а запалює величезного ліса!»

— **про клятву**: «А найперше, браття мої, не кляніться ні небом, ані землею, і ніякою іншою клятвою! *Слово* ж ваше хай буде: «Так, так» та «Ні, ні», щоб не впасти вам в осуд».

— **про хворих**: «Чи хворіє хто з вас? Хай покличе пресвітерів Церкви, і над ним хай помоляться, намастивши його оливою в Господнє Ім'я, і молитва віри вздоровить недужого, і Господь його підійме, а коли він гріхи був учинив, то вони йому простяться».

— **про каяття і молитву**: «Отже, признавайтесь один перед одним у *своїх* прогріхах, і моліться один за одного, щоб *вам* уздоровитись. Бо дуже могутня ревна молитва праведного!»

— **про любов до заблудлих**: «Браття мої, — коли хто з-поміж вас заблудить від правди, і його хто наверне, хай знає, що той, хто грішника навернув від його блудної дороги, той душу його спасає від смерти та безліч гріхів покриває!»

ПОСЛАННЯ ЯКОВА

O. Stemler.

ДВА ПОСЛАННЯ АПОСТОЛА ПЕТРА

Петро був одним із дванадцятьох апостолів Ісуса. Він написав два послання. Адресовані вони християнським Церквам у Малій Азії, що були розташовані на території сьогоднішньої Туреччини. Припускають, що Перше послання Петро написав у часи сильних гонінь на християн, щоб підбадьорити їх. Тоді християн мучили і вбивали. У Римській імперії, особливо за часів володарювання імператора Нерона (64–67 роки після народження Христа), хотіли знищити християнство.

Петро у Першому посланні до своїх християнських братів і сестер пише так: «І знайте, що не тлінним сріблом або золотом відкуплені ви були від марного вашого життя, що передане вам від батьків, але дорогоцінною кров'ю Христа, як непорочного й чистого Ягняти… Бо «кожне тіло — немов та трава, і всяка слава людини — як цвіт трав'яний: засохне трава — то й цвіт опаде, а Слово Господнє повік пробуває»! А це те Слово, яке звіщене вам в Євангелії… Благаю *вас*, любі, як приходьків та подорожніх, щоб ви здержувались від тілесних пожадливостей, що воюють проти душі. Поводьтеся поміж поганами добре… Бо й Христос постраждав за нас… Він тілом Своїм Сам підніс гріхи наші на дерево, щоб ми вмерли для гріхів та для праведности жили; Його «ранами ви вздоровилися». Ви-бо були як ті вівці заблукані, та ви повернулись до Пастиря й Опікуна ваших душ… Не платіть злом за зло, або лайкою за лайку, навпаки, — благословляйте, знавши, що на це вас покликано, щоб ви вспадкували благословення… А Господа Христа святіть у ваших серцях… Бо й Христос один раз постраждав був за наші гріхи, щоб привести нас до Бога, Праведний за неправедних, хоч умертвлений тілом, але Духом оживлений… Коли ж вас ганьблять за Христове Ім'я, то ви блаженні, бо на вас спочиває Дух слави й *Дух* Божий. Ніхто з вас хай не страждає, як душогуб, або злодій, або злочинець, або ворохобник, а коли — як християнин, то нехай не соромиться він, але хай прославляє Бога за те».

Згідно з переказом, Петро був засуджений на смерть і, за його власним бажанням, розіп'яли його на хресті головою донизу, бо він не вважав себе гідним бути розіп'ятим так само, як і Господь Ісус Христос.

ПЕРШЕ ПОСЛАННЯ ПЕТРА

ТРИ ПОСЛАННЯ ІВАНА

За давніми свідченнями та на думку богословів, ці три послання написав апостол та євангеліст Іван Богослов. Одним з ключових слів і в Євангелії від Івана, і в усіх трьох його посланнях є слово «любов».

Головне в Першому посланні Івана — любов, життя з Богом, радість, перемога, безпека, сенс життя:

— **перебування в світлі**: «Коли ж ходимо в світлі, як Сам Він у світлі, то маємо спільність один із одним, і кров Ісуса Христа, Його Сина, очищує нас від усякого гріха… Хто говорить, що він пробуває у світлі, та ненавидить брата свого, той у темряві досі».

— **ставлення до світу**: «Не любіть світу, ані того, що в світі. Коли любить хто світ, у тім немає любови Отцівської, бо все, що в світі: пожадливість тілесна, і пожадливість очам, і пиха життєва, — *це* не від Отця, а від світу. Минається і світ, і його пожадливість, а хто Божу волю виконує, той повік пробуває!»

— **антихрист**: «Хто неправдомовець, як не той, хто відкидає, що Ісус є Христос? Це антихрист, що відрікається Отця й Сина! Кожен, хто відрікається Сина, не має Отця; хто визнає Сина, той має Отця».

— **Ісус Спаситель**: «І ви знаєте, що Він був з'явився, щоб гріхи наші взяти, а гріха в Нім нема. Кожен, хто в Нім пробуває, не грішить…»

— **любов**: «Любов Божа до нас з'явилася тим, що Бог Сина Свого Однородженого послав у світ, щоб ми через Нього жили… Бог є любов, і хто пробуває в любові, пробуває той в Бозі, і в нім Бог пробуває!.. Ми любимо Його, бо Він перше нас полюбив… Кожен, хто вірує, що Ісус — то Христос, той родився від Бога… Бо то любов Божа, щоб ми додержували Його заповіді, Його ж заповіді не тяжкі».

— **лжепророки**: «Духа Божого цим пізнавайте: кожен дух, який визнає, що Ісус Христос прийшов був у тілі, той від Бога. А кожен дух, який не визнає Ісуса, той не від Бога, але він антихристів, про якого ви чули…»

— **вічне життя**: «Оце написав я до вас, що віруєте в Ім'я Божого Сина, щоб ви знали, що ви, віруючи в Ім'я Божого Сина, маєте вічне життя».

ПЕРШЕ ПОСЛАННЯ ІВАНА

ПОСЛАННЯ ЮДИ

Загальноприйнято, що це послання написав саме той апостол Юда, про якого згадується в Євангелії від Матвія (13:55). Юда умовляє християн «боротись за віру, раз дану святим». Прикладами зі Старого Заповіту Юда застерігає віруючих не наслідувати грішників у їхніх вчинках:

«А я хочу нагадати вам, що раз усе знаєте, що Господь визволив людей від землі єгипетської, а згодом вигубив тих, хто не вірував. І Анголів, що не зберегли початкового стану свого, але кинули житло своє, Він зберіг у вічних кайданах під темрявою на суд великого дня. Як Содом і Гоморра та міста коло них, що таким самим способом чинили перелюб та ходили за іншим тілом, понесли кару вічного огню, і поставлені в приклад, — так само *буде* й цим сновидам, що опоганюють тіло, погорджують владами, зневажають слави… А ці зневажають, чого не знають; а що знають із природи, як німа звірина, то й у тому псуються… Вони… люті хвилі морські, що з піною викидають власний сором; зорі блудні, що для них морок темряви бережеться повік».

Протиставляючи цьому безбожному шляху шлях праведності, Юда повчає християн, як треба жити й вірити: «А ви, улюблені, будуйте себе найсвятішою вашою вірою, моліться Духом Святим, бережіть себе самих у Божій любові, і чекайте милости Господа нашого Ісуса Христа для вічного життя. І до одних, хто вагається, будьте милостиві, спасайте і виривайте з огню, а до інших будьте милосердні зі страхом, і ненавидьте навіть одежу, опоганену від тіла».

Закінчується це послання чудовими словами, прославляючими Бога: «А Тому, Хто може вас зберегти від упадку, і поставити перед Своєю славою непорочними в радості, Єдиному премудрому Богові, Спасителеві нашому через Ісуса Христа, Господа нашого, слава, могутність, сила та влада перше всього віку, і тепер, і на всі віки! Амінь».

ПОСЛАННЯ ЮДИ

ПОСЛАННЯ АПОСТОЛА ПАВЛА

До Нового Заповіту входять 13 послань апостола Павла, написаних ним до християн Рима, Коринта, Ефеса, Филипів, Колосів, Солуня, провінції Галатії, а також до окремих християн — Тимофія, Тита, Филимона.

Послання Павла складають четверту частину Нового Заповіту. Просто неможливо передати все багатство Слова Божого, яке є в цих посланнях. Тому ми обмежимося лише декількома уривками з них:

ЛЮБОВ

«Бог є любов» — вчить Слово Боже.

У Першому посланні до Коринтян Павло пише про любов так:

«Коли я говорю мовами людськими й ангольськими, та любови не маю, — то став я як мідь *та* дзвінка або бубон гудячий!

І коли маю *дара* пророкувати, і знаю всі таємниці й усе знання, і коли маю всю віру, щоб навіть гори переставляти, та любови не маю, — то я ніщо!

І коли я роздам усі маєтки свої, і коли я віддам своє тіло на спалення, та любови не маю, — то пожитку не матиму жадного!» (1 Кор.13:1–3).

Любов — це суть вчення Ісуса Христа. Ісус сказав: «Люби Господа Бога свого всім серцем своїм, і всією душею своєю, і всією своєю думкою». Це найбільша й найперша заповідь. А друга однакова з нею: «Люби свого ближнього, як самого себе». На двох оцих заповідях увесь Закон і Пророки стоять» (Мт. 22:37–40).

А в іншому місці Біблії Ісус так говорить про любов Божу: «Так-бо Бог полюбив світ, що дав Сина Свого Однородженого, щоб кожен, хто вірує в Нього, не згинув, але мав життя вічне» (Ів. 3:16).

ЛЮБОВ

«Любов довготерпить,
любов милосердствує,
не заздрить,
любов не величається,
не надимається,
не поводиться нечемно,
не шукає тільки свого,
не рветься до гніву,
не думає лихого,
не радіє з неправди,
але тішиться правдою,
усе зносить,
вірить у все,
сподівається всього,
усе терпить!
Ніколи любов не перестає...
А тепер залишаються
віра, надія, любов, — оці три.
А найбільша між ними —
любов!»

1 Кор. 13:4–13

УЧИНКИ ТІЛА ТА ПЛІД ДУХА

Наш Господь Ісус Христос сказав своїм учням: «Я — Виноградина, ви — галуззя! Хто в Мені перебуває, а Я в ньому, той рясно зароджує, бо без Мене нічого чинити не можете ви».

Коли ми маємо живий зв'язок з Господом Ісусом Христом і зберігаємо його в нашому серці, тоді ми, як гілки виноградної лози, приносимо багато плодів. Ісус навів Своїм учням такий приклад: «Стережіться фальшивих пророків, що приходять до вас ув одежі овечій, а всередині — хижі вовки. По їхніх плодах ви пізнаєте їх. Бо хіба ж виноград на тернині збирають, або фіґи — із будяків? Так ото родить добрі плоди кожне дерево добре, а дерево зле плоди родить лихі».

У Посланні до Галатів апостол Павло пише про «учинки тіла» та про «плід духа»: «Учинки тіла явні, то є: перелюб, нечистість, розпуста, ідолослуження, чари, ворожнечі, сварка, заздрість, гнів, суперечки, незгоди, єресі, завидки, п'янство, гулянки й подібне до цього.

Я про це попереджую вас, як і попереджав був, що хто чинить таке, не вспадкують вони Царства Божого!

А плід духа: любов, радість, мир, довготерпіння, добрість, милосердя, віра, лагідність, здержливість».

Ів. 15:5, 6; Мт. 7:15–17 Гал. 5:19–23

МОЛОДИЙ ХРИСТИЯНИН ТИМОФІЙ

Коли апостол Павло під час своєї другої місіонерської подорожі дійшов до Дервії та Лістри, він зустрів там молодого послідовника Христа, Тимофія. Мати його, Евнікія, була єврейкою-християнкою, а батько — греком. Бабуся його, Лоіда, була також віруючою. Тимофій, як і євангеліст Лука, став постійним супутником апостола Павла і був із ним у Греції, Малій Азії і навіть у Римі. Переказ сповіщає, що після страти апостола Павла у Римі, Тимофій очолив велику Церкву в Ефесі і постраждав як мученик.

Апостол Павло написав до Тимофія два послання. Тут неможливо перерахувати всі головні думки цих послань. Ось лише деякі з них. Так, у Першому Посланні до Тимофія мовиться:

— **про молитву за всіх людей**: «Отже, перш над усе я благаю чинити молитви, благання, прохання, подяки за всіх людей, за царів та за всіх, хто при владі, щоб могли ми провадити тихе й мирне життя в усякій побожності та чистості. Бо це добре й приємне Спасителеві нашому Богові». Це Павло написав за часів імператора Нерона — фанатичного гонителя християн.

— **про останні тяжкі часи**: «А Дух ясно говорить, що від віри відступляться дехто в останні часи, ті, хто слухає духів підступних і наук демонів».

— **про багатство**: «Бо корінь усього лихого — то грошолюбство, якому віддавшись, дехто відбились від віри й поклали на себе великі страждання. Але ти, о Божа людино, утікай від такого, а женися за правдою, благочестям, вірою, любов'ю, терпеливістю, лагідністю!»

— **про життя праведне**: «Змагай добрим змагом віри, ухопися за вічне життя, до якого й покликаний ти, і визнав був добре визнання перед свідками багатьома».

— **про істинних служителів**: «Цурайся нечистих та бабських байок, а вправляйся в благочесті… будь зразком для вірних у слові, у житті, у любові, у дусі, у вірі, у чистості!… Пильнуй читання, нагадування *та* науки!»

Вважається, що Друге послання до Тимофія апостол Павло написав, знаходячись у в'язниці і чекаючи страти, за часів імператора Нерона. Він пише: «Я змагався добрим змагом, *свій* біг закінчив, віру зберіг. Наостанку мені призначається вінок праведности, якого мені того дня дасть Господь, Суддя праведний; і не тільки мені, але й усім, хто прихід Його полюбив».

«ОДИН ГОСПОДЬ, ОДНА ВІРА, ОДНЕ ХРИЩЕННЯ» ВІРШІ З ПОСЛАНЬ

«Всі згрішили, і позбавлені Божої слави» (Рим. 3:23).

«...Заплата за гріх — смерть, а дар Божий — вічне життя в Христі Ісусі, Господі нашім!» (Рим. 6:23).

«Один-бо є Бог, і один Посередник між Богом та людьми, — людина Христос Ісус» (1 Тим. 2:5).

«...Христос був умер ради наших гріхів...» (1 Кор. 15:3).

«Коли ти устами своїми визнаватимеш Ісуса за Господа, і будеш вірувати у своїм серці, що Бог воскресив Його з мертвих, то спасешся» (Рим. 10:9).

«Слово про хреста тим, що гинуть, — то глупота, а для нас, що спасаємось, — Сила Божа» (1 Кор. 1:18).

«Пильнуйте, стійте у вірі, будьте мужні, будьте міцні, хай з любов'ю все робиться у вас!» (1 Кор. 16:13, 14).

«Бо я не соромлюсь Євангелії, бо ж вона — сила Божа на спасіння кожному, хто вірує...» (Рим. 1:16).

«Не обманюйтеся, — Бог осміяний бути не може. Бо що тільки людина посіє, те саме й пожне!» (Гал. 6:7).

«...Кожне тіло — немов та трава, і всяка слава людини — як цвіт трав'яний: засохне трава — то й цвіт опаде» (1 Петр. 1:24).

«Бо мусимо всі ми з'явитися перед судовим престолом Христовим, щоб кожен прийняв згідно з тим, що в тілі робив він, — чи добре, чи лихе» (2 Кор. 5:10).

«Тому кожен із нас сам за себе дасть відповідь Богові» (Рим. 14:12).

«Сьогодні, як голос Його ви почуєте, не робіть затверділими ваших сердець...» (Євр. 3:15).

«Один Господь, одна віра, одне хрищення...» (Еф. 4:5).

O. STEMLER

ОБ'ЯВЛЕННЯ ІВАНА

Земля, на якій ми живемо, не буде існувати вічно. У багатьох місцях Біблії можна прочитати пророчі слова про це, але особливо багато їх в «Об'явленні святого Івана Богослова» — останній книзі Біблії.

Іван Богослов був одним із дванадцяти апостолів Ісуса Христа. Він був також одним з наймолодших апостолів. Згідно з переказами перших християн, усі апостоли, крім Івана, померли мученицькою смертю. Іван також постраждав за Христа. Коли він знаходився у засланні на грецькому острові Патмос, йому з'явився у видінні Господь і сказав: «Що бачиш, — напиши *те* до книги, і пошли до сімох Церков» (Об. 1:8–11).

У цій книзі пророцтва й події останніх часів змальовані, головним чином, символічно; наприклад, листи до сімох Церков, сім печаток, сім сурем, сім чаш гніву Божого, книга життя, число звіра — 666, Вавилон — велика блудниця, звір з сімома головами та десятьма рогами, десять царів, Новий Єрусалим… дорогоцінне каміння, дерево життя…

Об'явлення Івана містить глибокі таємниці. Але одне абсолютно ясно: Господь Ісус Христос прийде знову на землю. Він буде судити світ. Його чекали перші християни, Його чекаємо й ми.

Прочитаймо ж один із вищезгаданих листів до семи Церков. Ці сім Церков існували в той час, коли апостол Іван писав «Об'явлення», але листи відкривають і майбутній стан християнської Церкви та віруючих.

«ОСЬ Я СТОЮ ПІД ДВЕРИМА ТА СТУКАЮ...»

«Оце каже Амінь, Свідок вірний і правдивий, початок Божого творива:
Я знаю діла твої, що ти не холодний, ані гарячий. Якби-то холодний чи гарячий ти був! А що ти літеплий, і ні гарячий, ані холодний, то виплюну тебе з Своїх уст... Бо ти кажеш: «Я багатий, і збагатів, і не потребую нічого». А не знаєш, що ти нужденний, і мізерний, і вбогий, і сліпий, і голий! Раджу тобі купити в Мене золота, в огні перечищеного, щоб збагатитись, і білу одежу, щоб зодягтися, і щоб ганьба наготи твоєї не видна була, а мастю на очі намасти свої очі, щоб бачити. Кого Я люблю, тому докоряю й караю *того*. Будь же ревний і покайся!

Ось Я стою під дверима та стукаю: коли хто почує Мій голос і двері відчинить, Я до нього ввійду, і буду вечеряти з ним, а він зо Мною.

Переможцеві сісти Я дам на Моєму престолі зо Мною, як і Я переміг був, і з Отцем Своїм сів на престолі Його. Хто має вухо, хай чує, що Дух промовляє Церквам!

Об. 3:14–22

НОВЕ НЕБО Й НОВА ЗЕМЛЯ

Із декількох останніх розділів «Об'явлення Івана Богослова» вимальовується більш-менш символічна картина останнього суду, нового неба, нової землі та Нового Єрусалима.

«І я бачив престола великого білого, і Того, Хто на ньому сидів, що від лиця Його втекла земля й небо, і місця для них не знайшлося. І бачив я мертвих малих і великих, що стояли перед Богом. І розгорнулися книги, і розгорнулась інша книга, — то *книга* життя. І суджено мертвих, як написано в книгах, за вчинками їхніми. І дало море мертвих, що в ньому, і смерть і ад дали мертвих, що в них, — і суджено їх згідно з їхніми вчинками…

І бачив я небо нове й нову землю, перше-бо небо та перша земля проминули, і моря вже не було. І я, Іван, бачив місто святе, Новий Єрусалим, що сходив із неба від Бога, що був приготований, як невіста, прикрашена для чоловіка свого. І почув я гучний голос із престолу, який кликав: «Оце оселя Бога з людьми, і Він житиме з ними! Вони будуть народом Його, і Сам Бог буде з ними», «і Бог кожну сльозу з очей їхніх зітре», і не буде вже смерти. Ані смутку, ані крику, ані болю вже не буде, бо перше минулося!»

І сказав Той, Хто сидить на престолі: «Ось нове все творю!» І говорить: «Напиши, що слова ці правдиві та вірні!» І сказав Він мені: «Сталося! Я Альфа й Омега, Початок і Кінець. Хто прагне, тому дармо Я дам від джерела живої води. Переможець наслідить усе, і Я буду Богом для нього, а він Мені буде за сина! А лякливим, і невірним, і мерзким, і душогубам, і розпусникам, і чарівникам, і ідолянам, і всім неправдомовцям, — їхня частина в озері, що горить огнем та сіркою», а це — друга смерть!..

І місто не має потреби ні в сонці, ні в місяці, щоб у ньому світили, — слава-бо Божа його освітила, а світильник для нього — Агнець… І не ввійде до нього ніщо нечисте, ані той, хто чинить гидоту й неправду, але тільки ті, хто записаний у книзі життя Агнця».

Об. 20:11–13; 21:1–8, 23, 27

O. STEMLER

ОСТАННЯ СТОРІНКА БІБЛІЇ

Святе Писання, Біблія, закінчується згадкою про майбутнє, про друге пришестя Сина Божого, Ісуса Христа. Прочитаймо ж останній уривок з книги «Об'явлення Івана Богослова» — останню сторінку Біблії:

«І сказав він до мене: «Не запечатуй слів пророцтва цієї книги. Час-бо близький! Неправедний — нехай чинить неправду ще, і поганий — нехай ще опоганюється. А праведний — нехай ще чинить правду, а святий — нехай ще освячується! Ото, незабаром приходжу, і зо Мною заплата Моя, щоб кожному віддати згідно з ділами його.

Я Альфа й Омега, Перший і Останній, Початок і Кінець. Блаженні, хто випере шати свої, щоб мати право на дерево життя, і ввійти брамами в місто! А поза *ним будуть* пси, і чарівники, і розпусники, і душогуби, і ідоляни, і кожен, хто любить та чинить неправду.

Я, Ісус, послав Свого Ангола, щоб засвідчити вам це у Церквах. Я корінь і рід Давидів, зоря ясна і досвітня!

А Дух і невіста говорять: «Прийди!» А хто чує, хай каже: «Прийди!» І хто прагне, хай прийде, і хто хоче, хай воду життя бере дармо!»

Свідкую я кожному, хто чує слова пророцтва цієї книги: Коли хто до цього додасть *що*, то накладе на нього Бог кари, що написані в книзі оцій.

А коли хто *що* відійме від слів книги пророцтва цього, то відійме Бог частку його від дерева життя, і від міста святого, що написане в книзі оцій. Той, Хто свідкує, говорить оце: «Так, — незабаром прийду!» Амінь.

Прийди, Господи Ісусе! Благодать Господа нашого Ісуса Христа зо всіма вами! Амінь».

Об. 22:10–21

Καὶ λέγει μοι, "Μὴ σφραγίσῃς τοὺς λόγους τῆς προφητείας τοῦ βιβλίου τούτου, ὁ καιρὸς γὰρ ἐγγύς ἐστιν.

Ὁ ἀδικῶν ἀδικησάτω ἔτι, καὶ ὁ ῥυπαρὸς ῥυπαρευθήτω ἔτι, καὶ ὁ δίκαιος δικαιοσύνην ποιησάτω ἔτι, καὶ ὁ ἅγιος ἁγιασθήτω ἔτι."

"Ἰδού, ἔρχομαι ταχύ, καὶ ὁ μισθός μου μετ' ἐμοῦ, ἀποδοῦναι ἑκάστῳ ὡς τὸ ἔργον ἔσται αὐτοῦ. Ἐγὼ τὸ Ἄλφα καὶ τὸ Ὦ, ὁ Πρῶτος καὶ ὁ Ἔσχατος, ἡ Ἀρχὴ καὶ τὸ Τέλος.

"Μακάριοι οἱ ποιοῦντες τὰς ἐντολὰς αὐτοῦ, ἵνα ἔσται ἡ ἐξουσία αὐτῶν ἐπὶ τὸ ξύλον τῆς ζωῆς, καὶ τοῖς πυλῶσιν εἰσέλθωσιν εἰς τὴν πόλιν. Ἔξω οἱ κύνες καὶ οἱ φάρμακοι καὶ οἱ πόρνοι καὶ οἱ φονεῖς καὶ οἱ εἰδωλολάτραι καὶ πᾶς ὁ φιλῶν καὶ ποιῶν ψεῦδος.

"Ἐγὼ Ἰησοῦς ἔπεμψα τὸν ἄγγελόν μου μαρτυρῆσαι ὑμῖν ταῦτα ἐπὶ ταῖς ἐκκλησίαις. Ἐγώ εἰμι ἡ Ῥίζα καὶ τὸ Γένος Δαβίδ, ὁ Ἀστὴρ ὁ λαμπρὸς ὁ πρωϊνός."

Καὶ τὸ Πνεῦμα καὶ ἡ νύμφη λέγουσιν, "Ἔρχου!" Καὶ ὁ ἀκούων εἰπάτω, "Ἔρχου!" Καὶ ὁ διψῶν ἐρχέσθω. Ὁ θέλων, λαβέτω ὕδωρ ζωῆς δωρεάν.

Μαρτυρῶ ἐγὼ παντὶ τῷ ἀκούοντι τοὺς λόγους τῆς προφητείας τοῦ βιβλίου τούτου, ἐάν τις ἐπιθῇ ἐπ' αὐτά, ἐπιθήσαι ὁ Θεὸς ἐπ' αὐτὸν τὰς πληγὰς τὰς γεγραμμένας ἐν τῷ βιβλίῳ τούτῳ. Καὶ ἐάν τις ἀφέλῃ ἀπὸ τῶν λόγων τοῦ βιβλίου τῆς προφητείας ταύτης, ἀφέλοι ὁ Θεὸς τὸ μέρος αὐτοῦ ἀπὸ τοῦ ξύλου τῆς ζωῆς καὶ ἐκ τῆς Πόλεως τῆς Ἁγίας, τῶν γεγραμμένων ἐν τῷ βιβλίῳ τούτῳ.

Λέγει ὁ μαρτυρῶν ταῦτα, "Ναί, ἔρχομαι ταχύ." Ἀμήν. Ναί, ἔρχου, Κύριε Ἰησοῦ.

Ἡ χάρις τοῦ Κυρίου Ἰησοῦ Χριστοῦ μετὰ πάντων τῶν ἁγίων. Ἀμήν.

ОБ'ЯВЛЕННЯ 22:10–21
давньогрецькою мовою

«НАВЧІТЬ ВСІ НАРОДИ»

Прощаючись зі Своїми учнями перед вознесенням на небо, наш Спаситель, Ісус Христос, сказав: «Дана Мені всяка влада на небі й на землі. Тож ідіть, і навчіть всі народи, христячи їх в Ім'я Отця, і Сина, і Святого Духа, навчаючи їх зберігати все те, що Я вам заповів. І ото, Я *перебуватиму* з вами повсякденно аж до кінця віку!» Амінь».

З багатьох місць Євангелії видно, що Господь любить усі народи і хоче врятувати людей в усіх куточках нашої землі. Ось декілька місць зі Святого Писання, які підтверджують сказане:

«Ти був заколений, і кров'ю Своєю Ти викупив людей Богові з усякого племени, і язика, і народу, і люду…»

«Потому я глянув, — і ось натовп великий, що його зрахувати не може ніхто, з усякого люду, і племен, і народів, і язиків, стояв перед престолом і перед Агнцем, зодягнені в білу одежу, а в їхніх руках було пальмове віття».

«І побачив я іншого Ангола, що летів серед неба, і мав благовістити вічну Євангелію мешканцям землі, і кожному людові, і племені, і язику, і народові…»

Отож, любий читачу, ти дорогий Господу, незалежно від того, з якого народу ти вийшов: з великого чи з малого. Він любить тебе. Усі люди й усі народи мають однакову цінність перед Господом. Ісус Христос помер, щоб врятувати всіх людей на землі, і «кожен, хто покличе Господнє Ім'я, той спасеться».

Мт. 28:18–20; Об. 5:9; 7:9; 14:6; Дії 2:21

Дорогий читачу!

Ось ми й підійшли до кінця нашої книги. У ній описані, головним чином у скороченій формі, лише деякі події з Біблії. Біблія, тобто Святе Писання, — це Слово Боже, і ніяка інша книга (навіть і ця) не здатна замінити її. Радимо тобі, любий читачу, дістати повну Біблію або хоча б Новий Заповіт, тобто частину Біблії, написану після народження Ісуса Христа, Сина Божого.

Біблія є найбільш читаною книгою у всьому світі. Мільйони людей, молодих і похилого віку, простих і вчених, у всіх країнах світу читають Біблію щоденно. У ній вони знаходять шлях життя та спасіння, слово розради та підбадьорення.

Читай Слово Боже, друже мій. Господь сказав так:

«Небо й земля проминеться, але не минуться слова Мої!» (Мт. 24:35).

Уся Біблія, від першої до останньої сторінки, є Словом Божим. Лише Біблія, і ніяка інша книга, містить Слово Його. Інші книжки можуть лише тлумачити Біблію.

Читай же щоденно Слово Боже, і нехай завжди звучать у серці твоєму слова з Псалма:

«Для моєї ноги Твоє слово — світильник, то світло для стежки моєї» (Пс. 118:105).

З християнським привітом,

ВИДАВЕЦЬ

ГЕОГРАФІЧНІ КАРТИ
ТА
ФОТОГРАФІЇ ДЕЯКИХ БІБЛІЙНИХ МІСЦЬ

© Інститут перекладу Біблії. Палфот і Вікт. арх.н.е.х.ест.

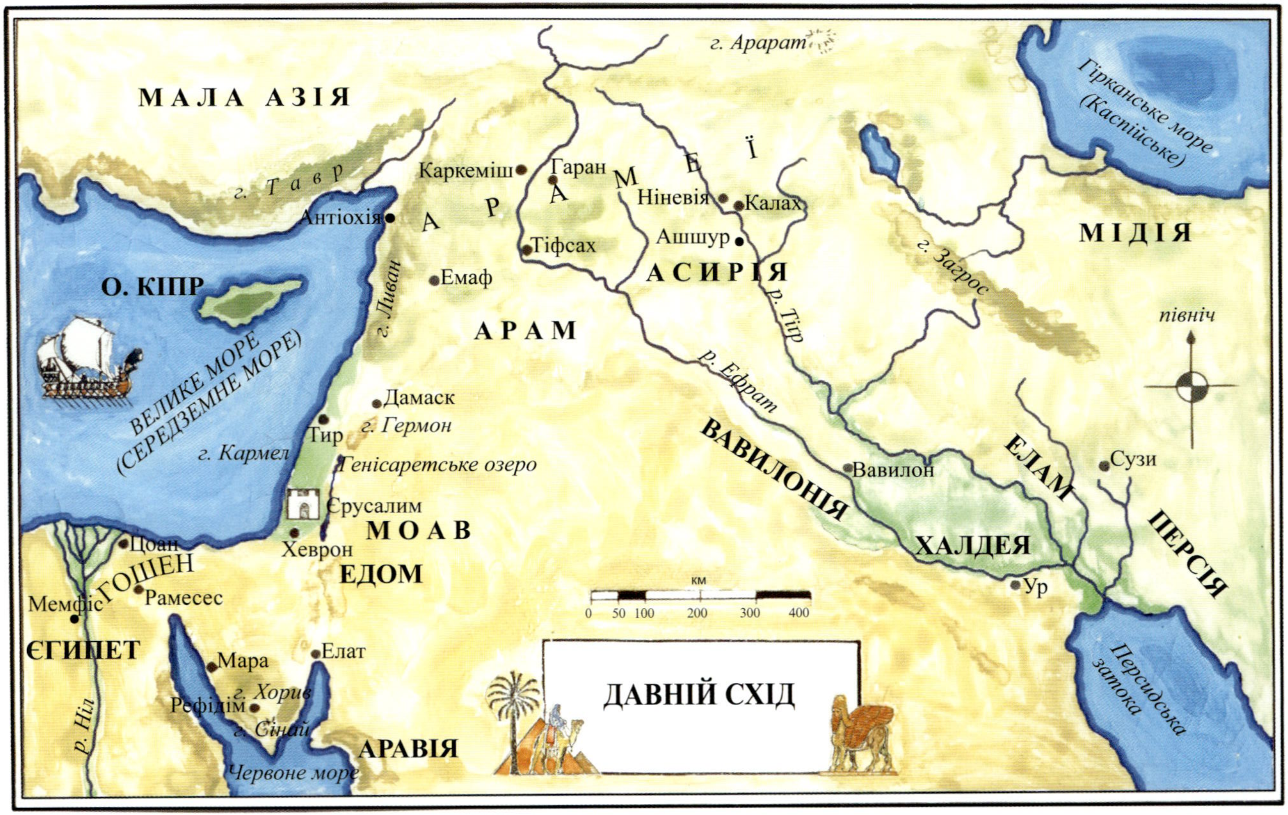
ДАВНІЙ СХІД
МАЛА АЗІЯ
г. Тавр
г. Арарат
АРАМЕЇ
Каркеміш
Гаран
Ніневія
Калах
Антіохія
Тіфсах
Ашшур
АСИРІЯ
Гірканське море (Каспійське)
МІДІЯ
г. Загрос
О. КІПР
г. Ливан
Емаф
АРАМ
р. Тіґр
північ
ВЕЛИКЕ МОРЕ (СЕРЕДЗЕМНЕ МОРЕ)
Дамаск
г. Гермон
р. Ефрат
Тир
г. Кармел
Ґенісаретське озеро
ВАВИЛОНІЯ
Вавилон
ЕЛАМ
Сузи
Єрусалим
МОАВ
Хеврон
Цоан
ГОШЕН
Рамесес
ЕДОМ
ХАЛДЕЯ
ПЕРСІЯ
Ур
км
0 50 100 200 300 400
Мемфіс
ЄГИПЕТ
Мара
Елат
г. Хорив
Рефідім
г. Сінай
р. Ніл
АРАВІЯ
Червоне море
Перська затока

ВЕЛИКЕ МОРЕ
(СЕРЕДЗЕМНЕ МОРЕ)
Сидон
Сарепта
ФІНІКІЯ
г. Ливан
г. Гермон
Дамаск
Тир
Кесарія Филипова
ГАЛІЛЕЯ
Капернаум
Магдала
Генісаретське озеро
(Галілейське море)
г. Кармел
Кана
Тиверіяда
Назарет
Наїн
ДЕСЯТИМІСТЯ
Кесарія
САМАРІЯ
р. Йордан
Себаста
Сіхар
Йоппа
Ариматея
Єфраїм
Лідда
Вефіл
Еммаус
Єрихон
Єрусалим
ПЕРЕЯ
Віфанія
Північ
Азот
Віфлеєм
ЮДЕЯ
Солоне море
(Мертве море)
Газа
Хеврон
Пустеля Юдейська
ІДУМЕЯ
Пустеля Сін
км
0
50
100
ЮДЕЯ
ЗА ЧАСІВ
ІСУСА ХРИСТА

© Інститут перекладу Біблії, Стокгольм

*Наше літочислення починається від народження Ісуса Христа.

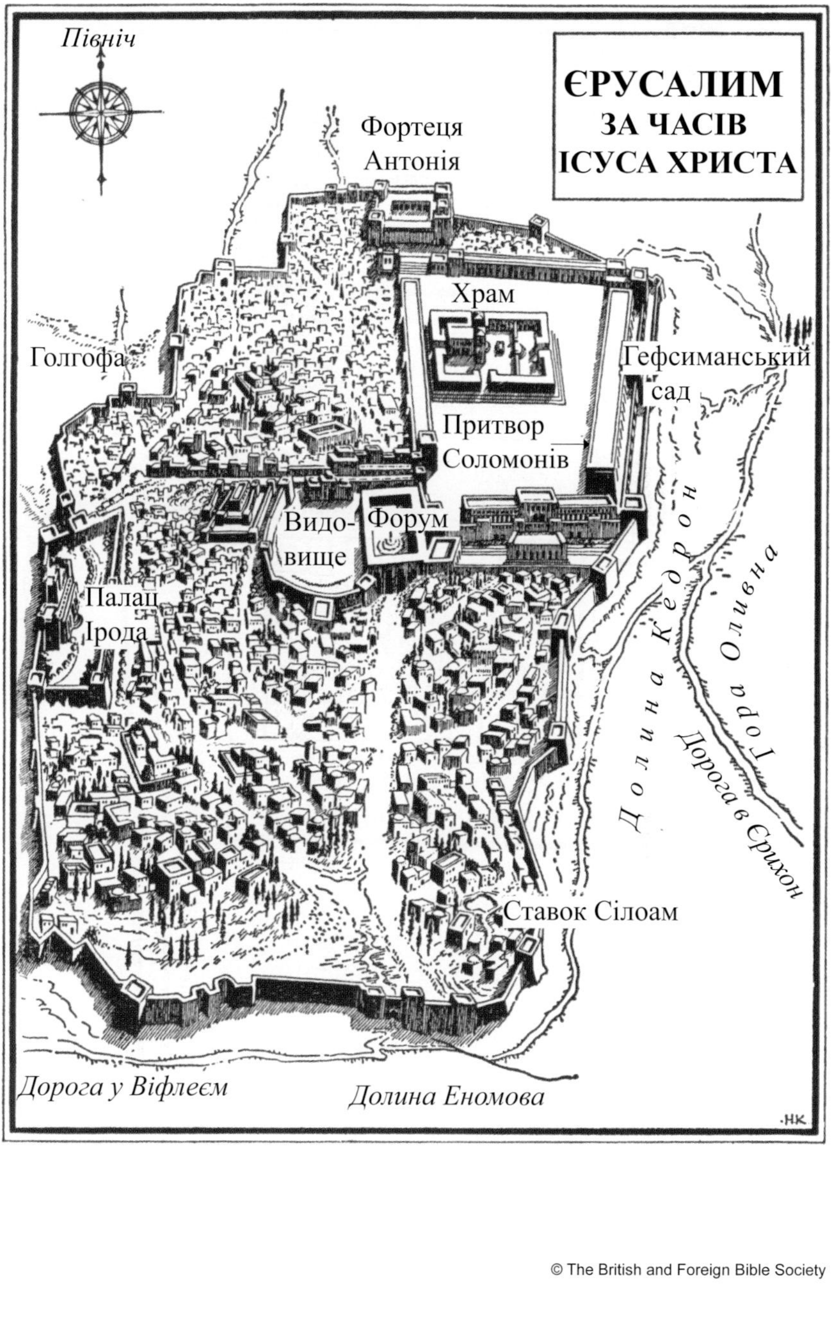

© The British and Foreign Bible Society

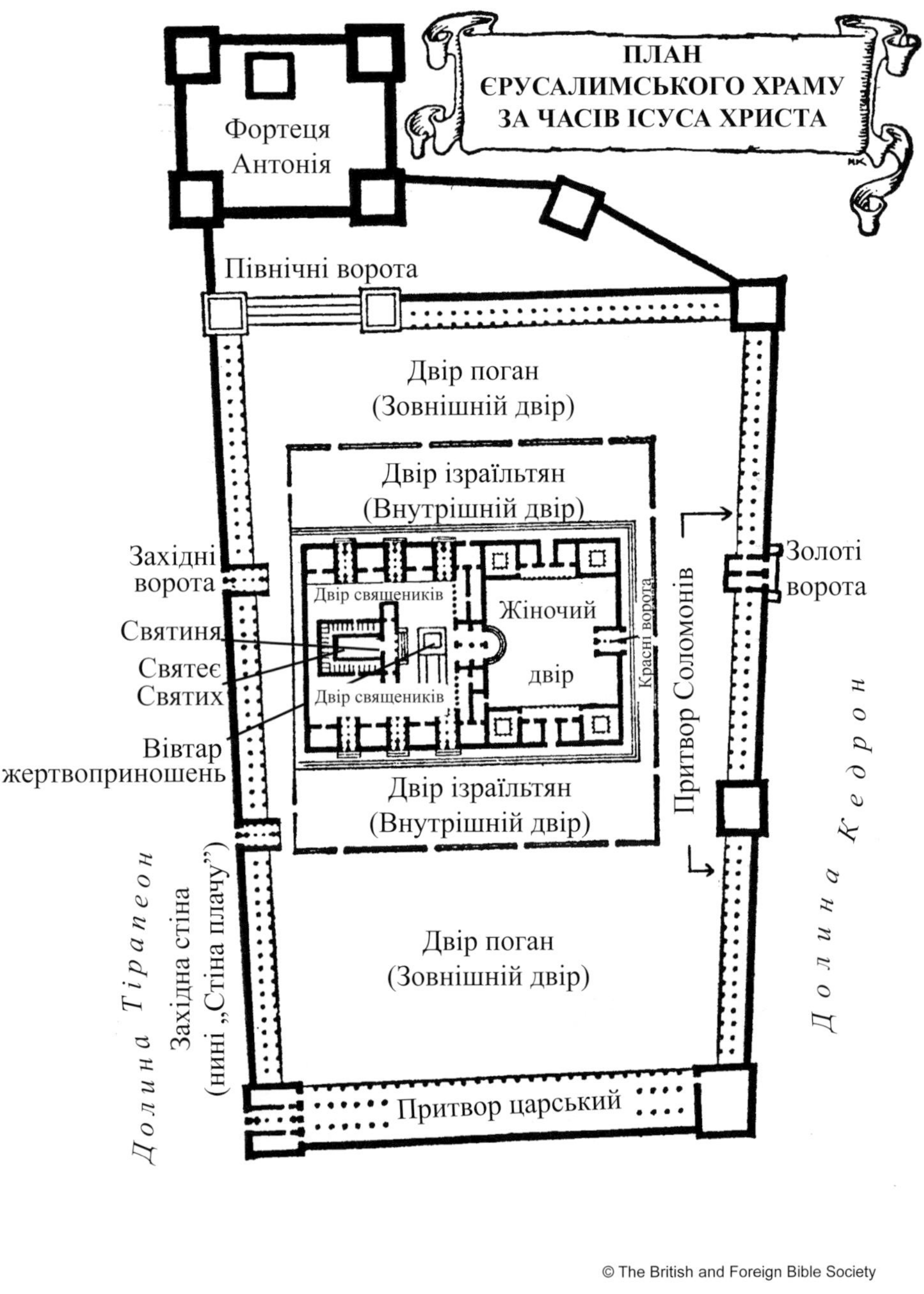

© The British and Foreign Bible Society

ЄРУСАЛИМ

Вид з Оливної гори (зі сходу).

Місце Храму Соломона. Зараз тут знаходиться мечеть Омара.

ЄРУСАЛИМ ТА ОЛИВНА ГОРА (з заходу)

«І коли Він наблизився і місто побачив, то заплакав за ним» (Лк.19:41).

ГОРА СІНАЙ

«І зійшов Господь на гору Сінай, на верхів'я гори. І покликав Господь Мойсея на верхів'я гори. І вийшов Мойсей» (2 М. 19:20).

СОЛОНЕ МОРЕ

«Усі ці зібрались були до долини Сіддім, — вона *тепер* море Солоне» (1 М. 14:3).

ГОРА ФАВОР

«Північ та південь — Ти їх створив, Фавор та Хермон співають про Ймення Твоє» (Пс. 88:13).

ГРОБ РАХІЛІ

«І вмерла Рахіль, і була похована на дорозі до Ефрати, це є Віфлеєм» (1 М. 35:19).

НАЗАРЕТ

«А шостого місяця від Бога був посланий Ангол Гавриїл у галілейське місто, що йому на ім'я Назарет, до діви, …а ім'я діві — Марія» (Лк. 1:26–27).

ВІФЛЕЄМ

«І ти, Віфлеєме, земле Юдина, не менший нічим між осадами Юдиними, бо з тебе з'явиться Вождь, що буде Він пасти народ Мій ізраїльський» (Мт. 2:6).

ЙОРДАН

«Тоді прибуває Ісус із Галілеї понад Йордан до Івана, щоб христитись від нього» (Мт. 3:13).

КАПЕРНАУМ

«І, покинувши Він Назарета, прийшов й оселився в Капернаумі приморськім, на границі країн Завулонової й Нефталимової» (Мт. 4:13).

КАНА

«А третього дня весілля справляли в Кані Галілейській, і була там Ісусова мати» (Ів. 2:1).

ШЛЯХ З ЮДЕЇ В САМАРІЮ

«Він покинув Юдею та знову пішов у Галілею. І потрібно було Самарію Йому переходити» (Ів. 4:3–4).

ГАЛІЛЕЙСЬКЕ МОРЕ

«І сталось, як тиснувся натовп до Нього, щоб почути Слово Боже, Він стояв біля озера Генісаретського» (Лк. 5:1).

ВІФАНІЯ

«Ісус же за шість день до Пасхи прибув до Віфанії, де жив Лазар, що його воскресив Ісус із мертвих» (Ів. 12:1).

КЕСАРІЯ

«І назавтра прийшли вони до Кесарії. А Корнилій чекав їх, рідню й близьких друзів покликавши» (Дії 10:24).

РИМСЬКИЙ КОЛІЗЕЙ — МІСЦЕ СМЕРТІ БАГАТЬОХ ХРИСТИЯНСЬКИХ МУЧЕНИКІВ

«І бачив я… душі стятих за свідчення про Ісуса й за Слово Боже, які не вклонились звірині, ані образові її…» (Об. 20:4).

ЗМІСТ

НОВИЙ ЗАПОВІТ